My Soul to Keep

TANANARIVE DUE

WITHDRAWN

■ HarperCollins*Publishers*

Grateful acknowledgment is made for permission to reprint the following:

"Call It Stormy Monday"
Words and Music by Aaron T-Bone Walker
©1947, 1958 and 1963 Gregmark Music Co.
All Rights Reserved

"Don't Explain"
Words and Music by Billie Holiday and Arthur Herzog
© Copyright 1946 by MCA-DUCHESS MUSIC CORPORATION
Copyright Renewed
International Copyright Secured All Rights Reserved

"Mother to Son"
From Selected Poems by Langston Hughes. Copyright ©1926
by Alfred A. Knopf Inc. and renewed ©1954 by Langston Hughes.
Reprinted by permission of the publisher.

"Tain't Nobody's Biz-ness If I Do"
Words and Music by Porter Grainger and Everett Robbins
© Copyright 1922, 1949, 1960 by MCA Music Publishing,
A Division of Universal Studios, Inc.
Copyright Renewed
International Copyright Secured All Rights Reserved

HarperCollins books may be purchased for educational, business, or sales promotional use. For information please write: Special Markets Department, HarperCollins Publishers, Inc., 10 East 53rd Street, New York, NY 10022.

FIRST EDITION

Designed by Alma Hochhauser Orenstein

Library of Congress Cataloging-in-Publication Data

Due, Tananarive.
   My soul to keep : a novel / Tananarive Due. — 1st ed.
     p.   cm.
   ISBN 0–06–018742–5
   I. Title.
 PS3554.U3143M9   1997
   813' .54—dc21   97–4992

97 98 99 00 01 ❖/RRD 10 9 8 7 6 5 4 3 2

For my father,
John Dorsey Due Jr.
I love you

Death will come to him
From every quarter, yet
Will he not die; and
In front of him will be
A chastisement unrelenting.

—THE HOLY QUR'AN
14:17

I'm your Forever Man,
You drive me crazy;
Your Forever Man,
I don't mean maybe.
Those others who hold you
Head straight for the door,
But I'm your Forever Man.

—THE JAZZ BRIGADE
WORDS AND MUSIC BY
SETH "SPIDER" TILLIS
CHICAGO (1926)

Prologue

Though his steps are not silent, no one hears the man walking down the darkened wing of Windsong Nursing Home in Chicago, his heavy soles echoing across the polished vinyl. His walk has the unhurried confidence of an administrator making his rounds, but since it is after nine o'clock, all of the administrators left hours ago, throwing on their coats and bracing their shoulders against Lake Michigan's unrelenting winds. Tonight's staff is small because of the snowstorm, which prompted some of the night nurses to call in sick. The man is alone in the wing.

He looks for 11-B uninterrupted, absently tapping each closed door with a leather-gloved hand as he passes. The halls are painted in shades of cheery peach and gold; the colors are an obvious attempt to brighten the silent, fading spirits hidden behind the doors. Inspirational posters line the walls, one picturing new daylight peeking behind a snow-dusted mountain range: TOMORROW, THERE IS ANOTHER SUNRISE.

He knows where to find the old woman because he asked for her room number at the reception desk earlier that day. He pauses before touching the doorknob, as though he expects someone to challenge him, but the only sound is the whir of the central heating system. He slips inside. The glow of a fluorescent light carelessly left on in the bathroom makes the room look frozen. The walls are bare. The only evidence of human occupation is a slight form shrouded beneath the sheets in the bed closest to him. The other bed, luckily, is empty.

The old woman's head snaps toward him when she sees his exaggerated shadow on the wall. He stands above the bed and can make out the lines that wrinkles have drawn across her face, the dryness of her lips, her sunken eyes surrounded by discolored skin. His stomach clenches and sinks.

Without meaning to, he says her name aloud. "Rosalie."

He knew she'd turned eighty on her last birthday, but he wasn't expecting this. Her face is a mask crumpled against the arcs of her hidden bones. Her white hair is so thin, it is nearly gone. And the backs of her hands . . . splotched and defaced by age. He is nearly forced to look away, his aversion to her appearance is so strong. He realizes her illness has done this to her, eating away at her insides until only this shell remains. She must weigh next to nothing; if he wanted to, he could lift her without straining himself and carry her in his arms into the night.

He must struggle to remember how she looked before, honey-complexioned and bright-cheeked. His eyes run over with tears. It is unconscionable that he has waited this long to come to her, his own flesh. Death, he decides, will be her friend.

Her eyes widen as she stares at his uncorrupted youth, the face of a thirty-year-old. Her moistureless lips tremble violently as she tries to speak. "You came," she says in a hoarse shadow of a voice. "We've been waiting. Folks tried to tell us you'd run off for good, but me and Rufus are waiting."

Rufus has been dead at least ten years, of congestive heart failure. He knows this because he saw the obituary while combing through the pages of the *Trib* in his ritualized search for familiar names among its pages. Rufus's was not the first he'd chanced upon, but seeing it had shocked him more than any other. His only consolation had been reading that Rufus had a survivor, his sister, Rosalie Tillis Banks of Chicago. Only then did he realize that Rosalie was still alive, that she had no one left except him.

What fanciful notion compelled him to call the Chicago operator to ask for Rosalie's telephone number now, after so long? Only to have it? No, of course not. He'd felt an overpowering need to hear her voice on the telephone, if only one or two syllables. But he'd waited nearly too long, confirmed the man who answered Rosalie's line. The old black woman who'd lived in the house before him was very sick, he said, and she'd moved to a nursing home. A day's searching brought him to her. Rosalie. She has seen his face, and she is receiving him with joy, nothing else. Rosalie must be living in her own world of delicate daydreams, where reality and imagination swap stories, he thinks. No wonder she doesn't have the sense to be afraid of him. Maybe, in her mind, he has come for her many times before.

"You know I couldn't leave you, Rosalie," he says, taking her frail hand into his. He shudders to touch her, repulsed and saddened when his fingers meet her sagging, unnatural flesh. This will not do for her, not at all. Not for Rosalie. This is only mockery of a human form!

For a precious few minutes, they speak about Chicago, State Street, the music that always filled the house. The piano and clarinet, his toys. Rosalie's giggles over the piano keys. He remembers Rufus and his temper tantrums. He imagines he can hear Christina's voice, straining for patience. All times from before, not long past. Everything she says makes his heart wring with old thoughts, forgotten regrets threatening to smother him. She sounds almost the way she did then, her voice rising with wonder as she stares, unblinkingly, into his face. She does not ask the first question about where he has been or how he has found her.

Finally, he sees her exhaustion as her eyes flit closed from time to time, so he says it is time for him to go. She clings to his hand tightly, clawlike, the way a child would.

"I have to do something, Rosalie," he says, leaning close. Even her scent, he notices, is unfamiliar to him. Time has made her a stranger in nearly every way. The countless reminders of what is different about her, what is ruined forever, make him tremble beside her.

"I know," she says, smiling. "I knew it when I saw you."

His teeth are locked tightly, hurting, as he walks to the neighboring bed to grasp the fresh white pillow. Now, all of his head hurts. When he walked into this room, all he'd anticipated was a secret visit while she slept. Not this. Not an unretractable impulse. But isn't this precisely what the word mercy was crafted to explain?

He stands over Rosalie for a moment, cradling the pillow against his abdomen. Is it possible that this lump of living remains is the same that fit easily into her favorite red gingham dress, the one she wears in his memories? Is Rosalie's essence preserved somewhere here still?

He blocks those thoughts. He cannot doubt what he must do. "Rest, Rosalie."

He can barely hear the parting whisper from her tattered larynx. "Goodbye, Daddy," she says.

PART ONE

■

Mr. Perfect

Hush now, Don't Explain
Just say you'll remain
I'm glad you're back
Don't Explain
Quiet, Don't Explain

—ARTHUR HERZOG JR. AND BILLIE HOLIDAY
(1946)

▪ 1

A low howl filled the two-story house, bleeding from the cracks in the knotty Dade County pinewood walls. There were intervals of peace, then the sound rose two octaves into a scream that splintered Jessica Jacobs-Wolde's sleep. She sat up, her eyes round. *Kira,* she thought. Was the awful noise coming through the wall from her daughter's room?

She reached out to touch her husband, but the space beside her in the bed was empty. The aloneness startled her, and she accidentally bit her tongue. When the scream came again, she realized the noise wasn't human. With wakefulness, logical thought began to wash over her like daylight.

Of course it wasn't Kira. Kira wasn't sick. Princess was sick. The dog was screaming from somewhere downstairs, probably the living room. Jessica closed her eyes, simultaneously relieved and dismayed. Nothing terrified her more than being roused from sleep by a faceless emergency. Her heart raced in dread whenever the phone rang at two A.M., as if the impending disaster she'd spent her life anticipating had arrived, just as expected. Sleep always made the unknown a tragedy, and this was bad in itself. There was something horribly wrong with the dog.

She heard clumping up the wooden stairs, then David's lanky form, in white briefs, appeared in the bedroom doorway. "We need to call the vet," he said, breathless. At certain times, like this, she could hear a buried lilt in his accent, showing his upbringing scattered between Africa and France. Usually, he sounded all-American bourgeois Negro, just like her. "We can't wait. I don't know what's wrong with her, Jess."

"I'll page him," she said, swinging her bare legs over the side of the bed to slip into her waiting Nikes. If you're a doctor, even a doggie doctor, you have to learn to expect calls at four in the morning, she told herself. She pulled the fading tassel on the black Oriental lamp on the nightstand, illuminating the helpless desperation on her husband's usually opal-smooth brown face. Worry lines were etched in his forehead. "See if Kira's awake, David. Don't wake her if she isn't."

He nodded, moving his lips to repeat her words before darting out of the doorway. His movements looked jerky, confused.

He was scared. She'd never seen him more scared in their seven years of marriage, aside from Kira's asthma attack the year before. They both lost their heads then, listening to their child gasping to breathe as they flew down the expressway. It was a wonder they hadn't crashed the car. To Jessica, that memory was still potent enough to make her chest tighten; she'd been convinced, for those endless minutes, that her child was dying in her arms and that she couldn't do a damn thing. No mother should know that feeling.

Yes, thank you, dear Lord, it's only Princess, she thought. I hate for the dog to be sick, but better the dog than my baby.

Poor Princess.

Princess, by pure size, had reached nearly human status in their family, especially with David. The Great Dane gave Kira rides and chased David's Frisbees on the beach with a red kerchief tied around her bulky neck. Truthfully, Jessica had never been able to muster the same affection for goofy Princess as she felt for her rust-orange tomcat, Teacake, when he crawled on top of her breastbone and folded his paws beneath his chin, meeting her eyes for silent conversations. Dogs were entertainers; cats, philosophers.

But to David, Princess was family. Jessica stared up at an eight-by-ten photograph of Princess that David had framed on their bedroom wall. The sleek black Dane was wearing a birthday hat and seemed to be grinning for the camera. Goofy, but lovable. Jessica smiled sadly. She'd better find that vet's number if she wanted to keep David from having a breakdown. She fumbled through her overstuffed woven African purse for her directory.

She didn't understand it. One moment, everything was fine; the next, life took on a mind of its own.

Princess, glad to be out of the kennel after their vacation, had been jogging up and down the street with David earlier, just before sunset. But after she wolfed down a can of dog food, she found a corner in the house and retreated there, coughing slightly as though trying to dislodge something irritating from her throat. It reminded Jessica of a person who'd eaten something that had gone bad and didn't feel well.

David wanted to call Dr. Roman right away, even before the

slight froth of dripping foam appeared at her jowls. But Jessica knew Princess couldn't be having a rabies attack, not just like that, and she'd had all of her shots. David wouldn't have let her bite a poisonous toad, and even if she had—as one of her family's two German shepherds had when Jessica was six—Princess would have died immediately. No, Princess was probably just nauseated. All she needed was a nap, and she'd be all better.

Let's give it until morning, she'd said.

Now, those words were ringing in Jessica's head with their stupidity. Again, she'd hoped to make something better by just ignoring it, hoping it would fix itself. She did it when her car made unfamiliar noises, when she got phone messages she didn't want to face, when she felt a strange ache or pain after a mishap. She should have learned better by now. She thought of the slogan at her dentist's office, which seemed to be posted for her benefit alone: IGNORE YOUR TEETH AND THEY'LL GO AWAY.

Princess wailed again, an agonizing plea that made tears find Jessica's eyes. What the hell could be hurting poor Princess so much? Why did the dog have to get sick now? In just hours, Jessica would need to perform emergency cosmetic surgery on her nursing-home stories for the newspaper. It was hard enough to drag into work the first day after a week's vacation, but she'd never be alert now, considering that they'd just made the five-hour drive back from Orlando that afternoon. Images of strolling costumed characters, endlessly winding lines, and fireworks spectacles were still glued to her brain. She grabbed a Minnie Mouse pencil from her purse to jab Dr. Roman's number on the telephone. Following the voice mail's recorded instructions, she punched the code to page him. Minnie's carefree grin stared up at her inanely.

Dr. Roman had been treating Princess since she was a puppy four years before. He was the one who patiently taped and re-taped Princess's ears for months to help them stand upright, despite the dog's irritable wriggling. He would understand.

"Did you call?" David shouted from downstairs.

Jessica sighed. She'd told him not to wake the baby, not that anyone could sleep through all of the noise in the house. Sure enough, Kira pulled her door open and stuck her fuzzy head out. Jessica still called her The Baby, forgetting she wasn't a baby at all. "Mommy," Kira demanded, whispering, "what's wrong?"

Jessica went to her and leaned over to kiss her forehead, then took Kira's hand to lead her back into the dark room. Kira's old *Beauty and the Beast* night-light glowed on the wall near her bed, a beacon against boogeymen. Jessica always felt like a little girl again in her daughter's room, with its happy colors and toys and the sweet smell of mini candy bars melting in their wrappers on her windowsill. David was a good artist, and he painted a new cartoon character on Kira's east wall each year; it was long past time to paint over the broad-chested, smirking blue genie from *Aladdin*. Before that, it had been Barney's wall. Jessica hadn't been sorry to see that sugar-coated purple beast go.

"Princess is still sick. You just stay in here, okay? Don't come out. Go back to sleep." Tears already. Kira bit her bottom lip hard. "What's wrong with Princess?" She would be sobbing soon unless Mommy said something reassuring.

"We don't know, honey," Jessica said. "We'll fix it."

"Mommy, will she die?"

Another yelp from downstairs, as though Princess had been struck sharply. Jessica tried to hold her expression blank, pretending she'd heard nothing, as though the dog's pain wasn't hurting her. She stroked the top of Kira's head. "Shhhh. Go to sleep, sweetheart. It'll be better soon."

Teacake warbled and bounded into the room. Jessica lifted the oversized cat and dropped him on top of Kira's bed as she slipped back beneath her blanket.

"Your job is to watch Teacake, okay?" Jessica asked.

"Okay. I'll do that," Kira said with an urgency of purpose.

Downstairs, David was kneeling beside Princess on a pallet he'd made from blankets and newspapers near the dining nook, the corner of the house he had converted into his office. His computer sat on the dining room table in the midst of piles of papers. He'd stacked history journals, music theory books, hardbound classic novels, and language books on shelves that reached the ceiling. Sometimes the clutter of their house made Jessica feel like she couldn't breathe, and she wondered if Princess was having the same reaction. Princess was lying prone, her head resting against the hardwood floor beyond the pallet, her eyes wide open. Foam was still dripping from her mouth. David stroked her neck, occasionally rubbing behind her upright ears.

"Maybe you shouldn't touch her. She may bite you. She's in agony," Jessica said, squatting beside him.

"She won't bite. She knows it's me."

"David, I wish I could figure out what happened."

"We missed something," David said, moving his hand to Princess's abdomen. "Feel here."

Gingerly, Jessica touched Princess. She drew her hand away quickly. Princess's abdomen was stone—bloated and tight. "Oh, my Lord. What's—"

"It's serious. We should have done something. It's not just her throat. It's something internal." David could barely speak.

Hindsight. Damn, damn, damn. It was her fault. An apology was forming on Jessica's lips when the phone rang, its sudden shrill making her jump. Their living room phone was an old-fashioned black antique with a rotary dial, and it rang with a jangling bell that reached every corner of the house. She grabbed it to silence it.

Dr. Roman sounded put out at first, but he drilled her with questions about Princess's condition. Had she eaten just before she got sick? Did her tummy feel bloated? When did it first start? The longer they spoke, the less sleepy his voice became, and the more rapid his words.

"I want you and your husband to get her to my office," Dr. Roman said, "but I feel obligated to prepare you. It sounds like it might be a stomach torsion, Jessica, and if it is, it's very grave. Princess may not make it. The only thing would be surgery, if it's not too late. And even then . . ."

She saw David staring up at her expectantly, and she could only listen with her mouth half open as the veterinarian's words assaulted her with their finality: Very grave. May not make it. "I don't think we can lift her," she said softly to Dr. Roman, filling a silence on the line she'd been unaware of for seconds.

"We'll lift her," David said, standing, sounding encouraged.

Jessica stared at him and shook her head slowly, the tears creeping to her cheeks. She watched David's boyish face change slowly, from puzzlement to gradual understanding to despair. He understood her eyes. Once again, he kneeled beside his dog and began to stroke her ears, speaking to her in low, soothing tones. Princess had been very quiet for a long time. "I'll meet you at the office," Dr. Roman said to Jessica.

Jessica told Kira not to worry and to stay in bed. They were opening the front door because Mommy and Daddy were putting Princess in the car, and then Mommy would be right back.

Luckily, the minivan was empty because Jessica had forced David to help her move their bags out so she wouldn't have to face the task in the morning. They folded the backseat forward to make room. Jessica hesitated to touch the dog at first, still thinking she might snap at them, but David was getting frantic, telling her to hurry up and to take the dog's haunches.

Sweet Jesus. The dog weighed nearly two hundred pounds and felt unbelievably heavy. They strained to half drag her across the aged marble tiles to the doorway, then they grabbed her at either end to lift her into the back of the minivan, which David had driven over their dirt pathway to back in as close as possible to the front door. Princess, wide-eyed, didn't utter a complaint. By the time David slammed the back hatch down, they were both perspiring and Jessica's forearms ached.

Jessica smelled something in the air besides the blend of their combined unshowered musk; it was sickness, turgid and bitter.

Jessica stood in the breeze and watched the vehicle rock as it drove up the steep driveway, the only sound on their quiet street of houses sleeping beneath a blanket of eucalyptus and ficus trees, and majestic old oaks buried with hanging moss. The red lights from the minivan's brakes lit up the street, illuminating clumps of the moss that appeared to be hanging from air. Then, with a screech, David was gone. Jessica heard the water from Little River lapping softly behind their house, and a dog from across the way barked into the dark. Princess's favorite basketball, riddled with teeth marks and half full of air, was on the front stoop beside Jessica, left behind.

Jessica sniffed and wiped her face with her nightshirt before she went back into the house. The sickness smell was on her. And she was alone. And, somehow, she already knew Princess would not be coming back.

Once inside, Jessica switched on the television set in the living room so a familiar noise would drive away her discomfort. As usual, David had the cable channel set to American Movie Classics. The black-and-white movie, one of those Fred Astaire dance spectacles, made the living room a safe bluish hue. The song was so cheerful that it made the moment feel more pronounced and ugly. Jessica went upstairs to look after her daughter, and to wait.

It was six-thirty, becoming light outside, when Jessica heard the front door open and knew David was back. She had been anxious, only half sleeping on top of the covers, and she felt equally wired and exhausted when he came up to the room. His eyes were pink from strain, vacant. His hair looked bunched.

"No?" Jessica asked.

David shook his head, not looking at her. He stepped out of the green University of Miami sweatpants he'd thrown on and folded them neatly to replace them in the drawer of their antique oak bureau. She knew he was acting out of habit; he should be putting them in the hamper in the bathroom instead.

"It's called a stomach torsion," David said mechanically, as though reading from a veterinary textbook. "It happens with big dogs. Especially Great Danes. Sometimes they're too active or they eat too fast, and their stomach just . . . twists . . ."

"I'm so sorry, baby," Jessica said. She replayed the dog's last hours in her mind; Princess tearing around the clear patch of grass on the side of their house, barking at their neighbor, then coughing, the foam at her mouth. How could they have known? "Did he say it would have made a difference if we'd . . ."

"I didn't ask," David said quickly, and Jessica knew then that he had asked, and that acting sooner might have saved Princess.

David sighed, shrugging, his back still to her. He was slender but toned, and his shoulder blades poked gently against the sinews of his back. "I guess it was us being out of town, her cooped up at the kennel all that time. A damn week. She was just so excited. I don't know. Maybe when she ate, it went down wrong. Something. Dr. Roman said it happens to Danes a lot."

Now, with confirmation, Jessica realized how bad, really bad, this was. Very soon, they would have to wake their five-year-old and tell her that the playmate she'd known as long as her world had existed was gone. Just like that.

David Wolde climbed into the bed beside his wife, hugged her tightly from behind, and began to cry.

▪ 2

Jessica had filed her story with her editors before leaving for Orlando, at midnight to be exact. It had seemed like a painfully long story even then, but now that she'd come back to find the drafts cluttered with highlighted memos and questions, every inch of it weighed on her brain. The main story and sidebar made up ninety solid inches of newspaper copy.

The last thing she'd said to David before she left for work at eight-thirty, after not even two hours of nervous sleep, was that she would be home early. Now, it was past noon and she realized that leaving early, or even on time, would be impossible. This might be one of those twelve- or fourteen-hour days, today of all days. The exposé was the Sunday showpiece, so it needed to shine.

Jessica had been on the elite investigative team of the *Miami Sun-News* for a year, and this was her first major contribution without sharing a byline with another reporter. She'd spent two months researching the abuse and neglect of the elderly in nursing homes, which was sparked by an anonymous tip-off from a former worker at a place called Riverview in Little Haiti. She'd visited there and talked to an old Haitian man, Frederic, who was so infected with bedsores that he was permanently disfigured, his right foot amputated from gangrene. David tagged along to both of her interviews with the toothless old man to translate his Creole, since Jessica didn't trust the nursing staff to accurately interpret his words. David was a master linguist, and Creole was one of eight languages he spoke fluently.

The old man's bedsores were mild compared to the tale he wove. Frederic claimed that the man who'd shared his room, a former school headmaster, had died after two days of unattended moaning and gasping. "He sick, *sick*," he'd told Jessica in broken English, his eyes running with water. "I say man sick. All day, all night. No listen. No listen." In Creole, he told of how helpless he'd felt, saying the world is on its head because the young ignore pleas from the old. His stories made Jessica's own eyes itchy with tears as she sat beside his bed, scribbling his words. After both visits, she and David went home and talked about Frederic late into the night. Those nights, she took special care to call her mother before she went to sleep.

Luckily, the dead man's family had demanded an autopsy, which uncovered a partial throat obstruction, and Jessica found a physician who confirmed that it could have been treated easily. Then, Jessica harangued the county medical examiner into conceding on the record that Riverview's handling of the man's death "on appearance, may not be shy of neglect."

Once printed, it would land Riverview in a state investigation. And this was only one of a half-dozen incidents she'd uncovered around the county, including one place that purportedly punished some of its more vocal wards by beating them with a strap.

The editors were excited. Jessica figured it was a long shot at best, but they were grooming her stories for a Pulitzer, which meant every sentence had been examined under a microscope. Her immediate editor, Sy Greene, had peppered the text with remarks like, Can't we get the medical examiner to say what he means? and Why don't you go back to Riverview and ask the old guy what he thinks about that?

Jessica sat in a far corner of the third-floor newsroom, which was filled with the clacking of computer keyboards, ringing phones, and the din from television sets playing the midday news on three channels. With each new question she read on her computer screen, Jessica's jaw tightened until the pressure reached the throbbing veins at her temples. She hated the editing process most of all. No matter what, the stories were never good enough. Her editors didn't seem to have the faith that she had pushed as hard as she could, since she'd come to the I-Team from the Features staff; there, her toughest assignments had been interviewing aerobics instructors who were occasionally too self-impressed to be civil. While Jessica was in Features, she couldn't help believing that she wasn't living up to her reasons for becoming a journalist in the first place: She wanted to change things.

One of the first assignments Jessica had as a new reporter in a suburban bureau was to write about a program for teenage boys that the county was about to cut. She'd spent only an hour talking to the administrator, got a quick tour, interviewed two teens too shy to do much more than mumble, and watched the photographer take a picture of them doing math homework with their tutor. She wrote the piece in an hour, then she forgot about it. Two months later, the administrator called her to tell her the county had changed its mind about cutting the program.

"Your story did it," he'd said.

Jessica then realized how much even the most casual touch could change people's lives, and she knew with certainty, for the first time, that she'd found her calling.

Sy was much less idealistic, an old-school relic, as though he'd styled himself after a brassy editor from a 1940s movie. Sy's tenacious eye for "hokey," as he called it—or bullshit, as Jessica called it—was the thing she both admired and hated about working for him. When he asked questions, three out of four times he raised good points. But it was turning into a long day, she'd already spent months on the stories, and Jessica wasn't in the mood for any more hokey-hunting.

Since Sy was in his office and out of her eyesight, Jessica typed an e-mail message to S. Greene:

NO WAY THEY'LL LET ME BACK IN RIVERVIEW. AND OUR GUY CAN'T GET TO A PHONE.

She waited for a response and smiled to herself when none came right away. Sy was usually quick to snap

THAT'S BULL

or

CALL THE ATTORNEYS.

His computer was signed on, so the electronic silence meant that she might have found one of his precious few throwaway questions, one he could live without. If she could only ferret out a few more of those, her headache might go away.

A message popped across the top of her screen:

WHY THE LONG FACE, GIRLFRIEND? NOT SO ROSY WITH MR. PERFECT? (P. DONOVITCH)

Peter Donovitch sat only three desks across from her, maybe twenty feet away, but messages had long ago replaced conversation in the newsroom. She smiled over at him wanly. She'd looked for Peter as soon as she walked in that morning, wanting to clasp a friend's warm hand to start her day, but he'd been out all morning and she'd been so preoccupied with her story that she hadn't noticed him come in.

In a newsroom filled with reporters who wore drab, frumpy clothes that never seemed to fit, Peter always stood out in his pastel shirts, paisley ties, and suspenders. His red-brown hair, cut short around his ears, was noticeably flecked with premature gray, as was his moustache, probably thanks to fifteen years as a reporter. Peter was her mentor on the I-Team. Thank goodness he was also a family friend who would understand.

She typed a response:

TERRIBLE NEWS. PRINCESS DIED LAST NIGHT. (J. WOLDE)

She heard her message beep to his screen, and saw his shoulders jump. He whirled around to mouth "I'm sorry" to her. She shrugged and typed another note:

MASSIVE DEADLINE. QUICK LUNCH LATER MAYBE?
(J. WOLDE)

SURE THING, SWEETHEART. GOD I'M SORRY.
(P. DONOVITCH)

Then, an instant later:

WELCOME BACK. WE MISSED YOU. (P. DONOVITCH)

She couldn't help smiling, this time from warm pleasure.

MISSED YOU TOO. NOW LEAVE ME ALONE. (J. WOLDE)

As soon as she sent the message, she laughed. He laughed, too, nodding as he read it. He understood. On deadline, all friendships were off.

Maybe she'd survive today, after all. Just having Peter nearby made her feel less anxious about the ordeal that morning. It wasn't even so bad with Kira, but David's sobbing anguish had really thrown her. He'd cried that way only once before, after a fight when they were still dating. She was frazzled from exams and she threatened to break up with him over some foolishness she couldn't even remember now. She'd dropped the words carelessly out of the side of her mouth, and they hit their mark—and then some. To her amazement, he began to weep, a mourning cry, not a wounded one. Just like he'd cried again that morning for Princess.

YOU NEED TO PIN DOWN THAT EXAMINER. (S. GREENE),

the next message on her computer said.

Jessica set her jaw. Pin him down? How many more times could she get that man on the phone to repeat his same tired old statement? Why was Sy purposely riding on her nerves?

F-U-C-K O-F-F,

she typed. She thought, then decided not to send the message. She could save that one for later in the day. She would probably need it.

"How's Mr. Perfect taking it?"

"Lousy. He cried all night," Jessica told Peter, stirring NutraSweet into the murky depths of her iced tea.

"All night?"

"You know how he is with that dog. How he was, I mean."

At nearly four o'clock, it was closer to dinnertime than lunchtime, but it was Jessica's first break all day. Peter convinced her to forgo the newspaper's cafeteria and eat at O'Leary's, a hotel bar across the street from their building, where they could sit on the patio in the muted warmth of the sun, which was emerging for the first time after a morning of rain. The only thing Irish about O'Leary's—which served glorified bar food, hamburgers, and buffalo wings—was its name. Their table sat just beyond the shimmering waters of the hotel's untroubled pool. The water was such a rich chlorine-blue, it seemed to glow. Jessica wanted to leap in—skirt, pumps, and all.

Thinking of Princess, Jessica was tempted to order a beer to go with her grilled chicken sandwich, but she held off. That would put her to sleep for sure. Caffeine would have to do.

"Jessica," Peter said, lifting his dripping water glass in a toast, "that man of yours is a saint. This seals it. Any man who can cry over losing a pet has the most special of souls. Mr. Perfect, once again, earns his sobriquet."

Jessica searched Peter's kind, faintly green eyes. He had bestowed David with that nickname almost immediately after he met Jessica in the newsroom. David sent her flowers at work in the early days, when she was most frustrated, and on late nights he came to deliver a hot dinner from home. Only now was Jessica beginning to detect a vague longing in Peter's voice when he spoke of David, a harmless envy.

Peter was intensely private, but she'd figured out that he must be gay even before she spotted him walking closely beside a bearded younger man at a Miami Beach festival two years before. He never mentioned a social life, a domestic life, any kind of life. His sentences were devoid of "we" when he discussed his weekends. He was so closeted that he wasn't out to her even after nearly seven years of working together at the *Sun-News*. He never posted his name on the bulletin board as a member of the Gay Journalists' Alliance, as a half-dozen other reporters had, but someone confided to her that while Peter never came to the meetings, he contributed generously and was on the mailing list. Despite that, there were rumors he'd been married once, and even had a son. He never talked about that either.

Peter's secrets made Jessica sad. As many times as Peter had brought Kira Christmas gifts (and black dolls, at that) and joined them in sampling David's honey wine in the backyard, she wondered when she would ever be entertained in Peter's home with his significant other, if he had one. She just didn't know, and she would never dare ask. Maybe Peter assumed that since she was a Bible toter, she'd fling passages on Sodom and Gomorrah at him. Christians got a bad rap for intolerance, and she just wasn't like that. She worried about her own conduct, no one else's, and she tried to live a good example if anybody cared to notice. But how could she bring up Peter's personal life if he wouldn't? She was becoming resigned to the fact that there was simply a great deal she would never know about her friend.

"What about Kira?" Peter asked.

"She was a mess, Peter. It broke my heart. We had to keep her home from school." She sighed. "Well, at least Daddy is there. Looks like he's the one who's always there . . ."

"Oh, no. Not the oh-god-I'm-such-a-lousy-parent speech."

"Listen, Peter, I'm serious. My mother had a job too. But she would have taken a day off if something like this had happened."

"You sound just like one of those guilt-complex moms on *Oprah*. Stop beating yourself up. You're a great mom to Kira. She knows you're there."

"Maybe I'm there in spirit."

"Being there in spirit is important too."

"Too bad spirits are invisible."

"She knows," Peter said with certainty, smiling.

David had quit his job teaching at the University of Miami as soon as Kira was born, two years after they married. Just like that. Now, he worked at home as a book translator and a contributing editor to a couple of foreign-language history journals, one in Madrid and one in Paris. He also earned some income from lecturing and from the textbook he'd written on jazz, *Body and Soul*, which was assigned to music students all over the country. It seemed to Jessica that David was accomplished enough to go anywhere and do anything, but he was perfectly content to sit in that tiny, 1,100-square-foot house and be a full-time daddy.

Was there something wrong with her because she couldn't do that? She'd never considered abandoning her hopes of being a journalist, even though it was a job that ate parents for lunch because of the time commitment. She was about to be nominated for a Pulitzer at age twenty-eight, exactly as she'd planned for herself. But what about the rest?

"Let me take your mind off Princess," Peter said, reaching under the table for his ragged brown leather briefcase.

"I wondered why you brought that . . ."

"I have a proposal I think is going to blow your socks off."

"Well, I'm already married," Jessica said, "so you can forget about that one."

"Hope springs eternal," Peter said, winking. He brought out a folder full of computer printouts she recognized from the newspaper's NEXIS network. He'd scrawled *elderly* on the folder in his sloppy script—the reporter's curse.

"What's all this?"

"Detroit. Chicago. Los Angeles. Look at this one: Poughkeepsie, New York. I found that in *Newsweek*. Appalling."

All of the stories were about abuse or neglect of the elderly in nursing homes, adult congregate living facilities, and hospitals. A headline from the *Chicago Tribune* arrested her attention and forced her to read: ELDERLY PATIENT SMOTHERED, CORONER SAYS. An eighty-year-old woman with cancer had apparently been asphyxiated while she slept, her nose broken. Rosalie Tillis Banks, a schoolteacher, daughter of a jazz musician from the 1920s. No suspects, no motives. The story quoted someone speculating the killer might have been a staffer, but administrators denied it. Windsong Nursing Home.

"Damn," Jessica said. "Suddenly, our Riverview is sounding like a five-star hotel."

"You're getting the picture."

"Why'd you pull these?"

"Because I read your story in the computer system while you were on vacation. I don't know why you're so shy about showing me your copy. It's amazing stuff, Jess. Sy is raving about you."

"That'll be the day."

"Behind your back, he does. Believe me," Peter said, smiling at her like an older brother. "Your pieces got me thinking about the treatment of the elderly. It reminded me of a housing minister I once met who was visiting from Brazil. The Miami social services people gave her a fancy tour, including a nursing home where all the old folks sang her a song. She burst out crying. They thought she was happy. But she was really crying because, in Brazil, she'd never seen such a thing. They take care of their elderly at home."

Jessica knew what he meant. Her mother was playing nurse-maid to Jessica's diabetic great-uncle at her house in north Dade; he'd had a stroke the year before, so he moved down from Georgia to stay with her. Bea Jacobs didn't believe in nursing homes. She'd taken Uncle Billy on cheerfully, even though Jessica told her she was crazy. So far, it was working out fine. And there was a certain sense to it, a cosmic logic: You take care of your own.

Jessica thought of Frederic losing his foot at Riverview, and the dead woman with the broken nose in Chicago. "Somewhere along the way," she mused, "family stopped mattering, didn't it?"

"It's a book," Peter said, pronouncing the words slowly as he held Jessica's eyes. "I already described your piece to my agent, and he likes the idea. All he needs is a proposal, and we have a publisher within a month."

"A book . . . ?" Jessica asked, puzzled.

"*Honor Thy Father and Mother: America's Abuse and Neglect of the Elderly.* We keep it simple. Some overview stuff, but mostly we concentrate on two dozen or so horrific cases from around the country. We interview friends, family. We interview advocates for the elderly, health professionals. We try to find out what's going wrong. We take a book leave for four months, even less, and then we're out. Bam."

Jessica felt a mild tingling sensation sweep across the hair on her arms, equal parts exhilaration and nerves. She'd forgotten how direct Peter could be when he wanted to. He'd already published two books, one on Florida's mob heyday, the other on a local serial murderer and rapist, and to him the process wasn't mystifying. To her, it was a sacred dream from childhood and therefore needed to be approached with caution.

"You don't need me for that," she said.

"Don't be crazy. Of course I do. These are your pieces. I have more experience in research, but you write with a grace I can only salivate over. Seriously. We do it together."

Jessica's thoughts scattered. "Four months? I can't stay away that long. I can't—"

Peter playfully slapped his palm on the tabletop, making the silverware on their empty plates clatter. "You're afraid of success. I keep telling you that. Well, I can't assure you this won't get us on the talk-show circuit, because it probably will. But the important thing is that somebody needs to write this book. And that somebody might as well be us."

To Jessica's relief, the waitress finally remembered them on the patio and brought out their check. Jessica tried to look like she was concentrating on figuring out her portion, but her mind was in a fit and her heart was pounding.

First Princess, now this. Her mother always said life rolls in cycles of good and bad, but sometimes even good news could be overwhelming. She wanted to run away from it. She wasn't even sure why. Maybe it was safer to run from both.

"I won't push for an answer today," Peter said as they crossed the street back toward the newspaper building, a six-story Art Deco monstrosity that resembled a staircase, painted lemon-yellow and facing Biscayne Bay.

"That's a shock."

"You have to think about it. Talk to David, but fight him if you have to. He's way too possessive of your time. You know that. He's not looking out for your career, Jess. But I am. I know these things. You have to trust me."

Jessica stared at the sidewalk as she walked, mumbling. "It's just that Kira's nearly finished kindergarten. . . and I wanted to know her teacher better, and already . . ."

Peter slipped his arm around her shoulder, and she was slightly embarrassed to realize that his lightly cologned scent was a comfort to her. She remembered how, early on, she'd mistaken his kindness for a crush, and how much that had flattered her. Not that she would ever consider another a man since she had David, but she'd always told herself she would have been nearly as lucky to end up with someone like Peter. Very nearly.

"You can do both, Mommy. You really can. You'll be based at home. Writing this book will be just like your job here, with a little more traveling. It's not a two-headed dragon. I promise."

Jessica laughed, imagining how naive she must sound to Peter. Here he was, practically handing her the one thing she'd longed for as long as she could remember, and she was stammering with excuses. That's the difference between us and white folks, she told herself. They don't stop to say "I can't" or "Should I," they just do. And it was a skill, sooner or later, she would need to pick up despite herself. *Honor Thy Father and Mother.* She liked the sound of it.

But David would be another matter.

"I'll talk to him," she promised. She was already dreading her return to the sadness at home, but now she had reason to dread it even more.

■ 3

If someone had told Jessica Jacobs, at twenty, that she had recently met the man she would marry, she wouldn't have thought to include David Wolde on her list of possibilities. Far from it.

She would have hoped he was Shane, the pro-bound UM fullback she'd had a frenzied petting session with after an Omega party at the beginning of the semester. Or even Lawrence, the lanky physics major who sat with her at the student union, but couldn't muster the nerve to ask her out. She might even have believed it was Michel, the tight-jawed president of the Black Student Caucus, who called her "little sister" and would have had potential if he'd remembered to sprinkle in some fun between bouts of righteous indignation.

But not David Wolde. He didn't fit any side of her at all, at least not any she'd discovered yet.

Granted, she couldn't concentrate on a word he said the first day she sat in his Intermediate Spanish tutorial because she was so absorbed by his face, and not just his startling beauty. (Beauty, she'd decided, even now, was the only word to describe his face's impression, an assortment of complementary features.) He simply looked unusual. He was black, that was certain. His unblemished skin was a rich clay-brown, and his tightly curled hair was kinky if somewhat wispy. But the slope of his forehead and nose, and his burnt-sienna lips, made him look nearly Middle Eastern, or some mix from somewhere far from the United States. Moorish descent, maybe. He spoke Spanish like a native, with a slight Castilian lisp. Yet, on the rare occasions he spoke English in class, the accent was touched by a ring of the unfamiliar. His face and his voice, in harmony, were a mystery that captivated Jessica from the start.

That aside, nothing else about Dr. Wolde (he pronounced it WOL-day, but everyone usually shortened it to WOLD) encouraged romantic thoughts. He almost never smiled, never flirted in the least, and his dark eyes lighted on male and female students with equal indifference. He looked young, possibly thirty, but carried himself as though he were at least forty. He was an old-fashioned black college professor, the kind her mother described from her days at Fisk in the 1950s. They don't play. They're only about business. They make that white guy on The Paper Chase look like a doddering old pushover.

There was no such thing as coasting in Dr. Wolde's class. And if you were absent a day, upon your return he asked you to stand up in front of everyone and, in Spanish, explain why. He spoke rapidly, his cadences trilling up and down and all around them, never mind that the language was always a hair away from sounding like babble to them.

Jessica had assumed Spanish was a blow-off course. In high school, she'd learned to conjugate verbs and her accent was all right, so she figured she'd slide by fine.

She was wrong. Midway through the term, Dr. Wolde's was the only class she was pulling a C in. She left his office near tears after an argument over a low mark on an essay she'd actually worked hard on. He'd marked off for accent marks that weren't slanted just the way he liked. This was a damn elective. She was going into journalism, not foreign service. She didn't need this shit.

"We're just learning," she complained, nearly shouting.

"If you're learning," he'd replied calmly, in English, "then what's the problem?"

During a flu epidemic that sidelined her other teachers at least one or two days, Dr. Wolde never got sick. The class prayed he would stay home just once. He never even got a sniffle.

She could no longer see the beauty in his face. ("Isn't that brother who teaches Spanish cute?" one of her friends asked her one day, and Jessica stared at the girl as if she'd lost her mind.) She no longer cared where the SOB was from; as far as she was concerned, he'd come from her worst nightmares. She found out he was some kind of expert from the music department, and he taught Spanish for fun. Just her luck. He was making her life miserable in her junior year, the year everyone said was supposed to be her most carefree, when the flow of college is under control and graduation is still a year away.

When all of her friends were at parties, she was up late writing in her Spanish workbook. She was reciting phrases into a tape recorder and playing them back, fearful of Dr. Wolde's reaction if she stumbled in class. He had a way of gazing at students when they made mistakes, eyebrows arched, that made Jessica want to curl under her desk. He was totally uncompromising. Jessica had always considered herself a perfectionist, and here was someone who made her feel like a slacker. She didn't like the feeling.

On the day of the final, Dr. Wolde had the nerve to encourage them to sign up for his Intermediate Spanish 2 course. "Honey, pleez . . ." the other black student, Rene, muttered just within Jessica's hearing. "This man must be on crack."

Jessica passed Dr. Wolde's class with a B-minus, souring a column of A's and B-pluses. She didn't know whether to shout with joy from her dorm rooftop or to slash Dr. Wolde's tires. She swore she'd had all the Spanish she could stand.

She didn't realize until a week later, chatting to a young man selling roses to motorists at a red light on South Dixie Highway, that she could speak Spanish with confident ease. "Are you Dominican?" the man asked her, in Spanish, indicating the dark skin of her forearm.

"No," she said. "Pero, tuve un buen profesor."

She'd had a good teacher.

That same day, Jessica signed up for Intermediate Spanish 2 with Dr. Wolde. The man from her nightmares, she thought ironically, smiling at herself.

Her life would never be the same.

"Mommy's home!"

Kira called through the screen door as Jessica climbed out of the minivan and let the door fall shut behind her. The driveway was a long, gravelly descent into a yard so overgrown with thick tree trunks, palm trees, and wide leafy plants that the two-story house was invisible from the street. A wooden marker pounded into the live oak just beyond the driveway identified their address, 376 Tequesta Road. They lived in El Portal, a secluded area west of busy Biscayne Boulevard, perched on the bank of the river.

It was long after dark, and Jessica heard a familiar whistling in the treetops overhead. The noise was half human, half something else, sometimes sounding like a war cry. When visitors asked about the high, persistent sound, as Peter had once, she explained it was the call of an old Indian woman's ghost.

If the visitor looked at her askance, as they almost always did, Jessica told them their house was on haunted Tequesta Indian ground, like in *Poltergeist*, except their haunts weren't in a pissy mood. Their property was across the street from a grassy burial mound with a prominent marker erected by the city decades before, and their yard even had a small cave built into a knoll near the street. Children and bent-over adults could actually walk into it and vanish into the solitude. The cave wasn't elaborate, just rough limestone walls and a pressed dirt floor. No hieroglyphics. Nothing sinister. The cave was one of Teacake's favorite daytime hiding places, and Kira took her playmates inside during neighborhood barbecues. Five or six could squeeze in at a time.

At first, Jessica had considered the added features to their seventy-year-old house only a novelty, but now she treated the ground with reverence. Was she superstitious? Whenever she drank outside, whether beer or Diet Coke or mineral water, she poured the first sip on the ground as a libation. Jessica had decided the ghost in the trees was a woman and named her Night Song. She heard her gentle call tonight. Night Song was their neighbor.

Jessica expected to hear Princess's barking next. Then she remembered, and the sadness was fresh. Her spirits ebbed as she walked down the path to the door.

"See? Look what I did," Kira said after Jessica lifted her up for a hug and kiss. While Jessica balanced Kira on one arm, heavy as she was, Kira handed her a dried watercolor painting of a house, clouds, and a black blob with wings soaring above. "It's Princess, Mommy, see?"

Then, she did see. Princess was in Heaven. Even their house looked obvious now in the painting. She should have known right away. Jessica kissed Kira's nose again. "You paint like Daddy."

Kira wriggled to be lowered back to the floor, and she danced from one socked foot to the other, smiling widely. She was wearing the Disney nightshirt they'd just bought her. Was it only the day before? "Daddy's going to paint Princess on my wall next. He said he'll do it tomorrow. It'll look just like this. He said so."

Jessica glanced at David then, who was sitting across the room at his computer. The pallet he'd made for Princess was cleared away. His face was drawn and weary, but he smiled faintly too. Undoubtedly, he'd had a long day with Kira, bringing this giddy smile of anticipation from the choking tears Jessica had heard as she left for work. Having Kira paint Princess had been a brilliant idea. Now, the grief she was feeling had a form, something she could touch and own herself.

David said he'd never spent much time around young children before Kira, but he was somehow a born father, just like he was a born teacher. Probably, she decided sadly, he gave so much precise attention to Kira—and maybe to her—to make up for all the things missing from his own childhood. Whatever the reason, she was just glad Kira had him. She was glad he was here, for Kira's sake as well as her own.

Jessica walked over to touch David's shoulders and roll her face in the honey-sweet scent of his hair. "You okay?" she whispered.

He nodded, clasping her hand. "It's past somebody's bedtime," he said, speaking more to Kira than to her.

"I tried so hard to get here sooner. I'm sorry."

"Don't be." David kissed her wrist. "But Kira needs to get up for school tomorrow. You can tuck her in."

It was a Miami-style winter, the temperature outside a cool seventy degrees, and all of the windows in the house were open. Built in the 1920s with high ceilings and plenty of windows, the house was designed for ventilation without air-conditioning, so they had never bought one. It was originally the neighborhood's pumphouse, but its line of owners since—including David—had added walls and other features to make its layout more conducive to a home. Before he met her, David had knocked out a wall to make more space for a proper living room.

Jessica flipped off the ceiling fan in Kira's room, afraid she would get too cold overnight. Kira's tiny denim jeans and T-shirt were laid out for school at the foot of her bed. David had already pulled her whitewashed pinewood desk away from the wall so he could begin painting his new mural.

"You won't be sad to see the genie go?"

Kira shook her head matter-of-factly. "That's old now." She climbed beneath her blankets, still grasping her painting.

"Why don't you give me that so it won't get wrinkled?"

Kira hesitated, then complied. Her smile was gone, replaced by a grown-up reflectiveness as she gazed at Jessica. "Is Princess in Heaven? Daddy said he didn't know."

"Daddy doesn't believe in Heaven, that's why," Jessica said, sitting by Kira's side after sliding the painting between two picture books standing on Kira's desk. David had never made his atheism a secret to their daughter. "But we do, right?"

Kira nodded, certain. "Right."

"Sunday, you can pray to Princess at church with me and Grandma and Uncle Billy."

Kira's eyelid winced, and she quickly wiped a tear away. She was probably thinking of what a poor substitute that would be for riding on the dog's back, or wrapping her arms around the dog's massive neck. The whole house still smelled like Princess. Jessica spotted some of the dog's straight black hairs on Kira's white bedspread and instinctively tried to brush them off.

"Mommy, why did Princess go away?"

So Peter had been right after all. She was having her moment, at last, to be a parent when Kira needed her. She gently rubbed Kira's forehead. "Princess died. That's how God calls you home, honey. You have to die to go to Heaven."

"Daddy won't go to Heaven?" Kira asked, alarmed.

Ouch. Did Kira understand already what Jessica, as a Christian, feared: That unless David accepted Christ, he would not be saved? That was a tough one to explain. Now was not the time.

"Of course he will. We all will."

"But you said he has to die. He won't die."

Jessica bit her lip, silent. She wasn't handling this right somehow, and she'd ventured into territory that frightened her. How could it be healthy for her to sit and insist that David was going to die, when Kira already felt insecure about losing Princess? "Every living thing God made," she said, still stroking Kira, "has to die someday. Heaven is the next place we go."

Kira scowled. "But Daddy's not going to die, Mommy. Not ever. He said so."

Jessica's stroking stopped. She cocked her head to the side. "When did Daddy say that?" Irritation had slipped into her voice.

Kira didn't answer, apparently sensing she'd said something wrong, that maybe she'd gotten her father in trouble. Jessica recognized the overwhelming loyalty Kira felt for David, the allegiance that hurt her sometimes because she felt shut out.

Jessica tried to sound more encouraging. "He said that today?"

Uncertain, Kira nodded. Then, as she was talented at doing, Kira recalled their conversation: "I said, 'Are you going to die too, Daddy?' and he said, 'No.' And I said, 'Not ever?' And he said, 'Not ever. I promise.'"

Kira's recitation helped Jessica understand a little better. It was only natural that David wouldn't want to scare her needlessly. Death was a big concept to teach a kindergartner. It had been a big concept at eight, when her own father died.

Her father. Damn it. Jessica felt her throat tighten as she saw her daughter's calm security in believing that David would always be here. Jessica had believed that too, those nights when she still wore pajamas and her parents tucked her in. The whole thing had baffled her. Her father drove away in the blue station wagon to buy them dinner from Burger King, and he didn't come back. Neither did the car. White policemen came instead.

Twenty years later, it baffled her anew.

"No, Kira," she whispered, "Daddy's not going to die."

"You see too much good in people," Dr. Wolde said, "even when there's no good to see."

The subject was Michael Corleone; a lofty conversation for the noisy 'Canes Keg, where they'd both ordered apple pie à la mode and coffee after an on-campus dollar showing of The Godfather. Jessica had never seen it, and hadn't planned to go, but the poster was tacked on the wall outside of Dr. Wolde's office when she stopped by to tell him how much she'd enjoyed his classes. As soon as he heard she was a Godfather virgin, his face lit up and he insisted on going with her. That way, he explained, he could experience it for the first time all over again. He'd discovered it for himself not so long ago, he said.

Jessica had had coffee with him once before, when she saw him sitting alone at the student union and, to her surprise, he invited her to join him. Usually, she didn't bond well with professors because authority figures made her tense. But Dr. Wolde had been pleasant, even laughing at some lame joke she made. She'd never have pegged him for a movie buff, which apparently he was.

"I think he's still a good person," Jessica said, defending Corleone. She pictured the young, clean-cut Al Pacino just home from World War II, not the solemn man whose ring was being kissed by the end of the film. And weren't they the same person?

Dr. Wolde snorted, sounding more like the professor she'd known in class. "In the first place, he's a murderer. Never mind the other crimes—all law is so subjective, I won't even count them against him. But he kills."

"Only to protect his family's interests," she said.

"Of course there's always a reason. All killers rationalize, or they couldn't kill. You saw how easily it came to him. Don't his acts make him soulless?"

"I don't think it's always that cut-and-dried, Dr. Wolde. What about self-defense? What about battered wives?" It occurred to her that she was on a strange side of this argument for a church-going Baptist girl. Part of the reason she was so eager to defend Michael Corleone was because Dr. Wolde had been so quick to condemn him. She'd grown to fiercely love Michael's character during the three-hour movie, no matter what he was.

"I really admire the film, Jessica, but he's idealized," Dr. Wolde said. "You're not seeing that, I think, because you're an innocent."

"An innocent?" Jessica said, repeating the archaic word with raised eyebrows.

"It's a wonderful quality. It's refreshing, like staring into a glass of clear water." He met her eyes, and she was unable to blink while he spoke. "*The Godfather* is about the death of a soul. You'll see what I mean. Next week, I'll rent you *Godfather II*. They're companion pieces. Then tell me what you think of your Michael Corleone." His tone was derisive. "In any case, you have to stop calling me Dr. Wolde," he said, "if we're going to continue to date."

"This is a date?" she asked, startled.

"Why not? Just because you wouldn't let me pay for your movie—"

"A whole dollar. Ooh."

"Well, that doesn't mean it's not a date. And I've already alluded to renting a movie for you to watch—and, given that you're not likely to own your own VCR, we would have to watch it in my living room. I'll invite you during the day, so you won't find me overly presumptuous. If it's not too late for that already."

Jessica felt distrustful of his glibness, imagining a guest sign-in book at his little bachelor love den. "Do you date a lot of former students?"

"I've never dated a former student," he said. "I don't date much at all."

"Why not?"

Dr. Wolde didn't answer. He opened his mouth as if to speak, then he changed his mind and ate another forkful of pie. "Say what you will about the 'Canes Keg," he said, "but they have good desserts."

"Is that your way of changing the subject?"

"That's my way of taking a lesson from you, trying to see the good in everything. Next time we eat out, I'm going to take you to a very fine restaurant. I promise."

∗

"That's two dates you're planning for us now," she said.

He smiled. She saw, for the first time since his opening class, the utter perfection of his face and teeth. Seeing it made her stomach jump.

"How old are you?" she asked.

"How old are you?"

"Twenty. As of January."

"I'm twenty-six."

"That's a lie," she said.

He pulled out his wallet, opened it, and found his Florida driver's license to show her his birthdate, a mere six years before hers. He was a Capricorn, like her. That meant he'd been only twenty-five when they met. Unbelievable. She noticed his address, somewhere in northeast Miami, and felt a charge at the idea of visiting his house. Dr. Wolde's house. But it was crazy.

"You seem . . . older . . ." she said. "Not that you look it, at least not much. But you act—"

"Like an old fogy?"

"You said it, not me."

"That comes from being a misanthrope," he said.

"Are you?"

"In general, yes. But not tonight."

Something in his gaze, an unchecked softness, frightened Jessica. It was almost as though her professor, inexplicably, had decided here at the campus bar and grill that he was in love with her. As though he couldn't see that he was brilliant, some kind of prodigy, and that she was a puny kid with common sense and a knack for throwing sentences together but who would never use a word like misanthrope in casual conversation. Hell, she'd be afraid of pronouncing it wrong. Whatever he believed he was seeing in her, he was bound to be disappointed. She'd be a fool to allow a remarkable man like David Wolde to work his way under her skin when she knew he would just get tired of her.

"Dr. Wolde," she said, "I don't think I can date one of my professors. It would feel weird."

"Call me David."

"David, I can't date one of my professors."

"Former professors," he corrected.

"Former professors," she repeated, her voice firm.

Dr. Wolde sighed, glancing down from her face to the scratched mock-wood Formica tabletop. He looked genuinely wounded, but also angry at himself. "I think I've overstepped some protocol here.

I'm no good at this. I thought since you're no longer my student, we could—" He sighed again, laughing nervously. "I'm sorry if I made you uncomfortable. I didn't mean to. I just enjoy this, being with you, and I thought . . ." He raised his palm to cover his eyelids, as though shielding his face from a sudden flash of light. "I'm embarrassed. *Ay Dios mío.* I'm sorry, Jessica."

In that instant, he'd transformed. She couldn't see a trace of the hard-edged man she'd known from the classroom, the man she'd very nearly feared. This was someone else entirely. Much later, when Jessica would try to pinpoint the moment David began to creep into her heart, this was the one she remembered, at the 'Canes Keg, his eyes covered with genuine shame.

She stammered reassurances and joked that she wouldn't file a sexual harassment suit, blurting, "I'd still like to see *Godfather II.* Even though it doesn't sound like it has a happy ending."

David smiled at her again, but his voice was sad. "There's no such thing as happy endings," he said.

Two weeks later, in David's huge nineteenth-century teak bed, they saw each other nude. Wordlessly, he cradled her, burying his face between her thighs. He eased her legs across his shoulders and hoisted her torso high, separating her buttocks, not leaving one spot where her body parted in two untouched by his lapping, gentle tongue. His mouth found places no one's mouth before his had ever dared, shocking her, delighting her. His moistness teased, retreated, plowed, circled. Rigid and shuddering, Jessica could only gasp as her mouth dropped into a startled, happy O.

Until that point, she realized, she had only made love to sloppy, adult-sized children. Sex with Terry, her short-lived freshman-year boyfriend, had been furious, making her think of a piston, and she remembered wincing while she watched his clenched buttocks thrust in and out of her eyeline in a blur as she stared over his shoulder. Terry had tried to explore her with his mouth, but not like this. Not like he was thirsty for all of her body's juices.

Jessica was so eager to return the pleasure that she massaged David's swollen maleness as though she could feel her own touch, and she tried, very nearly with success, to swallow its entire length whole. Like it was the most natural thing in the world.

Then David lay on top of her, grasping her wrists and planting her arms above her head. He arched his back and nudged himself inside of her, his breath whistling softly from behind his teeth. His heat blanketed her, filled her. When his pelvis began to dance, slowly at first but then with an urgent rolling motion, Jessica became lost from her body and thrashed against his weight as though she were having convulsions. Her cries were alien, primal.

"Damn. How are you so good?" she asked him, nearly demanding, when they finished in a bath of perspiration.

David laughed. "You make it sound like a complaint."

"Oh, no. It's not. But I wish . . . I could be like that. To make you feel those things."

He gazed at her, smiling. She could understand what people meant when they said they felt like they had known someone for years; the feeling was reflected back to her in that smile. He touched her hair. He didn't try to patronize her by telling her that she'd been just as good. They both knew that she'd mostly been helpless to his learned mouth, to the rhythms of his hips.

"I feel what you feel," David said.

"I hope I'm like that someday. Like you," Jessica said.

"Ah. You will be. You're a quick study. You know that old joke? How do you get to Carnegie Hall?"

Jessica smiled, and her fingers found him waiting, still wonderfully hard, beneath the sheets. She stroked. "Practice, practice, practice," she said, glad to hear him moan.

Alone while David showered, Jessica's heartbeat didn't slow. She realized she already felt a powerful glow in her chest, the kind that wouldn't go away soon. What had she gotten herself into? This guy had played her like a string bass. He'd always known exactly what to say, exactly what to do, and now here she was waiting for him in his bed. Was she being a naive schoolgirl to believe there was a special weight to this encounter, that she was more than a typical Saturday night lay to him?

But when David came back, she knew it was not typical for either of them.

"I don't believe in God," he announced, snuggling his dampness beside her. It came out of nowhere. Jessica suddenly felt acutely naked; she pulled the sheet across her chest to cover her breasts. David went on: "I'm only saying that because you do, because you wear that gold cross around your neck, because I see you say grace before you eat, almost in secret. I'm not vain enough to profess to know absolute truth, but I consider myself an atheist. I've seen too much to believe God has any hand in what goes on in this world. I'm not an antireligion zealot, but I wanted you to know that. In case it matters to you."

Jessica swallowed back her confusion. She was disappointed, but his honesty touched her. He was hurting for some reason, but Christ might still find him.

"It doesn't matter. Not now," she said, touching the springy curls that framed his face. Not ever? Oh, that face. David's parents were Ethiopian, which explained a great deal; Michel, who had visited Africa, told her many Ethiopians were exceedingly handsome. If David was any proof of that, Michel was right. She could still taste David's skin, his perspiration, on her lips. It was so strange how he'd always kept a careful distance before, not touching her even slightly when they walked or sat together, but now he was cleaved to her, cradling her against him, surrendering the whole of himself. She loved being wrapped inside him, and his confession hadn't changed that.

"No wonder you don't believe in happy endings," she said, trying to sound lighthearted.

He kissed her forehead, and she could almost swear she felt his jaw tremble above her. "I don't think about endings," he said.

The backyard, compact and on the bank of the river, was their place for special moments. This was where Jessica brought David when she knew she was pregnant, where she drew a crude stick-figure woman with a bloated belly tossing a rope into the sky, inscribing it with a variation of a line from one of his favorite movies, It's a Wonderful Life: David lassos stork, she wrote. She'd promised to stop taking birth control pills a year after they were married, and she did on the night of their anniversary without reminding him. Within three months, she'd conceived.

Despite the time that had passed since she'd moved in, the house still felt more like David's than hers. They married as soon as Jessica graduated from college, and since she didn't have any furniture of her own, she'd simply transferred herself into David's space, with his Victorian antiques and wood-carved bowls and African mud cloths. She was still sometimes afraid to touch things, the way she'd felt in her grandmother's house as a child. Soon after they were married, she accidentally stepped on one of David's favorite records, a seventy-eight RPM by an old group called The Jazz Brigade. She apologized, saying she'd find him another one, but he shook his head and brushed his finger against her cheek. It's irreplaceable, he told her, not scolding, stating a simple fact. His eyes were dim. She felt guilty about it for years.

Unlike the rest of the house, though, the backyard seemed to belong to her too. The sound of the water licking behind them was always soothing, as was the darkness, even the eerie call of Night Song. If she heard scurrying around them in the dark, she'd learned not to panic; it might be a raccoon or a possum, or simply a blue crab. The crabs left fist-sized burrows in the soft soil around their backyard bushes. The summer before, a crab crawled into the house. This was where she hoped David could begin to heal his grief over Princess, which was worrying her. He'd been despondent throughout dinner, so distracted while he served her that he even burned his forearm on a hot saucepan, leaving a dark-red leaf-shaped mark. Now his wound was dressed with tape and gauze from their first-aid kit, Kira was in bed, and they were alone.

"Sit down in front of me," she said. "Time for a backrub."

Silently, David complied, sitting cross-legged on the grass in front of the picnic bench. He was wearing combat fatigues, but no shirt. His skin was smooth, virtually hairless. Every time Jessica touched him, she wanted to follow through with gentle tastes with her mouth. Tonight, she resisted that urge and merely kneaded his tense shoulders.

"Relax, baby," she coaxed.

"I'm sorry. I'm trying."

The white from the bandage on David's arm glowed in the darkness. "I hope that scar won't be permanent. It's bad. I almost wish we'd gone to the doctor."

"I'm all right," David said. Jessica knew it would be pointless to argue. Aside from his trips with her during her pregnancy, and then during Kira's asthma attack, she'd never known David to go near any hospital or doctor. He was adamant to the point of annoying her. Once, she'd argued he was selfish to refuse to take an HIV test or to have a physical before they were married. Now she was left to wonder whether David was really as healthy as he looked. Or, could he have high blood sugar? Cancer? AIDS even? He never complained of so much as a toothache, but she didn't know. She'd decided to leave it to faith, but it was an uneasy faith.

Jessica felt some of the tightness of David's back melting away. He let his head dangle back, and he even moaned a soft approval. "Better?" she asked.

He nodded, his eyes closed.

"You know," Jessica began carefully, "this may not be the time you want to hear this, but I think we should consider driving up to the puppy farm in Naples." The tension returned, and David sat upright, about to speak. She cut him off. "I know it's early now, probably too early. But I'm thinking about Kira."

"No," David said, so firmly he sounded angry. "No more dogs."

"You're just saying that now . . ."

"It's cruel for kids. You give them pets, and then they die one by one. Teacake is next, you just watch. He won't stay indoors. It'll be a fight with a raccoon or a car or something, but he won't last much longer. I haven't even seen him tonight."

"He's sleeping in Kira's room. And he's fixed."

"That's not the point. The point is, you know I'm right." He sounded flustered. Jessica sighed, plying his skin with her fingers. She felt knots of stress in his muscles.

At times like this, Jessica was reminded of the super-gifted classmates she'd met when she was a kid, so bright and yet so socially and emotionally maladjusted. She figured David's moodiness, his tendency to tears, was part of the makeup that gave him such a capacity to love. Maybe he couldn't have one without the other. She'd learned it was best to appeal to his reason.

"So what you're saying is, because we're afraid of losing the things we cherish, we shouldn't allow ourselves to enjoy anything. Am I following you?"

"Something like that."

"But can't you see what that means? That's not right."

He didn't answer.

Jessica's own childhood losses had been overshadowed by David's, she learned soon after they began dating. His parents, sister, and brother died in a train wreck in France when he was twelve and away at boarding school. They'd all been en route to visit him as a surprise. He'd been too shattered to continue his studies and fell into state care, where he bounced between foster homes and ended up traveling with Catholic missionaries in Africa, never mind that he'd been raised a Muslim. That was how he'd come to learn Swahili and English in addition to French, Arabic, and his parents' native language of Amharic. Spanish came in college, which he finished in Madrid by age nineteen with an accelerated master's degree. He got his Ph.D. in music history from Harvard, and ever since he'd lived in Miami, where he learned Creole. Miami, he told her, had been his first home that felt lasting.

Maybe losing Princess was tearing at his fabric, proving to him that his newfound family was fragile too. Jessica did understand. Some mornings she woke up, gazed at David's sleeping form, and wondered when it would finally occur to him that he had twice her IQ and could do so much more with his life than spend it with her. She understood all too well.

"We should go away somewhere, all of us," David said.

"I can't take another vacation so soon. Not now."

"Not a vacation," he said, turning around to look at her. "I mean, we should leave. We should go to Zimbabwe or France or Des Moines, Iowa, and start everything fresh again. Let's just cash in some of my stocks, live on royalties. I can't understand your compulsion to anchor yourself to that newspaper. I'd really like to leave, Jess. I'd like for us to enjoy each other without any distractions. Kira will be grown up before we know it."

Jessica bit her lip, hoping the darkness would obscure the pain on her face. The career she was trying to build didn't mean anything to him. David had made this suggestion once before, when he was slightly tipsy, and it worried her then as it did now. Their visions for their lives were so different, how could their future possibly remain entwined?

"Why are you saying this, David? Because Princess died?"

"Yes," he said. "Because she spent the last six days of her life locked up with strangers, not with us. And because if we had known she would be dead in six days, we wouldn't have left her there. We would have done things differently. And I don't like to go through life counting the things I'd like to have done differently. The list is getting longer."

"Does that list include me?" Jessica whispered.

David's long silence frightened her. She saw his chest rise and fall as he breathed deeply. "As a matter of fact, yes," he said. "I wasted a year teaching you, another year courting you. I should have married you the day we met. And we should have had Kira sooner. Much sooner."

Jessica laughed at herself for the sentimental tears that sprang to her eyes. She should know David by now, that his words were capable of making her swell until she too was certain that it was all too good to last. David was too good to last.

She could nearly buy into his fantasy of the three of them immersed in one another, secluded from the world. She'd already drifted from most of her friends, and her mother had only a toe-hold on her, though she lived just thirty minutes away. Same for her sister, Alexis, a hematologist who lived on Miami Beach. Her fellow sorors in Alpha Kappa Alpha were threatening to boot her out of the alumnae chapter if she didn't start showing up at the meetings. All of her spare time was with David and Kira. A part of Jessica wanted to follow David wherever his dreams could take them, but then a voice whispered: What about your dreams?

When she was with him, the Sun-News always seemed far away. She hadn't thought of her nursing-home stories once since she'd been home, and only now did she remember Peter's book proposal with a sense of discomfort. She couldn't bring it up. To David's ears, the idea would sound appalling. She could almost see why. Almost.

"We don't have to leave everything to love each other, David," she said. "And we have plenty of time."

David didn't answer. Above them, Night Song's voice fluttered through the dry leaves, shaking them with a gentle rattling, and rose into the velvet, moonless dark.

▪ 4

Once again, he had killed.

Never kill again. That had been his vow. After the Century of Blood, the years of rage, he promised himself he would never again use his hands for killing. For a hundred years, Dawit had lived by his own law. Yet, in a moment's forgetting, he'd done it so easily. So effortlessly.

What aberration of nature would murder his own child?

He remembered a conversation he'd had with his Life brothers years ago, smoking opium and feeling full of themselves, when they'd compared themselves to the Yorubas' immortal *Orisha*, the Spirits. You, Dawit, a brother told him, are Ogun: Iron Spirit, warrior, lonely self-exile. "Oh! I am afraid of Ogun," they'd chanted in Yoruba, laughing in a mock prayer. "His long hands can save his children from the abyss. Save me!"

No, he was no god. He could not save anyone, not even little Rosalie. His only power was to bring death to others, despair to himself.

"This is damnation," Dawit whispered into the darkness, not loud enough to awaken the woman beside him. They were not touching at this moment, their nakedness was separated by several inches. Perhaps a taste of her navel with the tip of his tongue or a quick gaze at her sleeping face would wipe his mind free. But he did not move, so his mind remained hostage.

Never love again. That too had been his vow. How foolish he'd been to forsake it! He should have realized by now that, to him, love was much more perilous than mere killing.

Love that which is constant, like yourself, Khaldun had told them all when they consecrated themselves to the Living Blood in the underground temple in Lalibela. *The body heals itself, but the mind does not.*

Now, 450 years later, Dawit knew what Khaldun had meant. His suffering, his worries, his losses, would be his living death. Nature had been poised to take his child, and for the first time he'd been a witness to nature's inevitable triumph: his own child among the successsion of mortal lives constantly flickering out around him. In a blink of an eye, this was what became of a child. Every child. Always.

Was it more humane that he had taken Rosalie instead? No. It had been a selfish impulse, his shock at the profanity nature had made of her.

He should not have gone to see Rosalie. And he should not be sleeping beside this woman who had led him, again, to love, promising him a deeper abyss. Like Adele.

Before he could fight it, the horrible image swallowed Dawit's memories: Adele's naked corpse swinging from a rope tied around the thick branch of a tree. Adele's face, which had kissed his, wrenched in painful death; her fingers, which had owned his private parts, bumping lifeless against her hipbones. He hadn't remembered, until his eyes had seen Adele's twirling carcass, what a mortal's death meant. An end. A silenced voice. A stolen laugh. An emptied brain. Forever gone.

His own lynching had been sweet relief, for a precious moment. He swung beside Adele for a full day, moaning and sobbing, the rope slicing into his neck, always seeking to make him quiet. Three times, he gave the rope its victory; when his breath stopped, when he felt his cervical vertebra about to snap beneath his flesh, he did not fight. He let death come. And when he awakened, each time gasping to breathe, new tears waiting, he let death come again. And again. His last sight, always, was Adele.

Why must he always reawaken? Why couldn't the Living Blood inside of him ever rest?

At last, when it was nearly dawn, he'd given up and found the strength to grip the rope above his head, hoisting himself up by his arms until the deadly coil released him. He was free.

Free? Yes, he remembered, enslaved no more. Free with no reason to celebrate his freedom.

"Was this what you wanted, Adele?" he'd sobbed to her corpse, which remained frozen as though it still hung in the air even after he'd cut her down and rocked her in his arms. "Was this the freedom you followed me to find? I can't follow you where you've gone."

He'd become a killer, once again, to blot out his loss. When the Union regiment disturbed his hermit's camp after Adele died, Dawit's prayer for vengeance was answered. He was armed for battle with a striped flag, a ragged uniform of blue, and a bayonet, the wicked firearm that doubled as a spear's tip. He used his weapon well. He watered fields with blood.

And it was not enough. Never enough.

This new century, that much closer to the new millennium, had brought him hope. No more killing, he'd told himself. He earnestly tried to preserve his humanity; first through disciplined meditation and study under Khaldun, then by escaping to the mortal pleasures most of his Life Brothers did not care to know.

But his century of peace, clearly, was over.

Rosalie had shown him his own frailty. He could no longer navigate his path, imprisoned as he was by his emotions and an immortal's haughty whims.

One killing, one loss. One loss, one killing. Maybe loss was his price for Life.

Dawit smothered a hot sob in his throat, afraid to make a sound. He was not alone, and he could not explain his tears to this woman. That pact was his curse.

No, Dawit decided, he was not worthy of Ogun's name.

Prometheus was a better mythological soul mate. He was in chains, his innards picked at by an eagle, watching with disdain as his flesh, again and again, grew back to be freshly destroyed. Always. Loss had found him again, its talons and beak riving his liver, his heart, his soul. He would be forever stripped, reborn, stripped.

But reborn, Dawit wondered, as what?

▪ 5

David's burn mark had vanished by Sunday, less than a week later. Jessica noticed his bare arms as he slung his starched dress shirt across a chair and went outside in his undershirt, insisting on tuning up her mother's car after church. No sense paying a mechanic to rip you off, he told her. Searching for a scar—she couldn't remember if he'd burned his right or left arm—she tried to recall the last time she'd seen the bandage at all.

"What are you doing, baby?" he asked while she ran her fingertips across his unblemished skin. The day was unseasonably sunny, nearly eighty degrees, so David was clammy with a film of perspiration as he worked beneath the Honda Accord's hood in the unshaded driveway. Bright sunlight made his skin look brick-red.

"Your burn is gone."

"Maybe it's a miracle," he said. "Can you hand me that ratchet wrench on top of the toolbox?"

The miracle remark stung Jessica. Sunday was church day, and every other Sunday the family met at Bea Jacobs's house for an early dinner after the eleven o'clock service at New Life Bethel Baptist Church. The church was six blocks from Bea's house in the hedge-lined middle-class black neighborhood in northwest Dade where Jessica had grown up. The area was now in the shadow of Pro Player Stadium, the Miami Dolphins's football stadium, with horrific traffic jams on game days; during the football season, it was nearly impossible to make it to her mother's house on Sundays because of the steady flow of fans.

David rarely agreed to sit through a service, but he came today because he wanted to be with her and Kira. She'd glanced at him during the sermon for signs of acceptance, some enlightenment, but his face always grew stony in church. Once, she saw him staring at the painting of The Last Supper, especially the bearded Jesus figure in the middle, with nothing short of contempt. She'd seen that look before, prompting her to ask David if he hated God. He paused before answering.

"If there truly is one God, then it's God who's displeased with me," he said simply. He never answered when she asked why in the world he would say such a thing, claiming it was a joke. But she knew it wasn't.

Watching David methodically remove her mother's old spark plugs with counterclockwise twists of the wrench, Jessica told herself that her husband would never be saved. She would have to accept it. He'd been too poisoned against Christ as a Muslim orphan left to missionaries who were bent on converting rather than consoling him. He did not believe. If she trusted her Scriptures, that meant she would spend eternity without him.

Jessica had gone to church all her life, in her frilly pinafores and white gloves, but when she was young it was only another place she had to go. Home, school, church. She didn't really learn what faith was until after her father died, when she stood on her toes to see what was in the rose-colored casket. She didn't know what to expect, why she'd been so anxious to take her place in the line at the front of the church, clinging to her mother's hand. There, inside, was the grim, washed-out face of Daddy.

Daddy was going to stay in this box? And they were going to

bury this box in the ground? He had to be somewhere else, like her mother kept saying. That wasn't him at all.

On that day, Heaven kept Jessica's world from caving in.

David, somehow, lived without believing in a better place. And yet he could still wake up in the morning and carry out his day and go to sleep without being frozen awake with fears of death, of darkness, of nothing. She didn't understand how he could do that. She tried, telling herself one night *This is all, there is nothing after this*, but she felt swallowed by the vast barrenness. She thought of her father's bones, crumbling to black dust inside that beautiful casket beneath the ground.

Maybe David had a point. Religion was a crutch, a way people rationalized away their pain in life, like the slaves yearning for a better existence. A denial. When there is no fear of death, David had told her once, there is no need for religion.

For a moment, watching David examine her mother's dirty air filter and shake his head, she envied his strength. Here I am with a two-month-old scratch on my wrist from Teacake, but he heals by himself, she thought. His spirit, his body, everything. No wonder he never seemed to age a day.

"Din-ner!"

Her sister's shrill voice flew out of the open living room jalousie windows, a reminder of childhood. That was the same window where Jessica had stood vigil, waiting for her father to come home from his job working on the telephone lines; she'd probably been waiting by that window when he drove to Burger King in his billed Oakland Raiders cap, the one night he never came back. Jessica saw Alex's hazy figure in her place, in a bright-purple dress. Kira was beside her in the window, a ball of white taffeta and lace. "Dinner, Mommy! Dinner, Daddy!" she echoed. As usual, Kira needed to be a part of the production, whatever it was.

Bea Jacobs had fixed baked chicken, collard greens, cornbread, and two desserts, a sweet potato pie and a lemon pound cake. Jessica was amused by her mother's sudden culinary finesse. She'd never cooked this way for the family before, but she started in earnest after Kira was born, assuming a grandmother's role, and Uncle Billy had passed along some down-home Georgia recipes since he moved in, like peach cobbler and chicken feet stew. Bea was a neurotic cook, obsessed with kitchen details the way she'd fretted over the books before she retired as business manager of a chain of beauty shops. Like her daughters, she was a perfectionist. And she caught on fast.

"Where's David?" Bea asked, pulling her chair up to the head of the table after setting down the plate of cornbread. She'd always been thin, and she wore her hair in a silver natural, cut short the way Alexis wore hers. Only Jessica relaxed her hair, letting it grow in a straight page-boy style just past her ears.

"He's washing up," Jessica answered.

"Let's go on and say grace, then."

In a clash of wills with his in-law, David had once made a production of refusing to sit through grace at her table. Jessica thought her mother would bite through her lip, she was so angry. All things considered, Jessica thought with a smile, Bea was adjusting well to having a heathen in the family; both her father and grandfather had been pastors.

They grasped hands; Bea taking Jessica and Alexis's hands on either side of her, Jessica holding Kira's tiny fingers, and Alexis reaching over to Uncle Billy's wheelchair to touch his ruined left hand. Uncle Billy still couldn't move his left arm since his stroke. They murmured their amens in unison.

"You finished fooling with that car yet? I got something you need to listen to in back," Uncle Billy said when David joined them at the table. He'd dressed again and smelled of fresh cologne. The scent, whatever he'd found, suited him.

"Don't tell me you rooted out that old Jelly Roll record."

"Told you I had it somewhere up in all them boxes. Original recording, nineteen and twenty-five. Got me some Satchmo too." Uncle Billy's words slurred slightly, the stroke compounded by missing front teeth and a heavy Georgia accent. Sometimes Jessica couldn't understand him, but David never had a problem. A relative from Bea's mother's side, Uncle Billy had been born near the grounds of the same plantation where the family had been slaves for years.

"I'll be damned, Uncle Billy," David said, smiling. "I may just have to sneak in here one night and steal those away. And that old Victrola of yours too."

"Oh, no. You ain't stealin' nothin' from this old man. And I'ma still find that Jazz Brigade recording. My daddy left me that from when we was in Chicago, right 'fore the Depression. He used to watch those boys rehearse. Said they could cook. Seth 'Spider' Tillis, Lester Payne, all of them."

Something like rapture passed across David's face. He loved music. Whatever shelf space on their walls and in the closets that wasn't filled with books was dedicated to his vast record and CD collection, exclusively classical, blues, and jazz. He'd once told her that his CD collection alone numbered more than four thousand. But it was much more than a hobby to him; the New York Times had called David's book on the early jazz age, which he'd written at Harvard as his doctoral dissertation, the "definitive history of jazz."

David leaned closer to Uncle Billy, his chin resting on his palm. "Uncle Billy," he said slowly, "if you could find The Jazz Brigade . . . I lost all my originals. And it's so rare—"

"What's the . . . Depression?" Kira piped up.

David tapped her on top of her head. "It was a long time ago, Duchess. Many years before any of us were born."

"Now, hold up. I was born nineteen-seventeen," Uncle Billy corrected him.

"Yes, you'd better speak for yourself, David," Bea said. She always spoke a painstaking English, her T's sharp, a result of her upper-middle-class rearing upstate in Quincy.

"We sure got some old folks at this table, don't we?" Alexis asked. She shared a playful glance with Jessica; she and Jessica looked like twins, though Alex was thirty-four, six years older than Jessica, the same age as David.

"Old enough to know better," Bea said.

Bea's skin was a fair shade, though she'd told Jessica she was teased by her cousins as a child because she was the darkest one in her family. Maybe it was through rebellion that Bea married Raymond Jacobs, the darkest man she had ever known. Bea's pet name for him had been Blue, Jessica learned much later, because he was blue-black. Jessica and Alexis were mixtures of brown, though Jessica couldn't think of a time when anyone ever once felt a need to discuss the family complexions. In church school, when one of Jessica's young classmates pointed out that Bea was "light-skinded," like it was something special, Jessica didn't know what the girl was talking about.

Raymond was Bea's second husband. She'd divorced her first husband after ten years because of his drinking, then moved to Miami to begin a new life. She'd also hoped to have children, and her first husband had been sterile. Then, she met Raymond.

Raymond, who was six years younger than Bea and had only an eighth-grade education, won Jessica's college-educated mother through his sly wit and natural intelligence. His lack of formal schooling shut him out of many jobs, but Jessica had known he was a genius before she really knew what a genius was. She'd always looked forward to the day—maybe in fourth grade or fifth grade, she'd thought—when she could sit down and impress her father with how smart she was too. Fate had cheated her out of that chance.

Raymond had been young when he died, only forty. But Bea was no longer young. Jessica remembered, while sitting at the dinner table, that her mother had just turned sixty-six. She didn't look it, despite her silver hair; her skin was smooth and unwrinkled, splotched with only a few dark moles. Still, in just ten years, which no longer seemed like an eternity to Jessica, Bea would be seventy-six, close to Uncle Billy's age now.

Time passed so quickly. Jessica felt the disquieting sense, as she often did, of enjoying a fleeting moment before it was over as a memory, as though she were already reminiscing about Sunday dinner with Uncle Billy and her mother, way back when they were both still alive. Alexis's excited cry pulled Jessica from her thoughts. "Ooh, girl, I almost forgot," her sister said. "Tell us about that book you're writing."

The question was a surprise to everyone at the table, bringing a round of smiles and exclamations. Except from David.

"I was planning to tell you tonight. It's not in stone yet. Peter said something to his agent, and he thinks we can get a contract and take a leave of absence for a few months."

"Peter." David's tone was knowing, nearly scornful.

"What does that mean?"

David didn't answer, his eyes fixed on the road as he drove the minivan south on Biscayne Boulevard. It was raining again, unusual for February. Usually, the moody, sporadic storm clouds they'd experienced throughout the week appeared in summertime. It had been a gloomy and wet few days. Maybe that accounted some for David's sour mood, Jessica thought.

"Block . . . buster . . . Video," Kira said from the backseat. She'd taken to announcing all signs they passed. "I can read. Burger King. See? Star-dust Mo-tel."

"That's enough, Duchess. We know you're smart," he said.

"David, why are you so down on Peter?"

"We'll talk about that later." He tried to sound pleasant.

"Mommy, is Peter coming over?" Kira asked. Jessica allowed Kira to address Peter by his first name because her attempts to pronounce Mister Donovitch were hopeless. "He gave me a doll-baby. 'Member? For Christmas?"

"I remember."

David sighed shortly, no longer hiding his irritation. Jessica wondered if he was somehow jealous of Peter, if he felt threatened by her friendship with him. True, David was always simply courteous when Peter visited, holding himself at a slight distance only she could detect. But jealousy didn't make sense; she'd told him she thought Peter was gay. Did David have a problem with whites, then? She'd have to wait until they were home and Kira was bathed and tucked in before she could corner David in the bedroom for an explanation.

She found David spread-eagled across the bed, lying on his stomach. The bed, which David had imported, cost him twenty thousand dollars, he told her the first night they shared it. It was more than a hundred years old, a canopied opium bed that once belonged to some useless lord in China. The rich teak frame was engraved with intricate patterns of dragons. The bed was so high, David had explained, because its original owner probably rarely got up and wanted to meet visitors at eye level. Even now, whenever Jessica sat on the bed, which was built to rock slightly on a hinge, she felt like she'd entered an age-old sanctuary.

"Okay. Tell me what's bothering you," she said.

"I hate hearing secondhand about developments that affect our family," David said, his voice sounding muffled.

"You're right. I'm sorry. I just mentioned it to Alex—"

"I know what it takes to write a book, Jess. And traveling besides? I don't like it at all."

Jessica felt a stab of hurt, but it quickly turned to anger. "I planned to talk it over with you. I didn't know I'd also be asking permission."

"Apparently not. It sounds very much decided."

"You wrote a book, David. Remember?"

"Exactly my point. I wrote a book before I had a family or any life to speak of, and it ate up vast portions of my time. Four months, to me, sounds highly optimistic. I'd say at least six."

"So? What's six months?"

At this, David rolled over to look her in the eye. "Six months," he said, "is six months. A very short time, and yet a very long time."

She didn't understand him. No matter how long she lived with him and observed him and tried to think the way he did, he always confounded her somehow. Was it chauvinism? Selfishness?

"Peter says—"

David cut her off with a disgusted sound and rolled toward the wall. He was muttering to himself in another language, not Spanish this time, but Amharic or Arabic. She couldn't tell which. She thought of Ricky Ricardo having a tantrum on I Love Lucy.

"English, please," she said.

Groaning, he lifted himself and sat beside her so that their feet dangled together over the edge of the bed. He rubbed her thigh. "Do you watch my face when I listen to Mozart's Eine kleine Nacht-musik? Or Bessie Smith? Or when I look at you and Kira? Do you see the delight?"

She nodded. She'd seen that expression today, when he talked about music and his lost Jazz Brigade records with Uncle Billy.

"That's how your face looks," he said, "when Peter comes. Or any of your other reporter friends. You cloister in a corner and build a bonfire among yourselves, feeding it with analysis and supposition and gossip. The city commissioner's race. The presidential election. What's Peter's specialty? Oh, yes. The Mafia. Santo Trafficante and the rest. The sites of their summer homes, their illegitimate children, and so on. That's where we lose each other, Jess. You can sit with me and enjoy Mozart. And Bessie Smith. And Kira, of course. And you even tolerate my ramblings about the Crusades, or King Tewedros the Second in Ethiopia, or Francisco Pizarro, or the Huguenots in France—"

"Sometimes—" Jessica cut him off. As college faded behind her, Jessica realized her knowledge of world history was limited to Spain sending Columbus to "discover" America in 1492. When David went off, she felt like a moron.

"Try as I might—and I do, Jess, I really do—I can't muster that something you feel . . . that concern, or whatever it is, that drives you and your bonfire. But Peter does. And for that reason, he can move a part of you I can never hope to touch. The world is too much with him, to paraphrase Wordsworth . . . And I'm . . ." He paused, but didn't continue.

"The Brother from Another Planet," Jessica said, smiling, using Alex's nickname for him.

"Make light if you want, but I almost fell asleep when Peter was here last week. Bill Clinton, blah blah blah. Jesus Christ."

"I know," Jessica sighed, massaging his scalp with her fingertips. David was a history whiz, but he was so indifferent to current events, pop culture, and even racial issues. This barrier between them was getting harder to ignore. She could drop names like Louis Farrakhan or Clarence Thomas and get a blank gaze from David, so he definitely couldn't deal with discussions about anything her friends were talking about at work. Nothing. And forget about new music or television—except the sentimental old love stories, like *Casablanca*, that he watched on videotape. David lived in a world of books and jazz music.

She didn't understand how a man who was so damn smart could choose ignorance. She read her *Sun-News* and *New York Times* every morning before going to work, and when she came home she found the newspapers wherever she'd left them, untouched.

"Whether you admit it or not, Peter wants to pull you away. He wants to do it with this first book, and then another. He doesn't share our priorities, like family," David said.

"That's not fair."

"Isn't it? What does he have? Whom does he have?"

"David . . ."

"I'm only being honest. He has voter surveys and a yen for buried secrets. That's all, Jessica. That's all."

Jessica was surprised to realize that her eyes were stinging with tears. This was cutting to her core for some reason. She really wanted to write this book. Yes, maybe she did crave the chance to bond with Peter, who gave a damn about the things everyday folks talked about at the beauty shop and on their lunch breaks. So what? Why couldn't David see that their book might help people and make a difference? Was he really so oblivious to life outside their El Portal street?

Despite their differences, Jessica wanted to believe with her heart that she and David were soul mates. But sometimes their reliance upon each other scared her. Often, at bedtime, instead of making love or going to sleep, they spent hours talking about deep subjects like how the legacy of the African slave trade had transformed the world, or the essences of men and women, or the nature of love. And she learned something new from him every day, whether it was an unusual word in Spanish, the unsung conquests of some African emperor, or a verse from an Elizabethan sonnet. He even knew the Bible and the old-time spirituals inside and out. They had to work at it, but they found their common ground.

Ultimately, though, their differences returned, and she wondered how deeply they ran. How could she continue to overlook them, when they loomed so large?

Jessica didn't notice at first that David had slipped his arm around her shoulder, and that his head was nuzzled against her neck. "Don't go write a book now, Jess. Not now," he was repeating in her ear softly, barely audibly, as though begging for his life.

▪ 6

"Your man is tripping, Jessica."

"You're telling me."

Jessica had tried to reach Alexis at her job at the UM medical school's hematology lab all morning, and her sister finally called her back at the newspaper at ten minutes to noon. Peter planned to have lunch with Jessica to hammer out details for the book proposal he wanted to send his agent by midweek. She'd just seen him vanish into Sy's office. Lord, was he going to tell their boss already? Now she was nervous.

"I hate to talk about your husband, but you know what? He's always tried to monopolize you, from the beginning. I'll never forget how he carried on that time we wanted to see Janet Jackson. I mean, damn, he couldn't let you go for one night? And you were so afraid you wouldn't find a man that you put up with it."

Ouch. Alex was right, at least partially. Jessica was grateful she wasn't in her sister's shoes; Alexis was single now, and still looking. Jessica wondered if her sister would ever get married, or if it mattered to her anymore.

Considering Jessica's history with black men, David had been a godsend. Jessica and Alex won scholarships to a lily-white private school for gifted children when they were young, so they'd been socialized around whites except at church. When the scholarship money ran out, Jessica's adjustment to a mostly black public high school hadn't been easy. Huddles of black football players snickered at Jessica when she walked past, a gangly bookworm. One boy Jessica didn't even know sneered at her, saying she must want to be white since she was in honors classes with all of those white kids. To fit in, Alex had taken on a homegirl demeanor and found a boyfriend in high school, but Jessica never did. She'd felt like the same outcast in college, even with twenty pounds more shape and a sassy haircut.

Then she met David, who was so different himself. She thought many blacks were so quick to judge her based on nothing; but David never made hurtful assumptions about her, and that had been such a relief.

Alex never saw it that way. Jessica remembered the sting she'd felt after introducing her sister to David in the beginning; Alex had already ripped her ear open for going to bed with a professor, especially so fast, but Jessica had hoped her sister would be as impressed as she was by David's mind and manners, not to mention his incredible face. Didn't happen. After spending only one afternoon with her and David, Alex told her later: "Jessica, don't buy it. That man is running a game on you. He'll never really care about anybody but himself."

It had been a mean thing to say, Jessica thought. Mean and unjustified. Just because David had been shy with Alexis there? Because he wasn't good at chitchat? Or maybe he seemed a little arrogant? What about all of the *good* things? Alex admitted she still couldn't give Jessica a concrete reason for her first impression, and sometimes Jessica was convinced her sister had never learned to see past it.

"Look, it's not like I snapped up the first loser who came along. Is it?" Jessica asked.

Alexis sighed. "No, girl. That's not what I mean. You know David is something else. He's fine, he's intelligent, a model father. And he's good to you, too, most of the time. I just think you tolerate all his clinging because you don't think you have a choice."

"Well, I'll tell you what," Jessica said, "I'd rather have him clinging than walking out the door."

Alexis sighed, but didn't say anything.

"What?" Jessica asked.

When Alexis spoke, her voice was low and stern. "It just pisses me off," she said. "Look at the guilt trip that man has put on you. Like all you're supposed to do with your life is sit and hold his hand. I don't know where he gets that, but that's not the way it works. Here you are about to accomplish something meaningful, and instead of toasting you with champagne, your own husband is making you feel like shit."

"I know," Jessica said softly.

"You think Daddy was ever like that with Mom? Hell, no. David should be boosting you up, not holding you down. You write that damn book, girl. Do you hear me? You write it. And then you write a whole bunch more."

Jessica smiled, grateful to have Alexis to talk to. She'd learned long ago not to complain about her husband to her mother, since Bea remembered all slights long after Jessica had forgotten them. Bea would have a fit if she knew how much David opposed the book. Alexis, at least, was a little more objective. Not much, but a little.

"I will," Jessica said, deciding.

Once again, Peter suggested O'Leary's. He never got tired of the bar's greasy chicken wings. Jessica ordered a Ceasar salad and opted for a beer this time. She felt like she needed it. Since it was too hot on the patio, they sat inside beneath a television set playing The Young and the Restless, her mother's favorite soap. It was reassuring to glance up at the screen and recognize some of the actors playing the same characters she'd known when she was a devotee in high school; they were always there, year after year.

"Len had a surprise for me this morning," Peter said.

"Who's Len?"

"My agent. Leonard Stoltz. He mentioned our idea to an editor he knows, and she loves it. Len's guessing we might be able to swing a forty thousand dollar advance."

"A . . ."

"The snag is, we'd have to promise to use a case that's getting a lot of press up there in New York now, some guy who locked his father in the basement until he starved to death. It's not exactly within our purview of nursing facilities . . . and I know forty isn't a lot, divided in half . . ."

Jessica's mind was frozen. Somebody already wanted their book, and they hadn't even written a proposal. Half of forty thousand was nearly half her annual salary. " . . . Len wants us to overnight the proposal today, so he'll have something to show her while she's still excited. Jess? You with me?"

That instant, using her husband's nickname for her, Peter had sounded exactly like David. "I'm in shock," she said.

He smiled, and she noticed his face was drenched in red, probably from a weekend on the beach. She could see tiny age lines near those oddly green eyes. "I knew you would be. And I know how I felt when I sold my first book, so I got you something to put on top of your computer while you work—for inspiration."

He reached into his jacket pocket and brought out a paperweight, a six-inch troll with a wild tuft of purple hair, wearing glasses and holding a pencil. WRITE ON, it said.

"Oh, my god . . . Peter . . . you're so sweet . . ."

"I'm only being sweet now because I'm about to turn into a hard-ass. The editor said our chances for a sale are better if we promise a quick turnaround, maybe even by June."

"Four months . . ."

"Exactly. I want you to get to work on that Chicago case, the smothered woman. Maybe you should fly out there. In the meantime, at least get the police report. It's good material."

"I can't even believe this is happening."

Peter entwined their fingers across the tabletop and squeezed, one of his gestures that had confused Jessica in earlier days. He had a loving nature, like David, and he wasn't ashamed to express it. Other patrons at the bar could stare if they wanted to at this middle-aged white man clasping the hand of a black woman in the corner under the TV. Jessica would have hugged him if not for the table separating them. She remembered what David had said about Peter trying to pull her away, and she felt a hint of shame. Jessica hoped, fervently, that Peter had someone special and deserving in his life, but she guessed that David was right. He probably didn't. "We're going to do this, lady. Together."

Jessica smiled, but couldn't speak. Later, when she would think about this lunch with Peter, she would realize that she'd never even told him how much his encouragement and faith meant to her. And how much he'd brightened her life since the first day he introduced himself, showing her how to use the computer system when she was a nervous stranger in the newsroom. How even his friendly gaze, some days, meant the world.

Like a fool, she'd said nothing at all.

▪ 7

Even now, alone, Dawit knew he was being watched.

One of the Searchers had found him, perhaps months before. He'd noticed a cigarette butt half buried outside the back door a week ago, his first physical clue; but other clues had been present for some time, especially his awareness, his certainty, of eyes following him. Maybe Khaldun had sent more than one.

Their methods were undoubtedly sophisticated. They may have equipped themselves with wires planted throughout his house, ears listening on his telephone line, discerning eyes intercepting his mail. He could put nothing past them. All the better, he thought. It should be clear to them that he had not betrayed the Covenant with Khaldun. He had never betrayed it. Why was mere separation always considered such a dire threat? All he wanted was peace.

Maybe they would leave him be this time.

Accidentally, scouring the house for signs of intruders—he did this daily now—Dawit unearthed the scratched, frayed clarinet case he'd hidden away in the cabinet below the bookshelf, among his papers. It had been ten years since he'd last seen the case. He opened the rusting latches and saw the fine stained-wood instrument, each section nestled in its proper indentation against the fading magenta felt, and the memories deluged him in a crystalline rush that made him take a step backward.

blowdaddyblow spideryousuredomakethatbabysqueal

His memory was so sharp that he imagined he could smell mingled cigarette and cigar smoke and illegal whiskey soaking through wooden floorboards.

ihearitspiderihearit sohotman takemehome

Dawit touched the dusty Grenadilla wood of his B-flat Laube clarinet, and his heart raced. His armpits felt pricked with perspiration. His fingers trembled as he lifted the mouthpiece from its bed and examined the cracked, dry reed. More quickly, he began to fit the instrument together.

It was Khaldun who had taught Dawit the joy of creating sounds in the House of Music, while Dawit spent those first bewildered years wondering if he really would live forever. Ten years stretched to fifty, and fifty to a hundred, and by then he knew he would be privy to delights most men would never experience. The learning!

Of all the other houses that made up his brotherhood's community—the House of Mystics, the House of Science, the House of Meditation, the House of Tongues, and the House of History—Dawit had most treasured his studies in the House of Music. The first instrument Khaldun taught him to play was a simple, monochromatic flute carved from bamboo. Next, the stringed *krar*, with its wondrous ability to follow any human voice. And Khaldun had collected other instruments from around the continent: Egyptian lutes, bowl lyres from the lands south of them, the beautiful stringed *kora* from the far west coast, Bantu trumpets made from elephant tusks. And drums, of course, of every variety.

Dawit carried the love for music that Khaldun had cultivated in him wherever he went, always finding a way to indulge it. He'd bought this clarinet from a closet-sized music shop in Chicago in 1916, in January, his first day back in the States after his last short visit home.

How long had it been since he'd played his beloved instrument? At least fifty years, perhaps longer. He'd tried to make himself forget, but now the walls of his present were collapsing around him to clear space for the past, a happy past.

He moistened the reed with his lips and tongue, then blew. The aged reed spat at him. Too brittle. Damn it to hell. He searched the case for new reeds, or at least reeds that weren't already worn out. He found two wrapped in a small cardboard box.

He put on a recording by Satchmo with his Hot Five, "Cornet Chop Suey," turning up the volume until the music seemed to hold up the walls. After a breath to steel himself, he began to play. The reed and sticky keys fought against him. He was clumsy at first, stopping and starting as his head nodded to the music's flow. He lost the beat and honked when he should have found the notes, but then it began to fit back together again. Oh man, oh man.

His fingers played under, over, and around the cornet's lead. He had it, the way he had it then, just like that one precious time when the remarkable young cornet player from Kid Creole's band appeared from nowhere, climbing up onstage with Dawit and his boys—"Hey, lemme try this one, boys," the kid said with a wink. Then he gallantly pulled out the piano stool for Lil, his delicate-boned little wife—and they played their hearts out, almost enough to bring tears to the others' eyes, who were just trying to keep up. "Cornet Chop Suey," the kid told them it was called. Just wrote it, he said. Wanted to try it on for size.

That kid was something else. As much as Dawit loved to play with his own boys, he began looking forward to the end of their nightly gigs. And then he wasn't ashamed, like every other true musician he knew in town, to find that kid wherever he was play-ing and watch him hold a club in a trance late into the night. He reminded Dawit of Khaldun, the way he drew them all around him.

Goddamn, he could go!

To go back there again and hear Louis Armstrong with his Stompers at the Everleigh Club! No, the Sunset Café. Nineteen twenty-seven. No one could play like Satchmo. No one.

yougotitboy yougotit

Playing on, Dawit heard his clarinet's smooth notes swirling around his head. His flying fingers hurt. He blew until his face was dripping.

"You go on, Spider, show these cats something."
"What 'chu call this band?"
"The Jazz Brigade. Here every Friday and Sat'day night. Place jumps."
"What's that cat's name on horn? Blowing the stick?"
"Bandleader. Spider Tillis."
"His mama named him Spider?"
"Name of Seth Tillis. Hey, Spider! Man say we gon' make a recording!"

He knew it, he knew it, even then he knew it. The music they made was new, it was an invention of sound, an American-born hybrid; it was going to take hold of the world and not let it shake loose. From the moment he'd heard it, from the instant he'd picked up a clarinet or a saxophone or sat at a piano to imitate it, he knew it.

Seth was the name Dawit lived under then, left over from slave times. He found the name Tillis in a book—no way he'd go by Ole Master's vile surname—but Tillis was as agreeable as any other American name.

"How come they call him Spider?"
"Don't ask, just watch his fingers move."

He lived for that music. Lived for it. It woke him up in the mornings and would hardly let his brain go at night. For the first time in a century, he'd been happy to be alive, very nearly giddy, because the music was something fresh every time he played it. And it became something else again when the boys in his new band joined in, every voice distinct, their instruments conversing.

"Pumpkin seed, what are you doing in here?"
"Mama said I could watch you play, Daddy."

Rosalie.

The music stopped. The record had finished, and the only sound in the room with Dawit was the overloud popping and hissing from his speakers. The noise swallowed Dawit. His hands, suddenly fumbling and feeling too big, shook around his clarinet.

Rosalie.

She'd been at home in their apartment the whole time, she and Rufus, and his wife, Christina, while he was at the club making music. Then he'd left after the Searchers came. Just left, unquestioning, the way he'd been instructed long before, after taking his vow of Life.

And he'd killed her. Killed Rosalie. Crushed her face. Pressed the pillow hard even when her instincts willed her to fight against him to breathe. He'd killed her just as he'd killed so many before her, and would surely kill so many after.

Dawit howled and sobbed. The clarinet fell to his feet, the mouthpiece breaking loose. He nearly sank to his knees, but he lurched against the sofa and leaned against the armrest as he cried.

Were the Searchers watching him even now, in this state? Dawit, the fearless soldier, reduced to this?

The telephone rang on the coffee table beside him, and Dawit jumped. He let it ring three times, hoping that when he picked it up he would hear her voice, the voice that was his salvation.

Yes, it was her. The first word she spoke was his name, the name he'd told her, the Hebrew variation of the name his mother had given him in his first language, so long ago. She spoke it like a melody.

"David? It's me."

"Hey, baby," Dawit said.

"What's wrong? You sound awful."

"I was sleeping," he lied. He hated the lies. Everything he said or did was an utter, complete falsehood. Everything except what was in his heart, at its core. "What's up?"

"Uhm . . . there's been a development. Peter's agent has already talked to somebody who's really interested in our book."

He couldn't help pausing before he spoke. "You're kidding. That's wonderful," he said cheerfully, ignoring the vise wrapped around his chest.

His words, it seemed, had stunned her. Her end of the line was silent for a few seconds. "Really?"

"Jessica," he said, "I'm sorry for the way I've behaved. I've been an ass. There's no excuse. You're publishing a book, that's your dream, and I would be a fool not to be thrilled. I'll run to the store before school lets out to pick up some steaks for a special dinner. Does that sound good?"

She made a sound like a gasp. "Are you sure you're David Wolde? My husband? The voice is familiar, but . . ."

"Just hurry home. We've endured enough unhappiness in this house. It's time for a celebration." He knew he had found the right things to say. He wanted so much to be sincere in sharing her elation that he'd nearly fooled himself. She deserved happy words. She deserved all he could say and more.

"David, I love you," Jessica said.

Dawit closed his eyes. The vise, for that instant, was gone.

▪ 8

Lalibela, Abyssinia (Ethiopia)

SPRING, 1540

Two men on horseback gallop away from the colorful tents of a caravan of nearly two hundred merchants and their families, a traveling village. The sound of babies crying floats from inside a few of the tents. The caravan is flanked by dogs sniffing for scraps, camels, cows, and bleating goats, but the combined noises fall rapidly behind the men as their horses take them up the grassy hillside toward the stone city hidden in night's darkness. The rainy season is near, and cold droplets spray their faces.

Dawit's horse is swifter, pulling ahead. A convert to Islam, Dawit embraces the beliefs and language to trade silks and clothing from India. But he refuses to be called anything except Dawit, the name of the great emperor, the name his parents gave him. Dawit's allegiances are fickle. In battle, Dawit has killed both Muslims and Christians. Muslims kidnapped him and slew his father when Dawit was a child, selling him to a silk-draped Christian nobleman, yet Dawit has now befriended Muslims. When Dawit and Mahmoud's travels thrust them into unfriendly lands or the midst of skirmishes, they slay Christians from their horses. Both are good soldiers, but Dawit's spear is more sure. He kills, others say of him, without blinking his eyes.

Dawit earned his freedom because of his skills with a knife and spear protecting his nobleman's lands, and he has been free as an adult to travel and trade as he pleases. Many of his new Moorish companions are slavers, but Dawit refuses that trade, despite the rewards. After all, he'd been a slave himself, though lucky to be treated mildly by the man who'd bought him for a bar of salt. Dawit had been a child then, shamefully helpless, so that was his lot. The strong always overtake the weak, Dawit knows. But by their own laws, Christian merchants are forbidden to trade in slaves, and Dawit has come to agree with their thinking. Can people be considered cargo, like a bar of salt or a fabric?

Mahmoud, who rides three paces behind Dawit, is a skilled negotiator whom Dawit considers his brother. Dawit married his sister, but the pretty thirteen-year-old died with their baby during childbirth. Dawit's shared grief with Mahmoud over Rana's death sealed their bond. Tonight, they are bonded by a much stronger power they do not yet understand.

Lalibela is a city of priests and rock-hewn churches, so Dawit and Mahmoud hear chants in Ge'ez from dark corners as their horses' hooves clop across the rocky path toward the market square. Three hundred years ago, this was the capital of the country. Dawit and Mahmoud enter this Christian city with arrogance; they ride in silence until they reach a small garden behind a castle-like monastery, where they dismount and tie their horses. They walk barefoot to a stone stairway leading into the earth, but they wait before descending into the dense dark. Dawit calls down, and only his echo responds. The others have not yet arrived.

"We should not have come," Dawit says. He and Mahmoud wear nearly identical clothes, breeches with silk tunics. Dawit has a sheepskin slung over his chest as well, in the manner of his long-dead peasant father. Their scalps are covered with skullcaps.

"Are you losing your courage?" Mahmoud asks. He is from Arabia, younger and more fair-skinned than Dawit.

"Not my courage. It's my reason I've lost," Dawit says. "We should not have come to him again. This man is a trickster." Dawit notices the cross sculpted into the stone window of the church, meant to ward off evil. They might need its power tonight.

Mahmoud laughs, biting into an apple he has brought. "He has swallowed the blood of Christ," he chuckles.

"A lie," Dawit says, annoyed.

"I only repeat his claim."

"That is blasphemy to all of us, whether we follow the laws of Muhammad or Christ."

"Or both?" Mahmoud teases.

"Why do you mock me? I answer to Allah only."

"Today it is Allah. And tomorrow?" Mahmoud laughs, and Dawit must smile despite his anger. Mahmoud knows his heart; Dawit is drawn to the strong. Perhaps he has not given his heart to God at all, but only to the armies of warriors who cry out God's many names.

Mahmoud kicks pebbles from beneath his feet until they bounce loudly down the stairs. He feeds the rest of the apple to his horse. "Well, something brings you back here, Dawit."

Dawit sighs, examining the mysterious expanse of starlight above them through breaks in the clouds. The lights beckon him in the patterns of constellations he has now learned to see. There is the one that resembles a ladle! He sees it readily. "I'll tell you why. I like the pictures he shows us in the sky."

"And the symbols on a page he can read as words. That, too. We can learn to write, like the royalty. And the clergy."

"He is a good teacher," Dawit admits.

They hear the shuffle of feet, and soon they are joined by others at the top of the stairs; blacksmiths, carpenters, Christian traders, even two or three monks. One of the monks is responsible for their entry to this church tonight, Dawit knows. Soon, they number more than fifty, the youngest a boy of twelve. None of them wants to meet the eyes of the others near them. They are ashamed of their loose fellowship, seeking the voice of this mysterious man who speaks all tongues and calls himself by a Muslim name, Khaldun—meaning eternal.

Dawit gazes scornfully at the monks, who wear brass crosses on chains around their neck. They, like him, are hypocrites to seek audience with such a false prophet. "We should all be damned," Dawit mutters.

"Speak softly, Dawit. He comes."

Khaldun always walks with a torch, so he is visible from a distance. None of them can ever say with certainty from where he has come. His torchlight seems to appear at will in the night, traveling toward them in flickering orange that paints the bearer's form against the walls in a monstrous shadow. He wears a splendid white robe that drags in the dirt. Dawit's heart quickens.

Soon, Khaldun is close enough for them to see his face and the bushy black beard that hangs to his breastbone. He is a black African, not mixed with lighter bloods, though he has never told them which people are his. His strangely translucent eyes travel from face to face and he walks past, studying them. "You thirst," he says to each one after a gaze. "You thirst." He stands before Dawit, bearing into him with those soul-seeing eyes. Dawit struggles to meet his gaze, but loses his nerve and casts his eyes downward. He is a coward!

"You thirst," Khaldun says, rubbing Dawit's wrist.

In a silent line, they follow Khaldun down the stairs into the magnificent sanctuary carved from stone. Khaldun has told them how men broke their backs bringing the stone down from the Lasta Mountains under the reign of King Gebra Maskal Lalibela. Khaldun knows all that has come before. Dawit gazes at an archway as they pass beneath it, and he sees birds painted above the chiseled stone. Artists have covered the walls with images of saints and Christ, all of the figures' big brown eyes wide and full of piety.

In a corner of the church, they find seats in the rows of flat wooden benches. Khaldun mounts his torch in a hole carved in the wall and sits before them on the floor, his legs folded beneath him. They seem afraid even to stir as they wait for Khaldun to speak.

"My pupils," Khaldun begins in the voice that sounds ancient though his face is not much older than Dawit's, "your thirst for knowledge is the magnet that brings you to me. It is your brotherhood. You seek all knowledge, and all knowledge you shall attain. But to walk this path, you must follow with your heart as well as your mind. You must follow without fear, without doubt. This is a path from which no mortal man returns. There are no visitors to this home. Once you enter, it is yours to dwell in for all time."

They sit before Khaldun as if statues. His lessons do not usually begin this way. Dawit had hoped Khaldun would bring them the hollow bamboo instruments he is teaching them to blow to produce pleasing music, or that he would tell them more tales from African kingdoms. What is this he speaks of tonight?

Khaldun's voice floats between Dawit's ears like a magic balm. Dawit wants to move, yet he cannot. The voice fills his veins, seducing him. He knows he is hearing a sorcerer.

"You Christian brothers . . . remind us why Adam and Eve ate of the forbidden fruit," Khaldun says. "What was it they sought? Was it riches? Was it sins of the flesh? What did they seek?"

"Knowledge," one of the monks answers him.

Khaldun's face breaks into a smile of perfect teeth. "Yes. Knowledge. Knowledge, in the end, is the only prize."

"You drank Christ's blood?" Dawit blurts, interrupting.

The eyes of the others fall to him. Khaldun, instead of appearing angry, continues to smile. "Dawit . . . yes . . . the inquisitive one, the new son of Islam. What can I tell you of Christ's blood? There is more than you learned in your Scriptures. There is more than what you find in the Bible, or in Muhammad's Qur'an. There is much more. Did you know that precious ounces of Christ's blood were stolen from the fresh corpse, drained into a leather pouch? This is true. I was there when it was done."

"For what purpose?" Dawit asks, his mouth dry.

The flame's dance alters Khaldun's face slightly, shifting him into shadow. "Once, in my travels long ago, I joined a group of shepherds. We met another traveler—in the random manner in which all of you met me—who told us of a dream. He asked if we knew of this man called Jesus. We did. We had all heard stories of his claims. The traveler said he did not follow this man's teachings, yet in his dream he learned that Christ was among the prophets chosen to rise. The traveler told us of a plan. And we listened.

"Our hearts were not ready for faith, but we were greedy for life. The dreamer took us to Calvary, where Christ was nailed, and we stood among his followers to watch him suffer and die. His death was not so serene as these paintings you see all around you. When the corpse was brought down, I watched my companion help clean his wounds and steal blood from Christ's own veins. We sat vigil for two days over the cold pouch. Then, not long before the reports of the empty burial cave miles from where we sat, the blood in our pouch grew warm. We could feel the heat when we passed it between us. The blood lived."

With Khaldun's words, the room fills with gasps, murmurings of wonder. Khaldun silences them by raising his arm above his head. His voice grows as heavy as the rain pounding on the roof of the church.

"Our friend learned an incantation in his dream, a Ritual of Life for the Living Blood. He held up for us a vial of poison. Only through death, he said, could life return. He instructed us to drink the poison. At the instant of death, he told us, he would inflict a small wound and pour the Living Blood into our own veins to perform the Ritual of Life, repeating the words from his dream. There were six among us. One by one, we drank.

"Only I survived the Ritual. This, I believe, was in keeping with his design. The dreamer, who had not taken the poison, needed only one of us for his purposes. By morning, when I awoke, I cursed him. I thought him a devil, and a devil I now know he was. He asked me to perform the Ritual of Life on him, as I'd seen him attempt on the others, but my heart was overcome with fear. I had a vision that he would become a monster, perverting the blood to harm scores of men and make himself a god. After he drank the poison, I stood over him with the pouch of Living Blood in my hand, but I gave him none. I allowed him to die. Does that answer your question, Dawit?"

Dawit nods, transfixed and silent. "Why do you tell us this?" whispers Mahmoud. His voice shakes.

Khaldun studies their faces a moment before answering, his head turning from one side of the room to the other. "I have learned much in my years. I have been alone too long. I need obedient pupils who are willing to journey with me in Life for the purpose of knowledge, and knowledge alone."

"Do you have the blood still?" Dawit asks.

"The Ritual of Life awakened me from the dead, and I drank what little blood remained. Its saltiness coated my throat. The Blood of Life is inside me. I have lived much like a hermit for many years, asking God to forgive me. But He does not hear my prayers because I have stolen from one of His favored children. So, I no longer seek redemption. I seek knowledge instead, because knowledge is infinite. And I seek pupils. Two hundred years ago on this night, I found a lame dog. I poisoned his food and performed the Ritual of Life as I remembered it, emptying blood from my veins into a wound I made in the animal's flesh. That dog is with me still, and he has never been lame since. He guards me when I sleep." He paused, shrouding his voice in a near-whisper. "I can do the same for a man."

Another gasp fills the dank room. The men stare at one another, their eyes wide. Excited, Mahmoud squeezes Dawit's knee hard, peering at him with wonder. Dawit brushes his hand away, leaning close to Mahmoud's ear. "He lies," he whispers. "He says he has a dog. Where is the dog, then? What proof could we have of its age? He is a storyteller. These are Christian lies."

"Silence," Khaldun instructs, and they obey. He drops his robe past his shoulders until his hairless chest and abdomen are exposed. Then he pulls from his belt a long knife that gleams in the torchlight.

"Before I do what I must to show you the miracle of the Living Blood, you must promise to remain here the night, no matter what you see. You must wait as we waited. In the morning, all will be clear to you. Then you may choose to follow me."

They promise aloud, one by one, to remain the night.

Satisfied, Khaldun grasps the dagger so tightly that the muscles in his slight arm quiver. He closes his eyes, his face turned upward. Then, he plunges the knife into his own side. His mouth agape in a soundless scream, he drags the blade across his belly, leaving a yawning wound in his flesh. A river of blood gushes forward, releasing his coiled insides.

Frightened, the men leap to their feet and huddle in the back of the room. Khaldun looks like a slaughtered cow. He sits for a moment, watching his own innards escape through his wound, and then he crumples in a puddle of blood on the floor.

Instantly, two men break their promise and flee up the stairs. Dawit and Mahmoud watch them go, then they gaze at each other. They have promised to stay. With weak legs, they walk to the bench closest to Khaldun's corpse and sit before him, watching. Slowly, uncertainly, the others follow their example.

For hours, nothing happens. The torch is burning low.

"Look," one of the men whispers at last, pointing.

When did the bloody wound begin to close itself? Have they imagined this? Dawit leans close. He can see that, although Khaldun's innards and blood still lie around him, the long wound across his abdomen has sewn itself into a sealed, bloody scar.

"What Devil's work is this?" a monk mutters.

They wait, but still Khaldun does not stir. Dawit, like the others, dozes to sleep shortly before dawn, his chin resting against his chest. He awakens after someone places a warm hand on his shoulder.

Dawit opens his eyes to find Khaldun standing before him, wearing the smile of a father. His bloody scar is gone, his belly healed with barely a trace of the knife's treachery.

"Will you accept the Life gift, Dawit?" Khaldun whispers.

How can this be? A man can die and yet live again? And all wounds will heal as though by miracle? An army of such men would rule for eternity!

His mouth open with amazement, Dawit can only nod.

▪ 9

"Her name is Rosalie Tillis Banks. The nursing-home lady. I have a case number," Jessica said into the telephone receiver, trying to sound patient with the police clerk in Chicago. "I'd love to swing by, but I'm in Miami. If someone could just fax it to me . . ."

With their book deal signed and four days to go before her scheduled leave, Jessica wanted to get as many long-distance calls out of the way on the Sun-News's tab as she could. Sy was livid about losing two investigative reporters with only two weeks' notice, and she and Peter felt guilty, but it couldn't be helped. There was so much to do. They were trying to decide if Chicago should be one of their trips, and red tape had prevented her from getting the police report, which would have the names and telephone numbers of people she needed to talk to. Someone had supposedly mailed her a copy, but it never arrived.

Jessica had a sister on the phone. She'd have to play that card now, slipping into a more down-home vernacular. "Can't you hook me up? I see what you're saying about procedure, but it's a long way to Chicago. Sister, please."

The clerk, who sounded honestly harried, relented. "You better mention me in your book," she said.

Within an hour, the eight-page fax transmission began, and the old woman's death took shape. Banks, a widow, had no next-of-kin except an Indianapolis cousin who'd sent for her things. She'd suffered from advanced pancreatic cancer. Died January twelfth. The regular night nurse hadn't come in because of a storm the night of the murder, so the wing had been unattended for several hours longer than usual. (Made sense, Jessica thought. David had been in Evanston lecturing at Northwestern University that week, and he called home every night to complain about the snow.) Body wasn't discovered until morning. Only clue at all was an unfamiliar black male who'd asked about her the day she was murdered. Composite sketch to follow, the report said.

"Hey, Jessica, congrats on the book," a female reporter called to Jessica, walking past the wire room, where she hovered over the whirring fax machine.

"Thanks, Em."

Page eight was the composite sketch. The image on the fax was too dark and splotched to be helpful. All Jessica could see of the man was the curly outline of his hair and the whites of his eyes.

It figured the suspect was supposed to be black, she thought. That could be some staffer's convenient lie, like the white guy years ago who'd made up a story about a black attacker after he had killed his pregnant wife. That crazy woman who'd drowned her own sons, Susan Smith, had tried the same ploy. Pretty cozy, having a mystery visitor.

"The thing I like about Banks," Peter said, scanning the report over Jessica's shoulder at her desk, "is that her father was a legend in Chicago. Didn't the *Trib* say he was a jazz artist? Split, or vanished, when she was a kid. It's just interesting to me. The father vanishes, one of the great mysteries in jazz lore, and now the daughter is murdered."

"I don't know . . ." Jessica sighed. "This isn't *Unsolved Mysteries*. The question is, Do we think this was abuse? We don't want to include her and then have some nutcase step forward and say spacemen told him to do it."

"We can pin it on neglect, then, at the least. No night nurse. Someone comes in off the street and murders a patient."

Jessica still wasn't convinced. They'd heard about some heinous cases of long-term abuse in the past few weeks, and suddenly the Chicago incident seemed pretty mild. She scrawled the woman's name on a folder, slid the report inside, and dropped it on top of the pile of papers on her desk. "I don't think this is for us. Too many loose ends."

Peter shrugged, walking away. "I'll let you call it," he said. "By the way, would you please take those damn flowers home?"

"I'm saying," the courts reporter who sat behind her spoke up, "you're stinking the whole place up."

Jessica had two dozen purple-hued roses on her desk, awash in baby's breath, delivered Monday from David to commemorate her last week until her book leave. A cynical part of her told her it wasn't coincidence that David sent the flowers after he saw the troll Peter had given her, but the gesture was thoughtful anyway.

He was being a good sport. Today, he was out pricing computers for her. He'd already cleared enough space in their tiny bedroom—how, she didn't know—to furnish it with a small computer table. They would both be working at home, out of each other's way. He joked about erotic midafternoon "work breaks," when they could explore new areas of the house to ravage each other. The thought of it made her smile even now.

Her phone bleeped, and she expected it to be David. Their telepathy was frightening sometimes. But it wasn't him.

"Hey, Miss Wol-dee. This is Boo."

Boo. For long seconds, Jessica's brain was dumb with a lack of recognition. This man didn't sound like one of her usual sources, and she didn't recognize the street nickname.

The man lowered his voice slightly. From the hollow echo, she guessed he was at a pay phone. "Evergreen Courts projects. You don't 'member me?"

Boo. Evergreen Courts. Like microfilm, it all came into focus. He was a small-time crack dealer who'd called months earlier with a tip that the county's housing maintenance staff was involved in trafficking and dealing in the projects. He'd given her one lead that turned out to be good and promised more, but she never heard from him again.

Jessica couldn't believe the bad timing. Here she was on her way out the door, and a potentially great story had reappeared.

"What happened to you?" she asked.

"I'm just chillin'. I still got that stuff for you. You know, what we talked about."

"You mean names?" Jessica asked.

"Yeah. One of 'em just went up on a possession tip. But I don't trust the phone, if you know what I'm sayin'. I got it all wrote down for you. Then you can check and see if I'm lying."

"I know you're not lying. Everything you said panned out, but then you disappeared."

"Yeah, sorry about that, you know? But these muthafuckers don't play, so I gotta watch my back. 'Scuse my language. When we gon' get together?"

Jessica looked up at the newsroom clock. It was three. She wanted to tell him to forget it, she was about to go write a book, but she couldn't resist the easy lure of written information. She could make a few calls while she was on leave. If nothing else, she could file it away and have a great story waiting for her when she got back. That would be a nice peace offering for Sy.

"Now's good for me," she said.

He breathed hard. "Uh-uh. Bag that. I can't have you comin' 'round here. They already think I narced on 'em 'cause I went clean. I got a job now, a security gig at the mall, the one on Hundred Sixty-Third Street."

"You're out of drugs?"

"I been out. I got a little boy to worry 'bout, and he's old enough to start figurin' out shit for himself, Daddy standin' on the corner. I ain't raisin' him up like that. You know?"

"I hear you," Jessica said. "Good for you."

"I go on at eight. Meet me up there, if you want. I'll be at the gameroom 'til it closes, 'bout eleven. Then I patrol the lot."

Uh-oh. Another late night. David wouldn't like it. And if he knew where she was going, he'd insist on escorting her. But she'd been to that mall a hundred times, and there were plenty of people around at that time of night.

"Can I bring a tape recorder?"

"Bring what you want," Boo said.

They agreed to meet at eight o'clock. Jessica called David and told him she'd have to work late, covering a meeting of elderly residents in Miami Beach. It sounded a hell of lot safer than saying she was meeting a drug dealer at his night job. She considered her story an exaggeration rather than a lie, since sometimes she had to stretch the truth with David just to be free to do her job. He still grilled her on how late it could go, whether there would be any security, where she would park. Then he reminded her that Kira had asked to sleep over at Bea's because a teacher planning day had liberated her from school. With Kira gone, David had planned to come by to help Jessica load up some boxes from her office later that night.

"Tell you what, honey," she said, "I'll call you when the meeting lets out, then I can meet you at the paper. 'Kay?"

Reluctantly, still not sold on her safety, he agreed.

Peter, too, was finishing up some loose ends, she discovered. She found him sitting in the newspaper's library doing a property records check on the computer. He said he was in for a long haul.

"So maybe I'll see you and Mr. Perfect later?" he said. "I have some boxes that need loading too. Ha, ha."

She ignored his sarcasm. "What are you working on?"

"Mob stuff. The usual. You?" he asked.

"Drug dealers."

He laughed. "All in a day's work, right?"

"That's for sure." She paused, watching his fingers at work on the keyboard as he typed names onto the screen. Not knowing why, she drank in every detail about him that night: his white shirt, his Warner Brothers Sylvester and Tweetie tie, his gray slacks. Even the fine hair on his neck, just below his hairline. She felt a pull toward him that was not romantic, but as natural and bittersweet as could be. Like saying goodbye too soon.

She felt an impulse, as she had at O'Leary's, to hug him.

"Peter? Don't you ever get afraid of pissing them off?" she asked instead.

He chuckled, not looking up at her, his fingers tapping away. "You and David have watched those *Godfather* movies once too often," he said. "This isn't personal. It's business."

"That's what I'll tell my drug dealers," she said, laughing.

It was seven-thirty, an hour after a blazing sunset beckoned five reporters, all on deadline, away from their computers to the window facing the city's skyline. The cafeteria downstairs was serving carved roast, a staff favorite. There hadn't been any shootings on the police scanners all day, and there were no accidents on any major expressways.

All the signs indicated it would be an extraordinary night.

▪ 10

Dawit didn't make the decision right away. And when it came, it wasn't even a decision, really. It was a realization of what was to follow, a gently flowing current beneath him.

By ten o'clock, Jessica hadn't appeared at her office or left a message for him on the machine at home, and Dawit was anxious and more than a little frightened. The plate of beef stew and cornbread he'd brought her, wrapped in tinfoil, was only slightly warm now as it sat on her desk beneath the canopy of roses.

Her section of the newsroom, away from the commotion and light of the Metro section across the aisle, was deserted. The elite reporters don't work after dark, he surmised. He'd sat for a half hour undisturbed, unattended, growing more fretful as he watched the minutes pass on the clock overhead, and no sign of his wife.

He'd already exhausted the drivel in the *U.S. News and World Report* on her desk; the only thing that remotely interested him was a brief about Eritrean conflicts with Ethiopia, which made him marvel at how age-old quarrels could linger. But news of Ethiopia disturbed rather than comforted him. Recent signs of the Searchers told him that Khaldun wanted him back there, and soon he must go. He put the magazine away.

He didn't want to start moving Jessica's unmarked boxes without her instructions, so his eyes began wandering over her desk for lack of anything else to do. Her stack of folders was in front of his eyes, but he hadn't noticed them before. And he read, with the impact of a gunshot, Rosalie Tillis Banks.

Khaldun had said Mark me this: All words and deeds will find you, as a tightening noose finds the neck.

The sensation, at first, was like being yanked from the chair by his hair and flung headfirst into another existence. The Chicago world had never before crossed the Miami world, and yet his daughter's name was written before him like an indictment—and in his own wife's bouncy, feminine handwriting. For a full minute, as his mind lurched, he forgot to breathe.

He didn't touch the folder at first, fearing it was a hallucination, some visage conjured by Khaldun from his underground sanctuary. Khaldun was all-knowing, but all-powerful too? Was he a true sorcerer, as he and the others had always speculated? Was he even God himself, as more and more of his brothers, calling themselves Khaldunites, believed?

Dawit blinked several times, but Rosalie's name was still there. No, this was not Khaldun, he realized. This must be the work of a Searcher, intended as a cruel warning. Dawit's insides swelled with anger as he snatched the folder into his hand.

He was not prepared for what he found. Jessica herself had requested this document from Cook County Police, according to the handwriting on the cover page. His lips grew dry as he read. This was the actual police report written after his daughter's murder, detailing the evening and all its events. The report mentioned a stranger, a black male, who asked for her the day she died. (His own fault; he'd only planned to visit Rosalie then, so he had not been careful.) He nearly dropped the papers when he read that a composite sketch was included—his face, his own face—and he expected his senses to flee, leaving him faint, when he flipped to the page.

This was him. He could see it. A crude drawing, and too dark to readily recognize his features from a facsimile, but he could make out the angles of his jawline and his tufts of hair. The original, somewhere in Chicago, would certainly damn him.

Again, he wondered if sorcery was at work. How had this come to be? Why would Jessica know anything at all about Rosalie?

The answer was so simple, it was nearly fiendish. He'd killed Rosalie at a nursing home. Of all ironies, Jessica was writing about nursing homes. Was this not all the evidence he needed that Khaldun was a master of prophecy?

Sure enough, his deeds had found him. The noose.

Jessica's book would lead her to the truth. If she went to Chicago and found the report, wouldn't she certainly recognize her own husband's face? Might she already have seen enough traces to stimulate her curiosity? She might remember he had been very near Chicago, at the university, when Rosalie died. How would he explain this? How?

The Covenant, Dawit's mind screamed. *No one must know.* Dawit could not, under any circumstances, allow Jessica to continue her research. He closed his eyes, shutting out the inner voice that threatened, at any moment, to rip his life asunder.

"David? Jessica still not back?"

Peter. He knew the voice before he opened his eyes. Instinctively, he tried to shield the folder from Peter's view by closing it and resting his elbow on top of it.

"Not yet. You're working late." Dawit couldn't smile.

"I'm doing some record checks back in the library. Think I'll have to go soon, though. It's after ten. What smells so good?"

"I brought Jess some dinner. I wanted to surprise her."

Peter smiled in a way Dawit didn't understand, a nearly smug smile that infuriated him. This man, here, was the cause of his trouble. Yet, even at this time, the decision had not come.

"You're really too much," Peter said, walking to his own desk. He grabbed a notebook and began striding down the darkened aisle past him. "Oh, well. Back to work. Promised myself I could go home in ten minutes. You might try calling Jessica at your place. It's so late, maybe she decided to head straight there."

Did this mortal think he was a fool, stationed at Jessica's desk with a blind faith that she would appear? "I've been checking," Dawit said instead, keeping his tone even.

"I'm sure she'll be back soon. 'Night, David."

"Good night, Peter," Dawit said. He forced the pleasantry from his unhappy throat.

Once Peter was out of sight, Dawit once again picked up the telephone to check his messages at home. This time, thankfully, he heard Jessica's voice: "David? Baby? Are you out in the shed? I hope you haven't left yet. Listen, I'm so sorry. My meeting is running way late. Let's forget about the boxes tonight, okay? I'm getting some great stuff. I'll be home by eleven-fifteen, I promise. At least we can have a night alone, right? See you soon."

Dawit stood, surveying the empty section of the newsroom once again. Certain he was not being observed, he took the folder bearing Rosalie's name to a large yellow trash bin in the hallway and buried it there. Then he grabbed the dinner plate from Jessica's desk and made his way through a winding hallway to the service elevator. The main lobby was closed this late at night.

When the elevator doors opened, he met a boisterous group of blue-shirted men from the print room, but they took no notice of him. By the time the elevator rested on the ground floor, he was alone. A young, bespectacled black security guard at the window waved him past. The guard had allowed Dawit into the building without identification, or even signing him in, because he had seen him with Jessica before.

"'Night, man," the guard said. "Wife ain't back yet?"

"On her way home," Dawit shrugged.

"'Bout time, I guess, huh?" the guard laughed.

Dawit had the minivan today, which he'd parked at the curb just outside the service exit. Jessica had driven the smaller red Tempo, the family's second car, which they usually exchanged according to need. He left the plate of food on the seat beside him, turned on the engine, and coasted out of the newspaper's main lot toward Biscayne Boulevard.

The newspaper had four or five parking lots, he noted. The one closest to the building was full and had a guard on patrol, even at this hour, but the outlying lots were deserted. Nearly deserted. It was only when Dawit identified a faded green Ford Mustang parked alone in the lot nearest Biscayne that the thought began to take form in his mind, with clarity.

The Mustang was Peter's car. Dawit knew it because he'd seen it so often parked in his own driveway. He and Peter had even discussed it at length; it was a 1968 model, and Peter was the second owner. The car was somewhat abused, and had long ago lost its luster, but it was still a striking machine.

Hardly a second had passed before the thought became a plan.

Dawit drove two blocks past the lot and turned onto a side street lined with empty parking meters beneath coconut palms and yellow poinciana trees. He turned off the minivan's engine and headlights. Then he reached behind the seat for his toolbox, which he hadn't moved since tuning up Jessica's mother's car.

Dawit had perfect vision. He needed little light. His fingers deftly traveled without haste across his tools in their compartments. He passed up his screwdrivers, his bolts, his chisels. He stopped when he found the linoleum knife.

He clasped the thick handle and ran his fingertip across the wide blade, which was hooked at the tip. He'd used this knife to cut the new kitchen linoleum he'd installed the year before. Flooring was difficult to cut. The blade was sharp.

He had found his tool. Next, he slid on his work gloves.

Dawit left his keys in the minivan's ignition and closed the door, careful to leave it unlocked. Then he began a quick pace toward the parking lot, where Peter's car was waiting.

He marveled at the work of Providence; that tonight, of all nights, Peter should be working late. That his car should be parked in an unguarded empty lot, impossible to miss. He had searched his mind for answers to no avail, and suddenly they were displayed before him with the simple logic of physics or mathematics. All of the variables were in place.

Was this not simply a fulfillment of his Covenant? Wasn't Peter bringing Jessica, and perhaps others, that many steps closer to learning the truth about his Life gift?

The driver's side door of the Mustang was locked, which surprised Dawit. He remembered Peter telling him one of his door locks no longer worked. Was it the passenger's side, then? Yes. He opened the door, and a faint light went on inside.

Immaculate, except for a few papers on the passenger's seat. No camouflage, unfortunately, but perhaps he wouldn't need it.

Dawit flipped the seat forward and climbed into the cramped backseat, closing the door behind him. The bucket seat clicked when pulled back into place. In darkness, Dawit crouched as far down as he could across the leather. It smelled of mildew down there, perhaps from some long-ago rainstorm, but Dawit grasped the knife and ignored his nose. He was satisfied that he was hidden.

How odd, Dawit thought, that he felt no fear. He'd felt none with Rosalie, and he felt none now. Surely he must have felt nerves at one time, a time he'd forgotten, but all fear had left him now in association with this particular task.

Exactly twelve minutes passed before Dawit heard a footfall on the concrete beyond the parking lot's gate. Then he heard a scraping of soles on loose gravel, closer yet, until jingling keys signaled that his prey had come to him at last.

Peter unlocked the door, tossed his briefcase to the passenger's seat, and climbed inside his car. He slammed the door behind him.

Dawit was keenly aware of Peter's human presence now, the scent of his perspiration and sweet-smelling cologne. This is a man, Dawit reminded himself. You, too, are a man. This made them brothers, and he must respect this, Covenant or not. Peter had no immoral designs on Jessica. He only cared for her deeply, wanted to help her, much as Dawit did. There must be no joy in this.

For some reason, Peter sat still without slipping his key into the ignition. The closed vehicle was filled with a palpable, nearly physical, silence. Their shared presence mingled, at some level, knowing. Knowing.

If he wanted to, Dawit realized, he could give this mortal the scare of his life with the mere whisper of a word. They would both laugh heartily and allow this moment to drift behind them unlived. In those three to four seconds, knowing that he was presented with this choice, Dawit felt giddy with power.

Peter did not turn around even when Dawit sat up behind him. Instead of staring at the movement in his rearview mirror, Peter's gaze was directed at his steering wheel, reflecting. His bent form and submissive countenance seemed to be saying I know why you are here, what you must do, and I accept my fate in your hands.

Whether or not this was only in Dawit's imagination, it granted him the instant's resolution to swing his right arm around, almost as if to hug Peter, and sink the knife's hooked blade into the soft of his throat. Peter's entire frame froze and his head sank back slightly as he made a strangled sound. Dawit, using all his strength, carved the knife across the length of Peter's neck in a swift motion, through his larynx, his thyroid cartilage, his taut muscles. He felt warm blood seep through his glove, touching his fingertips.

Only now, through pure instinct, did Peter's hands fly to his throat, as if to try to pull the knife free. Dawit helped him, yanking the hooked blade loose from his torn flesh. Peter bent over the steering wheel, his chest hitting the rim but missing the horn. Blood from his opened arteries was spraying forward, painting the windshield red. Dawit felt hot droplets across his own face, even sitting behind Peter. Then, with an unpleasant gurgling sound, Peter thrashed backward in his seat, his weight giving Dawit a severe jolt.

"Be still. Let death come," Dawit whispered, feeling for him. He'd had his own throat slashed twice by lucky opponents, and he could well remember the astonishing horror of it, to be mortally wounded while fully conscious, unable to speak. Even to one who would reawaken, death was a traumatic surprise.

"Let it take you," Dawit breathed, close to Peter's ear.

As if in response, the horn sounded feebly as Peter's elbow brushed across the wheel and he slumped to a prone position across the passenger's seat. Peter's body spasms and twitches now were only nerve impulses, Dawit knew. He had killed again.

Dawit had no time for reflection. He glanced at his shirt and found it spotted with blood, and his right glove was damp and heavy with it. The smell of blood was so thick in the car, it was nearly smothering. Dawit strained against Peter's weight to push the passenger's seat forward and reach the door handle. With much effort, he climbed out of the car. Squatting beside the vehicle, he took off his gloves and hurriedly unbuttoned his shirt, using it to wipe his hand as clean as possible, then his face, and he wrapped the knife and gloves inside the soiled cotton.

The night air filled his lungs, replenished him. Some blood still clung to his skin, but not nearly so much as he'd feared. The smell was behind him, in the car, in Peter's tomb. Dawit heard traffic passing on Biscayne Boulevard just beyond the trees, but no one was in sight except, in the opposite direction, a few employees walking into the newspaper building from a closer parking lot.

As he crept in darkness toward his parked minivan, he pulled off his undershirt and wrapped that too around the bloody weapon. These would have to go in the backyard toolshed for now, until he could dispose of them somehow. Maybe in the river? He opened the van door and searched the floor for something he could wrap them in. A wrinkled plastic Publix shopping bag was shoved under the backseat. He fit his bloody bundle inside, put the bag next to Jessica's dinner plate, and started the engine.

Only 10:38. He would be home in fifteen minutes, or less, and he would beat Jessica with time to spare. That would give him time to shower. It would all work fine.

When traffic was clear at the stop sign, he drove off. He turned on his radio and found jazz playing on the public station. Billie Holiday was singing "Crazy He Calls Me." He turned the volume up high and sang along, surrendering his thoughts and deeds to the cleansing power of the music.

Peace. Yes, peace. In music, he found peace.

▪ 11

Running and running and running.

Jessica was lost in an exhausting dream about being chased with Kira. Kira was running far ahead of her, and Jessica flung out her arm to try to catch her. But she was too late, too late. Mommy, Kira called back to her over her shoulder, *are there good monsters, too?*

Jessica flipped over, waking, when David pulled his arm from beneath her to grab the ringing telephone. She felt agitated, not rested. It wasn't dark, as she'd believed. The sky, through their open curtains, was shedding its ink-blackness for the mingled gray and pink of new daylight.

"What time is it?" Jessica asked grumpily.

David shushed her, patting her leg beneath the blanket. "This is her husband," he was saying to the caller. "Who is this? . . . Okay, one sec. Jess? Honey, it's Sy Greene."

Jessica glared at the oak grandfather clock ticking against the wall across from their bed. She thought she'd left her days of being awakened by her boss long ago, back when she chased fire engines and was eager to please.

"Does that clock say six?" she asked with disbelief. "I know it's not somebody calling here at six o'clock."

"Ten 'til," David said, dangling the receiver near her face. "Honey, phone . . . Please?"

Jessica took the receiver. She didn't have a chance to say anything. She heard a muffled sound that she didn't recognize. After a moment, she realized with numbing trepidation that her boss was sobbing into her ear.

PART TWO

■

Spider

They Call it Stormy Monday,
But Tuesday's just as bad,
Wednesday's worse,
And Thursday's also sad.

    —WORDS AND MUSIC BY AARON T-BONE WALKER
                                     (1947)

▪ 12

At the start of her fourth month carrying Kira, in the bathroom, Jessica struck a deal with God: Make this bleeding go away, make it all right, and I will serve you for the rest of my life. No more of this half-ass church only on Sunday stuff. She vowed she would teach Sunday school, she would tithe, and she would never again think an un-Christian thought about anyone.

God, please just give me this baby.

She and David hadn't known, at that time, whether the child was a boy or a girl. But Jessica did know she had passed her first trimester, supposedly out of the woods for miscarriage, so she'd begun visualizing a real baby instead of a faceless, fragile embryo. When she stroked her stomach, she was stroking a child's head. If she felt a movement, anything at all, she spoke to the baby in response.

Is that you? You're growing, baby, aren't you?

So it was really the child, not she, who was bleeding.

Jessica was about to take a shower before going to work when she saw the brown spots of blood on her toilet paper. She wiped herself again, and this time the blood was clotted and fresh. It was red.

She screamed for David, and he came. He told her later he'd never been more scared, but she didn't see it in his face. He hugged her, giving her a robe, telling her it was okay, telling her not to cry. He called the obstetrician. He drove her to the hospital, rattling off assurances. "You're not in pain. You're all right. They'll fix it, Jess," he kept saying.

As it turned out, her placenta was hanging a bit too low. The doctor warned her that she would have to lie flat on her back for the next few days because he couldn't correct the condition. It would have to correct itself. If she hemorrhaged, he could not save the baby.

That was the first time Jessica, as an adult, really felt the fresh horror and helplessness of what it would mean to lose a person she was close to. In the moments her doctor described what was wrong—in the time between his warning about hemorrhaging and his reassurance that it was a common condition and she would probably be just fine—she felt a cruel randomness poised to slice away a part of her psyche.

And the question came: Why would God do this?

Because her faith was weak, she decided later, as she rested. Her faith was so weak and bare, it was ready to shred at the first sign of trouble. Feets, do your thing. She needed to trust Him. He wouldn't let her crash into the wall; He would steer her around.

And, yes, He had. Kira was the living proof.

"That's not me," Kira insisted, wrinkling her face when she saw a photo of Jessica holding a bright-red newborn in a hospital bed. Kira had started emphasizing words in sentences, enjoying the sound of her own conversation. "That's a Gremlin."

"Sure is a Gremlin. A Gremlin named Kira Alexis Wolde."

"Is that me?" Kira asked, pointing to the grainy photograph of a baby whose face was buried beneath a straw cowboy hat.

"Yes. You were about eighteen months old there," Jessica said, flipping to the next page in the photo album. "And here, you had just turned two. This is at Grandma's."

"The sailor dress!" Kira said. She dug through the pile of photos at the foot of Jessica's bed and found one that matched.

"Good work, Kira," Jessica said. Her daughter's eyes followed her fingers as she lifted the page's plastic sheet to fit the new photograph beside the one already there. The pictures were similar and had been taken the same day, with Kira in a navy sailor dress, which Bea had just bought her, playing on a rocking horse.

The photo albums had been a two-day project, and this was the last one. She'd filled five large albums so far. The piles of photographs in shoe boxes she and David kept under the bed were dwindling. David was the main photo junkie; he rarely went anywhere without a camera, and he had the walls of the house papered with framed photographs of family trips and backyard barbecues—him, Jessica, Kira, Teacake, and poor Princess.

The immersion in photographs and memories was a welcome sanctuary for Jessica. The photos showed her Kira's remarkable development from a wrinkled newborn to the thin, cinnamon-skinned child she was now. She had a round face, and her forehead sloped like David's. Working on the photographs with Kira was a simple pleasure Jessica had come to bask in.

"Are we almost done, Mommy?"

"Yep. Soon."

"Then you'll get up?" she asked, trying to crawl against Jessica's abdomen to snuggle beside her.

"Not-uh. Don't do that when I'm trying to work," Jessica said crossly. Kira's sudden movement had made the plastic crinkle; Jessica lifted the sheet back up, straightened the photographs on the page, and smoothed it carefully with her palm. The photos weren't quite right, angling toward one another. She'd wanted them to be just right, damn it.

"They're straight," Kira said.

"No, they're not. You call that straight?"

"Uh-huh. Will you get up when we're done, Mommy?"

At two in the afternoon on a Saturday, Kira was dressed in denim overalls, her hair combed for the day. But Jessica was still in the faded Jacksons' Victory Tour T-shirt she'd slept in, propped up in bed with crumpled sheets, and two or three paperback books lying facedown around her—James Baldwin, Jane Austen, Susan Taylor. David had found the battery-operated black-and-white TV, the one she'd bought after Hurricane Andrew knocked their power out for four days, and set it up for her on top of the bureau. She had no plans to get up. "I'm still tired, Kira," she said.

"You're always tired," Kira whined. "I want to see the movie about the big dog. Daddy said."

"Well . . ." Jessica said, squeezing her hand, " . . . either you can wait until I'm not tired anymore or you and Daddy can go. And I'll stay here."

"That's not going to work," Kira said with exasperation, a grown-up–sounding phrase Jessica figured Kira must have picked up from David.

David's voice came from the doorway. "Kira? Let Mommy rest. She said she's tired." He was changing the washers in the bathroom faucet. He'd stuck his head in and was gone just as quickly.

David's words silenced Kira, but her face was in full pout.

"I've told you about that. Don't make that ugly face," Jessica said. "It's okay if you and Daddy go. I'll be here."

The truth was, Jessica wanted to see the movie. She really did. She wanted a tub of popcorn, and she wouldn't mind sitting in a darkened theater all day. But she wanted to do it alone. It would take too much energy to go on an outing with David and Kira at this moment. Her mind was frayed, in retreat. Lately, half the time she adhered to her family, cleansing herself with them. Then, just as suddenly, she'd had enough. She would prefer silence now.

Small silence. And she would genuinely miss them, an ache, until they came back.

Maybe it was because the tears always followed a step behind her solitude. Any solitude. In the shower. On the toilet. Sitting alone in the backyard, watching the herons fuss over the water. The pain was still raw and the tears were always there; usually, they were only in hiding.

Nothing in her life, even the death of her father, had prepared Jessica for the murder of Peter Donovitch.

Even the word murder, when she thought it, drove into her mind like a hatchet. Her coworkers rarely used that word. They mentioned "losing Peter" or "Peter's death" when they talked to her; few wanted to call it by its horrible name. It was like processing two calamities; first, the grief over a friend dead so suddenly, then the added shock and anger at the bloody method of a killer who had gotten away without a clue except for a security videotape that was so dark and blurred it was useless.

Jessica did not go into the office the day Peter's body was discovered. "You don't need to be here," Sy kept saying on the phone. "It's best for you not to come here."

When the newscast came on—Peter's murder was the lead story on all three local channels, and even made the network evening news—she understood why. The first shot she saw, before she or David could think to turn off the television set, was the windshield of his car coated with dried blood. Sy had told her the killer cut his throat, but she'd managed the idea by thinking of an act that was somehow clean. She wasn't ready to see the shower of blood. Her friend's blood. She'd screamed. An hour later, she was still trembling.

And the old question came again: Why would God do this?

The memorial service three days after Peter's death, while difficult to face because of its finality, helped a little. Sy and some of the editors who had known Peter for nearly twenty years planned the service at the Unitarian Church, which he'd attended sporadically. At David's urging, Jessica hadn't been back to work, so the service helped her quench her need to know that others were as dazed and angry and miserable as she. She wanted to hug even clerks and editors she rarely spoke to.

For the first time, Peter's life took full shape for her. His doughfaced parents, who lived in Michigan, came to the service with a lanky teenager who kept his head bowed. The boy, it turned out, was Peter's son from a bitterly dissolved marriage. She heard someone behind her whisper that Peter's whole family, including his son, practically shut him out when he told them he was gay. Things had been better in recent years, but not much. She also discovered, in a testimony from the bearded man she'd seen with Peter at the festival, that Peter had nursed his lover, who'd had AIDS, until he died ten years before.

Learning these things, Jessica loved Peter more fiercely. But she was also hurt that he'd kept his life's sorrows from her, making himself a virtual stranger.

Despite the comfort of being with other people who cared about Peter, none of them could think of his death as a journey or a homecoming. It was a theft, plain and simple. A horrible, brutal theft. Jessica thought she felt better after the service, but when she tried to sleep that night, she envisioned Peter's Mustang and the blood-spattered windshield.

She dreamed she walked to Kira's bedroom window and saw the Mustang parked below in their driveway, the driver's side door open. In the dream, she gingerly walked outside to the car, to see what was inside. Someone she couldn't quite make out, not Peter, was sitting in the driver's seat.

Once, in her dream, the man sitting there was David.

On Monday, Sy called her to ask if she still planned to take a short leave. Jessica said she didn't know. Neither of them mentioned the book. She told Sy she'd gotten a good tip on drug dealing in the housing projects, but she stopped midsentence, remembering that she'd met Boo on the night of Peter's murder. Some crack addict or mob hit man or arbitrary psycho had been killing Peter at that precise moment.

Sy told her to take all the time she needed. He mentioned that the newspaper had decided to bring in some grief and trauma counselors for the employees. Everyone was taking it hard, having anxieties about their stories. Sy said he planned to go to the sessions, and he urged her to come too.

When Jessica asked David what he thought, he looked uncertain. "Do whatever you think will help," David said, "but I don't know if that would be good for you. There's a shadow over that place now. You have to stop thinking of Peter as a victim, Jess. The sum of his life was so much more than the awful way he happened to leave. That was only a split second in time. I think you're better off here with me."

She decided that he was right. She didn't know how she could have functioned without David's constant pampering and the wordless moments when he nestled beside her and pulled her head toward him until it rested on the familiar cradle of his shoulder. Occasionally she could let go enough to cry in front of him, and the world felt normal again for a time. Then, unexpectedly, the tears would come back later, worse than before.

David stuck his head into the bedroom doorway, drawing Jessica's attention away from flipping through her newly finished photo album pages. "Last call for the movie train," he said.

She shook her head, smiling. "I'll be okay."

"Want me to bring you some food after?"

She didn't have much of an appetite, but David would force her to eat. "Whatever you guys get is fine with me."

"'Bye, Mommy!" Kira called from behind him.

David told Kira to go find her jacket, since the temperature had dipped over the weekend. Kira came back wearing a heavy winter coat, and David sent her back to her room to find a lighter denim jacket. When she whined that she couldn't find it, he went after her. Jessica could hear them speaking in French through the wall of the adjoining bedroom.

David was trying to teach Kira languages early, and she was already doing well with rudimentary Spanish, which she was taking in school. Apparently, her French was improving too. Struck by Kira's stumbling grasp of the language, Jessica thought of how strange it was that her own daughter could speak words she herself didn't understand.

"*Marché,* Daddy," Kira said.

The two of them paraded one last time in front of Jessica's open doorway, waving as they passed. Jessica's face froze before she could smile. Seeing them walking away, David first and Kira trailing after, eagerly grasping her father's pant leg, Jessica's insides clenched with a cold dread that held her immobile.

She felt overpowered by a need to call out for Kira to stay home with her. Then she heard the door downstairs fall shut, and the uneasy feeling, after a moment, let her go.

Her tears came, right on time.

▪ 13

Barcelona

1710

In the shadows, five figures stumble noisily in the stairwell, exchanging fondles and muffled laughter as they approach a rented room on the top-floor landing. The air is heavy with the salty perfume of the Mediterranean through the open windows.

"Wait. Be silent," Dawit whispers as they reach a closed door, annoyed with the three whores' noisemaking. "I'll bring Chinja out first."

"Chinja?" Mahmoud cries sloppily, louder than necessary. Dawit cannot see Mahmoud's face in the darkness, but he can smell his wine-laden breath. "Let that cur watch!"

"Who is Chinja?" asks one of the whores.

Dawit ignores her, unwilling to be burdened by inquiries. He continues to speak to Mahmoud in Spanish, the musical language they have assumed with ease since their arrival. "And have his eyes staring on? It's unappetizing, Mahmoud."

"I've appetite enough to carry on without you, but do as you like. Send him out, then." Before Dawit can open their door, they hear a loud creaking below them, at the bottom of the stairs, and a swinging lamp fills the stairwell with a rocking glow. "Who's there?" calls an old man's voice, the innkeeper.

"Your tenants, sir," Mahmoud says mockingly, exaggerating his Spanish lisp, "and our new raven-haired friends."

The old man curses, climbing closer to them. Dawit can make out the grizzled white of his beard behind the light. "You come at this hour, closer to dawn than dusk, waking my wife? With whores?"

"Dawit . . ." Mahmoud says, just within the innkeeper's hearing, "his wife, the poor creature, is young and well favored. Would he allow us to borrow her for the night?"

"For a coin, he might," Dawit says, joining Mahmoud's game. "Or, she might be so grateful she'll offer payment to us."

The whores join them in laughing at their ridicule of the old man. One of the women shrieks as Mahmoud's hand roves beneath her bodice.

The innkeeper's voice rises to a bellow. "What did you say?"

"Dawit, he is so loud. He makes my head hurt," Mahmoud says.

"We have only said that we apologize, sir," Dawit responds respectfully to the man. "And we wish your wife a good night."

Contemplating this for a moment, the innkeeper does not speak further. Perhaps, Dawit hopes, he will return to his quarters so that he and Mahmoud can relish these females' talents; one of them has crushed her soft haunches against him, and his rigid anticipation has grown uncomfortable in his breeches.

"Well said, Dawit," Mahmoud says, again too loudly. "You're so graceful a liar, you could convince a buzzard he is a peacock."

"Devils! Your tongues are vile!" the innkeeper shouts.

"How my head aches," Mahmoud moans. "Please persuade him to be silent, Dawit, or I swear I'll tumble him down the stairs and send him to his mortal God."

"Sir, you misunderstand—" Dawit begins.

"Moorish devils!"

"Moorish devils?" At this, Mahmoud takes a step down toward the innkeeper despite impatient pats on the shoulder from Dawit. Why does Mahmoud insist on engaging in silly political debates at every turn? "The black Moors were Spain's salvation, with all your ignorance here, you old fool. If you're fortunate, you'll be conquered again."

The old man makes flustered sounds, then his voice returns. "Let's see how boastful you'll be when my neighbors tear your limbs apart!" Surprisingly agile, he leaps away from them to the door below, which opens to the street.

The women are no longer laughing. As soon as the innkeeper vanishes, they raise their skirts and descend the stairs behind him, frightened. Like a flock of turtledoves, Dawit thinks. Curse Mahmoud! Yet again, he has sabotaged a promising evening. Can't Mahmoud even pretend civility toward mortals, in the quest of pleasure if nothing else?

"We are forsaken," Dawit says, sighing.

"Oh, let them go. They are terribly ordinary, like this place. Spain is inhospitable, Dawit. Let's set out now."

"We just arrived!"

"Reason enough to leave. Besides, I fear that the innkeeper's threats are sincere, and I've had too much wine to be a good ally to you. I couldn't bear to see you strangled senseless on my account."

"As if I haven't suffered worse for your sake," Dawit says, smiling. "If you're so charitable, you should have considered that before exercising your tongue. Of all times—"

"Oh, don't berate me like a wife. Let us go."

"Then wake Chinja," Dawit sighs, "and we'll find a ship. Arguing with you is futile."

Mahmoud suddenly takes Dawit's arm and urges him down the frail wooden stairs, away from their room. "Why go back? We have our coin purses, so we lose nothing except a handful of clothes. Chinja is too worrisome. We'll leave him to live by his wits."

"What wits?" Dawit asks, chuckling, resisting.

"All the worse for him, then."

"But he serves us well, Mahmoud. Or tries to."

"He vexes me. We'll find another valet."

"You see? I asked why you troubled yourself to steal him in the first place."

At this, the door above them opens slightly, and Chinja is there; he has been awakened by the shouting and voices. Despite the child's mother's pleading, Mahmoud abducted the boy two years ago to travel with them as a servant. The woman had begged Mahmoud to marry her and take them both; she was the loveliest daughter of a merchant whom Dawit and Mahmoud had business with in Bombay. She told Mahmoud her son by him had ruined her for any other man. "I'll remove him, then," Mahmoud had said, hoisting the wailing boy over his shoulder. "You are ruined no more, my flower."

It was a playful coup for Mahmoud, but an instant annoyance to Dawit. Like all mortals, the child seemed to adopt a new illness at every turn and was maddeningly inept.

But, somehow, Dawit has grown accustomed to him. Dawit can see Chinja's brown nose and baleful eyes through the crack in the doorway. Mahmoud's son's age, Dawit guesses, is seven or eight years old. A ghastly age, Dawit recalls.

"Were you summoned?" Mahmoud asks Chinja.

"No, Father," he says, very softly.

Dawit is weary of Chinja's sad face. "Well, go, then," he tells him sharply. "Close the door."

"I'm sorry, Uncle," Chinja says, and quickly obeys.

Yes, Dawit decides, Mahmoud is right. It's best for them to leave him. They have no place for any child.

"Ah!" Mahmoud says, grabbing Dawit's shoulder, excited by a thought. "Morocco! I count thirty years since we were there."

"Yes, and it's a short journey," Dawit says, suddenly heartened. "Agreed."

As the two men descend the stairs, they plan their adventures at the next port. The mortal child who listens to their fading footsteps from behind the closed door, like his mother, has already been forgotten.

▪ 14

"Like this, Daddy?" Kira asked, stirring a wooden spoon in cake batter from a bar stool he'd brought to the kitchen counter. His stewed chicken and lentils with rice were simmering on the stove, ready to eat. Next, dessert.

Dawit's head, for the moment, was quiet. "Just like that, Duchess," he said. He wrapped his larger fingers around hers to guide the spoon. "Scrape the sides. The blender didn't get it all."

"Can I lick it after?"

He cocked his ear, leaning closer to her. "Excuse me?"

"I mean . . . *May* I lick it after? Please?"

"Yes," Dawit said, squeezing her shoulder with a wistful smile, "of course you may."

If this small pleasure is a crime, Dawit thought, no man has ever been more guilty. He had not come back to North America intending to collect another family. Yet, he had done it.

He'd only left Lalibela again because the rigors of study in the House of Science had proven too monotonous, too dissatisfying; his brothers had teased him, saying he'd adopted the mortal's laziness. After his stay at Harvard to write a small part of what he knew of jazz history, he'd bought this house in a simple neighborhood, envisioning it as a private retreat where he would organize his ideas and grade a few students' papers, nothing more. He'd chosen a city near his beloved ocean, whose waters he'd missed while living in Lalibala's seclusion. And Miami, he knew, was large enough to provide him any anonymous delight he might crave. That aside, he'd planned a quiet life as a teacher, just as he'd promised Khaldun when he left.

How had it all changed so quickly? He had not only a wife but this child to call his. He was certain he'd sired countless children before—one or two who had even known his face well enough to recognize him and, upon chance meeting, call him Father—but this was something else again. This was not supposed to be.

Shortly before his departure, a very wise Life brother, Melaku, had come to him and politely suggested that Dawit was the victim of an addiction; he hungered for his old way of life, the mortal's way, and he was unwilling to accept Khaldun's guidance to a higher consciousness. As always, he'd advised Dawit to practice his meditations. "The meditative state is a Life brother's highest, and happiest, existence," Melaku told him.

Dawit had heard this said many times before, especially by Khaldun himself, but he could not abide it. Endless meditating? He had visited the House of Meditation and seen for himself how the brothers there were frozen, barely breathing, their eyes fixed on nothing. That was the same as not living, Dawit thought.

So, he'd thanked Melaku for his advice, but told him not to worry. "Believe me, I understand better than most how frivolous the mortals' world is," he'd said. "My only addiction is diversion, and there's no hazard in that."

"Dawit . . ." his brother had said, as if he'd never spoken to anyone so confused, "Don't you see that Khaldun has only *prepared* your mind with languages, sciences, and lessons from the old ways? That had its place in the beginning, to teach discipline, but it is only a means, not an end. You are ready to absorb much more, if you stay and allow it. When will you make your life's home with your own kind?"

His own kind? Whom could Dawit claim as truly his kind? Only Mahmoud had seemed kindred to him; they both enjoyed study, but they also needed their time away, and Mahmoud had shared his zeal for pleasure. The other Life brothers who traveled abroad too often behaved like cheerless archaeologists afraid to leave any markings. One brother, Teferi, had made homes with mortal families for ages—even Dawit had once joined his brothers' complaints to Khaldun that such an act was akin to living with primates—but by now, Teferi had simply gone mad.

No, Dawit knew, his Life brothers were not like him. He had not spoken to Mahmoud in many years, since he'd left Chicago to return to Lalibela in the late 1920s—and then Mahmoud had been embarrassed to learn of Dawit's brief time spent with a mortal wife and children. It seemed to have come between them, Dawit thought sadly. He and his friend had shared a few happy reminiscences, but then Mahmoud cloistered himself in the House of Mystics, a group whom Dawit considered a pack of fanatics. Dawit hadn't even had an opportunity to say goodbye to Mahmoud before he left again.

Dawit cringed to imagine what Mahmoud would think of him now. Yes, he loved these mortals. Not all mortals, certainly, but *these*. He was learning lessons Khaldun did not teach, then. He was finally exercising not his mind but his heart.

What a farce his family in Chicago had been, he realized, a mere backdrop for the dizzy pace of his life. His sole love then had been music. Christina surely had lived to curse the day she'd first heard him on his clarinet at the supper club, her watchful parents by her side. He'd noticed her rapt eyes while his fingers were possessed on the keys. Was anyone else hearing the music as he heard it? Yes, *she* was, a lone listener in a room drowned in chatter and tinkling silverware. Later, she would tell him that was when she'd fallen in love; she'd been fooled by the passion in his breathing, the beauty of his sounds. She'd failed to realize that, at that moment, all the humanity he had to offer was on the stage with him, leaving his lips.

Christina had kept his bed warm with her tentative surrender to his desires, and Rosalie and Rufus were mere products of those couplings, nothing more. Often, instead of coming home to her, he'd visited many other willing beds. He had never cooked a meal with Rosalie the way he did now with Kira. Despite his son's begging, he'd never taught Rufus to play even a simple scale on the clarinet. He'd had no notion that it should be any other way.

Now this. Unasked for, unanticipated.

Jessica had captured his eye when he first spotted her in the front row of the tutorial—the seats chosen by only the most serious students—and he'd taken note of her feigned cockiness, her lovely full lips, her breasts pressed tight against a Lycra top, her hair combed back into an efficient ponytail. *Teach me something, I dare you,* her face said.

Still, he'd never sought out any of it. He'd made no effort to socialize with her, yet there she was one day, in the student union, joining him for coffee. He never meant to ask her out, but he couldn't resist when she said she'd never seen *The Godfather,* his latest discovery in the world of film that he'd ignored for so long. (He'd sworn off movies after seeing only a half hour of the infuriating distortions in *The Birth of a Nation* with Christina in 1916; it had taken him sixty-four years to venture back to a theater.) He had tried to make only polite conversation with Jessica, and something else, unexpectedly winning or frightfully boyish, emerged from his lips instead.

When he knew he wanted her, he told himself it would be sex only. His manhood had gone too long untended—he'd realized, with disbelief, that he'd so segregated himself that fourteen years had gone by without a woman in his arms—and he wanted to possess her. He wanted to cup her appealing young breasts in his hands. He wanted to feel her skin against his. He wanted to be swallowed by her.

He'd been so deluded by his desires. How could he have believed once their flesh joined that he could disentangle himself from her? Hadn't it been the same with Adele? It wasn't merely these women's bodies he wanted, it was their souls. Their love.

Mortals he'd encountered in years past had learned only to despise him. And why not? He was so different from them in his thinking, in his deeds. Living among them, he'd come to see how altered he was; at painful moments, even how terrible he was.

But he'd never seemed so to Adele. Nor to Jessica.

And certainly never to Kira. Kira's love, wholly unconditional, was an enchantment.

In Kira, Dawit understood how reborn Khaldun must have felt when he collected the Life brothers as pupils, so many fertile minds ready for seeds. Kira wanted to know everything, to learn everything, and she learned so quickly! And her love for him was so profound that even the smallest things he taught her governed her life.

For a flickering instant, he'd seen a glimpse of a child's love once before, in Chicago. Not in Rufus, who'd been so young that Dawit never considered him anything but a nuisance, but in Rosalie. There'd been one time—he couldn't remember the circumstances nor what words had been spoken between them—when he looked at her and comprehended that she was not merely an accident who carried his genes and traces of his face, but a treasure. That was the first time he'd looked upon any of his offspring the way he knew many other mortals did, with a tenderness that had shaken him with its power.

Adele, years before, had been scarred by the pain of losing so many children to slavery. But even as he'd tried to console her, Dawit had regarded her stories with the dispassionate knowledge that many children were sold, lost, discarded; it had been so since the beginning of time, and it would always be so.

It shocked him when he found himself so touched by Rosalie, the gentle way she yearned for his love. And he'd seen it so late! Before he'd had an opportunity to explore this new depth of feeling for her, the Searchers came. He had joined them without argument, even with some eagerness, because he knew his life with that family and those musicians was only an illusion. Within a month of his return to Lalibela, Chicago seemed like a distant, pleasant dream. He'd been happy to enjoy it all while he could, but there was no point in languishing. Those mortals had their world, he had his.

Even now, he could never permit himself to forget that his sep-arateness was his essence.

He'd known all along it was unnatural to make a home with mortals, to tether himself to any mortal's ever-dying heart. Know-ing this was what kept him sane; it enabled him to leave those he was fond of when he needed to, and to kill those he was indiffer-ent to when the Covenant of secrecy compelled it.

But this time, he knew, he was treading a dangerous path. There were moments—particularly soon after Princess died, and only a dog!—when he feared that he'd taken his attachments too far. That perhaps he was like an addict, after all, propelling himself toward an eternal hell.

Yes, the feelings Jessica and Kira awoke in him were intoxicating. He wanted to drink his fill of them, to revel in them, to learn what it was to feel as they did, with life pared down to its emotional simplicities.

But he must never forget his limits.

He could not expose himself to the emotional ravages he'd suffered with Adele. That period and its circumstances had been too violent, and her death too horrid.

Now, his only enemy was passing years. Living with mortals again, Dawit couldn't help noticing how quickly they aged. Jessica was thinner, her face drawing more tightly at her cheekbones and betraying the life experience of a woman at the end of her twenties, not the beginning. And Kira! Kira, so recently an infant, was nothing like she had been. Already, her head reached the kitchen countertop.

Suddenly, as if to punish him, Dawit's mind transported him back to snowy Chicago, to Rosalie's room in the nursing home, to her wrinkled skin and ravaged, weightless form. The mere image, surfacing in his head, unsettled his stomach with near nausea.

Kira would be deformed the same way one day. And Jessica.

He must not be here to see it. No matter how much it might grieve him to leave, and even if he were permitted to stay, he could not bear to witness their slow deaths to time.

But, if . . .

"See, Daddy?" Kira had left only a few lumps in the cake batter.

"Perfect," Dawit said. Even simple conversation with his daughter drew out the gentleness in his voice, on his face, no matter what his thoughts. Jessica, too, had this effect on him.

"Can I go up and get Mommy?"

"Not yet. Let's give her a few more minutes."

Dawit's hands trembled as he found the aluminum cake pans in the storage bin beneath the oven door. In an instant, he had allowed his mind to venture to the place he fought against so hard, and he could not arrest the poisonous idea.

What if Jessica and Kira never had to age or die? What if they could share his blood?

It was so simple a solution. It would create a scandal, and Khaldun's most severe punishment might await him, but would those things be worse than losing Kira and Jessica so soon? Jessica, at last, could be his true life mate, no longer separate. And Kira would have the world at her disposal for all of time.

He knew of no precedents. Of all the brethren who had come under Khaldun's tutelage when he had, he knew of none who had broken the Covenant, passing on the Living Blood to a mortal. Could that be? Had even Teferi felt consigned to watch family after family fade away? No wonder his senses had fled!

Speaking emphatically, with his reasons listed from dusk until dawn, Khaldun had made the Covenant the clearest lesson of all. Passing on the Living Blood was a defiance against God, or Allah, or Yahweh, the Life Force who made the blood live. Larger numbers would be dangerous to all, Khaldun said, inviting the scrutiny of outsiders. They might all find themselves imprisoned, studied, exploited. Moreover, any newcomer not first approved by Khaldun might be reborn as a monster to humankind.

And absolutely no women could receive the blood, he said— because women might carry it in their wombs, passing it on to children. Immortals must not become a race ungoverned, Khaldun said. They would remain a select few.

Your only Covenant to me in exchange for the Life gift is this: No one must know. No one must join. We are the last.

They had each sworn it, invoking whichever deities ruled their lives. They had sworn it with their own blood, which they spilled in ceremony to meet death. They had sworn their word to Khaldun, the savior who transformed their passing deaths into eternal life.

Dawit had watched his beloved Adele, swinging beside him on a tree, her neck snapped in two at the hands of mortal demons. Yet, he had never thought about defying the Covenant. He had never before struggled, as he did now, to remember the Hebrew words Khaldun recited while performing the Ritual of Life on one of the dead while Dawit, beside him, was still semiconscious. Dawit had always been true to Khaldun. He loved Khaldun, as they all did. Why was Dawit's mind now tormenting him so with thoughts of disobedience?

As if sensing his inner struggle, Kira gazed at Dawit with solemn, unblinking eyes as she watched him pour the batter into the pan. "Daddy . . . Why is Mommy sick?"

Dawit cursed himself, as he had many times before tonight. He'd so often wished he could relive that moment in the parking lot, at Peter's Mustang, and let that mortal live. Killing his wife's friend, he now realized, had been a hasty mistake. A mortal's life was nothing to him, but everything to his mortal wife. He'd made what should have been his last resort the first.

But could he otherwise have prevented them from learning what happened to Rosalie? He'd believed killing Peter would halt Jessica's research in Chicago, and he'd been right. But he was to blame for making it necessary. Wretched impulse! If he had let nature take Rosalie instead, their book would not have endangered him. Peter would be living still.

Dawit had wanted Jessica and Kira with him at home, away from the newspaper and her passions she wasted there—yet, this was not his wife. Her friend was two weeks dead, and so was she. As often as mortals confronted death, Dawit was intrigued by how it affected them. Any deaths they endured seemed to serve as further evidence that theirs was coming too. Now, Jessica seemed afraid to live.

"She's not really sick, honey. She's sad. A good friend of hers died. You remember how we felt when Princess died and you stayed home from school? That's what's happened to Mommy. When you're sad, you don't like to do the things you usually do."

"Will she be sad forever?" Kira asked, looking alarmed.

"No. Are you still sad about Princess?"

Kira nodded emphatically.

"But not as sad as you were the very first day. Remember how you cried? And me too? We'll always be sad inside a little, but not the same way. It gets better. Mommy will get better too."

Kira leaned closer to Dawit, lowering her voice. "Is it Peter?" she whispered.

Dawit paused, his hands on his hips. More and more, he and Jessica had learned that it was useless to try to keep a secret from their daughter. "Now, why would you ask that?"

"I heard her talk about him on the phone. She thought I was asleep."

Dawit sighed. He slid the cake pans into the oven, then closed the door quickly to avoid the blasting heat. He, like all his Life brothers, was sensitive to all physical sensations. The brothers in the House of Science had determined that the Living Blood's rejuvenation process affected the body's nerve endings, invigorating them as well. It was a small sacrifice, Dawit had decided. He could no longer remember the time when all touch had been duller, less exquisite. He had lived only thirty years as a mortal. Since then, he had lived more than a dozen times that.

"Yes, Kira," Dawit said, "Peter is her friend who died. We didn't tell you because we thought it would make you sad, too."

"Peter was very nice," Kira said. "He gave me presents."

"He was nice to Mommy, too."

"So, nice people go to Heaven. That's what Mommy says."

Heaven. Even the concept made Dawit's lips curl with distaste, but he tried to check himself for Kira's sake. Heaven was the only answer Khaldun did not offer, because Khaldun's knowledge was only of the world. So, Dawit had decided, Heaven was a lie. He refused to believe he had forfeited his soul's salvation as the price for the Living Blood. Was he expected to live in guilt, craving forgiveness? Should he cower before an invisible God like a primitive who expects lightning bolts to be flung from the skies by rain spirits? All because of a tale of Christ's blood?

The storyteller whom Khaldun met those many centuries ago may have lied about the blood's origin from the start. Or, perhaps Khaldun had fabricated it all. Who could prove that Khaldun himself was not the only source?

Dozens of years after joining the Life brothers, Dawit had finally sought Khaldun for an answer to his question: *Was the story you told us the truth?*

This question had teased Dawit since his first reawakening. He'd waited so long to broach it only because he dreaded the answer, not because he feared Khaldun. And it was uncommon to have a private audience with Khaldun, who was usually occupied with teaching or in an unreachable meditative state. That day, however, Dawit had his teacher's full attention. One thing Dawit admired most about Khaldun was the supreme objectivity he had gained through mastery of his emotions; he was not quick to anger nor to judgment, and he was always just. That day, Khaldun had even gazed at Dawit with what might have been a gentle smile. Dawit had not yet asked the question aloud, but Khaldun could hear even what was unspoken. That was another of his gifts.

If you believe it, Khaldun had said, *I could never convince you otherwise. If you do not, nothing I tell you could sway you. I am the one who should be asking you: Is it the truth?*

No, Dawit said, certain within himself. And Khaldun, still smiling faintly, had not addressed the subject again.

Why should he believe it? His brothers in the House of Science could devise a half-dozen explanations for the Living Blood's regenerative properties. And the Khaldunites were convinced Khaldun himself was a deity, despite Khaldun's insistence that his gifts could be attained by any of them, given enough time and study. No, Dawit had decided, he would not be a prisoner to Christ or Allah or Satan, or any other of humankind's imaginary guardians or tormentors. He would not mourn his exclusion from a fabled Heaven. The world was all he knew and ever would know, so he would worship only worldly things.

How much breath did he waste on Adele and other slaves who traded their lives away in the hope of a redemption after death? How often did he urge them to come to his Sunday reading lessons rather than flock to church meetings where their masters would have them pray and sing? Adele tried to explain to him how it made their troubles more bearable, but it only infuriated Dawit. Had the slaves' belief in salvation erased the misery of their lives?

Oh, sweet Adele, Dawit thought, I would build a Heaven for you if it meant you could rest there. I would gather the bricks and carry them on my shoulders, if only you could be at peace. To Adele, a slave from birth, a mother to children stolen from her breast, death was Heaven enough. Perhaps, indeed, Dawit thought, death was Heaven after all.

"Peter was a very nice person," Dawit told Kira. "If you believe he is in Heaven, then perhaps that is where he is."

"He is," Kira said. "Heaven is a good place, Daddy. I think it's a very good place. Jesus lives there."

A Christian for a daughter, and already bent on converting him! Dawit sighed, wishing Jessica and her zealot of a mother would stop filling his child's head with such nonsense.

The telephone rang. "Keep away from the oven, Kira," Dawit said, rushing to pick up the living room phone so Jessica would not be disturbed. He wished they could live without a telephone altogether. The invention had brought nothing but interruptions.

Dawit recognized Uncle Billy's breathing and the meandering of his drawl immediately. "Boy, you ain't gon' b'lieve the stuff I'm digging out. Some of these old records I ain't seen since my daddy died. He's even got photographs in here, ticket stubs from all the big shows. And we're talking a long way back."

"Like what?"

"Jelly Roll Morton, one thing. And I think my daddy must have bought every Louis Armstrong record they put out. One of 'em got an autograph right across the label and I never even knew it. And I'ma get you that Jazz Brigade you looking for. You need to come 'round here sometime."

"I will. This week," Dawit promised, "and if you find The Jazz

Brigade, I'll come right away, no matter what time of day or night. They only pressed a handful of records."

"Damn shame . . ." Uncle Billy said. "Some of 'em didn't press no records at all. And once it's gone, it's gone."

Dawit wished more mortals shared Uncle Billy's sense of history. Jessica's great-uncle had a sincere appreciation of music that made Dawit long to forge a more meaningful relationship with him, beyond casual phone calls or banter after Sunday dinner. But, then, what was the point? The old man would surely be dead soon. Dawit had learned that he might as well be a visage, like all mortals. What point was there in befriending ghosts?

"You're all right, Uncle Billy," was all he said.

The phone call put Dawit in a better mood. He brought his clarinet out of the cabinet and began to fit it together while Kira watched. He had denied himself this joy with his new family, but no more. He had proven his devotion.

"What's that for?" Kira asked. Was it possible she'd never seen a clarinet?

"It makes music. I'm going to go upstairs and surprise Mommy. *Avec moi.* Come with me."

Like bandits, they crept up the stairs. Dawit held Kira's hand so she wouldn't betray them and go leaping into the open bedroom doorway. Safely hidden around the corner, he brought his clarinet to his lips and began to breathe out the soulful melody of "My Funny Valentine," one of Jessica's favorite songs. He allowed the resonance of the deep, long notes to pierce the air, then took deep breaths to begin the next strains. The music overpowered the chatter from the news on her television set.

Jessica leaped out of bed and ran out of the room to find the source of the music. She was still in bedclothes, a faded T-shirt that reached her thighs. He could see the loose curves of her bare breasts beneath the thin material, the spread of her hips, and he longed to drop to his knees and kiss every smooth inch of her torso. Even with her hair uncombed, sticking straight up near her temples, she was impossible to resist. She stood riveted with a smile.

When the song was finished, Kira cheered and clapped. Jessica clapped too, squinting in confusion. "David . . . when did you . . ."

"My old clarinet from college. Got it from an antiques shop in Cambridge. I haven't seen it in ages."

"Amazing," Jessica said, still intrigued. She touched the instrument, then drew her hand away as though she were afraid of harming it. "I mean, you sound *good*. I can't believe you never told me you play. What else don't I know about you?"

He winked at her and kissed her lips lightly, then whispered in her ear. "You don't know how horny I get when I play."

"Really?" she said, kissing his earlobe in response. Her warm breath lingered there, journeying to his loins until he squirmed. She also lowered her voice to a breath. "Well, you don't know how horny I get when I'm serenaded."

"I can't hear!" Kira complained.

Jessica and Dawit ignored her, sharing a playful gaze. That night, for the first time since Peter's death, they made love. Dawit would not let her rest until she was whimpering his name.

▪ 15

One Sunday Jessica decided, with unexpected resolve, that she would drag her butt back in to work the next week. She'd been away nearly three weeks, munching on Doritos, gaining weight, half reading books, avoiding church, reflecting on her life, and she decided it was enough. She couldn't just run away.

David and Kira were at the Dade County Youth Fair. Jessica had planned to go with them, but at the last minute the promise of an empty house overshadowed her desire to be a good sport. She'd outgrown the fair and its farm smells, loud music, and expensive snack foods. She loved rides, but hated lines. Better for David to go. He had more patience. She didn't know where in the world he got it from.

Strolling beneath her neighborhood's hundred-year-old live oaks with Teacake slung agreeably across her shoulder, Jessica felt lonely. More than lonely. She felt alone. At midafternoon, Night Song's voice was quiet. The day was hot, and the shade only make-believe. The cooler weather was probably behind them now; the climate was charging into a mean summertime mode on the eve of spring.

"Guess I won't be writing that book," she said aloud, surprising herself with the straightforwardness in her voice. It wasn't the statement itself that made her happy; it was her ability to say it and live with it. *Honor Thy Father and Mother* had been Peter's book, both in inception and inspiration. Without Peter, it felt like a dress fitting two sizes too big.

She could write a book more true to herself. She'd always wanted to write a memoir about her great-grandfather Lucius Benton, who'd come to Miami from the Bahamas to work on Henry Flagler's railroads. She'd been told his name could be found on the 1896 charter that incorporated Miami into a city. Jessica had always meant to sit down with her mother and pay close attention to all of the stories about her most immediate ancestors. It was time to do it. She wouldn't need a book leave. She could do it in her spare time and bring Kira along to hear Grandma's stories too. Wasn't that the only way the stories got passed along? She couldn't keep waiting forever.

Today would not be a crying day, Jessica realized, and she passed the granite Tequesta ground marker on the hill across the street from their house. Even when the image of the bloody Mustang tried to assault her, she fought it away. Instead, she remembered the troll Peter had given her, which she'd hidden from sight in the closet, and smiled.

Was she finally coping with losing him?

This had been hard, harder than she'd imagined anything could be. How would she ever survive if something happened to David? She wouldn't, that was all. Jessica still couldn't understand how in the world Bea had managed.

Her father's death had destroyed their family, in small bits falling out of place. Alexis nearly flunked out of school that year, locking herself in her room and discovering the escape of marijuana with her friends. And Bea was always sad and nearly always silent, never trying to make anyone laugh with her flip comments. She'd had to take a second job, and she never wanted to sit still anymore. After the accident, Jessica couldn't help feeling she'd lost her mother too.

It wasn't until her senior year in college, finally grown, that Jessica had felt enough like her mother's friend to finally ask her what she'd gone through when she was widowed.

"There's a lot of hurt in life, Jessica," Bea had said, almost matter-of-factly. "My mother had a hard life. A very hard life. You remember the story."

Jessica nodded. After her grandmother's funeral two months before, Jessica had been shocked when Bea told her that Grammy had been raped by her white employer in Quincy. She'd gotten pregnant, and Grandpa, a pastor, wouldn't hear of an abortion, even if it had been legal. So, she had a son—Bea's brother, Jessica's Uncle Joe. Grammy and Bea were so light themselves that no one paid any attention to how fair-skinned the new child was, and Grandpa always claimed Joe was his. As far as Jessica knew, only the women in the family ever told the story, passing on a painful heirloom.

Bea went on: "For the longest time, after my mother told me that, I looked at her differently. The way you look at someone who's lived through something you can't imagine. The most severe test of all. But see, my mother never saw it like that. She treated Joe exactly the way she did me, like he was a blessing. So there is light, but only if you can see past the pain."

"Did you ever see a light, Mom? After Daddy?"

Bea had given Jessica a fragile, wounded smile. Then, she sighed. "Seemed like I spent whole days cursing the Lord out, just asking why. Raymond was the kind of man who, after you met him, made any other man ruined in your eyes. He was that to me. What did I learn? I learned I could lose even that and still survive. One day I looked in the mirror and thought, hardly believing it, I'm all right. Doesn't sound like much, does it? I wouldn't have minded living my whole life without knowing it, but I guess it's something. My mother used to say to me that she collected sorrows and put them in her pocket. Walking around with them that way, by and by, you just learn to carry them all a bit better, to stand up a bit straighter. That's all life is, on this earth anyway. You'll see it, too, when your trials come. I wish I could tell you they won't come, Jessica, but they always do."

That's exactly what Jessica was afraid of. Losing her father had ended her childhood, but the rest of her life had been so easy. She'd met David before she began to worry about becoming an Unmarried Black Woman statistic, and he had never failed her. She got the first job she applied for, the only one she'd ever wanted. Kira was healthy except for the asthma that seemed to improve each year.

Why, then, did it all feel so temporal? Their life was like a dream, and she'd learned young that dreams always end.

Would she be strong enough for her trials? Was Peter's death meant, in some way, to help her learn to carry her sorrows?

When Jessica reached the gravel path at the top of their driveway, Teacake complained and wriggled to spring out of her arms. As usual, he trotted straight for the darkness of the cave and vanished inside. After watching the cave's mouth for a half-minute, her mind drifting, Jessica found herself walking on the thin dirt path through her yard's incline of rocks and plants, following Teacake. The cave was at the highest point in their yard, shielded from the street by a cluster of palms, a tangle of staghorns and elephant-ear plants, and the broad trunk of the oak tree that displayed their address to passers-by on the other side.

Holding the wall with her fingertips for balance, Jessica climbed down the cave's steep, narrow steps, three of them, until she entered the wider space below. At first, all she could see of Teacake was a red flash from the reflection of his eyes. Teacake, not in the mood for company, meowed in protest and darted past her back outside. Jessica let him go. She hadn't come to the cave for Teacake.

She'd come because of the feeling.

When anybody asked Jessica if she believed in visits from ghosts, she laughed the way she did when she watched those television programs about folks claiming they'd been kidnapped by UFOs. And she didn't count her believing in Night Song and the spirits from the burial ground, because a few unexplained whistles from the trees wasn't the same as having a face-to-face conversation with Aunt Josephina.

But alone, during reflective moments, she felt it. The cave had been built to store arrowroot, David told her, but all of the Tequesta neighborhood stories made her think of it as a burial cave instead. Now, she knew why. She could feel it as she crouched, balancing herself with one knee touching the rough floor. She could admit it to herself at this moment, but not again anytime soon—not to herself, not to Bea, not to Alex, and, most of all, not to David:

Jessica believed her father was in this cave.

She couldn't pinpoint the first time the feeling had come, but she'd felt such an attachment to David's house because of the cave. He hadn't even mentioned it until they'd been dating for two months, but she was hooked the moment she explored it with him. Visiting it by herself, she'd always found that the cave made her feel more alive and yet calm, as if she'd been nestled in someone's arms. And she'd thought it was only coincidence that when she was inside, she always thought of her father at least once. She'd even caught herself thinking "Goodbye, Daddy" whenever she left.

But something had happened a few months before, when David had been on his music lecture in Chicago and Kira was taking a nap in the house. Jessica had wandered into the cave and allowed herself to believe that her father was in there with her. As soon as she thought it, she felt comforted. And on that day, when she'd realized how late it was and whispered "Goodbye, Daddy," she thought she'd heard not even a whisper, but an echo in her head:

Goodbye, Baby Girl.

It had startled her, making her pause before she climbed the steps, but then she pushed it out of her head. Just like that. Maybe it was so natural to her that she hadn't even given it half a thought.

Until now.

As her eyes adjusted to the diminished light in the cave, Jessica studied the pockmarked, flaking limestone. She saw bugs crawling in a line around around tiny roots and moss that had made their way down here. She felt stupid suddenly, like Alice crouching in a miniature room. It's just a cave, she thought, disappointed.

Jessica waited a long three minutes before she spoke. "Hey, Daddy," she whispered halfheartedly, hopefully. She was so desperate to hear a response that her brain gave her one: Hey, Baby Girl.

That hadn't been a voice, not this time, not like before. It was just a thought, a memory. That's what her father had always called her. To him, Alex had been Big Girl and Jessica had been Baby Girl, as if they didn't have given names.

"Hot in here today," Jessica muttered, thinking aloud.

Just thick-blooded, an interior voice of her mind said. Thick-blooded? Oh, yes. She remembered how she used to always complain about being too hot when she was young, so Bea had told her she was "thick-blooded," the opposite of thin-blooded. "To match your thick head," Bea used to say.

Yours is the warmest blood, Baby Girl.

A voice. She heard the distinct roll of her father's timbre in the voice, all seven words spoken with a schoolteacher's slow deliberateness. She'd nearly forgotten the true sound of that voice. She hadn't heard it in more than twenty years until this moment when she heard it so perfectly in her mind. Jessica's breathing slowed. Could it really have come from her head?

No, she decided. No, it hadn't.

As if in confirmation, there was a low-pitched laugh from somewhere. Below her? Above her? It might have come from across the street, camouflaged in a breeze, but Jessica heard it with her ears, not her mind. A loving laugh. Her father's laugh.

Staring at the wall, Jessica thought she might be seeing something, so faint that it was like a fleck out the corner of her eye that would be gone if she blinked or looked too hard. Her father could be sitting right across from her, cross-legged, wearing his old Oakland Raiders cap and dusty work boots with the bright red laces, the ones she remembered. And she almost imagined she could see him eating a Whopper with Cheese, still nestled in the wrapper. Smiling at her.

Was it really seeing, or was it just wanting to see? She couldn't tell.

You're a big girl now, Jessica.

The voice was so unexpected and clear this time that goosebumps bloomed across Jessica's arms. Her blood didn't feel warm now.

"I know I'm a big girl," she whispered, not knowing what else to say.

Big girls have to walk with their eyes open. Wide enough to see.

"I do, Daddy," Jessica said, again very softly, not wanting to spoil it. She was afraid to move. She winced when she heard a bird squawk outside, wondering if the noise would chase him away. Here she was, a grown woman talking to herself in a cave in the middle of the afternoon, but she couldn't walk away. She couldn't pretend she didn't hear.

Your strength is the strength of stones.

Suddenly, Jessica wanted to cry. Was he going to leave her now? She didn't want to be alone again, not yet. "No it's not, Daddy," she whispered, blinking away tears.

For a long time after that, there was silence. Jessica felt as though she were waiting for something, so she was still, breathing patiently. He wasn't gone. She knew that. She could feel him here, loving her. For a moment, the cave seemed to breathe around her, as though it were sighing.

And then the fluid feeling left, as abruptly as the end of an embrace. She didn't feel like crying anymore. A contentment spread through her chest, making her feel flushed.

The apparition, or whatever it had been, was gone. All she could see was the cave wall.

Hold tight to Kira for me, Baby Girl. Until it splits your heart and soul.

The voice—or at least it still seemed like a voice—was fading. Now, Jessica could only hear a distant rambling, spoken unhurriedly, just within her hearing.

There are no good monsters. Tell her.

Then, nothing. Jessica suddenly felt uneasy, not comforted. The last words had confused her. Even scared her.

Quickly, Jessica stood up and practically stumbled back up toward the light outside. Emerging from the cave and gazing around her yard as though she were seeing it for the first time, Jessica realized her heart was thrashing from her chest to her throat. She felt a headache coming on. Served her right. Irritated with herself, Jessica wiped gray dust and mulch from her knees. Already, her rational mind was telling her she'd been in there making it all up, like the nonsensical thoughts that buzzed through her mind right before she fell asleep at night.

Guess you can believe in anything if you want it badly enough, Jessica thought.

She stood at the top of the hill, gazing at the shadowed, empty windows of her house until a feeling of solitude began to stifle her. Why did she feel like someone was watching her? Not her father or a friendly spirit, but someone who didn't belong?

She'd hold tight to Kira, all right, Jessica decided. As soon as David and Kira got back, she was going to hug them both like they'd been out at sea.

"Come on, Teacake," she said, scooping the cat into her arms from a bed of dry leaves near the mouth of the cave.

Jessica was walking at an unhurried pace as she began to make her way down the driveway, but by the time she reached the front porch she was in full sprint, clinging tightly to Teacake. There are no good monsters, she kept thinking, that cryptic phrase she thought she'd heard in the cave swimming around in her head.

All afternoon, while she waited, it wouldn't go away.

▪ 16

502 State Street
Apartment B
Chicago, Illinois

MAY 1926
"No, it's like this: one-two, one-two. You have to listen. I told you, it's up-tempo."

"What you wanna go change the tempo for, Spider? Thought this was a ballad. It's late, nigger. I gotta split. It's a wonder your neighbors don't lynch you."

"Let's run through this new intro real fast, see how it sounds. Let's go. One-two . . ."

"Daddy?"

". . . One-two, one-two, ready, play—"

"Daddy . . ." A voice, an interruption.

Dawit freezes, his clarinet reed a half inch from his waiting lips. The oxygen seeps unaccompanied from his lungs, and the inspiration vanishes from his head. The Joplin-style chords and syncopation that had been tumbling inside his imagination, waiting for release, fall silent. Lester sighs and plinks a few sour keys on the Baldwin. The piano needs tuning, and Dawit keeps forgetting to make the time to do it. The flat sound will soon grate on Lester's nerves and give him another excuse to insist he has to go, Dawit knows. Lester is so damn temperamental. It's nine-thirty. They'll only be able to play for another half-hour before the landlord comes knocking about the noise. They're scheduled in the recording studio by midmorning, and he won't be able to pull in Al, Tommy, and Cleve before eight to rehearse.

That's only three hours to make it work. At the most.

"Daddy."

For the first time, Dawit notices Rosalie standing at his elbow. She's wearing a plaid nightgown that reaches her ankles, her jet-black hair hanging loose to her shoulders. She's tall for eight, looking just like her mother. Damn. That's right. Christina is spending the night at her parents' house because her father is sick, which explains why Rosalie is standing here talking to him at this precise moment. She's going on about something Dawit can't understand because she's talking so fast.

". . . Right, Daddy? Remember how you were telling me and Mama about how you saw him in New York last week?"

"Who?" Dawit asks, confused.

"Langston Hughes. The poet. You said he came up and—"

"He always sees the show when we're in Harlem," Dawit says, still not comprehending. "What does that have to do with anything?"

Rosalie smiles, waving a piece of paper in the air. "Our teacher brought us one of his poems in a magazine, and I memorized it already. Want to hear? It's called 'Mother to Son.' 'Well, son, I'll tell you: Life for me ain't been no crystal—'"

Lester is giving Dawit one of his vitriolic looks, which means his hands will be jelly on the piano keys for certain. Dawit is stunned; under different circumstances, he might have to laugh. He's working on a fresh arrangement the night before his group makes its first recording—and they've waited long enough, God knows—and this child is standing here reciting a poem.

"Rosalie," he interrupts her breathless presentation, his temples tight with anger, "what am I doing?"

Rosalie is silent, staring at him with a pleading expression.

"What am I doing?" he asks again, refraining from shouting only because Rufus is asleep. That kid can never keep still, so if he gets up there'll be no peace the rest of the night.

"Practicing," Rosalie whispers.

"That's right. And you know good and damn well you're not supposed to come in here distracting me when I'm working. How many times do I have to say it?"

"I just wanted to do it for you because I'm going to bed," Rosalie says, sticking out her lip. She rubs her wrist against her eyelid.

"Not now," Dawit tells her. "Go on."

Rosalie mumbles something about being sorry and leaves them alone. Dawit glances back at Lester, and the glare is still there behind Lester's round wire-frame spectacles. "Hey, maybe she can tell us some Brer Rabbit stories, too," Lester says with flat sarcasm.

"Sorry."

"You know," Lester says, wiping his fingers on his slacks, "I'd like to git while I still have a home to git to. My house ain't like yours, where you do what you want. My wife already told me about this, being out here all hours——"

"I said sorry. Let's go."

One-two, one-two. The new intro is an homage to ragtime; the rest is fresh, modern, improvisational. The piece is snappier, catchier, has more character this way. It's an entirely different song! It might be innovative enough to draw attention to the record, win The Jazz Brigade a little more notice. Then they'll be able to get out of the gin mill where they're gigging—they're backing up two-bit singers and enjoying only occasional opportunities to showcase the band—and secure something permanent at the Sunset Café. Playing it up-tempo, they could open with this one at the Summer Stomp next month. I'm your Forever Man, You drive me crazy . . .

The landlord knocks at fifteen minutes to ten. Dawit can see in Lester's face as he waves goodbye, even though he's still complaining, that he likes it, too. He won't admit it, but he knows the music is worth the trouble.

Dawit doesn't think he'll be able to sleep, not with the chord structure playing in his head and his anticipation pumping him full of adrenaline. He sits at the piano for twenty minutes, soundlessly fingering the keys, humming to himself. But he needs to rest.

On his way to bed, he passes the children's room, which looks bright from the moonlight between the parted draperies. For some reason, seeing the light across their beds, Dawit stops in their doorway. Rufus is sound asleep, but Rosalie's hands are folded across her chest and he can see her eyes gleaming.

Dawit feels a twinge of conscience. His daughter has complained in the past that the music keeps her up; apparently, she doesn't have

Rufus's talent for sleeping through late rehearsals. Dawit walks into the room, standing in front of the window at the foot of her bed. He gazes down at the dark street, where three automobiles rumble below him in succession. State Street is always busy, no matter what the hour. That's why he insisted on living here. When Dawit strains, he can hear laughter and even music from the club blocks away. He wishes he were there playing, just to get it—

Who's that?

Dawit's eyes shift to the spot directly beneath his building, searching for a movement; he was certain he'd seen a man dressed in white, someone standing against the railing, but he is gone.

Could it be . . . ? Dawit won't permit himself to think it.

Not yet. Not now. It's too soon.

"Rosalie," he says quietly, still peering outside, not turning to her, "I'm really excited about this record."

"I know," Rosalie says.

Why is it so difficult to apologize to her? Dawit can barely think of words. "Well . . . That's what made me so short with you. I'd like to hear Langston's poem, though. Maybe tomorrow, you know, at breakfast, you can recite it. Early."

"I can say it now," she whispers.

Dawit glances at Rufus, who hasn't stirred, curled up and facing the wall in a fetal position. It's better not to risk waking him. "No, not now. It's late. I'll listen to it tomorrow."

"'Kay," Rosalie says. She is smiling, satisfied. It takes so little to please her, Dawit realizes, awed. He wonders why he so rarely takes notice of what a pretty child she is.

"It must be difficult, having a musician for a daddy," he says, thinking aloud.

Rosalie doesn't say anything, shrugging beneath her bedsheet, so they are wordless for a long time in the moonlight. Dawit leans across the sill and sweeps his eyes from one end of the street to the other. The man he thought he'd seen is not there. It must have been his imagination.

Forever Man, I don't mean maybe . . .

Dawit is still hearing his song. He taps the beat on the windowsill with his index finger and hums. The time for The Jazz Brigade has dawned, he realizes. So get accustomed to it, Rosalie, Dawit thinks as he gazes at the anxious night. It's going to get worse before it gets better. He could no more control his destiny than he could the luminescence of the moon or the path of a tropical storm.

In that instant, startling himself, Dawit feels sad, even panicked, in a way he doesn't understand immediately. He has something to lose now, in this life he has made for himself. How frightening it is, he realizes, when fate is at liberty to take over what will has begun. He leans over Rosalie to kiss her forehead, and his lips linger on his beautiful child's smooth skin.

"Good night, Duchess." He pauses. "Love you."

Rosalie's eyes are closed, and Dawit is glad. She must, at last, be falling asleep, savoring the temporary silence.

▪ 17

William Emmet Gillis had seen many things in his eighty years of life. As a boy of six, alone with his mother in their lean-to outside Macon, he saw his baby sister born feet first from between her bloody thighs. During the war, liberating a concentration camp, he saw walking skeletons with tattooed numbers on their paper-thin white skin—the work of Satan himself. He'd lived to see his parents, his wife, his daughter, his sister, and his two nephews go on to Glory before him.

But until this very day, he'd never seen a ghost.

There was no denying it was a ghost in the photograph, staring him dead in the face with a wide smile. The ghost was wearing a white tuxedo and bow tie, and he held before him, in both hands, a dark clarinet.

It was Jessica's husband, David. Same pretty face, comely as a woman's. Same skin that looked like it had never seen a blackhead. Same perfect, perfect teeth. And those eyes that always looked like they were somewhere else, even when they were on you. Uncle Billy swore those eyes had always given him bone-chills, since he first met the boy. Dead eyes. Except when he talked about music, when they sprang to life.

It was David in the photo, eyes and all. The thing was, according to the date painted on the bass drum in the far right corner, the yellowing black-and-white photograph was from The Jazz Brigade's Summer Stomp, 1926. The ghost looked about thirty, just like David looked now. He was holding up well for a man going on a hundred years old. Damn well.

This was a good day for seeing ghosts. He'd seen another one just that morning, when he woke up and noticed a woman standing at the foot of his bed in the not-yet morning light. He'd have known her even without the white calico dress she was wearing, the best she'd been able to afford for their wedding sixty-two years before. It was his dead wife, Sadie, smiling at him and reaching out her hand as if to touch him.

It had pained Uncle Billy to see her, especially looking as young and pretty as she did, as fresh as their wedding day, but something held him back from wanting to touch her. He knew what that touch would mean. He'd had a blinding headache the day before, and his breaths were starting to feel stopped up in his throat. He slept with the humidifier on to try to clear out his lungs, but it didn't seem to help; less and less seemed to ease his ailments the older he got. Since the stroke, his body had never been near right. The doctor said he could still be having ministrokes, even if he couldn't feel them, and he figured the tiny shocks were wearing his old body down.

Seeing Sadie, he knew what she was there for. It wasn't that he was afraid; and Lord knows he was weary. He just couldn't bring himself to try to sit up in the bed and swing his good arm over to touch her just then. Just couldn't.

Later, when her figure vanished, he'd felt ashamed. Glory wasn't anything to shy away from. No, Lord. Not if it meant being with Sadie, and she'd made a special trip to fetch him. Better for him to be out of poor Bea's hair. He decided that the next time he saw Sadie, he would go with her.

Then, he saw the second ghost, and he understood it all.

Going through the last box from his closet right after lunch, he'd found the photo. He'd just put down the phone from talking to David when he pulled that rare Jazz Brigade record out of its faded jacket and the photograph fell out. His father must have put it there for safekeeping and forgotten it. His father's gaunt figure was in the middle of the picture, the young man he'd been back then with pomade in his hair, surrounded by the grinning musicians. His father, Uncle Billy remembered, had been beside himself when his favorite jazz group agreed to pose for this photograph with him after their show. Excited as he could be.

David, the ghost, was at his father's side.

It scared Uncle Billy so much at first that he'd dropped the photo on the floor. It landed faceup, staring right back at him. No mistaking who it was, what it meant. His journey to Glory had begun as far back as when Bea carried him down here to stay with her. It had begun the moment David first shook his hand and said hello.

You were in Chicago in the 'twenties? Ever hear of The Jazz Brigade?

He'd forgone Sadie's ghost, the gentle ghost. He would have to go with this one, the one who'd been toying with him all this time, who was tired of waiting. He would be here soon.

Uncle Billy was wearing only his robe, which he'd worn at lunch with Bea before she ran off to her church to lead the choir practice for Sunday's Easter service. He would bathe himself today. No sense in a fully grown man waiting for some woman to bathe him.

He was wheeling toward the bathroom when he heard David's knock, his fingertips tapping across the jalousie windows at the door leading out to the backyard. He saw a muddy shadow.

Uncle Billy figured he could forget about his bath. David's coming here would probably change everything.

"Uncle Billy?" David's voice called.

"Open," Uncle Billy called back, his voice hoarse.

David walked in, grinning at him. "Bea's car is gone," he observed. "You're not in here making trouble, are you?"

Uncle Billy didn't answer, looking David up and down. It was one thing to see him in the photograph, but another to see him in the flesh. Spider Tillis was right here in the room with him, real as could be. Gazing back at the picture in his lap, Uncle Billy felt his bare toes tingling on the footrests of his wheelchair.

"You all right?" David asked.

Without speaking, Uncle Billy lifted the photo with his good hand and held it out to David. Let him see for himself.

David took the photograph, grasping it with both hands. His grin disappeared real quick, soon as he saw it. Whole face changed, in fact. He looked scared at first, glancing at Uncle Billy, then his eyes went back to the photo and Uncle Billy could see how his jawline was getting hard. He didn't move.

"Where'd you find this, Uncle Billy?" David asked from where he stood two feet in front of the wheelchair.

David's eyes were alive now, too, but with a calm that was too calm, more like a mask for something else. When Uncle Billy didn't answer him, David asked two more times, the same exact words. Seemed like he was losing his patience.

Three times, Uncle Billy didn't answer. He sat in his wheelchair and studied David's eyes. He'd never really stopped to stare a ghost in the eye before, and he figured it was an opportunity he should make the most of. His left arm was tickling, the way it always did since the stroke, itching to move but forgetting how. He should have left the humidifier on. His lungs still felt tight, like no air could come in or out.

David took a step toward him, then sat at the edge of Uncle Billy's made bed. He didn't say anything, making Uncle Billy remember his grade-school teacher Mr. Morley, who used to allow five minutes to pass without saying a word when the class disappointed him or didn't act right, letting his eyes sweep across the room like a judgment. Same as Mr. Morley, David seemed to be mulling over just which punishment best fit the crime.

David let out a long, hard sigh. He looked toward the window, out at the empty clothesline in the backyard. Bea had taken in the wash just before she left, saying, "I'd better do this now in case of rain. I'll be a long while, Uncle Billy. You sure you don't want me to call for a day nurse?"

Uncle Billy just about cursed her out then. Hell, no, he didn't need no damn day nurse to be alone for a few hours. Get your smart behind out that door, he said to Bea. He'd made her laugh. That was the last thing he'd heard before the door slammed shut behind her, a girlish-sounding laugh that reminded him of Sadie.

"Let's talk about this picture, Uncle Billy," the ghost said. He was trying to sound patient, but he couldn't quite pull it off. Uncle Billy could see through that nonsense. He wasn't a fool.

"Ain't nothing to say," Uncle Billy said.

"Well, you can't possibly believe this is me."

"Didn't say a word about you, now did I?" Uncle Billy answered. He had him there.

David waited a moment before speaking again. "You just seem disturbed," he said. "That's what led me to think perhaps something was bothering you."

Lord, sometimes this boy strung sentences together in ways that made no kind of sense, like he had to search for the longest way around to the end of his thoughts. Keeping company with white folks, that was where it came from, and all those universities besides.

"I ain't disturbed about a thing," Uncle Billy said.

There. Uncle Billy saw it that time, a flinching in David's jaw. His teeth must be grinding hard, ready to crack.

"You see," David said, speaking syrup-slow, "this photograph was taken in nineteen twenty-six. That was seventy-one years ago. Do you see now why that can't be me? That would have to be my grandfather, wouldn't it? Can we come to that understanding, Uncle Billy? And I'll just take this home."

Understanding? What did he mean by that? Some trickery?

"All I know is what I see; what I see is what I know," Uncle

Billy said. Suddenly, he felt bold. "Tell the truth, I knew there was something funny with you the first time I laid eyes on you. I sure did. Just ask Bea. I even told her, I said, 'That sure is a strange one got your youngest daughter, ain't it, Bea?' And she said, 'What you mean?' And I said, 'It's just what I see. I ain't got much else, but I got eyes.'"

Uncle Billy felt good to say it, to bring it out in the open. "So I guess you got to do what you got to do," he said as clear as he could muster.

The ghost wrung his hands between his knees and sat staring down at the colorful carpet Bea bought Uncle Billy, a Moroccan woven rug she'd found on sale. Uncle Billy had never before had a rug—or anything else, for that matter—from Morocco. He'd had nothing but the most special treatment since he'd moved in with her. He couldn't complain about a thing.

David sat, not moving, for what seemed like a long time. Something was working hard in his mind, knitting his brow. Hell, the man looked like he was about to cry.

Without saying anything, David stood and picked up the Jazz Brigade record from the stack in front of Uncle Billy's wheelchair. He ran his finger across the hard vinyl edge, then he made his way to the Victrola on top of the bureau. When he put the record on, the music was nearly covered over by the noise from age. The music sounded far, far away, like this ghost's sullen brown eyes.

Uncle Billy didn't know the name of the song that was playing, but he'd heard it many times before, in Chicago, when his father used to play it. His father was never so proud as when that record came out, and he played it every night when he came home from bellhopping at the hotels. These boys are like family, his father used to say. I remember them when they was nothing. Now, look. And he'd put it on again.

Uncle Billy hadn't remembered a conversation with his father for a long, long time. Maybe the remembering was all a part of it.

"From your looks, I'd say you were about to take your bath when I interrupted you," David said, like he was about to leave. But he didn't leave. Instead, he walked behind Uncle Billy and gripped the wheelchair's handles, slowly pulling in a half circle until he was backing Uncle Billy out of his room, into the hallway.

"That could be," Uncle Billy said. He had to admit it, he was just the tiniest bit scared now. He didn't like it when people pulled his wheelchair backward. He always liked to know where he was going, and he wanted to see it before he got there.

"I'm sorry I sidetracked you, Uncle Billy," David said, just as nice as could be.

"Ain't no trouble," Uncle Billy said. His lungs were really fooling with him, likely to burst from the strain of breathing.

They were in the bathroom. Uncle Billy noticed they could hear the tinny-sounding music even here, as faint as could be. Uncle Billy heard the creak and whine of the faucet, and a small cloud of steam began to rise behind him as water drove against the porcelain tub. Just like that, Uncle Billy's breathing was easier. It was all better, with one small dose of sweet, hot steam.

"If you don't mind," David said to him, "I'm going to help you take your bath today. Is that okay, Uncle Billy? May I do that?"

And he stood behind him, out of Uncle Billy's sight, as though he really were waiting for an answer. Uncle Billy would have smiled for sure this time, but his nerves were holding his face still in the silence while David waited behind him. Just waited.

As if a ghost hadn't already made up his mind what he was going to do from the moment his shadow touched the door.

▪ 18

"It wasn't his heart or another stroke. From what we can piece together, he must have slipped in the tub and banged his head," Alex said, speaking in a near whisper.

The family was assembled in the waiting area at Jackson Memorial Hospital's emergency room, ushered by Alex, who was wearing her white lab coat with a brass nametag reading ALEXIS JACOBS, M.D., HEMATOLOGY. Jessica forced herself to stare at the grooves on the nametag, virtually shutting out the words flowing from her sister's lips. Jessica wanted to feel pain and shock at the suddenness of Uncle Billy's hospitalization, but her rational mind wouldn't allow it, as though it were afraid of shutting down.

What was it her grandmother had always said? Bad luck comes in threes. Princess, Peter, and now Uncle Billy. Was the run over now? Please, Jesus? Was this awful season of sadness finally behind them?

"The result is a brain hemorrage and swelling, complicated by the earlier bleeding and tissue damage from his stroke. He's in a coma, but I don't think he's going to last long," Alex said. "He can't breathe unassisted."

Bea sniffed, wiping her nose with a crumpled Kleenex she'd been turning over in her hand for the past two hours, since they'd all arrived at the hospital with Kira in tow. Bea nodded at every other word from Alex, her face set and impossible to read. Jessica hoped her mother wasn't blaming herself because Uncle Billy had his accident while she was away.

"It'll come down to the life support. His primary physician is Dr. Guerra, and he'll explain it in more detail," Alex said, squeezing Bea's elbow. "You may have to make a very hard decision, Mom. You know that, right?"

Bea nodded again, this time with a momentary gaze at the ceiling before closing her eyes. "Doesn't seem right," she muttered, "deciding whether people will live or die."

"Life support isn't life, Mom. It's machines."

"I know."

Feeling David's arm draw more closely around her waist, Jessica looked over her shoulder for Kira. She was sitting across the room, giggling with a blonde boy her own age while the boy's mother sat in a teary, red-faced daze. The other woman apparently had her own unexpected tragedy to sort through.

"Kira," Jessica called sharply. Kira snapped to look at her, slightly startled. "Come over here."

"It's better if she doesn't hear this," David said, close to Jessica's ear, forever Kira's diplomat.

"I just want her here. I want to hold her hand."

When Kira came to her side, Jessica hugged her daughter close to her with one arm, stroking her cheek with her fingers. Jessica suddenly felt like crying, but she didn't think it was because of Uncle Billy. She hadn't had a chance to get close to him because she'd never met him before he moved to Miami. As bad as it sounded, none of them had expected him to live long, and Bea wanted him to die peacefully, with family.

Something else, deep inside Jessica, was tugging at her tears. Maybe it was the collection of misery in this room, where so much bad news had come for so many.

"I'm hungry, Mommy," Kira said.

"We'll get something to eat in a little bit," she promised.

Bea had called them as soon as she came home and found Uncle Billy sprawled across the bathtub's porcelain rim, with a bleeding gash at his temple. Water had been running over the sides of the tub, soaking the hallway. It was pure chance he hadn't drowned. That might have been better, more merciful, Jessica thought. A quick death had to be preferable to an artificially prolonged life.

In the hospital cafeteria, where they waited while Alex took Bea to the intensive-care unit, David read Jessica's thoughts. "It would be better for Uncle Billy, and your mom too, if it was over," he said. Kira was too mesmerized by dipping her steak-cut french fries in her mound of ketchup, covering all possible angles, to pay any attention to their more subdued adult preoccupations.

"I was thinking the same thing, but I feel sort of guilty."

"I don't understand how he survived at all," David mused. "He should have died right away, from hitting his head. Or he should have drowned right after. It's inconceivable."

"David," Jessica scolded softly, indicating Kira with a nod of her head, "please."

He half smiled, embarrassed. "Sorry," he said, playing with the wilting lettuce in his chef's salad.

Of all ironies, David had planned to visit Uncle Billy that afternoon. She'd heard David on the phone with him, and he'd been anxious to see some records Uncle Billy found. Uncle Billy called when the three of them were walking out of the house to pick up school supplies at the mall for Kira—they'd promised her a new bookbag, since her plastic strap was broken. After Uncle Billy's call, Jessica told David she'd take Kira herself. Go on and enjoy your music, she said.

If only he'd gone as he planned.

But David was still at home at his computer when they got back less than two hours later. As they walked through the door, the frantic phone call came from her mother.

"What made you change your mind about going to Uncle Billy's before?" Jessica asked David in the cafeteria. She felt penned in by the white lab coats and the incessant announcements, a sheen of sterility covering a building brimming with suffering. No wonder David hated hospitals. She wanted to leave this place, and soon.

David shrugged absently. "Goddamn copyeditors in France. They had questions on a piece I sent them three weeks ago. Wouldn't let me get off of the phone."

"Daddy, you cussed," Kira pointed out.

It was so weird how the mind could play tricks. When she first came home, Jessica was convinced that David had visited Uncle Billy because of the music. Finally, she thought she was redeemed for breaking David's record; as she and Kira walked down into the yard, she believed she heard vintage music floating through the open living room window, a Jazz Brigade song called "Forever Man" she recognized from her early days with David. She'd been so sure of it, she imagined she could make out the energetic clarinet solo.

But by the time she opened the front door, the music was gone. And there was David, sitting at his desk, hard at work, amid utter and sudden silence.

▪ 19

MR. PERFECT IS A TRIP. (P. DONOVITCH)

It wasn't until after noon that Jessica finished making her rounds in the newsroom, greeting colleagues she hadn't seen in weeks. Surprisingly, she'd missed them. She'd even missed the comfort of the sameness, the clutter, and the routine tasks being performed around her. She was glad to be back.

She purposely tried not to notice Peter's desk, which was cleared of papers and already robbed of its chair. She instead spent a half hour talking about good news with Emily, a young GA reporter who'd just found out she was pregnant after doctors had told her she would never conceive. That was the way God worked. One life gone, one miraculously created. Mysterious and wonderful.

So Jessica was in a good mood. She thought she was ready when she sat at her desk, turned on her computer, and pressed the keys to retrieve her e-mail messages. She braced herself for the possibility of finding old messages from Peter that she'd never erased; to avoid that, her fingers were poised to clear her screen as soon as she read the new ones. She found one message from Sy that morning, asking her to stop by his office when she had some free time; a system-wide announcement about the grief counseling, which had ended by now; and older messages from coworkers, mostly condolences and disbelief.

Then, she scrolled to the messages from her last day at work. There it was. The time displayed alongside the message was 10:22 P.M., so close to the coroner's estimated time of death. One of the last things Peter had done before he died was to send her a message.

MR. PERFECT IS A TRIP.

She didn't even know what it meant.

Before she realized it, a sob had risen in Jessica's throat. Matt, the black courts reporter who sat in front of her, glanced around. "Sis? You okay back there?" he asked.

Jessica nodded, forcing her lips into a smile, but she stumbled to her feet and made her way to the ladies' room, where she sat on the toilet seat, fully clothed, and waited for the spell to pass. Her knees were trembling. Goddamnit. Goddamnit. Forgive me, Lord, but I'm using your name in vain today. Will this ever be over?

The message was so cryptic.

MR. PERFECT IS A TRIP.

Why would he send her that message so late at night? What could have prompted it? Had he taken a last glance at her roses from David, which were now shriveled and completely brown?

"Peter sent me one of his crazy messages the night he was killed. I just now saw it, and it makes no kind of sense," she told her boss later. "You know how he was with messages."

"Stop thinking about it, kiddo. You'll drive yourself nuts with wondering," Sy told her. His office was cramped, but he had a tranquil view of Biscayne Bay and the causeways stretching eastward to Miami Beach. At one time, Sy had been a sports reporter, and on his wall he'd framed photographs of himself posing with Muhammad Ali, Bob Greise, O.J. Simpson.

Sy, who was nearly fifty, seemed to have aged several years in her absence. His skin looked pale and dry, and he had dark marks under his eyes. He looked like he hadn't been getting much sleep. It probably didn't help that her disappearance, and Peter's death, cut his I-Team in half.

"Do the police know anything else?" Jessica asked him softly.

Sy looked at her, one eyebrow arched. "You sure you're up to hearing it?"

She nodded. "Not knowing is killing me."

"You and me both." He swung around in his swivel chair, resting his folded hands on his desktop. "Well . . . they know for sure the guy was waiting in the backseat. There's a flash on the surveillance tape where you can see someone climbing into the car five or ten minutes before the guard says he saw Peter leave. Unfortunately, the fucking street lamp was out. If not for that, the whole thing would be on tape. As it is, all we can see is a light-colored shirt, and that's about it. Dumb luck. They're not thinking robbery, because nothing was taken. That's one weird thing. And the wound was real clean. Professional. From the wound, they're saying the blade was a strange shape. Curved. The M.E. said he thought it was a hook-bill knife."

"What's that?" Jessica asked, her insides sinking.

"You know, like a flooring knife. For linoleum."

How bizarre, Jessica thought. She pictured the monstrous wide blade and hook curling at the tip. "I've seen one of those, from when we redid the floors in the kitchen. Damn," Jessica said, swallowing hard, struggling not to imagine the knife at her friend's throat. "That's a weird weapon for a hit man, isn't it?"

"It's a weird weapon for anybody."

"So, basically, we don't know anything."

Sy sighed, smiling sadly. "Right," he said. "By the way, I heard about your uncle. My condolences. Feel free to take off early if you need to."

Jessica gazed at him, puzzled. "Uncle Billy? My great-uncle, really. How did you hear about that?"

"Let's just say you have a thoughtful husband. He called to tell me he died, that you might be upset about it."

Jessica shook her head. "He's amazing," she muttered. "Thanks, Sy, but I'm fine. It's horrible the way he hit his head on the tub. But I'm okay. Nothing surprises me anymore."

"I know the feeling, kiddo."

Bea had decided to stop Uncle Billy's life support the night before, as soon as his doctor determined he was brain-dead. Bea squeezed the old man's hand and peered once more at his strangely bloated face while machines forced him to breathe. Then Jessica and David led her out so the doctors could do their work.

She couldn't believe David actually took the initiative to call Sy on his own. He'd tried to convince her to tell her boss that she'd had a death in the family and to take off another day, but she really felt she needed to get back to work. The funeral wasn't until Wednesday, and it was Monday. She was fine, she'd told David.

But he called Sy anyway.

Mr. Perfect is a trip, Jessica thought. He really was. Jessica understood the probable meaning behind Peter's last message to her. She just couldn't figure out why in the world he sent it.

▪ 20

Trees, whenever he contemplated them, reminded Dawit of Adele.

While Kira played with Teacake and one of her dolls at the mouth of the cave below, Dawit straddled the V-curve where the trunk of the front yard's thirty-foot orchid tree diverged upward into sturdy branches. He angled his lopping shears to prune away withering, dead branches above him, slicing with precision above the dark rings at each branch's base. He was careful not to cut below the rings, or else the tree would not be able to mend its wounds properly. In the fall, the tree would awaken with lavender blooms that would make them the envy of their block.

There was nothing quite so splendid and reliable as nature.

Dawit could not ruminate long on the tree's beauty, however, because memories interrupted. He was never able to look upon a tree with the same fondness after one had been conscripted as an agent in his eternal separation from Adele.

> *goddamn nigger bitch scratched my face*
> *gimme that rope, Will*

That one had been a sinister tree, devoid of leaves, with thick branches grasping like claws, a lone tree at the bank of the Mississippi. Dawit could remember, as soon as he'd seen it, that the tree's look unsettled him. It was dead, nearly black, yet it stood upright. The dead tree in the waist-high saw grass was an omen, he knew. Best they shouldn't rest near that tree.

> *Seth, I'm thirsty. We ain't gon' stop but a minute.*

It was Adele's stubbornness he'd loved. Her stubbornness brought her with him, trailing after him a full six hours before she let on with her birdcall that she'd come too. She wanted to go to freedom, despite his argument that she should not risk her life to escape when he could surely arrange to buy her himself in a short time. Dawit's heart had stopped when he heard the whistle from the brush behind him. His legs ached from fatigue and his heart ached from missing her, and he'd thought of going back to fetch her. Could that be Adele's call . . . ?

> *Adele?*
> *You sho' ain't gon' leave me that easy, is you?*

Dawit had often wondered, for more than a century since, how his life might have been different if they had never stopped beneath that wretched tree.

"Daddy, it's getting dark," Kira called up. "The ghost will be here soon. You're in her tree."

"It's not dark yet. Just a bit longer and I'll be finished, Kira. Night Song won't mind having me here."

Even Kira's voice could not pull Dawit away from reliving that horrible day, the day he mourned in vivid dreams, replaying the short sequence of events as though hindsight could alter the past.

It was clear from the surprised faces of the white men—five of them—who emerged from the woods that they were not patrollers. They were random laborers—loggers, he guessed, from the ropes coiled across their shoulders. They were sharing a jug of liquor, on their way to rest at the riverbank. The men walked toward them, nearly jolly in their manner, already perilously close.

Well, lookie here
We got us some runaways?

It would be foolish to try to outrun them. Better to negotiate, Dawit decided. He hadn't added Adele's name to his pass, but he could convince them so long as he played his role and didn't insult them. They probably couldn't read themselves.

Then, before he could speak, the situation became grave.

The youngest, barely a man yet, sidled behind Adele and wrapped a thick arm around her middle. He playfully planted his hand across her chest, squeezing her breast. "You wanna nurse me, Auntie?"

Dawit knew then, from the expression on Adele's face, that he would have no opportunity to intervene. Another woman might have simply trembled or tolerated the man's touch. Adele could not.

Goddamn!

Without turning, Adele had whipped her arm around to rake her sharpened thumbnail across the man's face, drawing a strip of bright blood from his cheekbone to his forehead.

All smiles and mirth were gone. As a warrior, Dawit knew that whenever blood was drawn, talking was finished.

You see that?
Nigger bitch

He and Adele could stand to fight, or they could flee. Without weapons, could they hope to prevail against five men? No. They could not.

Adele, run!

In the end, was it his own act—and not Adele's—that sealed the day's horror? He'd hoped to frighten the men, or at least to draw attention away from Adele so she could escape. After all, his death meant very little.

He'd leaped onto the man closest to him, the biggest, and cracked his neck with a simple, skillful twist of his arm. All of them heard the sound. There was no doubt, when the wide-eyed man slumped to the ground, that he was dead.

It did not frighten the men away. Instead, it roused a fevered fury. And Adele, whose skirts were soggy and heavy from the river, could not be quick enough.

Git her 'fore she swims away

Dawit was halfway bound, wincing beneath their blows, as he watched the bleeding man drag Adele to the riverbank, beneath the solitary tree. He was pulling at her clothing. One of the men tossed a heavy hemp rope across the tree's sturdiest branch.

Bring her here

Dawit knew what was going to happen next. He saw it happening in his imagination beforehand, and he could not stop it.

You like killin', nigger? You 'bout to see some

Adele did not call for him. She never once made a sound.

Watching what the four men did to her while he was bound and helpless, Dawit's reason dissolved. He kicked and shouted and writhed, spittle flying across his face. He sometimes imagined he'd won his senses back since then; more often, he knew he had not.

Dawit's own lynching was a comfort to him after what he had seen. Death put his sick heart to sleep.

Why did he have to reawaken? Why?

No wonder his love for Christina had felt so weak. He'd no room in his heart left for Christina then, only sixty years after Adele's death. Christina's father, who ran a thriving funeral home in Chicago, gave them the best wedding he could afford. Hundreds of colored men and women turned out to witness their union, to see Christina's lithe form in a splendid white gown.

He'd had no such wedding with Adele. They made silent vows to each other, sharing their flesh in love. He always kept his seed away from her so they could not make a child who would never truly belong to her. And so, though he'd been instructed to stud her, he'd been enabled to love her instead. Often, they merely lay together in an embrace, not sleeping, not fully awake.

When he met Jessica at last, he had long ago soothed away his hurt. He had been ready for her, a woman nearly unblemished by life's tragedies, for whom he could become anyone he chose. In the process, he could forget his own sorrows. He had been waiting for her.

"Daddy, you're going to fall," Kira called, sounding troubled.

"I have a ladder, sweetheart. I'm not going to fall."

Dawit's perch was twenty feet above the ground. The tall, aluminum stepladder was at least four feet beneath his dangling black combat boots. From here, he could survey the nuances of the house he had refurbished inside and out when he bought it ten years before. The paint was cracking near the base of his second-story bedroom window, he observed. He would need to touch it up after the blistering heat of the upcoming summer.

Dawit realized that Kira was right, however. It was seven-thirty, nearly too dark to see by now, even with his superb vision. Jessica would be home from work soon, assuming she hadn't stopped at her mother's place first to help her plan Uncle Billy's funeral.

Dawit snipped his shears once more, clipping the final piece of dead wood he hoped would make room for a bud in the fall. Only as he watched the wood drop, spinning toward the ground, did he pause to ponder his own unfathomable indifference.

Uncle Billy. With his own hands, he had killed a sickly old man who had done him no harm. Even game animals, he reminded himself, know they can often elicit mercy from some predators if they pretend to be sick or lame. Uncle Billy had not been afforded even this measure of natural decency when Dawit cracked his head against the bathtub rim with all of his might, he thought.

Yet, at this moment, Dawit felt no shame. Why would any man want to live as he'd been, so shriveled and useless? And it was justified! Uncle Billy had found a damning photograph, a precious treasure. That photograph, one Dawit didn't even remember posing for, clearly begged for him to fulfill his Covenant. The resemblance was too precise to pass off as even a relation. His face looked the same now as it had then; as it had since the 1500s.

He could not bring himself to destroy the photo, though. He packed it inside of the small stack of records he took—after all, Uncle Billy certainly wouldn't miss them now—and hid it away in the cabinet next to his clarinet. He couldn't resist listening to the "Forever Man" record once he got home, and it served him right that Jessica had returned so quickly and nearly caught him playing it. He had been thinking of her as he listened. "I'm your Forever Man." Jessica had not even been born when its lyrics first found his pen, but in his heart Dawit had written the song for her.

Behind him, from a taller live oak far above his reach, Dawit heard a whispered hissing growing higher pitched, to nearly a screech. Night Song was here, and her song sounded unusually disconsolate.

"Daddy! It's the ghost in the tree!"

"I'm coming, Duchess," Dawit said. He rested the shears across the branches in front of him and used his arms to support himself as he began to climb downward, his foot angling toward the top of the stepladder.

Before he could touch the ladder, a movement from the side of the house visible through the branches—something white—held Dawit rigid. Someone was there. A dark man in a white shirt had darted behind the toolshed, out of his sight in a simple instant. Dawit processed what he had seen, and he realized the man had been wearing a skullcap. He heard a rattling from his neighbor's gate.

A Searcher!

Dawit's mind was seized with so many conflicting impulses—to chase him, to shout, to climb higher so he could try to see him better, to take Kira and hide with her—that it dizzied him. He lost control of his heart's frenetic pumping.

It wasn't until Dawit heard Kira's terrified shriek that he realized he was falling.

He bumped the ladder with his flailing arm on the way down, toppling it over, and inside tangled aluminum he felt his shoulder and forearm explode against the hard soil on the pathway below. His body bounced, ribs crunching, and then his head bumped so hard against the soil that his teeth clicked violently, slicing into his tongue, and he lost his vision to a shower of red sparks.

For a blissful instant, he felt nothing.

Then, the pain came.

At once, his senses seized upon every aspect of his frame that had been scraped, jounced, broken. His shoulder was horribly twisted out of place, paralyzing him. His ribs felt shattered.

Dawit howled.

The first thing Jessica noticed of the commotion in her front yard when she drove up was the toppled stepladder at the base of the tree, and she knew what had happened.

She knew why their elderly next-door neighbor, Mrs. DeNight, was stroking Kira's head, trying to calm her red-faced sobs; she knew why David was lying prone beneath the tree while Mr. DeNight stood above him, his arms crossed before him.

David had said he would prune the orchid tree today. He had fallen, and he was dead.

"No!" she screamed, fumbling to open the car door while her engine still idled. "Oh, *Jesus*."

Jessica fell to her knees at David's side. She saw that his eyes were wide open, thank Jesus, and he was swallowing hard. "I'm all right," he whispered, blinking back tears of pain.

Jessica's heart leaped with momentary relief. David wasn't dead. But he wasn't all right. His shirt was torn, he was bleeding from his mouth, and there was something wrong with the way his arm was twisted behind him.

"Did someone call an ambulance?" she asked breathlessly.

"He wouldn't let us," Mr. DeNight said, pushing his thick tortoiseshell glasses higher on his nose. He spoke with a fading Irish lilt and sounded nearly amused. "Says he'll sue us."

"What?" Jessica cried. She looked down at David with disbelief. "Are you crazy?"

"I'm fine. I don't need an ambulance." At this, with Mr. DeNight's assistance, David struggled to sit upright. He held his injured arm, gritting his teeth.

Kira sobbed, running into Jessica's arms. "Night Song pushed Daddy out of the tree."

"Shhhhh, Kira. Don't worry. That's not what happened," Jessica said absently, studying David to try to analyze his wounds. He was still wincing violently, possibly from some kind of internal injury. She would have to be insistent this time. His aversion to doctors was ridiculous. "David, what's wrong with your arm?"

"I just banged it up. It's sore. I'll put some ice on it, and I'll be okay," David said, finding his voice a bit more.

"We heard him yelling all the way across the street. We knew something horrible happened," Mrs. DeNight said to Jessica.

"I just lost my balance and fell off the ladder. That's all. Just wait until tomorrow. Tomorrow, it'll be okay." David was mumbling, sounding nearly incoherent. "Tomorrow morning."

"Want me to help you inside?" Mr. DeNight asked David, extending his arm. "That is, if you won't sue me . . ."

"He didn't mean that, Mr. DeNight. Excuse him."

Jessica was thankful that David didn't seem to have trouble walking, but she wasn't very reassured. He was obviously in a lot of pain, and his shoulder looked absolutely deformed, as though he had a hump in his back. The bleeding from his mouth also worried her. The thin trail of blood had reached his chin.

As soon as David was inside, he collapsed against the couch and promptly moaned, his eyes closed. He'd scraped his left cheekbone in the fall, leaving it raw. God only knew what else could be wrong with him.

"That shoulder's dislocated, David," Mr. DeNight was saying as Jessica leaned over her husband to unbutton his shirt. "Look there. See? You need someone to fix that up for you."

"Mommy, Daddy's bleeding," Kira said, still crying, as she climbed beside David and grasped his hand.

"I'll find a cloth and some cold water to clean up his face," Mrs. DeNight said, ducking back toward the kitchen.

Jessica's hands were trembling, she realized. Once David's shoulder was bare, there was no mistaking how badly he'd twisted it; the shoulder was pushed back so far, it had nearly vanished. Maybe his arm was broken too.

"I'm calling 911," Jessica announced firmly.

David gave her a wild-eyed, foreign look that made her shrink away from him. "I already told you—no fucking doctors!" he shouted, nearly screaming the words. "I said *no fucking doctors.*"

There was silence in the house except for a glass tumbling into the aluminum kitchen sink. Mr. DeNight was frozen, his arms folded across his chest. Kira's sobs had stopped as she gazed up at David, fearful. Jessica herself could not move, she was so shocked at the venom in David's voice. She couldn't remember his ever shouting at her this way. Not ever.

"Maybe we'd better leave," Mr. DeNight said cheerfully, as though nothing had happened. "Lottie? Let's go on home."

Jessica's bottom lip shook. She was close to tears, but she fought them back. "Thank you for everything," she said, anxious to help guide her neighbors out to the porch. "I'm so sorry about . . . I mean, I don't know what . . . David's never . . ."

Mr. DeNight squeezed her arm reassuringly. "Give him some time. He may have a concussion, or even be in shock. He'll come to his senses soon, after the pain gets to him. Take care he doesn't try to sue you, though. I still get a kick out of that."

"And he sure meant it," Mrs. DeNight piped up.

"He'll be all right. Could be just a tad embarrassed too," Mr. DeNight said privately to Jessica as he waved goodbye.

When Jessica returned to the sofa, David was resting his head against the cushion, his eyes closed. She immediately felt tense, but she noticed that his breaths were falling evenly up and down.

"David?" she said.

"Shhhhhh," Kira said, raising her finger to her lips. "Daddy said he's going to rest now."

"David, did you hit your head? I don't think you're supposed to try to sleep after a head injury."

"I'm fine," David said, not sounding any kinder. He didn't open his eyes to look at her. "Put Kira to bed. Can you handle that? She doesn't need to be up now."

Don't talk to me like that, you damned sonofabitch, Jessica thought in a rage, but she kept her mouth firmly closed. That's his pain talking, she told herself. And if he wanted to be so stubborn, she decided, then let him sit there and suffer.

"Come on, Kira," she said instead, taking her daughter's hand.

Her own hand was still unsteady. David's outburst reminded Jessica of why she'd never felt fully at ease with Princess in the house. The giant dog had been playful and adored them all, but Jessica could never forget that she was an animal. One day, without thinking, Jessica tried to snatch a chicken bone from Princess's mouth so she wouldn't choke on it; the dog snapped, her sharp teeth clicking only an inch from Jessica's fingers. Those gnashing teeth hadn't been intended as a warning. Princess wanted to bite her, and hard. Jessica felt alienated from her, like a stranger. Just now, David had made her feel the same way. The trauma of his fall had uncovered someone she had never met.

While Jessica bathed Kira upstairs, she heard David flick on the television set and turn up the volume to *Casablanca*. Then she heard the faucet go on in the kitchen. He must be all right if he's walking around, she thought. Still, after Kira was tucked in, it might not hurt to call Alexis from the bedroom phone.

Hurriedly, Kira recited her nightly prayer before climbing beneath her sheets. "Now I lay me down to sleep . . . I pray the Lord my soul to keep . . . If I should die before I wake . . . I pray the Lord my soul to take." Bea had taught Kira that prayer, the way she'd taught Jessica as a girl, but Jessica never liked it. What a scary idea to send into a child's head at bedtime, she thought. "And please bless Mommy and make Daddy okay again. Amen."

"Honey, did Daddy fall off the ladder or out of the tree?" Jessica asked Kira, pulling her bedsheet up to her chin.

"The tree. Night Song pushed him, Mommy. Just like I said."

How high was that? Twenty feet, maybe? More? Sweet Jesus, he might have been killed. It was a miracle he was even conscious. Jessica smoothed Kira's sheets across her belly. "Night Song didn't push him," she said.

"Yes she did, 'cause she's a ghost."

It probably hadn't been a good idea to pass on to Kira the folklore about their neighborhood's long-dead Tequesta haunts. Kira sometimes had nightmares and came scrambling into their room at night, though it was happening less often as she got older.

"Yes, but Night Song is a good ghost. A good ghost wouldn't do anything to hurt anyone. We don't have to be afraid of Night Song. She can't hurt us."

Kira lowered her voice to a whisper. "Mommy, are there good monsters too?" she asked.

Jessica stared hard at Kira's face, her heart stilled. The question stunned her. Then, Jessica remembered her own cadre of monsters who used to terrorize her from under her bed when she was younger. Apparently, they'd found her daughter too.

She kissed Kira's forehead. "There's no such thing as monsters, Kira. Monsters aren't real."

"Oh, yes they are," Kira said with deep certainty, then she inexplicably grinned her widest grin and swept her shining eyes away from Jessica. "Hi, Daddy!" Kira cried, sitting up in bed.

David was standing in the doorway, smiling back.

Finally, the fog of agony that had overrun Dawit's mind had lifted, releasing his rational self. How he loathed pain! His tolerance for discomfort was nearly nonexistent, and he'd been so long without pain he'd almost forgotten its treachery.

But it was the Searcher, not his fall, that had thrown his senses into disarray. Dawit had been certain the Searchers were here all along, but without confirmation he'd allowed himself to hope he might be wrong. Whichever of his brethren had been sent to discover his whereabouts must have been bold enough to wish to be seen, Dawit knew. Searchers valued stealth above all else. They would never be so careless as to be spotted accidentally.

What did it mean? Had the dreaded time come so soon?

Dawit hissed slightly as he reached over to turn off the beating water of the shower, where he'd stood for long minutes as though the water could wash away his hurting. The water from the showerhead was by now only lukewarm. Dawit's body was stiff, and his shoulder still throbbed at intervals that were sometimes better, then horribly worse. And what of his ribs . . . ?

Dawit rubbed away the steam clouding the full-length mirror behind the bathroom door so he could examine his naked flesh. Ah. Just as he'd feared, the bruise on his rib cage where he'd broken at least two ribs was deep brown already, very visible. The bruise would not go away for many hours. He would have to hide his ribs from Jessica.

His face had not fared much better, especially his swollen tongue he'd nearly severed when he bit down on it upon impact. It was hard for him to speak, and painful. He'd also scraped some skin from his face along his jawbone. He would have to fix it.

After drying his face with a towel, dabbing at the tender spot one-handed, Dawit found cotton gauze in the bathroom first-aid kit and secured it to his face with white surgical tape. The bandage was unsightly, but at least it would hide the damage to his face.

There was nothing he could do to improve his shoulder. He considered an attempt to snap it back into place, but the thought of new pain dissuaded him, especially since his ribs were already stabbing his insides. Better to let it heal itself.

"David? Are you okay in there?" Jessica called, knocking on the closed door.

"I'll be right out, baby," he called back.

He wrapped himself in his white terry cloth robe and took one last look. He'd cleaned his blood away and covered his bruises with clothing or bandages, so there was no more to be done. This night would be his test. He must make it through this one night.

In the bedroom, Jessica had lighted candles on either side of the bed and put on a tape of music from India that she'd bought from a yoga center years before when Dawit was helping her experiment with basic meditation. He recognized the instruments right away, the flute and tambura. He had played the mystical-sounding stringed tambura for a time with his brethren in the House of Music. Sometimes, he missed those days. He missed Mahmoud and Khaldun most of all.

Jessica had selected the right music to calm him. Dawit shuddered with regret, thinking of her. Surely, he had scared her. What must she think of him?

Jessica patted the space on the bed beside her. "Come," she said. "I want to talk."

He leaned over to kiss her cheek, lingering despite the pain. "I have only two words: I'm sorry," he said. "I really am."

"I know," she said. When he sat, she slid beside him and slowly slipped her arm around his waist. He wanted to scream when she brushed his rib cage slightly, but he repressed the urge. She rested her chin on his good shoulder. "David . . . we have to go to a doctor. You know that, right?"

Dawit sighed. "Yes," he said. "Tomorrow."

"I don't want to wait that long. I'll have Mom come over right now to sit, and we can drive to North Shore Hospital."

"Darling . . ." David said, wishing he could rest his aching tongue. "I know you don't believe me, but I'm fine. Even the shoulder isn't as bad as it looks. I know what I'm talking about. It's happened before. Let's give it until morning. If you're still worried in the morning, I'll go. I promise."

For a long time, Jessica didn't speak. He knew she was not happy, but she seemed to realize this was the biggest compromise she had ever won from him. "I called the DeNights to apologize," Dawit went on, to prove he'd recovered his mind. "I freaked, as you would say. The fall scared me, more than anything. But it's okay. It really is."

Jessica kissed his good shoulder, nudging her lips past his robe to his skin. "Okay," she said. "You know this is all just because I love you, don't you? Because if you let anything bad happen from being stubborn and stupid, I'm going to kill you. You know that, right?"

"Yes," he said. Now, it was he who felt tears, both from the wretched pain and from his depths of love for this woman, this mortal woman—a woman he must soon leave or convince to join him in Life forever. And how could he do either?

The hypnotizing sound of the tambura and its gentle Eastern strings reminded him of the incongruity of their worlds.

"I'll never leave you, Jessica," he said, not realizing until later, as he tried to sleep despite the diminishing shocks of pain, that he had come to his decision at last.

▪ 21

"David, wake up, honey. Look who stopped by."

Confused, Dawit blinked into the daylight from his canopied sleep sanctuary. For a moment, unreasonably, he expected to see Christina's face above him. Or Adele's. But neither of those women called him David, of course. David was Jessica's name only.

And so she was here, dressed for work in an orange silk blouse and houndstooth skirt, smiling down at him nervously. Dawit shifted in the bed and felt a dull, distant throbbing behind his shoulder blade—a residue of pain rather than the pain itself. His body had done its work, leaving him depleted of energy. Once while traveling through Ethiopia, after losing his right hand in swordplay with a nobleman in Gonder whose wife he'd conquested with his charms, Dawit fell unconscious and found a fully formed hand in its place by morning; but the new limb nonetheless ached for a full two days. Regeneration was a strain on his system, and that hardship had not improved with time. Dawit felt groggy and disconnected, lost in the patchwork of his own ancient histories.

"Babe?" Jessica asked, sounding worried this time because he didn't respond. Dawit scowled at her, half sitting up in the bed. "I said there's someone here to see you."

Alexis, Jessica's sister, stood in the doorway in a white lab coat. She too was apparently on her way to work and had no doubt stopped by at Jessica's urging. Dawit tightened his fingers around the silk bedsheet, rigid with anger.

"What's up, David?" Alexis said cheerfully.

Dawit nodded. "'Morning," he mumbled.

"Hear through the grapevine you took a fall out of a tree. My price is right, so Jessica wanted me to come check you out."

Jessica looked at Alexis, grateful, and then back at Dawit, with pleading, apologetic eyes. She bit her bottom lip, waiting for Dawit to respond. Of all wretched luck, marrying a woman with a physician in her family! He had never met anyone who hounded him about doctors' care as much as Jessica. Americans had grown far more pampered in recent decades. Perhaps the Searchers were right in what they had told him the night they came to bid him to leave his family in Chicago; perhaps it was no longer possible, in modern times, to blend with mortals.

But Dawit decided to acquiesce. After his mean-spirited temperament the night before, Jessica had earned his cooperation. "Well, I know a deal when I hear one," he said, mustering a smile. "It's not every day you can find a doctor willing to make house calls. I have only one rule, Sis: no needles."

"Deal," Alexis said.

Once Dawit's robe was off and his torso bare, Alexis examined him in the bright morning sunlight from the bedroom window. She ran her fingers across his back, his shoulders, his ribs. Her fingers tickled, sometimes finding a vague soreness, but Dawit sat without moving, his eyes occupied with watching his toes wriggling absently inches above the floor. Jessica stood beside them, her hands folded across her chest as she watched.

"Which shoulder is it?" Alexis asked at last.

"The left shoulder," Jessica said.

Alexis probed with her palm. Dawit winced, more for display than out of discomfort. "Let's look at your abrasion," Alexis said unexpectedly, and before Dawit could protest she zipped his bandage away from his cheekbone. Jessica leaned closer, and Dawit sat beneath the two women's eyes. From their faces, and from past experience, he knew that they could not see evidence of the raw skin from the night before.

"It was just a scratch," Dawit said.

Alexis chuckled. "I don't see no damn scratch."

Dawit looked at Jessica and tried to make her smile with a wink, but her face remained taciturn. She was silent, crossing and uncrossing her arms. Dawit wondered what dangerous thoughts were unsettling her. "Jess, I told you I'd be fine," he said, squeezing her hand.

Jessica accepted his hand, but he noticed she didn't squeeze back. In the past, Jessica had always been very good about ignoring his vanishing scratches and scars. For the sake of them both, he hoped that was not changing. This was the worst possible time for a change.

Or was it? Perhaps this was the best time, after all, an avenue for all of the unlikely possibilities ahead to come to fruition. Even the subconscious thought of disclosure, brushing the edge of his mind, made Dawit's spirits soar.

"Do you hurt anywhere?" Alexis asked him.

"My ribs are sore, but just a little. They're not broken or anything . . . See?" he said, poking his rib cage to make his point.

"David, your shoulder was completely out of whack," Jessica said. "Mr. DeNight said it was dislocated."

Slowly, Dawit raised his arm and wound it in an exaggerated propeller motion. "No dislocated shoulder here," he said.

"You got that right," Alexis said. "You're damn lucky, David. That tree out there is no joke."

"Of course I'm lucky. I married your sister, and I get free exams to boot. I'd call that damned lucky."

Alexis laughed, but Jessica's gaze was hard and analytical, with set eyes that had finally seen too much.

Jessica convinced David to fix Kira's breakfast and dress her for school so she could follow her sister outside to her white Beamer to steal a moment with her. Not that she had the first idea what she planned to say. She just wanted to tell her sister she had goosebumps, even despite the morning heat.

"Look at you, Jessica, all worried for nothing. I'm glad it wasn't serious," Alex said.

"Yes, Lord," Jessica said, swallowing hard, standing over her sister's open driver's side door. She knew Alexis was late to the hematology lab already, but she stood planted there.

"You okay?"

Jessica shook her head. "No. I have to ask you something."

Alex dropped her arms to her sides, gazing at her expectantly. "What?"

Jessica sighed. What was the best way to tackle this so she wouldn't sound like an idiot? Alexis had legitimate business at her lab and didn't have time for foolishness. Besides, Alex wouldn't have any qualms about laughing right in her face.

Jessica began, staring at the ground. "Uhm . . . Is there any medical condition that would explain a hyperactive immune system? Or accelerate somebody's recovery rate?"

"Some people have very strong natural defenses, if that's what you mean," Alex said. "I assume you're talking about David?"

Instinctively, Jessica glanced at the house to see if they were being watched or overheard. No one was standing at any of the windows, and she'd been careful to close the whitewashed wooden front door before pulling the screen shut.

"Alex, this whole thing is weird. I saw him last night. He had much more than a scratch on his face. He scraped a bunch of the skin off. It was bleeding. And his shoulder was so jammed out of place, he looked deformed. Look up there," she said, pointing up at the orchid tree, where the shears David had left were still nestled high in the branches. "He fell from there. He banged the hell out of himself. Last night, I was scared to death he'd broken half of the bones in his body. This morning, he's fine."

Repeating aloud what her brain had been telling her all morning, Jessica felt a tingling sensation on her arms and at the nape of her neck. The words sounded ridiculous, but they were true. All true. She realized her heart was pounding, making her feel weak. She wondered if the uneasiness in her belly was because she hadn't yet eaten breakfast, or if it was from confronting the impossible.

Alex gazed at her a moment, then her eyes wandered to her dashboard. "It's not that weird to me. David's fall scared the devil out of you last night. Maybe it just seemed worse."

Jessica leaned so close to her sister that their faces nearly touched. "I know blood when I see it. I know a bruise when I see it. How can he be bleeding one night, and then there's not a trace this morning? And he *knew*. Even with his shoulder, he kept saying 'Wait until morning, wait until morning,' like he knew the whole time that he'd be all better. What about his shoulder? How did it get fixed?"

"People can pop their dislocated shoulders back in. Although, if he did, he should really see a doctor because there's probably ligament damage. I'm surprised he's not sore . . ."

"Sore? Why should he be sore? He doesn't have a mark anywhere on his body. What about that bandage on his face? Alex, there was nothing there. Absolutely nothing."

"So you should be happy, right?" Alex asked.

"Yes, I'm happy. I'm ecstatic. I just want to understand it, that's all. I want to know how he can do that. I want you to explain it. I'm a journalist. We need to know these things."

"I don't know what to tell you. Granted, maybe another specialist would know something more, but I don't think so. Unless your immune system is suppressed or impaired, recovery pretty much takes place at the same pace. We cut ourselves, our blood clots, we form scars."

"And the scars last," Jessica said.

"Yes," Alex said. "Not long, usually. But they last."

Jessica lowered her voice to a hush. She was revealing things she'd never allowed herself to think about, much less shared with another person. Teacake had scratched the bridge of David's nose as a scared stray kitten, drawing blood. During a hike on a trail in El Yunque in Puerto Rico before Kira was born, David tripped in his boots and scraped his elbow against a jutting tree stump. And he'd had a burn mark on his arm just a few weeks before. All of the marks were gone before she realized it. Why hadn't she ever wondered about it before?

"His scars don't last," she said aloud, in wonderment. "They never do. Right now, I'm trying to remember even one time he's had a scar longer than a day. I'm telling you, they don't last."

Alex's eyes darted upward, and Jessica followed her gaze. David was staring down at them from the open second-story bedroom window, Kira's room. He waved.

Jessica waved back, smiling, but her voice was free of mirth as she spoke to her sister in the same guarded tone. "I don't get it. He's my husband, I love him to death, but I have to be honest. It's freaking me out."

"So get him to a doctor. Have some blood tests done," Alex said. "Hell, I'll do it myself. About time he saw somebody."

Jessica shook her head. "Won't happen," she said ruefully. "You know better."

"Ain't you learned how to handle that man yet?" Alex asked playfully. "Listen, tell him you won't give up any you-know-what if he won't take his tail to a doctor."

"You're so vulgar. You should be ashamed," Jessica said, slapping her sister's shoulder. "I'm serious, Alex."

"Shoot. Me, too."

Jessica's didn't answer; her eyes were fixed on David's form as he stood in the window watching them. Alex got into her car and turned the key in the ignition.

"Look, I'm late. Don't worry about Superman up there. Some people are blessed, that's all. And science ain't got nothing to do with it," Alex said. "Wish I had a dose of whatever he's got."

"Amen to that," Jessica said.

▪ 22

Lowell Mason Farm South of Baton Rouge

1844

A shock of cold water droplets against Dawit's cheek makes him cringe and claw at the dirt to retreat farther into the sawdust-filled corner. He has spilled water on himself after batting his arm against the sudden appearance of a corroded tin cup in front of his face. The cup clanks, a hollow sound, against the packed dirt floor. He does not know where the cup came from. He does not care. His senses are drowned in agony.

A woman's voice. "Damned if he ain't—"

Next, a gruff man speaks. "Can't make him drink if he don't want to."

"He gots to drink, Ben. He been bound up in the sun two hours. Miracle he ain't bleed to death."

Be quiet, Dawit's mind screams. *Go away and leave me alone.* He would strangle the voices with his bare hands if he had the strength to move or to even open his eyes again. His back is raging with pain, as if it is on fire. He is curled against the wooden wall, but he cannot move even to relieve the suffering of his tender skin against the wall's rough texture.

The smell of blood fills his nostrils. His own blood, he realizes. His stomach lurches, and suddenly his mouth is running over. Unable to turn his head, he begins to cough uncontrollably, swallowing back the warm, meal-like vomit.

"Lawd, now he's gon' choke hisself," the woman's voice says, and he feels his head pushed to the side so he can cough his mouth clear. A sour-smelling dry rag moves across his lips.

"Damn," the man says, sounding more distant than before, "I ain't seen nobody take a hunnert with the cowhide in a long while. And him hollering like a girl. Bet you he can't talk from raising all that Cain."

"Talking ain't gon' be his problem. You hush and fetch me that balm I keep in the washbucket. Lord Jesus, look at how his back's cut to pieces," the woman said.

"I ain't gon' look at him no mo' myself. Turns my stomach. What he try to run from Ole Master for? Nigger ain't got no sense. Wonder where he from. Sound like he was hollerin' in African."

"Uh huh. Wild as can be." The woman sighs. "But he won't try to run no mo'. He sho' ain't."

Dawit feels a flame of pain across his back and writhes weakly, trying to scream. He can make no sound. His throat is raw and tattered. The woman's voice is close to his ear, soothing. "Hold yo'self still, now," she says. "I ain't no roots woman, but this the best I can do. It hurt now, but yo' back ain't never gon' mend without it."

"Ain't gon' mend noway," the man mutters.

Another blaze of pain. The woman's fingers are smearing something sticky on his back, across the open wounds. Dawit grits his teeth so hard together he is certain they will dislodge from the pressure. He longs to strike out at this woman, the one who is bringing him renewed pain, but he knows she must be a friend.

"Shhhhh. That's right. Just hush. Don't know what p'ssessed you to run like that, straight from the block. You ain't even seen the farm, don't know nothin' 'bout Ole Master. There's lots worse than him, when you get sold this far south. You could be in the rice swamp, you ain't careful. Mason Farm ain't so bad."

"He crazy, like I say," the man says. "You all right here, Clara? I'ma go eat 'fore it's all gone."

"Bring him some corn pone back?" the woman calls after him, her own voice sounding far away, like an angel's.

The man laughs. "He ain't gon' be eatin' for a long while. Shoot, Ole Master might've done outsmarted hisself this time. He finally git some luck at the poker table, and what he do with it? He buy this crazy nigger. Ole Missus say he set down some fifteen hunnert for this one, and then whips him so bad he might not last the night. She fit to be tied. Would serve Ole Master right, too."

"Hush, Ben. He can hear you."

"He ain't hearin' a thing I got to say, or no one else," the man says. "Not for a long while."

Suddenly, Dawit hears nothing. He is in Lalibela, sitting at the ashen bare feet of Khaldun, who smiles warmly and touches the top of his head. Then Khaldun is gone, and Dawit is scaling the slopes of the great Kilimanjaro mountain with Mahmoud—exhausted, laughing, goading each other to be the first to the top. No, it's Ife; he and Mahmoud are guests of a chieftain, delighting him with the stringed instruments they have made. To win his favor and access to his lovely daughters, they join his people in fighting off the neighboring rivals who have raided the village in hopes of capturing them to sell to white traders as slaves.

Slaves.

Mahmoud, Dawit says, I'm very curious about America. Let's go there.

America? Nonsense, Mahmoud retorts. They are barbarians. They slaughter natives and Africans there for sport. *Believe what I say,* Mahmoud warns with a finger close to Dawit's nose, *America will be worse than death for you, Dawit.*

Dawit tours Philadelphia first, where his love for music leads him to a hall to hear a Negro orchestra as fine as any in Europe. The founder, a free man named Frank Johnson, offers to grant him an audition. What a discovery Mahmoud has missed!

But Dawit is not ready to settle. He has a keen curiosity to see how Africans live in the South. Dawit has never visited a slave plantation, to see what became of the children of Africans he has seen sold, traded, and kidnapped over so many years. In Europe, he read claims that the North American slaves are pampered and content. Can that possibly be so?

And so he goes. At the dock on the river in Missouri, the steamboat *Carlton* blusters toward Dawit. A white man on the ramp blocks Dawit's path. "Hold up there, nigger. You can't purchase a ticket for passage on this boat."

"I have money," Dawit says, displaying the coins in his palm.

"We don't have room for no free niggers," the mate says, and Dawit watches the powerful boat thrust a lather in the water as it inches away from him. Dawit is amazed. He has been refused seating in train cars and theaters, and glared at by whites offended by his fine dress in the marketplace, but his money has always served him in some capacity until now. He has tried to adopt the manner of other North American blacks, addressing whites with what sounds to him like a comically condescending deference. But he had forgotten himself with the steamboat mate, failing to call him "Sir"—a mere ship's mate!—and gazing at him straight in the eye as he tried to board. Servility does not suit him, Dawit decides.

Perhaps he has seen enough.

Then . . . what?

That is the last he knows. Much of the rest is gone.

Dawit awakens stripped of his fine clothes and his papers, shirtless, and wearing soiled breeches. The back of his head is throbbing. Has he been robbed? Abducted? He is locked in a dark room, pinched from hunger, as though he has not eaten in days. There are chains at his feet, binding him to dozens of other brown-skinned men and women of all ages in a cargo hold with him. He feels the motion of a steamboat.

Everyone is waiting, stone silent. Their fright is palpable. "Where are we?" he asks them.

This Louisiana. We goin' to auction.

Dawit opens his eyes, confused by the distinction between memory and the present. He is at the threshold of both. He is alone, shivering beneath a coarse blanket on a dirt floor. There is no motion, so he is no longer on the water. Brilliant daylight streams through the cracks in the wooden walls. He is in a corner. There are barrels all around him, and yokes and bits and other farming supplies: hoes, shovels, plows. The smell of manure is strong in the air. Where is he now?

Lowell Mason. The name comes to his mind, but Dawit has no memories attached to it. He reflects, straining his dulled mind. Soon, he can visualize a white-haired man with a moustache who raises his cane into the air, bobbing it, a face in a crowd.

Fifteen hundred. Sold.

Then, Dawit remembers. He remembers shackles bound so tightly that his ankles are rubbed raw. He remembers a bumpy ride in back of a horse-pulled wagon. He remembers running as soon as his ankles are free, as soon as his feet touch the ground. The impulse to run is all his bewildered mind knows.

Then, his wrists are bound, suspending him from iron hooks on the side of a long wooden building. He dangles, his toes barely reaching the dusty earth. The sun beats against his back. A younger, bigger man with pale skin is calling him names. He has rarely heard this odd English word: nigger. He hears a whip snap behind him, and then he feels it bite sharply into his back, tearing away his flesh.

Dawit cries out, sitting up straight, full of rage.

He is no longer bound to the hooks. He is beneath a blanket in this crowded farm storeroom, tortured by memories only. He is breathing hard, his body gleaming with perspiration. Instinctively, he swings his arm around to touch himself between his shoulder blades.

The skin itches, but the bloody gaps are gone. His skin is smooth and familiar.

He is tired, so tired.

Dawit hears a creak as an unseen door opens, and the room is flooded with sunlight. He crouches in the corner, hiding behind a barrel, to see who comes. He is determined to kill the intruder. No one will whip him again, not ever.

A silver-haired dark woman appears in front of him. She is old, with teeth missing and skin wrinkled like a raisin. She wears a dress with frilled sleeves that looks as though it might have been very pretty once, but it is so grimy with dirt that it is a mockery of what it was. She offers him a tin cup, standing at a distance. Dawit realizes she is afraid of him.

"You must have an awful thirst by now. You didn't want it last night," she says, barely keeping her voice steady.

Dawit studies her and decides to trust her. He remembers, in a remote way, that this woman has been kind to him. He nods at her and takes the cup, hurriedly slurping the tepid water.

"Couldn't steal you no food, so you gon' have to wait 'til evening," the woman says. "I'm Ole Master's cookwoman. There's meat tonight."

Dawit does not speak. He has so many questions for her, but he cannot bear to hear her answers. And she must have as many questions for him, he realizes. Dawit scratches his itching shoulder blade, and he sees the woman's eyes following his motions. He drops his hand away from his healed back.

"Look here," the woman says, speaking softly, her eyes probing into his, "I'ma keep you out of sight long as I can. Ole Master know you got to mend, so he prolly won't call after you for some days. I'll tell him you getting better, by and by. And I'ma find you a shirt to cover your back with. But you gots to keep covered. Else, everyone can see."

She reaches toward him to take the cup back, and Dawit sees the violent trembling of her fingers. He must kill her, he thinks. He has no choice. She knows he has healed. But he does not move. He wants to hear what she has come to say.

"My name Clara," the woman says. "I'm too old for fieldwork and ain't no mo' babies to tend after, so I'se the nurse for coloreds in these parts. Ole Master known me since he was a boy. We was raised up together on this farm."

Dawit gives the cup back to her, wiping droplets of water from his lips. Clara goes on. "I saw yo' back from last night, and then from today, when I brought the blanket. I saw how all the blood is gone, 'cept from on the wall."

At this, she swallows hard, and she is so nervous that Dawit expects her to spring backward at any moment. She holds the tin cup in one hand, but extends her other palm for inspection. "Week ago, I drew blood on this hand cutting some cane Ole Master say I could have. Cut was awful deep, hurt me bad. Balm didn't help much, so I beared my pain. Can't do much else. Last night, I still had a red cut sore as could be, swelled up. Big one. You can see the mark for yo'self."

Dawit leans slightly closer, and he can make out a closed, dark scar on her palm. It is small, the length and width of a blade of grass. The scar looks old, and he sees no swelling.

Clara is breathing faster as she goes on. "This mornin' I wake up 'fore sunrise and first thing comes to my mind is, 'Clara, something different today.' And it's my hand. I look at my hand and see the cut all mended, not nearly sore as it was, and I thought it was a miracle from God. Then I came in to see if you made it through the night, to put some balm on your back. But when I come in, all your marks is gone. Like you ain't never been whipped a day in yo' life.

"Then I look on the wall and I see your blood, and it's still red, ain't dried up like blood do. I touch it, and it feel warm to me. I knew it, then. It's in your blood. That's how your back mend itself. My hand touched your blood last night, so my hand mended and my pain is less. Maybe you a devil. Maybe you got some voodoo. Don't know which. You got healing in your blood."

Dawit's thoughts are overwhelmed by the quick analysis of this old slave woman. Her claim intrigues him: Can it be that the Living Blood has healing properties outside his body? The Life gift is only attainable through Khaldun's ritual—the blood-giving at the moment of death—but this old woman's tale seems to be proof that the blood can function at some small level even without a ritual. Naturally, Khaldun has forbidden experiments to understand the blood's effect on mortals.

By accident, it seems, this woman has discovered in one night what Khaldun himself has not learned in hundreds of years. The thought makes Dawit's heart's pace quicken. He wonders if he should share with Khaldun what he has learned.

Then, Dawit is overcome by grief. He cannot share anything with Khaldun, he realizes. Khaldun is many miles from here, and Dawit is a prisoner on a slave plantation in America. And this old woman, for what she has learned in innocence, must die.

Clara's eyes widen, as though she can hear his thoughts. She holds up one bent, wizened finger. "I ain't gon' say nothin' 'bout you, voodoo man. Ole Master would have you sold for sho'. I know why you'se come. You'se come 'cause I prayed for it."

With that, tears brimming in her eyes, she tells Dawit that her young great-grandson lives on a plantation two miles from Mason Farm. At night, she travels there to try to tend to him because his foot was crushed beneath a wagon wheel and nearly severed. The wound is not healing, she says. His foot is turning black, and he has a terrible fever. He no longer recognizes anyone. She is afraid he will die soon, and a boy of only ten.

"I got this cup here, voodoo man, and I got a razor hid in my skirt. You can bleed yo'self into this. Not much. Just a bit. I'ma go tonight and take him the blood to see if it won't help. And then you and me ain't got nothin' mo' to say 'bout it. You unnerstan me, voodoo man?"

A razor in her skirt. Dawit realizes how easy it would be to overtake this old woman, steal her razor, and empty the blood from her own bold throat. Imagine such a request! She must be mad.

But Dawit doesn't move. This woman has cared for him and shown him kindness. She does not know all the truth about him, so it is not a direct betrayal of the Covenant to help her. It is risky, yes, and perhaps foolish. But, he thinks, why not? Why should he withhold a few harmless drops of blood?

"If you ever tell anyone what you have seen," Dawit says, his voice rough, "I will kill you, old woman."

He sees Clara's face draining, her features falling limp, as she stares at him. She has taken his words as a refusal. He senses that she is a woman whose life has ill afforded her the luxury of tears, but tears run across her face nonetheless.

Dawit lifts his palm to her. "Give me the cup," he says.

Dawit's first meeting with Ole Master comes nearly a week after his whipping, when the door to the storeroom opens and the man

Dawit saw at the auction strides in. It is a Sunday, so the man is dressed in a black suit. Clara has said they were raised together, but despite the droopiness beneath his eyes, he looks decades younger than Clara. He drops a small burlap sack at Dawit's feet. Dawit glares at him.

"These are your clothes and a pair of shoes for the year," Lowell Mason says, not looking at Dawit's face, ignoring the insolence in his eyes. He speaks with yet another accent—drawling and difficult—unfamiliar to Dawit's ears. "There's no need to run from here. You ask either of my niggers—Ben or Clara—and they'll tell you that."

Dawit doesn't answer. His mind is reeling with curses, but he holds his tongue. The man glances at Dawit's eyes, then quickly away, and Dawit believes he is ashamed.

"I heard what you said, that story 'bout being a freeman and being sold down the river, and I can't say if that's true or not. You talk real proper, not like any slave I ever heard. All I know is you were at the auction, and I bought you because me and my son can't get on here alone. Mayhap you can read and write, and I can't unlearn you that. But if I hear of you trying to teach it here, or anywhere else nearby, you'll be back on the wall. And if my son can't break you, I know someone who can. I hope it won't come to that."

How tempting it is, Dawit thinks, to wrap his fingers around this man's throat and silence him forever. But what then? He does not know his surroundings well enough to make himself a fugitive murderer. Foolishness has brought him too much danger already.

"What you said you call yourself?" Ole Master asks him.

"Dawit," he answers.

Ole Master shakes his head. "Name on your papers is Seth, so that's what you'll answer to. Your life before, whatever it was, that's all over now. Sunday is rest day. Tomorrow, you work. I've hired you out to Turner's farm, and he'll expect two hundred pounds a day in your sack. And pick it clean, no bolls. Picking started in August, so you've lost me a fortune in just one week."

Lowell Mason, Dawit soon realizes, is not a rich man. Gambling losses have taken their toll, he learns from the one who calls himself Nigger Ben. The farm was once grand, but it now provides only the barest sustenance; the majority of its horse stalls and six slave quarters are now empty. He has the old man and woman, Clara and Nigger Ben, but that is all. Both are too old to do much work, so Dawit alone must make farm repairs and tend the three mares. Dawit works from dawn until long after daylight, with twenty minutes to eat at midday and Clara's cornmeal waiting for him at night. Dawit always wears his towcloth shirt to cover his back, no matter how hot the sun in the endless cotton fields.

He is never whipped again, aside from a halfhearted lash from Ole Master's son, Gil, when he was drunk with power and whiskey. Dawit caught the rough cowhide, coiled it around his bare hand, and yanked hard until the whip was taut, silently daring Gil to strike again. Gil looked startled. "Let loose of that, nigger," he said, and when Dawit threw it aside, Gil only leaned over to pick it up and walked away. He never raised it to Dawit again, even as a threat. Dawit has never encountered such weak-willed cowards!

Soon, Clara dies in her sleep. Dawit regrets that a woman of her years lived her life in bondage, but he is glad his secret has died with her. The blood healed her hand, but it did not give her the Life gift. So Dawit realizes that her great-grandson, Franklin, who survived his foot injury with the Living Blood she brought him but walks with a limp like Nigger Ben, must still be a mortal too.

Exploring when he can, Dawit quickly learns the local geography, the outlying woods and bayous, and he knows he can write himself a pass that might let him travel to the North at any time. But he has taken an interest in Franklin and some of the Turner slaves. On Sundays, their free day, he has begun to teach a group of them to read and write by drawing letters of the alphabet in the dirt. Later, someone steals a Bible to read from. The group has grown steadily, and word of Dawit's gift of knowledge passes quickly among them. They are as eager to learn as Dawit was when he first met Khaldun, and that desire touches him. That is why he has decided, at least for a while, to remain here.

One day, the news comes that Ole Master's brother in Virginia has died and left him a new slave. It is a woman, Dawit hears. In the afternoon, Ole Master brings out his carriage for Nigger Ben to drive him into town. He whistles for Dawit to come to him. Dawit, exhausted from labor and the sun, stands before him.

"Seth," Ole Master says, "the woman I'm bringing is yours. She'll sleep beneath your blanket. If I had a way of thinking like my neighbors, I would take her for my own bed. Or leave her to Gil. But I'm a pious man, and I don't allow that here. So I leave your work to you. This is your mate." And he smiles in a way that makes them conspirators, as though the woman is a gift.

Watching the carriage raise dust as it ambles along the path toward town, Dawit is so enraged that he is shaking. Assigning him a wife! Expecting him to lie down with her, to breed with her as though they are no more than livestock! I must leave this place, Dawit says to himself—the thought that plagues his mind so many times a day. The Searchers may come soon, and he does not wish to be seen this way. Property of such a low creature as this, a hypocrite who believes himself a saint!

After nightfall, as Dawit eats ashcake and bacon on the stool in his one-room log quarters, the door flies open. Ole Master stands there, still grinning, with a dark woman taller than he at his side. Her hair is in tight braids wound across her scalp, her cheekbones jut sharply, and she wears a plain, coarse dress with frayed black shoes. The woman is glaring at him, her arms wrapped around herself. Her face has no fear, only indignation.

"Seth," Ole Master says, nudging the woman inside his bare, tiny room, "This here is Adele. I want her belly big by winter."

Then Ole Master is gone, and they are alone in darkness. Dawit can no longer even see the statuesque woman left for him, except the memory of her face. Despite her status, she is bitterly proud; her face is so hard, the beauty beneath is nearly masked. Nearly, but not quite. She is clearly Yoruba, a marvel!

Suddenly, Dawit is afraid of himself. He is afraid to be locked in darkness with this woman, this Adele, expected to behave as a beast. He has not held a woman in a long time.

She seems to hear his mind. "If you take me, nigger, it's only gon' be with a fight," her raspy voice comes from before him. "I ain't having no more babies. I've had three sold from under me. You hear? No more."

Dawit contemplates her words in silence. He finishes his food and slaps his palms together to rid them of crumbs. "Adele is a lovely name," he says at last. "Fitting for a lovely woman."

"I've whupped bigger menfolk than you, niggers and buckras too. Don't try that pretty talk on me."

Dawit sighs. "Adele," he says, "are you a human being or a beast? Answer me that."

"What you sayin'?"

"I said, are you a human being or a beast?"

She exhales, self-righteous and slightly bewildered. "A human being. You?"

"A human being," he says. He finds his blanket on the floor and tosses it toward her, then slides away to sit against the wall. "Go to sleep, Adele. Lovely Adele. With me, sleep is safe."

At first, there is no movement. Then he hears the scraping of her feet on the floor, feels the air from the blanket as she allows it to float down, and hears her dress crinkle as she curls on top of it, fully clothed. Still, he listens. A few moments later, he hears her breathing slow as she begins to sleep.

Dawit's heart pounds. For long minutes, he sits in the dark wondering what shameful acts he is capable of committing against this mortal woman. Then he, too, closes his eyes and wills sleep to come.

▪ 23

Jessica wasn't sure how long David had been behind her, his skin pressed to her buttocks, plying himself between her thighs to gently rub his hardened flesh against her. He glided and retreated until her body's moisture cleaved to him and cleared his path, and then he was inside of her, rocking from behind as if in a sleep-trance. She moaned softly, barely awake herself as his solid warmth crept through her and filled her up.

Through the window, light was glowing faintly as the curtains trembled in a sudden breeze. Dawn was Jessica's favorite time to make love. Every time she awakened to David's morning touch, or made him stir from hers, it was startling, unfamiliar. A secret seduction.

She felt David's hands wander across her stomach beneath her T-shirt, then he found her nipples and plied them until they stood, sending starts of pleasure to her loins. His fingers followed a path across her body's nerves until they rested against her clitoris, tickling it lightly, just enough to make her squirm and gasp. David's touch was always just right, just so. She writhed, pressing herself against him so he could push himself farther inside her. She wanted to feel him bump against her full bladder, as far as her flesh would allow.

Even after nearly eight years of marriage, David's sensuality was so strong that her heart still raced, and her body still jumped beneath David's fingers. He never seemed to make love the same way twice, always reinventing himself. Sometimes, under the heat of his weight, she felt herself transcending beyond orgasm to another place entirely. Before Kira was born, Jessica could scream without control; the more noise she made, the more inspired David's efforts. Now, since Kira's bedroom was directly beside theirs, the strain to be silent sometimes broke her concentration just when her pleasure was sweetest.

This time, once again, Jessica had to grit her teeth as her body below her waist melted away. She quivered inside, bucking against him.

"Yes . . ." David whispered, enjoying her gratification.

Behind her, she felt David's abdomen spasm and knew he was coming too. He breathed hard against her ear, biting her earlobe gently, and his hot breath made her shiver to her curled toes.

"Je t'aime beaucoup . . ." he whispered.

There was just something about French, Jessica thought. "Damn . . . I love you too."

Her face and flesh felt fevered. She turned to face him, entwining herself around him, pulling his head against her breastbone to cradle it. She held him with fascination, thinking of how vulnerable he'd been as a child, the orphan. Now, all he had was her.

"I want to take you to France," David whispered. "I want to show you Paris and Versailles. We can live there."

"Mmmmm . . ." she mumbled, already fading from wakefulness.

"Will you and Kira go away with me?" He'd been asking her this question daily for the past week; the phrasing made it sound like he might go somewhere without them.

"Of course," she breathed.

"I mean it, Jess," he said, his voice louder, more urgent.

"Me, too," she muttered, and she was asleep.

When Kira came downstairs for breakfast after the second call, her T-shirt was untucked and her shoelaces were flapping on the floor. She marched to the table and waited for Jessica to pour milk over her bowl of cornflakes. David was in the kitchen making toast for all of them, and coffee for the groggy grown-ups.

"I don't want to go to school," Kira announced.

Jessica hadn't heard this complaint in a long time, since Kira's first week in Ms. Raymond's kindergarten class. She took a comb and began to fluff out the natural shape of Kira's hair. Kira would need a haircut soon—she was beginning to look like Angela Davis, circa 1968. When the comb pulled her head back slightly, Kira missed her mouth with the spoonful of cereal. "Mommy, I don't want to go to school," she repeated.

"I heard you."

"You didn't answer."

"You know what I'm going to say," Jessica told her.

Kira sighed, clicking her tongue insolently. Then, she laughed when she missed her mouth with her spoon again. Jessica didn't even have time to scold Kira for being sassy before her laugh dulled the sting. This kid has an on and off switch, she thought.

David appeared, resting the plate of toast behind his plastic-covered computer. "What'd you do to your face? You look like a milk monster," David said, and Kira's laugh turned to peals.

Jessica peeked around at Kira's face. Splashes of milk dotted her nose, cheek, and chin. She couldn't help laughing herself.

"Are you sick?" David asked, dabbing her face with a napkin.

"Well . . . maybe a little sick . . ." she said. "Yes, I think so."

"Don't tell stories, Kira," Jessica said.

"I think I am a little, Mommy. I feel bad."

"What's wrong?" David and Jessica asked in unison.

For a long time, Kira didn't answer. She worked her face around, exaggerating her thought process, then she shrugged. "I don't know," she said.

Jessica shared a knowing glance with David. This child could be such a bullshit artist. Maybe someone at school had called her a name, or the teacher had told her to stop talking so much. Only Kira knew best what was going on in her little head.

"When are we going away, Daddy?" Kira asked.

Jessica paused midchew, wondering if Kira had overheard their bedroom conversation, but the guilty expression on David's face told her he must have discussed a trip with her too.

"Don't know yet. That's for Mommy to decide."

Jessica felt her old mechanisms warming up, shifting into gear. Out of the question. They weren't going anywhere. She'd invested too much time at the paper and would miss her family too much to simply pack up and leave. Bea would skin her alive for taking her granddaughter so far away, even for only a year.

"Remember, we have money stashed away," David kept reminding her.

David's father, who'd been an importer in France, left him a nice-sized estate and a lump of cash. David had been forced into state care, but the money became his when he was twenty-one, and he promptly invested it. The way he described it, one year he was virtually a pauper, living on student loans and macaroni and cheese, and then a letter from the French government informed him that, as of his birthday, he had a quarter of a million dollars sitting in the bank. He'd bought this Miami house, and just about everything he owned, with cash.

As soon as Jessica graduated from college, David tried to tempt her to forget about a career and backpack across the world with him. But in those days, when she still couldn't get used to the M-R-S in front of her name and the hyphen that joined their surnames, David felt temporary. She just knew he would get bored, leave, or cheat, so she decided to get her own act together fast. The backpacking could come later, if it came at all.

And it *was* later, Jessica realized. David was dying for her to have another baby, which would make traveling a lost cause. But Kira was old enough to handle it now. It's not a two-headed dragon, she thought, remembering Peter's words to her.

Europe had culture, variety, freshness, and Africa even more. It would give Kira a foundation she would never find in the States, and give Jessica a new start.

What if she was standing at the threshold between a good life and a *remarkable* life? Her father told her once, in a secret-telling voice he used every time he read fairy tales, that her life was going to be remarkable. That was the first time she'd heard the word, in fact. Of course, he'd probably said that to Alex, too, but Jessica had grown up assuming it was prophecy. She planned to write a story that would change the world—or a book, like David's, that would make a profound historical contribution. So far, that wasn't happening in Miami.

Maybe God's plan would present itself if she had the courage to break away. Courage was all it would take.

Jessica folded her hands to look her daughter in the eye. "Kira . . . You really want to go away? Even if you wouldn't see Ms. Raymond or your friends or Grandma or Aunt Alex for a long time?"

Kira nodded, not hesitating. She looked earnest.

"But why, sweetheart? Because Daddy says so?"

"No," Kira said. "'Cause Grandpa says so."

Jessica and David scowled and glanced at each other, puzzled. Kira had never known a grandfather a day in her life.

"Grandpa likes Burger King. Just like me," Kira went on, and Jessica's heart froze as she thought of her father's trip to Burger King the night he died. She grasped the edge of the table as though she believed she would fall if she let it go.

"He says you and me have to leave, Mommy. Just you and me, he says. But I want Daddy to come too. Grandpa says if we don't leave, bad things will happen. Very, very bad things."

"What kind of bad things, Duchess?" David asked, seeming unaware of the fright that was making Jessica feel dizzy. Maybe he thought Kira had invented an imaginary friend. Good Lord, could that be?

"Very, very bad things," Kira repeated, and the way she said it, as though she truly *were* repeating careful instructions, locked Jessica's muscles. "Like what happened to Peter and Uncle Billy. A monster will come for us."

At this, Jessica could clearly see the color draining from her husband's face, leaving his lips looking dry. He'd figured out that something wasn't right. It wasn't just her imagination. She wasn't the only one rendered breathless by Kira's recitation.

What the hell was going on?

A dream, David mouthed to Jessica after his head snapped with the realization. "What kind of monster, Kira?" David asked her.

Kira shrugged and didn't answer at first, as though she couldn't think of the words. She looked directly at Jessica. "A mean monster," she said. "Or, maybe a good monster too."

"There are no good monsters, Kira," Jessica said suddenly, her voice barely a breath.

"That's what Grandpa says too," Kira said sadly, and she brought a spoonful of soggy cereal to her lips.

Jessica's quickened heartbeat had given her an instant headache, and she couldn't think of what else to say. Should she ask Kira if she'd seen Grandpa in the cave? Did she really want to hear her daughter's answer?

Abruptly, as soon as Kira finished eating, David tied her shoelaces and sent her upstairs to brush her teeth. Jessica saw his eyes, glassy with worry, as he watched her go.

"What was she talking about?" David asked.

"I don't know," Jessica whispered. Her mind was still stuck on Kira's words: *He likes Burger King, like me.* How could Kira know her grandfather liked Burger King, that he'd been eating a Whopper when . . . ? When what? Jessica had to force herself to finish the thought: When she'd talked to him in the cave. When he'd told her to warn Kira that there were no good monsters.

"You okay, Jess?" David asked, hugging her with one arm.

She shook her head. "I don't know."

"She's afraid of something. We've had so many bad things happen, first Princess, then Peter and Uncle Billy. Maybe that's what it is. I've tried to shield her, but . . ." He sounded so down on himself, Jessica squeezed his hand.

"Well, Lord, there's only so much you can do, David. We've both tried."

"This environment is bad for her, Jess."

Jessica blinked. "Maybe it wouldn't be a bad thing to leave.

Maybe we should. There are too many bad memories for her right now. If we plan for this summer . . ."

"We shouldn't wait until summer. We'll enroll her in an American school in Paris. The sooner we go, the better. That's very clear now."

His face was uncompromising. This was no longer a discussion of a remote possibility; it was becoming a plan, full of details and weight. It sat heavy on her shoulders. She'd felt this way with Peter, when she realized their book idea was more than talk.

"It just feels like we're running away," she said.

"Sometimes the only choice is to run away," David said, and kissed her.

Jessica knew some of her coworkers were still grumbling about her quick rise to the I-Team, the most coveted position for idealistic reporters with visions of *All the President's Men* dancing in their heads. When she'd interviewed with Sy the year before, she'd known full well she had a decent shot at the job, not only because she was good, but because the team had never had a black reporter in its existence. As her mother put it, the system had been working for everybody else for so long, it was damn well time it worked for her.

So, here she was. The state was investigating the facilities she'd exposed in her nursing-home package, which was still being complimented and believed to be a shoo-in for the Pulitzer finals. And her tips from Boo on drug dealing by county maintenance workers were panning out better than a dream. She'd just contacted a former low-level Dade County HUD supervisor who'd moved to Arizona and seemed willing to talk off the record. She'd felt a little like Bob Woodward during their telephone conversation, which he cut short when his son had to leave for school: "Knowledge of this goes high. Higher than you'd think," the man said before he hung up. What more could she want?

A month ago, a development like this would have sent her into an adrenaline fury, and she'd be pulling twelve-hour days to knock on public housing residents' doors, probe her sources in the local DEA office, and swap information with her police buddies at Metro.

Instead, Jessica found herself halfheartedly scribbling down her telephone messages from HUD bureaucrats and stifling a yawn at her desk. She checked her watch. Only noon. Either the days were getting longer or she was just getting plain bored.

And she was alarmed at herself. Could it really be that she'd reached her career goal and had no idea what she wanted to do next? Her job was beginning to feel like a forty-hour-a-week distraction from her life at home with Kira and David, the part that mattered.

"It's hard to explain," Jessica said to Alex on the phone during their customary lunchtime conversation. At the UM lab ten minutes away, near the hospital, Alex was no doubt sitting on a stool with a tuna fish sandwich in one hand and a Diet Coke in the other. Jessica had stolen away to sit with her sister enough times to know her daily menu. "It's like we're courting again. He's trying so hard. But not in the way that makes me feel smothered. He's starting to let me inside."

"Inside what?"

"His head. His thoughts. Showing me the clarinet is only part of it. There's so much more to him. I really feel that."

"Uh-huh," Alex said, sounding slightly skeptical as she shoved food into her mouth. "Can I throw up now?"

"Don't be cynical. David is really deep. You know that. Don't tell me you've forgotten the time he shocked you by going off on microbiology at Christmas dinner."

"The man knows his stuff. No doubt about it."

"And, Alex . . . He's so good on clarinet. You should have heard him last night playing this song by Billie Holiday, 'My Man.' I thought I was dreaming."

"Watch it. He's just trying to get into your pants," Alex said, and they both laughed. It wasn't so far from the truth, really; David was trying to get his way. Suddenly, there was silence on the line. Their thoughts, momentarily, had merged.

"So, I don't know what to do . . ." Jessica said.

"And I don't know how to counsel you on this one, either. It's kind of scary to drop the J-O-B, move to a foreign country, and start over. You don't even speak French."

"I know," Jessica sighed.

"But, heck, James Baldwin went to France. All the writers go to France. Maybe it's a rite of passage for you."

"Yeah . . . I was thinking something like that too . . ." Jessica said, chewing on the cap of her Bic pen. Listening to Alex munching on her food was making her hungry. Maybe she'd swing by the house and surprise David for lunch. David's leftover curried chicken sounded a lot more appealing than whatever was waiting in the cafeteria.

Another short silence. "So you're scared, huh?" Alex asked.

"It's for real now. It's definitely for real. He even talks about going to Africa someday, to Ethiopia. Exotic places. It's really tempting."

"Mom's going to have a fit."

"Oh, Lord, yes." And who could blame her, really? One year away could turn into two or three, or more, and Bea Jacobs didn't believe in airplanes. Once, while Bea was visiting her brother in New York, a traffic jam made her miss Flight 401 back to Miami. The plane crashed into the Everglades swamps. More than anything else, that was what made Jessica believe in miracles.

"But you have to live for yourself, Jessica. Life's too short, you know? Here I am still in Miami, and I've been talking about going to South Africa since way back when Mandela was voted in. I have an application to direct a clinic at a township just sitting in my drawer. I wish I had somebody to carry my tired butt out of here, to spur me on. Safe and comfortable is also very boring."

"I know that's right."

"I've always known you had bigger fish to fry than the *Sun-News*. I mean that."

Jessica's stomach jumped. Alex was right. Her destiny had nothing at all to do with the *Sun-News* and drug dealers or corrupt politicians. All of that was very small compared to whatever it was the Lord had waiting for her. "I guess I'm going to swing by home and get some food," Jessica said.

"Y'all better not go nowhere without telling me goodbye."

"Oh, please," Jessica said. "Get back to work finding the cure for sickle-cell. I'll catch you later, Dr. Jacobs."

After Jessica hung up, she looked up and saw one of the young mail clerks standing over her. He smiled at her sheepishly, tossing a manila envelope on top of her desk. The envelope was scuffed and wrinkled at the corners.

"What's this?"

"Sorry," the clerk shrugged. "It fell behind the cabinet. If I hadn't dropped a dollar back there, it would have been buried until Christmas."

Jessica glanced at the envelope's return address. It was from the Cook County Police Department, with someone's initials scrawled from Media Relations. Confused, Jessica looked at the postmark; it had been mailed nearly two months before.

Of course. The Chicago nursing-home lady. No wonder the original copy of the police report never arrived. Jessica had forced the poor sister to fax the whole report for nothing, and then she'd misplaced the fax anyway.

"Well, damn. Thanks a bunch, Rick," Jessica said.

"Sorry," he said, blowing her a kiss as he turned to walk away. "Hope it's not important."

In her hand, the envelope felt like an unearthed memento from an era long past. Jessica could remember the woman's name, Rosalie Tillis Banks, but she could barely relate to the time when her story had seemed so vitally important. The time when Peter was so anxious to have her fly to Chicago.

Her stomach churned slightly at the thought of her meetings with Peter to discuss the book idea that had died with him. Some things were not meant to be, she mused. Only Jesus knew the master plan. Peter's death had shaken her faith, a tremor at the roots, which time had stilled, but Jessica was stubborn in her belief that everything happened for a reason. She had to believe it. God wouldn't create a random world.

"Rest in peace, Rosalie Tillis Banks," Jessica muttered, leaning over to search for her trash can.

Shit. Missing again. Trash cans, telephone directories, and chairs were valuable commodities in the newsroom, and one or the other was likely to vanish at any time. Jessica wasn't in the mood to search for it. Instead, she slid the unopened envelope into the overcrowded mess of her bottom desk drawer.

Soon, it would all be trash to her anyway. Just papers. Very soon, Jessica realized, she might be cleaning out her desk in Miami for good.

▪ 24

The music arrested Dawit's attention, making him pause his fingers above the keys of his computer and crane his neck toward the stairway. He heard the mystical, soothing sound of the tambura and flute playing from the tape in the bedroom, casting a spell. Neither he nor Jessica had touched that tape in days. Dawit stood, forcing the cat to leap from its resting place on his lap. Someone was there.

Dawit was not afraid. After all the waiting, it was a relief.

Dawit found him lying in the precise center of the bed, propped up on a bank of pillows, his arms folded behind his head, and his bare feet crossed before him. He wore only white drawstring pants and a skullcap, and his eyes were closed as though he were in deep concentration. He wore a closely trimmed beard, new for him.

Was it a happy irony, or a cruel one, that he should be the one?

"Mahmoud," Dawit said, grinning. The grin was sincere. He did not move from the doorway, but he wished to hug his dear friend close to him. The sight of Mahmoud, more than anything, always reminded him of his real life, the other life, life in innocence, before the Living Blood.

Languidly, Mahmoud opened his eyes. His mouth, too, gave way to a warm smile on his bearded face. "At last, my brother," he said in Arabic. He sat up, dangling his legs one by one over the edge of the massive bed.

They did not speak, the two of them, for many seconds. There was much love between them, innumerable shared experiences. Yet, they stood before each other now as adversaries. To Dawit, Mahmoud's eyes looked sad as he studied him. The tambura player's sure fingers glided along the strings, filling the room's silence.

"You're very fit," Dawit said, noticing the ridges of the tight muscles in Mahmoud's forearms as he lowered his palms to the mattress. He knew the Searchers had rigorous routines of fasting and exercise to give them a mental and physical advantage in their work.

Mahmoud nodded, accepting the compliment with a gracious smile.

"How did you find me?" Dawit asked.

"You are predictable, my friend. And your name is known here. I enjoyed Body and Soul. This music, jazz, sounds like a cruder cousin of what you and I improvised three centuries ago in the House of Music. Do you remember?"

"Of course," Dawit said. Their music had a stronger North African influence, but the rhythms and chord patterns were strikingly similar. "I wish I could have written of it too."

Mahmoud's smile, that quickly, was gone. "Our music is not for them," he said curtly. "You insult me with the thought, Dawit."

Dawit knew he should have expected no other response. Mahmoud had always been conscientious about any undertaking, so he was certain to be as rigid as any other Searcher. They treated their work as a religion, with strict adherence to Khaldun's words: *As immortals, we are this planet's only true inhabitants. The others are only visitors, and our place is not with them. Their concerns are not our concerns. As the sun shuns the night, so too shall we be separate.*

"I would never write about what belongs to us," Dawit said, hoping to ease the silence that now separated them. "You know that much about me, I hope."

Mahmoud's face didn't soften. "Well, perhaps you've already written too much for your own good, Dawit. Your book jacket listed Miami as your home—I found this house the first day I set out."

Dawit nodded regretfully. "I was not hiding," he said, but he knew he had not been careful. He'd attempted to learn from the mistakes of his reckless days in Chicago by living in anonymity, or close to it; but his expertise still brought attention to him, even when he did not seek it. Foolishly, he had led the Searchers to his family's doorstep.

Long ago, Khaldun had even asked Dawit to join the Searchers. Despite being honored at the invitation—and although he'd never then imagined he might one day make a home with a mortal— Dawit knew he had too much fondness for the mortal's way of life. He would be too sympathetic to those, like himself, who could not live long away from it. How could he agree to restrict others who shared his own taste for exploration?

Dawit's refusal had visibly disappointed Khaldun:

Dawit, I fear the knowledge you value most is experience. You must learn that, to an immortal, worldly experience spells lasting emotional ruin.

Learn to relish the clouds, to marvel at the sunrise. The clouds and the sunrise are constant, like yourself, and will never cause you grief. Do not underestimate the tyranny of grief. Humans were not meant to bear the grief of hundreds of years, and mortals do not. But living among them you will, Dawit. And then you will know Hell.

How could he have told his beloved teacher the truth, that he had already been tainted?

He'd once shared his Life brothers' pleasure in life for life's sake, but he needed external stimulation; his heart, his hungry loins, all of his being. He could not unlearn it, no matter how much Khaldun entreated him and how hard he tried.

Up to twenty of his brothers took periodic breaks to live in the larger mortal world, at least for a short time, usually traveling in groups. The fortunes their colony had received over time from the sale of crafts and artifacts, useless to most of the Life brothers, were used liberally by those who traveled. Two or three others, like Dawit, had even taken wives for a time. How had they not been changed by it?

Dawit was embarrassed to realize that his concept of time was now so altered, so much like a mortal's, that even a mere year or two passed slowly for him. He could no longer enjoy four months' debate on a single passage from Spinoza the way his brothers could. And several years' silent meditation—commonly practiced in the House of Meditation, where Life brothers refused meals and instead breathed nutrients from vapors in the air—was out of the question. For as much as Dawit loved his home and his own kind, Lalibela had become tiresome to him.

And Mahmoud, whether or not he would admit it today, had once shared his mind. Had he also shared his weakness? What of the child he'd abducted from India, his son who had traveled with him? What had the boy's name been? He couldn't remember. But he remembered one thing well: Mahmoud had abandoned the boy, left him penniless, most likely to starve.

Dawit did not even think of the incident until two hundred years later, when he was summoned from his Chicago family's side and escorted back to Lalibela. How, Dawit wondered, could Mahmoud have been so unfeeling? Of course, he had a scattering of his own children through the years, but at least they'd always had their mothers to care for them. Hadn't Mahmoud worried for his child at all?

When Dawit had asked Mahmoud about it those many years later, he thought he'd detected sorrow, but then the expression melted into Mahmoud's matter-of-fact gaze. "Why do you think we left him?" Mahmoud asked. "That boy you speak of has been dead nearly two hundred years. It's an absurdity he was ever born."

That boy, Dawit realized, might have awakened something in Mahmoud that frightened him. Could that explain why, in time, he had joined the Searchers? And why he was so changed now, his demeanor toward Dawit so different? Which of them, Dawit wondered, had changed more?

As if he knew his thoughts, Mahmoud sighed, looking away from Dawit to study the interwoven figures carved into the bedpost. "This visit grieves me, Dawit."

"And me." Dawit tried to salvage a smile.

"We were brothers, you and I, before the rest. Your love for Rana made us that."

"Yes," Dawit said, remembering Mahmoud's sister, a smooth-skinned, brown-eyed girl of thirteen with black hair that shone like silk. She'd held his face in her tiny hands like a wonder. His first wife. His first love. Oh, to go back there and start again!

"We have shared much," Mahmoud went on.

"And many," Dawit added, thinking of the brothels they frequented, delighting in prostitutes who could make their female parts squeeze like fists and fling coins into the air.

"That was all long ago," Mahmoud said, still not looking at him. "I am happily celibate now. My head is more clear."

"Ah, yes. I forgot about that. Forgive me if it's hard for me to imagine that you are a Searcher. You out of everyone else, Mahmoud."

"Oh?" Mahmoud asked, his head snapping back so that their eyes were level. "It is not so hard to believe. First we are children, clinging to toys. And then we become men."

Dawit did not answer the remark, though it stung and made him angry. The time for reminiscences had passed, he realized.

"Tell me why you have come," Dawit said.

"You know why, my brother."

There. It was said. Dawit's jaw trembled slightly. "Then I have a message for Khaldun—I have not broken the Covenant and I am not ready to leave. With his permission, I would like to remain several more years with my wife and child."

"That I cannot grant," Mahmoud said evenly.

"How long, then?"

"One month. Two, if I choose to be generous."

"When did you become so pompous? You speak for Khaldun?"

"I've told Khaldun what I have witnessed. He agrees that you are a danger to yourself and to all of us. The time for your return is overdue. Perhaps, then . . . you can be helped."

Dawit frowned. "Helped?"

"Dawit," Mahmoud said, features softening, "you are a madman, or very nearly one."

At this, surprised, Dawit took a step closer to Mahmoud. "Explain what you mean."

"What explanation is necessary? Do not think I am as gullible as these mortals you play with. I know what happened to the old woman in Chicago, your own flesh. I know what happened to your wife's friend. And to the sick old man."

So, he knew. Mahmoud had been vigilant in his watch, apparently. Dawit's first impulse was to deny the charges, but he could not. It was true he had killed, and killed many. He crossed his arms before him. "I remember a time when blood did not make you squeamish," he said.

Mahmoud's eyes seared him. "Don't mistake my concern for

squeamishness. For the sake of the Covenant, I would take a life with less conscience than even you. But I would not be so careless. I would not rely on the stupidity of mortals to cover my deeds. Even the stupid can see what is obvious, with time. You are too obvious. And it has become sport to you."

"I kill only for the Covenant," Dawit said indignantly.

"Even if that is so, you are misguided. The Covenant was never intended as an excuse to slay mortals at will. Our Covenant compels secrecy. Which path is straightest to secrecy? Leaving mortals to themselves, or mingling among them and killing them when they recognize what we cannot hide? You build a fire only to stamp it out when the flames dance too close to your face, Dawit. It is foolish. It is childish weakness."

Dawit heard the cat cry from the doorway, then it trotted into the room and leaped onto the bed, rubbing against Mahmoud with a raised tail. Mahmoud massaged the cat's chin, keeping his eyes smugly on Dawit. Mahmoud must have been near their home for a long time to have won Teacake's fickle friendship.

"If you like," Mahmoud said, "you may bring the cat."

"It has been a blessing to see you, Mahmoud," Dawit said, ignoring his words. "Now, I must ask you to leave."

Defiantly, Mahmoud leaned against the bedpost and bent his knee, one foot raised to the mattress. The cat licked Mahmoud's chin and curled into his lap. "Dawit . . . I hate to point out how much you remind me of Teferi."

Teferi! Teferi, the misery of Khaldun, was the reason the Searchers had been created. In the earliest days, fewer than a hundred years after the brotherhood's creation, it was reported that Teferi had mortal wives and families in several countries—three wives and twelve children in the Kingdom of Ghana alone. He remained in their midst for so many years, the brothers complained to Khaldun, that his families would have to be blind not to notice that he did not age as they did. It was also rumored he gave them advanced knowledge from the House of Science—battery-powered lights!—to help them improve their lives. This was also forbidden; obviously, it would only bring attention to him. Teferi was simply a heretic.

Khaldun decided Searchers would be designated to find and monitor Life brothers who were abroad. And, when it was deemed necessary, they would bring them back.

It had done nothing to improve Teferi. During Dawit's last visit to Lalibela after leaving Chicago, he learned Teferi had lost his powers of reason while living in Turkey and slaughtered a dozen mortals in a marketplace. "I liberate you!" he had shouted, hacking indiscriminately. Searchers had been dispatched to free him from the Turkish prison, or else he might confess his Life gift. Teferi was brought back in chains to Lalibela; Dawit stared into his eyes as he shuffled past under guard, and absolute emptiness stared back at him.

After forty long years among his brothers, Dawit told Khaldun that he intended to return to North America. Khaldun urged him to think about Teferi, who was still imprisoned at the colony. He had daily meditations with Khaldun. Often, Khaldun confided to Dawit, Teferi cried like a child:

Shortly before his madness, our Teferi heard news that his mortal wife had been killed. This is what you seek, Dawit? The flesh lives forever, but not so the soul, the psyche, of man.

"How dare you compare me to Teferi!" Dawit said to Mahmoud. "I'm no madman, leaving the bodies of mothers and infants in my wake. He sickens me. I have done no harm. I simply wish to be left alone."

"Then you are a fool, Dawit. You would rot in an American prison when they come for you? We cannot allow it. You jeopardize all of us with your sloppiness. You have a history here, like before. You must go."

"Mahmoud," Dawit said gently, standing directly before his friend, "you know I can be trusted. What of Christina and my children? I left when the Searchers found me because I knew my face was too well known. I have proven my loyalty. My loyalty even overrules my love. But it is too soon!"

"How can you speak of love? Love for mortals?" Mahmoud said. "There are plenty of nests for your cock. Visit brothels in Addis Ababa, if physical lusts guide you. But you should have love for Khaldun and your brothers only."

Dawit stood rigid, angry. "As always, you mock what you do not understand. And you are coarse."

"I understand more than I care to confess, Dawit. You know my past conduct like no one else. But I do not crave to be what I am not."

"What do you crave to be, then? A silly clairvoyant in the House of Mystics? Or worse, aspiring to spend dozens of years at a time in meditation, content with a breathing death?"

"Now it is you who mocks what he does not understand," Mahmoud said.

"Tell me, looking into my eyes, you prefer trances and mind exercises to all else."

"I prefer my own kind," Mahmoud said, his gaze unblinking. Impatiently, he scooped the cat out of his lap and tossed it to the floor. The cat turned to hiss at him over his shoulder, then scampered away. Mahmoud stood, brushing fur from his trousers. "Enough of this talk. You have heard my message. I will wait, but not very long. And remember this: I can take measures to convince you."

"Now you threaten me?"

"No threat, my brother, merely an observation," Mahmoud said, standing close to Dawit to probe his eyes. "Without the woman and child, you have no reason to stay."

"State your meaning," Dawit whispered, enraged.

"My meaning is clear. This trip you propose with them is unacceptable. You cannot flee to France. I know you, Dawit . . . I am unhappy to think it, but I am afraid you are tempted to break the Covenant. I will not permit it. Begin to accept that you must leave."

"I'll say this," Dawit said, raising his finger near Mahmoud's nose. "Your life will be a living hell if you hurt either one of them. You will die a new death daily. Teferi's fate will be a respite compared to yours, you whore's son."

Mahmoud's face seemed to narrow. "My mother may have been a whore, as you well know, but I never took one for a wife!"

Dawit's arms flew up to push Mahmoud, but Mahmoud's hands were quicker, taking a firm grip of Dawit's wrists to hold them still. Mahmoud, Dawit realized with surprise, was stronger. "Do not incite me, Dawit, or you will leave today. Only our friendship makes me wait."

"I have to leave them soon enough, in years to come! Leave me in peace! I have a right to love my wife and daughter!" Dawit cried, ashamed to find himself so distraught in his friend's presence. There were tears in his voice. He was so angry that his Arabic felt sluggish in his mind as he tried to find the right words to express himself.

"What you speak is betrayal, nothing less."

"Betrayal? What I speak is human!"

"And are you human?" Mahmoud asked with curled lips, flinging Dawit's wrists away from him.

"We are humans, all of us. The Life gift does not make us other than human. We were born to mortal humans. We bleed and hurt like humans. We are immortal, but human still!"

Suddenly, inexplicably, Mahmoud grinned. His eyes shone with a mean-spirited delight. "Incidentally, your mortal pet is home early, Dawit. You didn't hear her car drive up?"

Dawit gasped. His peripheral vision told him someone was in the doorway. It was Jessica. She stood with her lips parted, clinging tightly to her purse, her expression lost in alarm and confusion. How long had she been standing there? What had she overheard? Dawit was paralyzed where he stood.

"David . . ." Jessica said in a faint breath, "who is this?"

The Arabic! She could not understand. Relieved, Dawit attempted to recover himself and raised his palm to press it against his forehead, where he could feel the race of his heart in his veins. "I didn't see you there, baby," he told her in English. "I'm sorry. This is a friend. Mahmoud, this is—"

Mahmoud only sneered at Dawit and pushed his way past. "I have no time for nonsense, Dawit," he said in Arabic. "You heard what I came to say. Tell your plaything goodbye."

When Mahmoud didn't slow his stride, as though he could not see Jessica and intended to walk through her, she darted to the side of the doorway to give him room to pass. Dawit and Jessica stood motionless, gazing at each other, as they heard Mahmoud's bare feet thump down the stairs, and then the front door opened and closed with a slam. Jessica's face was drawn, stunned. The gentle music swirled around them, swathing their silence with its deceptive calm.

▪ 25

It was a beautiful night, with a bright moon reflecting from behind a patchwork of dramatic clouds, a painting in the sky. And yet it was a horrible night. Jessica wished she could be anywhere but where she was, doing anything else.

"You were fighting. I saw him push you," she said wearily, resting her head on her arms, which were folded across the picnic table. At last count, this was her sixth attempt to have a conversation with David that would smooth away the mystery of the afternoon. She'd tried three times before she went back to her office, and three more times since she'd been home. By now, she was tired and scared to her core.

The hamburgers David had grilled for dinner were still stacked on a plate in front of her, cold and congealing with grease. Kira had scarfed down her own hamburger, and now she was amusing herself by probing the gardenia bushes for lizards with a twig from the backyard rubber tree. Teacake skulked alongside her, waiting to pounce at anything that moved. It would be very dark soon.

"Yes, we were arguing," David said tonelessly, staring at his clean, untouched plate.

"Tell me again who it was."

"His name is Mahmoud. He's a former student. He was upset about a grade."

Jessica, enraged, sighed and closed her eyes. Who the fuck did he think he was talking to? He was lying.

"I know I haven't taught in many years," David went on quietly. "He's been out of the country. He's held a grudge. Can I help it if he's unbalanced?"

Jessica didn't answer, her eyes still closed. She was surprised that she'd managed to keep from shouting or screaming or crying this long. She'd come home for lunch and found her husband arguing with a half-naked man in their bedroom, and his explanation—when she finally managed to pull it out of him—was the lamest one she could imagine. Jessica had interviewed enough people who openly lied to her face to recognize crap when she heard it.

"When you first introduced him," Jessica said, one careful word at a time, "you claimed he was a friend."

David gazed out at the water, and she followed his gaze. The lamps in their next-door neighbor's backyard were reflecting in the current, writhing snakes of faint red and green. David swallowed hard. Lord, Jessica observed, he was really no good at this. She wished he could muster a better lie, so she wouldn't be forced to push for whatever the truth was.

"Tell me, then, what you think," David said.

Jessica glanced at Kira, who was engaged in a lively conversation with Teacake yards away from them, near the back door leading to the screened-in porch. Jessica called out, warning her not to kneel in the mud beneath the bushes. "I won't, Mommy," Kira called back. Hearing Kira's voice brought Jessica much closer to tears.

"I don't know what to think, David," she said, returning her eyes to him. "What should I think?"

David tried a hollow smile. "At the risk of sounding very trite, it isn't what it looked like. He's not a lover, if that's what you're thinking. Is that what you're thinking?"

Jessica sighed, wiping the stinging corner of her eye. "I'll tell you something I learned from my mother. After my father died, she and Alex had horrible fights. Alex was going through this Rasta phase, when she wouldn't comb her hair and smoked weed in her bedroom with the door locked. The shouting made me crazy. The anger was so big, it was everywhere. One day I asked my mother why they were saying such hateful things to each other. And my mother stroked my head and explained something I truly believe: We only waste energy to have horrible fights with the people we love the most. And that fight I saw today was not between a teacher and a student. It just wasn't. So you're going to have to come up with something better than that."

David hung his head, silent. He, too, wiped away a tear.

So, this was it. She'd broken through. Lord help her.

Jessica took a deep breath, gathering her courage. "And you need to come up with it soon. Because you know what? I just realized I'm sitting here trying to figure out where my daughter and I are going to spend the night."

David made a pained sound and reached out to squeeze her hand. She felt sick to her stomach. She didn't have the strength to move her hand away, so she left it beneath his, immobile.

"Don't do that, Jess."

"Then talk to me, David. Right now."

He nodded emphatically. "I'll do my best. I don't know what I can tell you."

"How about something that isn't complete bullshit? That would be a good start."

Studying him, she believed she could actually see the wheels turning in his head, his struggle to decide what to reveal and what not to reveal. It infuriated her, frightened her. How much was there inside him that was as foreign as this barefoot Middle Eastern man who nearly tried to knock her over? As tempted as she was, Jessica hadn't even called Alex to share the latest bizarre twist to her life. Alex probably would have told her to pack her bags and get an AIDS test, which wasn't what she wanted to hear.

David held his hands in front of him, almost as though to pray, and he absently tapped his fingers together, one after the other, beginning with his pinkies and moving to his thumbs. Nerves, she knew. She was nervous too.

"I will admit," David said with difficulty, "that there are some aspects of my life you know nothing about."

Jessica felt a severe cramp in her stomach, and she winced. David went on, his voice very low. "But those aspects do not include another lover; male, female, or otherwise. I have to ask for your trust on this point. If I lied about Mahmoud, it's only because explaining him would mean having to explain vast complications that I never intended to share with anyone. And I hope you don't take that as a personal affront, Jessica. But you know I have had a difficult and scattered life. There are many parts of it I intended to leave behind me."

"And he's one of them?"

David nodded slowly. "Yes. Very much so. I haven't seen him in years, and he suddenly dropped in today unannounced."

"Who is he?" Jessica asked.

David blinked rapidly. "We grew up together. We both spent years with the missionaries in Africa, in Egypt. He is like a brother to me, both in good ways and bad. We had a falling out many years ago. He is like blood, and you can't escape blood."

"What made you fight?" Jessica asked.

"My father's money," David answered painfully. "He grew jealous that I was suddenly so well off. We'd both been penniless before that. I tried to help him, to encourage him to go to school—and I even offered to pay—but he made unreasonable demands. So, we don't speak now. Until today. You see how it went."

That was all. Slowly, Jessica felt her stomach unwinding. Her breathing, once again, felt unrestrained in her lungs. "Why didn't you just say that before?" she asked.

David shrugged. "I've noticed that Americans seem to enjoy living in their unhappy pasts, Jessica," he said. "I do not."

At this, Jessica almost smiled. True, David often complained he didn't understand the rationale behind TV talk shows where guests paraded their miseries for entertainment. He derided the thought of most therapy, insisting that people should learn to grow past traumas and rely on inner strength to become reborn. She agreed with him, in part, but she also wished he could learn to be more open about himself and his life before he met her. Sometimes, she had to admit that they were still virtual strangers.

But this crisis had passed. Thank you, Jesus.

Jessica squeezed David's hand and raised it to her lips to kiss his fingers. "Thank you. That's all I wanted. We'll leave it, for now," she said. She glanced at Kira and found her patting the mud with her hands. She thought about scolding her, but didn't. Kira was wearing her after-school grunge clothes, and there wasn't really any way to keep kids away from mud.

"I'm still worried about Kira," she said. "Do you think we should call a specialist?"

David shook his head. "We should go to France. We should start again. Distance from troubles eases them."

"Not all the time, David," she said, noticing the layers of sadness wearing at his face, his lips. Seeing Mahmoud had really shaken him, she could see. Please let me in, David, her mind implored. Just once, let me inside. "But I've been thinking about it, and I think France is a good idea. I'm getting excited."

David brightened, but only slightly, as he leaned over to kiss her cheek. "Good. I'll start making some calls," he said, picking up the spatula to lift a cold hamburger to his plate. His expression was unreadable as he fumbled to open the twist-tie on the bag of buns.

She believed his story about Mahmoud. It wasn't just wanting to believe, she told herself. She believed.

Jessica's stomach growled. Her appetite was back, too. "One day, David, I want you to tell me all about Mahmoud. I want you to tell me everything. Okay?"

David nodded, meeting her eyes. "Yes," he whispered, meaning it. "Very soon, I'll tell you everything. I promise you that."

Jessica smiled.

PART THREE

The Covenant

Love me, honey, love me true?
Love me well ez I love you?
An' she answe'd, "'Cose I do"—
Jump back, honey, jump back.

—"A Negro Love Song"
Paul Laurence Dunbar
1890s

▪ 26

"Teacake? Here, kitty. Come here, kitty, kitty."

Dawit's whisper-call was the loudest sound in the calm of the yard, which was wrapped in a darkness reminiscent of the heart of a woodland. It was two o'clock in the morning, and when Dawit awakened he'd expected to find the creature curled at the foot of their bed in his usual spot. But he was gone, tonight of all nights. He wasn't in the bedroom chair, he wasn't sleeping on his favorite bookshelf at the foot of the stairs, he wasn't flopped across Kira, and he wasn't warming himself against the refrigerator vent on the shiny kitchen linoleum.

Was the animal psychic? Teacake always seemed to know exactly when Jessica's car would drive up in the evenings, no matter how early or late. He posted himself at the front window to wait for her. Even Kira had noticed this, and she would shout, "Teacake says Mommy's coming!" Perhaps Teacake had altered his habits because he sensed what was to come.

"Teacake, where are you?"

Dawit's Durabeam flashlight, part of the hurricane-season stockpile collected by Jessica, swept across the yard's countless leaves and blooms, pebbles on the pathway, isolated blades of grass, and the rims of the Tempo's tires. Dawit crouched beneath the vehicle to search for the cat, smelling the pungence of collected motor oil. Only asphalt and pebbles. The same beneath the van.

Goddamnit. He shouldn't have waited this long, until the night before the weekend trip. He should have done this sooner.

Dawit wiped nervous perspiration from his face and glanced at the glowing hands of his watch. He'd already been up for ten minutes. If Jessica sensed, even subconsciously, that he'd left the bed, she would ask him questions. So far, he'd been pretty good about limiting his work to twenty minutes a night—or, even better, to the daylight hours when Jessica and Kira were away. Jessica was a sound sleeper, but he didn't want to risk making her suspicious of him at the one time she would need to trust him most of all.

Where was that fucking cat? Mr. DeNight or someone would probably call the police if he kept creeping around his yard with a flashlight. At the last homeowners' association meeting, the Neighborhood Watch president warned them that an intruder had been sighted lingering on the streets after dark. Probably Mahmoud, Dawit thought. Mahmoud was no doubt observing him at this very instant, wondering what he was up to.

"Teee-cake . . ."

As he climbed the rocky embankment in the center of the yard, the flashlight's wide beam found the mouth of the cave, drawing exaggerated shadows cast from overgrown weeds, moss, and jutting stone. The cave was another of Teacake's favorite spots, but usually during the day. Would he have come at night?

Dawit squatted at the entrance and poked the flashlight inside. He heard a loud hissssss even before the light sought out the corner where Teacake was crouched, his tail puffed like a chimney brush. The cat bared his teeth and hissed again. Teacake's eyes glowed a luminescent red in the beam.

"It's just me, dummy," Dawit said in a soothing tone. "This is how you show your gratitude for six years of free room and board, you little miscreant?"

Teacake recognized his voice. He flicked his tail around himself and mewed, then gnawed at something irritating his front paw. "So, are you coming out or am I coming in?" Dawit asked.

Teacake licked himself, not moving otherwise. Cats were so blasted contrary. Dawit steadied himself with one hand against the low-hanging stone at the mouth and climbed down the narrow, makeshift steps into the cave.

Dawit kneeled and scratched Teacake beneath his chin, eliciting a garbled purr, then he scooped the cat under one arm. "You should be grateful to me," Dawit muttered, kissing Teacake's nose as he grabbed his flashlight with his free hand before standing. "I have an invaluable gift for you."

The shed on the north side of the house was a tacky remnant of the previous owner, fashioned after a wooden barn painted dark red. Inside, Dawit housed the lawn mower, his toolbox, the pruning shears, the stepladder, and an array of items that didn't fit in the house, including the tricycle Kira had outgrown. She'd been promised a bigger bicycle with training wheels for Christmas.

After flicking on the overhead sixty-watt bulb, Dawit closed the shed door and dropped Teacake on top of a cracked plastic outdoor table they had replaced years before. Immediately, Teacake jumped down to the floor to sniff at a half-dozen withering dead lizards scattered across the concrete. He began to sniff at one of the petrified carcasses.

"Don't do that. It's poisonous," Dawit warned from habit, shooing the cat away from the lizard with his foot.

In the past week, Dawit had made a new work space in the shed. He'd arranged the table, a wooden folding chair, and a radio he kept tuned to a music station that played jazz after midnight. The shed resembled a laboratory at this point, making Dawit wonder if he wasn't some sort of mad scientist. Was Mahmoud right in his assessment? Was he a madman by now?

Dawit peeked under the lid of a hole-poked shoe box he'd left on top of the chair. Inside, resting on a bed of dry grass, was a large gray lizard Dawit had named Satchmo. Satchmo scurried around in the box, a noise that prompted Teacake to prop himself up on his hind legs to try to see inside.

"Evening, Satchmo," Dawit said, smiling. Still alive. But he'd known the lizard would be fine. The morning before, when he'd found Satchmo's belly contracting with rapid breaths, those shiny black eyes wide open, Dawit had trembled with disbelief. Then, he'd felt an overwhelming sense of power as he understood what it meant. He had done it. Satchmo would always be fine.

Dawit lifted the box and cracked the door of the shed open so he could toss the lizard to freedom. "Go, Satchmo," Dawit said, flinging the contents of the box out into the dark. "Have a good life, my friend."

Teacake tried to race out to chase the lizard, but Dawit closed the door before the cat could escape. "Sorry, compadre," he apologized. "You'll leave a bit later. I promise."

Dawit reached behind the ladder in the corner to find the paper bag hiding his cache of hypodermic needles, housecleaning chemicals, and pesticides. He'd killed at least ten lizards so far in his quest to find an injection that was quickly lethal, yet not so instantaneous that his subject would be dead before Dawit could complete the most critical portion of his task. Satchmo, with a bellyful of ammonia, had been the first to live.

Ammonia would not do for Teacake, Dawit had decided. He had no way of determining how much of the chemical would be necessary to induce a quick death, so he'd chosen another compound that killed the lizards quickly—rubbing alcohol, with its deadly isopropanol. He'd considered turpentine and rat poison, which he believed would act more quickly, but those agents might be more painful to Teacake's system. Not that the alcohol would be painless, he surmised; but it would impair Teacake's central nervous system and lead to a coma, so the animal's pain might be brief. He hoped so, at least; the less noise Teacake made, the better—his wails might awaken Jessica and Kira, which would be disastrous.

Dawit laid both needles he had prepared on the weathered patio table. One contained the full dose of the isopropyl alcohol, the other a small sample of Dawit's blood, which he had drawn earlier that day. The blood, inside the hypodermic's plastic casing, was still noticeably warm to his touch. Dawit rested his index finger against it, savoring the heat, still fascinated by its mysterious properties.

Next, Dawit turned on the radio and heard the deliciously lazy tenor saxophone of John Coltrane. He sat in the chair, listening to the piece to identify it. It took him two seconds. "A Love Supreme," of course. And wasn't it fitting?

He wished he could relax and enjoy the music rather than face the task ahead. Dawit gazed across the shed at Teacake, who was still sitting in front of the closed door, looking back at Dawit expectantly. Seeing that Dawit had noticed him, Teacake cried to be let out. His voice sounded like a child's.

A single tear ran down Dawit's cheek. What insanity was this? He would torture and possibly murder a beloved family pet, and for what? On the belief, perhaps mistaken, that he had recalled the Life incantation he first heard pass from Khaldun's lips?

And what next? Would he do the same to his wife and child?

From habit, under his breath, Dawit began to recite the simple Hebrew phrases he had dragged from the recesses of his memory: "The Blood is the vessel for Life. The Blood flows without end, as a river through the Valley of Death."

Khaldun, no doubt, had believed Dawit remained unconscious when he performed the Life ritual on the last of his brethren in the underground temple. Dawit was not supposed to have heard those words. None of his other brethren had, he imagined, so perhaps that was why none had attempted to bring anyone into their Life fellowship. He alone had heard.

The instant Satchmo's ammonia-filled belly stopped its faint movement, Dawit had injected him with the blood from his veins and recited those simple words. By morning, when Dawit returned, Satchmo was awake.

Again, Dawit glanced at his watch. He had already been away from Jessica for nearly twenty minutes. He must begin his work, or else the Ritual might find him still here by morning.

Dawit played with the plunger of the clear syringe until the liquid inside crept to the tip of the needle in a bead. He held it steady in his right hand and kneeled beside Teacake, stroking the cat's head. "I wish there were another way," Dawit said to Jessica's cat.

And what was the harm of it, really? Why hadn't he done the same with Princess, when he watched his dog writhe on the veterinarian's exam table and take her last, shallow breaths? He should have had his blood waiting for Princess. Or dear Adele.

By now, Dawit's vision was blurred by tears. In a quick motion, with one arm, he lifted Teacake beneath the front legs to expose the soft fur of his underbelly. Estimating where the cat's stomach rested, he jabbed the needle deeply into it, pushing the plunger in with all his might.

Teacake howled, and Dawit felt the cat's claws slash furiously against his face, near his eyes, before Teacake thrust himself away from Dawit with his strong hind legs. Teacake nearly stumbled over himself in his terrified effort to run from Dawit, scrambling behind a cardboard Christmas tree box in a corner of the shed. He made low, threatening sounds that resembled growling.

Cursing, Dawit touched his face. Bleeding. He was lucky the animal hadn't scratched his eyes out. Would one injection be enough to work quickly? He didn't know. He wanted to inject Teacake once more, to be certain, but he didn't relish the thought of another encounter with those sharp claws. Teacake was a much heartier opponent than any of the lizards had been.

From his sanctuary, Teacake's growls turned to frightened cries. Perhaps he was already in pain, or simply confused. Dawit prayed he would not be too loud, or he would have to chase Teacake and knock the beast unconscious. This was already difficult.

Mahmoud was wrong; there was no sport in killing for him. And killing a loved one, even a pet, was more daunting than he had imagined. Why hadn't he simply asked for a tranquilizer from the vet so Teacake would not suffer? It would have required an explanation, but he should have gone to the trouble for Teacake's sake. He would need more merciful methods in the future, he decided. Much more merciful.

Thankfully, after a few more minutes, Teacake was silent. Then,

Dawit heard the animal make retching noises. The first dose of poison was doing its work.

"What are you doing?" Jessica asked Dawit, trailing after him as he walked out of the house carrying two UM duffel bags to the minivan. She'd been watching morning cartoons with Kira in the living room when she noticed him pass through with the bags. He detected accusation in her voice.

"We're taking a trip," he announced, smiling.

"Who is?"

"You and me, babe. It's all set up." He hoisted the bags into the van's cargo bin, grunting. "Bea's taking Kira for the weekend. Then, you and I are camping out in the Everglades for two days away from civilization. I found a guy who rents a cabin out there. It's great. You have to ride an airboat to get there."

Behind Jessica, Kira giggled. "Did you know about this?" Jessica asked, turning to look at her.

Kira nodded, smiling. "I'm sleeping at Grandma's."

It took all of Dawit's energy to maintain his jovial exterior, since his spirits had been crushed all morning. He'd been so methodical—holding a mirror up to Teacake's nose to gauge exactly when his breathing stopped, checking for the cat's pulse, injecting the blood exactly as he had with Satchmo. He'd said the incantation slowly, not stumbling over his words.

Yet, at dawn, when he'd stolen back outside to check on the cat's progress in the shed, he lifted the towel he'd spread over Teacake and found him lying motionless, his glazed-over eyes open, his joints already stiff with oncoming rigor mortis. Still dead.

Only five hours had passed. Perhaps it was still too early.

No, Dawit told himself, he had to face facts. He had killed the fucking cat, another family catastrophe he would have to deal with when he returned from the weekend with Jessica. That is, if Jessica would return with him at all after he found the courage to reveal what he intended. Teacake's death, realistically, was the least of his worries at the moment. The future of his family was very much at stake.

He had not mentioned the trip in the house, nor used any of the household telephones to plan or discuss it, because he hoped to keep their destination a secret from Mahmoud. Mahmoud's ears were everywhere. Dawit would need privacy for his days away with Jessica. He hoped Mahmoud did not suspect what he was up to.

If only Teacake had lived! That could have served as evidence enough in his own mind, and in Jessica's, that he could be trusted to carry out the Life ritual on human beings. What now? What was the purpose of revealing everything to Jessica if he could not ask her to join him with Kira?

But he must. Mahmoud would surely return. Clearly, he had threatened to harm Jessica and Kira, and Dawit did not doubt his sincerity. Mahmoud had been softhearted when Dawit first met him, often hesitating with his spear when he should have struck, but the years had changed Mahmoud. The years had changed them all.

He would have to explain why their departure must be sudden, and not to France, after all. The Searchers would find them without much trouble in France. He must take them to Africa, somewhere they could easily vanish for years.

Could he expect Jessica to agree to such a thing?

"I like your nerve, planning a trip without even asking me," Jessica said, startling Dawit from his thoughts as he arranged the duffel bags. "What if I had big plans for this weekend?"

"You don't have any plans and you know it."

"Isn't the Everglades a swamp? We're camping in a swamp?"

"Swamps are very romantic and secluded. There aren't many people there. Only alligators," Dawit said, and Kira squealed in mock fright.

Jessica nodded. "Uh-huh. Well, do you know that quote by Jerry Seinfeld? 'Sometimes the road less traveled is less traveled for a reason.'"

"Who's Jerry Seinfeld?" Dawit asked.

Jessica rolled her eyes. "Never mind."

Kira tugged on Dawit's belt loop. "Is it time to go, Daddy?"

"Stand back, Pumpkin," Dawit said, and he slammed the rear hatch closed on the van before turning to Jessica to hold her shoulders. "You're not mad, are you?"

She shook her head. "I guess most people would kill to have a husband who'd plan a surprise weekend trip. I'm slightly speechless, that's all."

"Good," he said, kissing her forehead. "Then, go upstairs and get dressed. I think I packed most of what you need, but you can see what I overlooked. Hurry, though. We have to drive way out west, about sixty miles. The guy's meeting us at the Big Cypress National Preserve with his airboat at noon. If we miss him, we'll never get to the island."

"What about—"

"I've packed plenty of food. Plus, it's an island, so there's fishing, and he said he has poles at the cabin."

"What about Teacake, Daddy?" Kira asked suddenly.

Dawit's stomach sank, but his smile remained frozen on his face as he massaged Kira's scalp. "We'll leave the kitty-door unlatched for him. I've left two days' worth of food and water. Let's just trust the raccoons won't get to it first."

"I'm going to find him and say bye-bye," Kira said, turning to sprint back into the house.

Jessica wrapped her arms around Dawit's middle and snuggled her face against his bare chest. She kissed his nipple. "A secluded island, David? You're amazing. And what a great public relations tactic, letting Kira stay with Mom for the weekend. Mom, of course, won't say anything, but she's very upset about this idea that we could move."

"That we will move."

"That's what I meant," Jessica said.

Dawit patted Jessica's firm backside. "Go on in and get dressed, mi vida. I need to put a few more things in the van, then we can get out of here."

"'Kay," Jessica said, looking up at him with a girlish smile. "This is going to be great. You shall be adequately rewarded for your creativity and spontaneity. Did you pack the massage oil?"

Her eagerness made Dawit sad. He shook his head slowly.

"Then you didn't think of everything, did you?" she asked, squeezing his cheek, and she jogged back into the house with a giddy step that reminded Dawit of Kira's. His wife, in so many ways, was still so much like a child. She possessed the sort of abandon he'd forgotten many natural lifetimes ago, and he loved that about her. He wished he could lose himself inside of it.

Very soon, Jessica would be forced to grow up in a fashion most people could never imagine. How would it change her?

To keep worries from afflicting him, Dawit concentrated on details. He had his hiking boots. His razors. The flashlight. Bread, fruit, leftover KFC fried chicken, crackers, sodas, flour to fry up any fish he might catch, the cast-iron skillet, a saucepan. The cabin's owner said he had cooking utensils, but Dawit wanted to bring his own to be sure. He wanted dinner tonight to be special, because it could very well be the last pleasant moment he might share with his wife for a long time.

What else would he need for this trip, miracles aside? Ah, yes. His battery-operated CD player and radio. They must have music.

"David?" Jessica's voice floated to him from Kira's bedroom window as he stood in the front yard. He looked up, but could not see her behind the gray screen. "Have you seen the cat?"

"I'll take a quick look around," he said, waving up to her.

No, he had not seen that cat in at least an hour. Perhaps that hour had made a difference. Dawit prayed it had, but he knew he was only fooling himself as he trudged to the shed.

Inside, he gazed at the lump beneath the fading beach towel. No change. To be sure, he lifted the towel to examine the cat. Teacake's eyes were still open, muddy pupils completely dilated—which meant the light was not affecting them. He gently poked at Teacake's rib cage and shoulder blade. He lifted one paw and watched it flip back to the concrete floor as though it were elastic. Unless it was his imagination, Teacake's joints seemed slightly more pliant, offering less resistance, but he couldn't be certain. He was probably seeing only what he wanted to see.

"Better you than my wife or child," he muttered to the corpse. "But I wish you'd lived, Teacake. You don't know how much."

Dawit sighed and once again buried the animal beneath the towel. He lifted his portable CD player and was about to leave when he remembered his most valuable supply: an eight-inch hunting knife with a wide blade. He pushed aside wood scraps, goggles, and dust masks on his tool table until he found the knife, which he'd bought two years before and never removed from its leather sheath. The purchase had been on a whim.

This weekend, he would finally need the knife. The thought, by itself, made Dawit shudder with dread.

"Did you find him, Daddy?" Kira asked Dawit when he walked into the house through the back door. She had her Minnie Mouse overnight bag slung over her shoulder, and she'd taken an impatient stance with one hand planted on her little hip and her head cocked far to the side. Dawit wished he had time to find his camera, so he could take a photograph of her.

"No sign of Teacake. I'm sure he'll turn up. He's probably just out making friends." Hearing this, Kira looked downhearted, biting her bottom lip.

"Did you look in the cave, too?" Jessica asked, appearing with her African purse and a handful of paperbacks.

"I looked everywhere, Jess. But I'm sure he's fine. You know, animals can sense changes like an impending trip. Maybe this is Teacake's way of voicing his displeasure."

"Well, he never has before . . ." Jessica murmured.

After a last search of all of the closets and cabinets to make sure Teacake hadn't locked himself up somewhere, the lights were turned off, the house was closed up, and the three of them piled into the van to begin their weekend adventures. Dawit noticed Kira's face in his rearview mirror; she was staring out of the backseat window at the yard, obviously hoping to catch a glance of the cat. Guilt-ridden, Dawit looked away and started the engine.

"Don't worry about Teacake, hon," Dawit said softly.

Jessica lifted the hunting knife from the dashboard, turning the sheath over in her hands. "Uhm . . . Yo, Running Deer, what's this for? Planning to track some game in the wilds?"

"Don't underestimate my hunting prowess, my love."

"Well, my grandmother used to fix us squirrel and rabbit, but I think I'll stick to more conventional stuff, if you don't mind."

"You ate bunnies?" Kira asked, making a face.

"A long time ago. Wabbit stew, like Elmer Fudd. But I'm not going to let Daddy force me to eat any rabbits. Squirrels, either. Any chance you might catch a wild filet mignon out there, David?"

Again, Dawit tried to smile, but he didn't answer. As he backed to the end of the driveway and swerved around to follow their winding street, he felt momentary release, unexpected promise. His family was with him in the safety of this enclosed vehicle, and he could simply drive them anywhere, if he chose. Teacake, in this isolated moment, was not yet gone for good in their minds. His family loved him, and he was still David, if only for now.

Would they love Dawit, too, or would they think him a monster? And truthfully wasn't he only a monster, an abomination, in the end?

"When are you and Mommy coming back?" Kira asked, leaning behind Dawit to whisper in his ear as he drove. Dawit nearly chastised Kira for not wearing her seatbelt, but he enjoyed the scent of the baby shampoo from her hair, a sweet lemon, and he could not bring himself to ask her to move away.

"Very soon, hon," Dawit said, his throat tight. "We'll be back so soon, you won't even realize we were gone."

▪ 27

Soon after David drove past the campus of Florida International University on State Road 41, Tamiami Trail, the sprawl of the suburbs flew behind them, replaced by a canal running alongside the two-lane road and nothing but trees and brush ahead as far as Jessica could see. She smiled, resting her hand on David's knee. Did he feel the sudden freedom, too, like taking a gasp of pure air after being locked in a musty room? She felt a liberation that was like a dose of some sort of drug, a euphoric high.

The wilderness of the Everglades had always been nearby, even when she was a child, but she'd never explored it, never ventured far from the safety of what she knew. She'd come out here a few years before to write a story about a Miccosukee activist, but she never came to camp; hell, she hadn't camped since she was a Girl Scout. The idea of camping made her imagine the scent of marshmallows roasted with chocolate, sandwiched between graham crackers. Good old s'mores.

The memories also evoked the scent of bug spray.

"Shit," she said, tightening her fingers around David's kneecap. He, too, was in a trance. He looked at her, his eyebrows arched. "Did you pack bug spray? The mosquitoes will be murder."

"I think so. If not, we'll pick some up," he said.

Jessica would have preferred a flight to the Bahamas or Jamaica, truth be told. An Everglades island hideaway was a romantic thought, but not necessarily in the middle of May. She was surprised David hadn't considered what a pain the mosquitoes would be.

But, then again, she knew this trip wasn't going to be a vacation in the truest sense. David hadn't been the same since that visit from Mahmoud, so he wasn't exactly in a fun-and-sun mood. And David's silence today definitely meant he had something on his mind. That was all right. She'd learned that if she gave him enough time, he'd finally bring up whatever was bothering him. Maybe he wanted seclusion to do it. She figured he was going to try to push her to leave Miami within the next two weeks, as he'd hinted, but she couldn't agree to that. Kira's school term would be finished in a month, and she couldn't understand his hurry. It didn't make sense to pull Kira out of school early. A month wouldn't matter.

Signs along the roadway—most of them gaudy billboards, but a few hand-painted and charming—advertised airboat tours, alligator wrestling, Miccosukee and Seminole crafts, and campsites. Their vehicle was part of a steady convoy of cars and campers, she noticed, many with out-of-state plates. So they weren't the only ones out here, after all.

"Thank you for this, David," she said.

He smiled, still staring straight ahead. "Don't thank me yet. Let's see how you like it."

"So, what kind of cabin is this? It has electricity, right?"

"There's a generator. It's like a tiny house, the way he described it. Bathroom, kitchen, a bed with a mattress. But there's no TV and no phone. So, in our society, I believe that constitutes a cave and a supply of flint, right?"

Jessica laughed, but the idea of not having access to a telephone for two days bothered her. She would miss Kira, and she was certain Bea would want to hear from her. "We should have brought Kira," she said. "I'm sorry she's missing this."

"Look at that," David said suddenly, nodding toward a road sign. PANTHER CROSSING, it read. Jessica felt a thrill surge through her frame, making her sit up straight.

"There aren't that many Florida panthers left," she said. "Think we'll see one?"

"Who knows what we'll see?"

They made it twenty minutes early to the Glades Air-Jet Tours dock in Ochopee, off Tamiami Trail. The minisized office with a thatched roof was painted bright cobalt blue, the same shade as a sample airboat elevated on display beneath a billboard on the highway. The colorful billboard pictured a grinning cartoon alligator waving a Western-style hat as he steered an airboat through a spray of water. On the real-life airboat beneath, three weathered mannequins sat in the passenger's seats; two adult-sized and one child-sized. Rain and sun had faded their clothes and any discernible facial features, even their eyes.

"Can we spell T-A-C-K-Y?" Jessica asked, shielding her eyes from the midday sun as she climbed out of the van and gazed up at the billboard and the airboat's faceless family.

"Watch that idle talk. The guy who owns the cabin runs this place, Jess, and he gave us a good deal."

"I hope he can give us a good deal on bug spray," Jessica said, slapping at a huge mosquito that had already found her bare calf. Her palm left a small smear of bright red blood behind. "Damn these things. I thought they disappeared until summer. Are there any mosquitoes in Paris?"

"Not that I can recall, no."

"Good."

David slid on his sunglasses with his middle finger, and Jessica paused to admire his face. He always looked good in shades, but with his jaw set with a sense of purpose, and dressed in camouflage-pattern shorts and a matching T-shirt, she felt an impulse to drag him into the backseat and molest him. Jessica wondered how long it would take before they were settled on the island. And alone. This was seeming more and more like a good idea.

"Y'all are a shade early, but that's perfect. How are you? Rick Mantooth. Ready to roll on out?"

The man who met them on the wooden dock was stocky, crisped red from the sun—especially the rolls of fatty flesh on the back of his neck—and wore his silver hair shaved in a crew cut. He had a genuine Southern accent, the kind Jessica rarely heard south of Ocala and north of Homestead; most people in between, it seemed, were transplants from places anywhere but Southern. Jessica usually told visitors that Miami was more Caribbean than Dixieland; but they were no longer in Miami, she remembered. Their guide sounded like a genuine Florida cracker, one who would be proud to display the title on a bumper sticker.

"Mantooth. Where is that from?" Jessica asked him.

He grinned with rows of straight, tobacco-stained teeth. "Seminole, on my dad's side. He was a logger, started running airboats out here before nobody knew what one was hardly. Fact, that cabin we're heading out to is his too. Not afraid of snakes, are you?"

Jessica leveled a no-nonsense gaze at Mantooth, then glanced back at David. "What kind of snakes?"

Mantooth only laughed, reaching to take her duffel bag from her shoulder and nestle it inside the hollow of the airboat tied closest to them. The painted boat was aluminum, the size of a large powerboat, with a monstrous fan propeller and an elevated operator's seat at the rear. At the front, it had two rows of four aluminum seats with foam backs for passengers. While he helped them load, Mantooth explained that airboats were best for traveling through the hammocks and marshes because they could glide across very shallow water.

Despite her nervousness at climbing into the unfamiliar boat, Jessica was in such a good mood that she found herself humming, of all things, John Denver's "Take Me Home Country Roads." No girlhood camping trip had ever been complete without it. After finding her seat, which was slightly damp, she sprayed herself with the can of Deep Woods Off David had rooted out of his duffel bag.

The boat bobbed while David and Mantooth loaded the last bag and climbed on board. The engine started with a deafening rush of wind and the churn of the motor. Mantooth pulled back on a long metal stick beneath his right hand, and the boat lurched backward.

"Oh, shit . . ." Jessica muttered, grasping her aluminum handrail. She looked at David, who sat unsmiling beside her. "You okay?" she asked into his ear.

He nodded, smiling faintly, and held her hand so tightly that it almost hurt as the boat sped away from the dock. Jessica admired the sight of the massive cypress tree trunks growing submerged alongside the boat's path. The trunks were adorned with air plants, like mammoth mutant spiders, much bigger than the ones that grew in their yard.

"Island's a good fifteen miles out!" Mantooth said over the airboat's engine. Some of his words were nearly lost in the wind as the boat skated over the water. "Take us about thirty minutes in, and another thirty when I bring you back. Government owns most of the land, but some of the islands, like mine, are still private. There's plenty of island to keep you occupied this weekend, most likely. It's two, three square miles."

When David didn't respond, staring straight ahead through his impenetrable sunglasses, Jessica turned around in her seat to shout up at Mantooth. "What kind of wildlife is out there?"

Mantooth revved the engine to increase the boat's speed. "Let's see . . . Lots of egrets—there's one there. Wood storks. The occasional 'gators. You'll want to steer clear if you see any waist-high mounds, since it's late spring—'gator egg-hatching time. Don't try to feed 'em, that's for sure."

"Don't worry!" Jessica shouted back.

"No panthers or deer on the island. Sorry. Lots of birds, though. You'll see blue heron and ibis. And fishing's great. I got cane poles in back of the cabin, if you want to try your luck with the bluegill and largemouth bass. There's crayfish too."

"You hear that, David?" Jessica asked, concerned because he was so quiet. David only nodded, his eyes still straight ahead. Granted, David was usually withdrawn around people he didn't know, but she thought he'd be more interested in hearing what their guide had to say. He was the one who'd brought up fishing before. What could be bugging him?

"Other than that, it's pretty much like a standard beach," Mantooth went on. "Lots of sand for you to take in the sun. Not that either of y'all really needs a tan, I guess."

Very funny, Jessica thought, but decided to let the remark slide. "With all of these mosquitoes," she called, sounding slightly hoarse, "I don't think I'll want to spend too much time lying out there anyway!"

"Yep, the skeeters are bad," Mantooth said. "There's lots more spray in the cabin, case you run out."

Jessica liked Mantooth's easy manner and cheerful features. She would feel so much more at ease if she knew she could pick up a telephone or a radio and find him ready to glide back to them in his airboat. She found herself wishing he wouldn't be so far away.

"How come there's no phone?" she shouted, and she had to repeat the question because it was drowned out in the noise as the boat skimmed over a bed of waterlogged saw grass.

"No lines," Mantooth shouted back, and Jessica nodded.

"We don't need a phone," David said in her ear, the first words he had spoken since the boat began its journey. "It's a vacation, remember?"

As the airboat pitched her deeper into the unknown and the wind whipped her short hair across her forehead, Jessica could think of a couple hundred reasons she might need a telephone— snakebite, alligator attack, sunstroke, broken limb, compulsive mother's urge to speak to Kira. She couldn't remember the last time she had been anywhere without a telephone. Suddenly, she felt as though the boat were transporting her hundreds of miles away from civilization rather than a few short miles from a road- way that led straight back to Dade County.

"What if something happens?" she called back to Mantooth.

He winked at her, his face still broad with a smile. "Then you better hold on 'til about five o'clock tomorrow. That's when I'm coming to pick y'all up."

Jessica bit her lip. "Listen . . . Do you think you could swing by before then, maybe, just to—" David cut her off before she could finish her sentence, wrapping a heavy arm around her shoul- der. His abrupt movement annoyed her—just a little. Instead of affectionate, the gesture felt almost rough.

"No need for that, Rick," David called to Mantooth, overpow- ering her words. "I'm sure we'll be just fine."

"I don't believe this. The light doesn't work," Jessica said, flipping up and down on the exposed switch built into the wooden wall of the cabin, which was in a woodsy, elevated portion of island. The house was built high on what looked like stilts, probably in case of flooding. They'd climbed twelve steps to get to the unlocked door.

"David, go run and try to catch that Mantooth guy. I can't believe he left us here without—"

"We have to crank up the generator first, baby."

David took off his sunglasses and put them in his T-shirt breast pocket, gazing around the tiny room. There was a bed, all right; queen-sized, made up with a tightly pulled brown blanket in the middle of the open room, devouring most of the space. A small pine table for two was pushed against the far wall, and then there was a tiny kitchen space with a two-burner range and small oven, with a miniature aluminum sink beside them. A portable refrigerator stood in a corner adjacent to the oven. The only ornament in the room was a replica of an eighteenth-century musket mounted on the wall above the table.

Jessica sneezed. The room needed airing out. She made her way to the picture window across the east wall, hoping the screen was intact to keep the mosquitoes out. They'd been swarmed with the buggers while their shoes got soggy as they climbed across the grassy shoal to the shore. Through the window, she saw a majestic array of cypress, royal palm, and pine trees; and, in the distance, aqua green of the water surrounding them. This would be a nice cabin, with some A.C.

"Okay. Found it," David called from the kitchenette, and she heard him fussing with machinery. "Guess we'll need power for the fridge, mainly. The stove is propane."

"Do we have any?"

David held up an aluminum can. "Ye of little faith . . ."

The generator began to whir noisily. Much better, she thought. Some sign of the twentieth century.

Actually, the room was sort of quaint, built completely from wood. It was clean-swept and practical, almost like a lodge. From the outside, they'd been able to make out where the individual logs were secured together to build the walls.

Jessica walked past the bed to the bathroom and flicked on the switch. Wooden walls, a smooth wood toilet seat, linoleum floor. The sink was tiny and makeshift, but she was struck by the old-fashioned porcelain tub on brass legs. Nice touch, she thought, but a strangely sentimental detail in such a spare place.

"Well?" David asked her, bending over to unload the fried chicken and drinks into the fridge.

"It's cute. Daddy Mantooth had simple needs, I guess."

"I can't wait to take a look around the island," David said, and the cheeriness of the statement made Jessica notice his improved mood. "First, I'm going to find a fishing hole. Rick told me about a marsh near where he dropped us off."

"A marsh? Which one? It's all a marsh."

"Quiet, you. Here's our plan: I'll hunt and gather, and meanwhile you can pound our clothes with some stones to wash them. A return to the primal couple."

The primal couple. It had a nice ring to it. Smiling, Jessica surveyed David's smooth behind as he leaned over the refrigerator. She felt a glow of arousal, but ignored it. It was too damn hot for sex just now. That would have to wait.

"I'll pound the colors first, then the permanent press," she said instead. "I wonder which marsh is the cold water and which is the warm . . . ?"

"Now, you're in the spirit."

Hand in hand, sticky and stinking from bug spray, they explored. The island was big enough that they could forget, at long intervals, they were on an island at all. On the edges of the water, where the saw grass and partially submerged trees grew, there was no doubt it was a swamp. But then the stretches of fine, dark sand began, followed by the brush and the woods. They found overgrown trails twisting through the wooded areas, and one path led to a rusting water pump built beside an oak tree.

"Think it works?" Jessica asked, enchanted.

David began to pump the handle, which squeaked loudly. Then water began to dribble out, growing into a thin stream. On an impulse, she raised her palm to catch the water, which was warm; but when she slurped it, the flavor was fresh and wholly clean, like the island, which smelled of dense growth. David drank too.

"I like this place," Jessica said.

"I'm glad."

There was movement all around them; lizards, butterflies, scurrying bugs they couldn't see. In the trees above, they could hear the untamed chatter and nagging of birds out of their sight. Jessica saw a quick movement on the ground in front of her, and she glanced just quickly enough to see a small brown rabbit hide behind a fallen pine tree. She'd actually never seen a wild rabbit.

"There's your dinner," David whispered in her ear, and she slapped his shoulder, scolding him. Then, David kissed her lips. After he slowly pulled his mouth away, they wrapped their arms around each other tightly and pressed close, waiting for the simultaneous moment when the heat and perspiration between them would force them to let go. They waited a long time, standing in the shade of the oak, until it seemed the moment would never come.

▪ 28

Their lovemaking steered between moments of tenderness—with David above her with such love on his face that he looked like he was in pain—and raw, hard sex that made her cling to the hand-made oak bed frame so David's thrusts wouldn't send her off-balance, flying onto the floor as he pounded her from behind.

The sounds they made were part song, part call and response—from gasps to screams to whimpers. As their sounds mingled with the other night noises drifting through the open window, with her dripping perspiration and the damp scent diffused inside the breeze in the room, Jessica felt like one of the creatures outside, unashamed in the wildnerness, doing what God intended creatures to do.

Afterward, they were both breathing hard, their slick chests rising and falling fast, and their flesh burned so hot that they couldn't bear to touch. They fell away from each other and lay still on the blanket, smelling their heavy sex scent, their lower bodies moist from each other.

The only light in the room was from the moon. David looked like a shadow beside her, as though she could reach her arm out and it would pass right through him.

"I love you so much, Jess," he said, a whine.

"Me, too," she said.

He'd caught only one bass for dinner, using bread for bait since he'd forgotten to buy worms. They cut the fish in half after he fried it up. She'd eaten fresh fish and day-old fried chicken with a slice of bread, and it had tasted like a feast. They'd sat on the cabin's steps, watching the blaze of the sunset light up their island in an orange bath while David's radio played static-filled jazz that sounded like a broadcast from a time long ago. This is a dream, her mind had told her as she witnessed the too-perfect sunset. I'm going to wake up soon.

David turned over in bed, facing her. She felt his rapid breaths against her forehead. "I have so many things I need to tell you," he whispered, "but I'm scared out of my mind."

She'd expected this. A part of her had realized from the start that the purpose of this unexpected vacation was to give David whatever he needed—whether it was distance or guts or escape—to tell her more about himself. So, even without realizing it, she'd been prepared. His words did not alarm her. She touched his damp hair with her fingertips.

"You don't have to be scared."

"There's so much you don't know," he said.

"I know that," she said. "But I need to. Right?"

A nearby owl hooted so loudly that it sounded like it was in the room with them, perched at the head of the bed. When the owl fell silent, she noticed the chaotic chirping of the crickets.

Everything around them was awake, it seemed. So was she. Her eyes were wide, trying to make out David's features in the dark.

"I've tried to imagine a life without you and Kira," David said. "I can't. I hardly remember my life before you. The only future I could bear would be the three of us together. Always. But you have to know things about me first. This is going to be so hard. Nothing will ever be harder than tonight."

"Hard for you or me?" she asked, trying to make a joke, but she realized that her throat was parched nearly mute.

"Mostly for you, I think," he said.

"Maybe I'll surprise you," she said, accepting within herself that she could stand to hear about an affair with another woman—or even a man. She could, so long as it was over. If David was bisexual, so be it; so long as he was honest, he didn't cheat, and they could fulfill each other's needs. She could stand to hear about a criminal record, even, which might explain his financial independence. Hell, the Kennedys had been bootleggers and nobody hassled them. That story about an inheritance from David's father had never rung completely true to her, or to Bea. People can change, she told herself. Jessica decided she could stand to hear any of those things because none of that would be worth losing David over. Not even close.

David took a long, labored breath. "You remember when I fell out of the tree?" he whispered. "How my bruises went away?"

The bruises. Jessica's lips parted. She realized that David was going to take her to a deeper place than she had imagined, a place she herself had buried since his fall. She felt scared.

"I remember," she said.

"Well, I saw the look on your face, the wondering. And you've probably noticed other times, too. How I don't stay scratched. You've noticed, haven't you?"

"I've noticed." Jessica became aware of how hard her nipples had grown, teased by the breeze. The back of her neck felt hot.

"There's a reason for that," David said. "I have a very unusual makeup. Not just me. There are others like me. Mahmoud is another. There's something different about our blood."

Jessica allowed his words to wash over her, and she struggled to hold her panic at bay. What could be different about his blood?

"Are you sick?" she asked.

"No," he said soothingly, brushing his palm across her collarbone. "I'm perfectly healthy. I promise you that. It only means that I heal very quickly. That I never get sick. Wounds vanish overnight.

That's why I avoid doctors. I already understand my blood chemistry, and doctors would only be confused."

Unless she imagined it, Jessica was certain she could hear the thumping of David's heart near her. Yes, she could. Or was it her own? She wanted to hug him and tell him it was all right, that he didn't need to go on. But she had to know more.

"So, that's your big secret . . . ?"

"Part of it," David said.

"What's the other part? I'm with you so far."

She heard him swallow hard. "What you have to understand is, I'm sharing something with you I've never shared with anyone. Not because I cherish secrecy, but because I've been instructed not to. This is all so delicate, Jessica."

"Who told you not to? Is it like a . . . government thing?" The question sounded silly to her, but what else could it be?

"No," he said. "Not like that. It's hard for me to explain. In fact . . . I can't really explain, not verbally. If I told you everything now, flat out, you'd think me insane. You'd have me put away. But the alternative will be very traumatic for you. And I'm sorry for that. I wish I knew of another way."

"David . . ." she said. "Now, you're scaring me."

"I know," he said quietly. "I'm sorry."

For a long time, they were silent. Jessica no longer heard the generator or the flurry of nocturnal life outside. All she heard was the silence of her waiting. Their hearts danced.

"You know," he said, "this is one instance I'm glad you're a woman of faith. I really am. I'm going to ask you to believe in something tonight that your mind will tell you not to believe. But you must. I can't tell you how imperative that is. You must know that I would not lie to you, that you can have faith in my word to you. And in the morning, everything will be all right. Just like I told you when I fell from the tree. Do you remember that?"

Jessica nodded, not speaking.

"We're going to make a passage tonight, Jessica. Both of us. Our faith in each other, and our love, will be our light on this path. By morning, we'll have witnessed a true miracle. I guarantee you that. We will."

Jessica couldn't think of anything to say. She realized that her toes and knuckles were curled tight. Her entire frame was tense. David had never spoken this way to her. No one had ever spoken this way to her. Her mind was too unsettled to process what he was saying, to respond at all.

Abruptly, David sat up. She saw him hang his head, staring at the floor. She saw him wipe his eyes. Then, painstakingly, he stood naked at his full height beside the bed, a far-off shadow.

"Mi vida," he said, "I have to stop talking now. I'm going to draw myself a cool bath and sit in the tub for a few moments. Okay?"

Jessica was relieved. Taking a bath was a very normal thing to do, and the thought of the routine returned her to the sense of reality that had been fleeing as David spoke.

"Sounds like a good idea to me," she said.

He leaned over the bed and kissed her forehead, so gently she could barely feel his lips. "We'll talk some more a little later. And remember—by morning, everything will be fine. Just like before. I promise you."

Jessica watched him walk, in darkness, to the bathroom. He closed the door, then she saw warm light stream across the wooden floor. It seemed to her that a long time had passed before she heard him turn on the water for the tub.

In that time, inexplicably, she had the sense that she could open the bathroom door and he wouldn't be there at all.

Dawit sat on the rim of the tub, struggling to calm his shaking fingers as he grasped the hunting knife he'd hidden beneath the tub earlier, while Jessica was reading outside. He saw his own face, elongated and exaggerated, reflected in the shiny blade. Tonight, he would experience his personal moment of self-discovery.

Among his Life brothers, a small number had learned to worship and conquer pain. They conducted drumming ceremonies with swords and knives, amputating their own limbs, sawing through flesh and bone with maniacal grins on their faces. They culminated with disembowelment, mimicking what they had all witnessed Khaldun perform on himself the first night in the temple. A few of them went further, subjecting themselves to decapitation, a gruesomeness that turned Dawit's stomach. The severed head always withered away, and, over a period of twenty-four hours, a new one grew at its old stump. During its formation, the new head was a mass of bloody flesh and bones. For some reason, severed heads always grew back without hair, even eyebrows. Bald Life brothers, the beheaded, were highly respected.

These acts were considered the height of bravery.

Each rebirth, these exhibitionists believed, helped cleanse their souls. Dawit had always considered them foolish, and Khaldun himself never watched their bloody rituals, dismissing them as childish spectacle. But Dawit recalled their ceremonies and grins now, and he admired their courage.

Dawit had considered many methods of proving his condition to Jessica; a gunshot to his head, poisoning himself, leaping from a great height. No method, he believed, would be so effective as what Khaldun had done. His recovery would defy all explanation, and she would have no choice but to believe.

The tub was already a quarter filled with water. He must hurry, since the beating water was meant to cover the sound of his own cries. He, who had killed so many, must find the will to commit the same butchery against his own flesh. He must not shy from the pain. He must welcome it. He must revel in it.

Dawit extended his arms fully outward, grasping the knife with both hands, its blade pointing at his belly. The Japanese variation was hara-kiri, the ultimate act of sacrifice. His Life brothers called it The Cleansing. A union with the knife.

"I do not fear the pain," Dawit said aloud.

A full minute passed. Then, he plunged.

"David? Did you call me?"

Jessica wondered if she had dozed off, but she wasn't sure. She heard the water running in the bathroom, the monotony of the sound growing overbearing. She was more sleepy than she'd imagined she would be, considering the strange things David had just said. Even though he'd only been gone a few minutes (that's what it felt like, anyway; she couldn't be sure), already their conversation had taken on a surreal texture in her memory—as though, just maybe, she'd dreamed it.

Suddenly, a practical consideration swept Jessica's consciousness, bad news to complement bad news. She'd left her birth control pills at home, and she hadn't taken one that morning. Damn. She was so good about remembering, but David hadn't thought to pack her peach-colored daily dispenser and she hadn't thought to check. Realistically, she could get pregnant this weekend; her doctor had warned her that the minipills she used, which didn't have estrogen, needed to be taken religiously at the same time every day to be effective. So much for that. David's sperm was roaming unchecked inside of her now.

But that thought, as soon as it came, was forgotten.

David's sperm. David's blood. If something was different about David's blood, did that mean it might affect Kira? Did he have some sort of genetic defect, like sickle-cell anemia? Was it something Alex should study?

I never get sick. Wounds vanish overnight.

Jessica's naked body was overrun by goosepimples. He had much more to tell her, he'd said. What could it be? What could sound more crazy than what he had already said? She no longer knew what to prepare for. There was no way to prepare at all.

Again, Jessica was certain she heard David's voice from the bathroom. Not calling her, exactly. A sound.

"David?" she called, propping herself on her elbows.

Only the stream of water answered. She wondered, for the first time, exactly how long he had been in there. It seemed to her that the water had been running for a long time, maybe fifteen minutes. Why did it seem he'd been gone so long?

Suddenly, Jessica thought of Uncle Billy in her mother's tub, dying, the water running over the rim and into the hallway. She remembered the way Bea had described the bloody gash at his temple. The thought scared her. She felt a momentary panic as she realized she was alone and nude in a strange place, in the dark.

Why hadn't David answered?

Jessica found David's T-shirt at the foot of the bed and slid it over her head, wearing it inside out. She slipped her feet into her Nikes, which were still damp from the afternoon, and stood up to shuffle toward the bathroom. This close, the sound of the water was nearly deafening. She knocked twice on the door.

"David? I thought I heard you say something."

The door was unlocked. She eased it open and peeked inside.

David had fallen asleep in the tub, his head turned away from her, and the running water was creeping up to his chin. Another inch and the water would be running onto the floor, just like with Uncle Billy. How had David managed to turn the water pink?

Jessica took two steps forward. She meant to turn off the faucet. She meant to lean over and tousle David's hair to wake him. She'd thought it might be nice to climb in with him.

That was when David's head snapped around and she finally saw his face. He was slack-jawed, his eyes wide but fluttering oddly. Though he was looking right at her, he wasn't seeing her. He raised his arm from the tub, pulling out a dripping knife he allowed to clatter to the floor.

The water wasn't pink, she could see now. Near David, it swirled deep red. The closer she moved, the more red and murky the water. The red was coming from him.

"I'm sorry, Jessica," David gasped.

She stared back down at the knife, and she knew.

Jessica couldn't stop screaming.

▪ 29

Jessica was startled by the sound of a fanatical woman's wounded wailing echoing against the trees behind her, until she realized the sound was coming from her. She sloshed through the saw grass, nearly losing her footing in the knee-high water when she stumbled across something hard beneath the muddy surface. The beam from her flashlight skipped wildly from lilypads to grass stalks to isolated tree trunks, all looking large and forbidding. Another wrenching sob made her shoulders heave, and she had to wipe her eyes with her forearm because she couldn't see for her tears. The flashlight pointed uselessly into the dense, dark sky.

"Help me . . ." she said hoarsely. "Oh, Jesus . . . someone please come help me . . . David is . . ."

Her mind wouldn't finish the thought. Instead, another sob rose from her chest and nearly doubled her over.

She didn't know what she'd expected to find out here at the water's edge. It was as though she'd thought this was a movie where she would run to the beach and see an ocean liner floating in the distance, and all she would have to do was build a bonfire and wave her flashlight, and paratroopers would come floating down. Or she could peer out and spot a nearby island with a fireplace flickering through someone's window, and she could yell out—water carried voices farther, didn't it?—and someone would peek out and say *Joe-Bob, I think I hear something.*

Something unseen splashed in the water five feet in front of Jessica, and the sound made her scream and leap back. No, she wasn't in one of those movies. She was in a fucking swamp, surrounded by snakes and alligators and God-knows-what-else. It seemed unbelievable that an airboat from the mainland had dropped them off here just a few hours before. A few hours. And now everything was all wrong, and no airboat would come to her no matter how long she screamed into the night.

Her feet were being sucked into the soft mud, and each time she took a step, the gunk nearly pulled off her untied shoes. Mosquitoes were biting her all over, and viciously—her face, her arms, her legs, her bare buttocks. Mosquitoes were raining on her.

Sucking her blood.

She thought about the blood everywhere, on the bathroom linoleum, in the tub, on the bedsheet she'd tied around his middle to hold his insides in because, yes, his insides were falling out through that mess he'd made in his belly, and when she finished vomiting in the sink she tied the sheet into a tight, tight knot around David's middle like they would have done on *Emergency!* when she watched it as a kid. And the white sheet soaked through, just like that, into crimson. The Quicker Picker-Upper.

She could smell it even here, the blood. It was on her hands, on her shirt. The blood smell blended with the smell of wet rot all around her, and she imagined her feet were drowned in blood. She shined the flashlight at the water to be sure, and all she could see was a pool of black filled with white specks.

The mosquitoes pulled her from her trance. Eating her alive, her mother always said. Yes, they were. With another scream, she ran out of the saw-grass bed until she reached the beach. Her feet kicked up sand, which clung to her damp legs and pelted her face.

Then, somehow, she was on her knees. She'd fallen. She collapsed onto her palms and wept. She remembered to pray again. She had been praying so long and so hard.

Help me, Jesus. Please don't let him be dead. Please, oh please, let him make it through the night.

At that moment, Jessica had forgotten that David would have to make it through the night and all of the next day, and through an airboat ride, and through a journey to some hospital bound to be far, far away. She kept thinking he needed to make it through the night, until morning, that was all. And he'd be all right. Hadn't he said something like that? If he just made it to morning, everything would be fine.

She needed to check on him. She needed to go back.

Jessica was gasping to breathe when she made it up to the cabin and kneeled on the blood-spattered floor beside the bathtub. She hadn't realized she'd been thinking *please, please, please* over and over again until David's eyes opened and the thought turned into *thank you, thank you, thank you.*

David didn't say anything, but he looked like he was trying to smile. His head was still resting on the pillow she'd propped up on the rim because she couldn't think of how else to make him comfortable after she drained out the tub. She would have liked to carry him out of the tub herself, but she didn't think she would be strong enough even if she acquired that superhuman strength people get in a crisis that she'd read about in *Reader's Digest*; and, besides, what if she was carrying him across the room and his intestines spilled out? She'd seen something—she didn't know what—some soft, bloody organ poking through the hole in his belly.

David hadn't said anything in a long time, since he'd told her that he was sorry, right in the beginning when she first found him. He'd been crying before, with her, the two of them crying hysterically, but he looked too weak to cry now. It wasn't all the blood or even her shock that made Jessica cry. It was David looking so scared, writhing when she touched him, screaming for the pain to go away.

Jessica squeezed his hand, and she felt him move his fingers inside of hers. "I'm here now. I won't leave you," she said. "You just hold on. Okay? Just hold on."

David was fighting to swallow. Then, when he did, he opened his mouth to try to speak. No sound came out. *I waited*, his silent lips said. His head sank back into the damp pillow, and his mouth closed again.

Jessica didn't know what else to do, so she began to sing the most cheerful church song she could think of: "Jee-sus loves me . . . This I know . . ."—she swallowed back a sob—"Cuz the Bi-ble . . . Tells me so . . ."

A very rational voice in Jessica's mind spoke to her in such a calm tone that it transfixed her. Your husband is about to die, the voice said, and there is nothing you can do about it except sit here and hold his hand, so that is what you must do.

Jessica squeezed David's fingers, but he didn't squeeze back. Pursing her lips, she gazed at his eyes. They had fallen shut. His eyes had been closed when she came back, she remembered. His eyes had never been closed before she went outside.

I waited, he said.

"David?" she whispered. "Honey, please . . ."

No, he would not open his eyes again. His chest had stopped moving, so his breathing was gone. Most of his blood was in the tub, dripping down the open drain. His heartbeat was gone.

David was gone.

Jessica cradled her husband's head against her breastbone. "You don't have to be scared anymore, baby," she said. "See? See? The hurt's all gone. It's all gone now."

That was all that mattered to her shutdown mind. Then the rational voice inside whispered to her, nudging: David is dead.

The fanatical woman's strange wailing jarred her again.

*　　　*　　　*

Dawit's first sight when he opened his eyes was Jessica. She was sitting half naked on the bathroom floor in a bloody T-shirt, her legs spread straight out in front of her, her head resting against the wall as she slept. Her face was not at rest. In fact, he barely knew that face; it was ashen and crusty, her eyelids swollen, her mouth half open as though she'd fallen asleep in the midst of a moan.

Still, Dawit smiled. He could not move his head yet to do much more, or reach out to touch her, but he smiled. It was a privilege to be so loved. An honor. His eyes overran with tears he didn't have the strength to wipe away. He felt as though he would need to sleep for days, but he knew he could not. It must be dawn, and there was so much to do. So much to say.

"Jessica," he rasped.

Her eyelids flinched, but she did not answer.

A few minutes passed. Finally, Dawit strained to raise his hand to his tender stomach, where he felt so much pressure that it was a labor to breathe. She must have tied something around him, a tourniquet. Bless her, she had been so desperate to help him! His fingers found a knot in the sheet beneath his rib cage, and he fussed with it until it loosened slightly. There.

The next time Dawit glanced back at Jessica, her eyes were open, regarding him. Her expression had not changed, as though she were dispassionately watching a hallucination.

He smiled again. "I'm sorry I scared you," he whispered.

Jessica sat bolt upright, her eyes darting frantically from her hands to her bloodied shirt to him again. All her confusion and gratitude and fear were written in her face, in her trembling mouth. "I thought I'd lost you," she said with wonder, kneeling beside him, pressing a warm palm to his face. New tears streamed down her cheeks, clearing a path through the the old ones.

Dawit struggled with the knot to untie it, summoning all his strength to arch his back so he could pull the blood-soaked sheet away from his flesh. Alarmed, Jessica grabbed his hands.

"No," she said, holding him with a firm grip. "Shhhh. Don't do that. You're hurt. David, don't. Baby, stop that."

He stared into her eyes. "My wounds heal, Jessica. It's morning now. It's all right." She looked at him, frozen, her eyes squinting with bewilderment. She didn't move as he clawed at the sheet to expose his abdomen. "Look. I heal."

Above his protruding navel, there was a jagged, closed scar. Fading signs of a wider lesion remained at one end, where Dawit had first stabbed himself and twisted the blade while he struggled, through the pain, to carve across his abdomen. It had not been pretty work. He'd only progressed seven or eight inches, roughly halfway, before he began to feel faint from the agony of his task.

The scars looked old, as if they were from many years before. The blood that remained on Dawit's skin, while it still appeared fresh, was not seeping from the closed wounds. He wiped his palm across his stomach, cleaning some of the blood away.

Jessica was leaning over the tub, peering at his flesh closely. She touched him, gently at first, running her hand across the scar, then she began to prod. Dawit felt a burning sensation and hissed. "*Cuidado.* I'm still sore, Jess," he said.

Jessica drew her hand away, staring wild-eyed at his face. Her mouth fell open and closed as she struggled for words. "I don't . . . But I saw . . ."

Dawit took her hand and kissed it. "Remember what I said? My blood isn't normal. My body isn't normal. My wounds heal. In an hour or so, even these scars will be gone. I'm all right, Jessica. Just like I said, remember? I said that by morning, I would be all right. I had to show you."

" . . . Show me?" she whimpered, still helplessly confused.

He nodded. "I'm sorry. It was the only way."

Jessica blinked uncontrollably. Then, a guttural sound rose in her throat, turning into a rage-filled scream, and she began to pound Dawit's chest with her fists. Her blows hurt, sapping away what little energy Dawit had gained. He cried out and fumbled to grab her fists, to hold them tightly. "No, baby," he said. "Please don't. That hurts."

Jessica gasped, as though he'd struck her. She stared at David with reddened eyes that were wide, frantic. Then, her pupils drifted upward, gazing toward the ceiling, and she collapsed against the tub with heaving, wretched sobs.

"It's all right, Jess. It's all right. I'm here. I'm never going to leave you," Dawit said, reaching over to drape one arm across her shoulder. Jessica flung her arms around him, burying him, and sobbed into his ear. Her grip around his neck was so tight that he felt he would choke, but he tolerated the discomfort. He stroked her matted, sandy hair. His own tears stung his eyes.

"It's okay, baby. I'm sorry. I'm here. I'm here forever."

Though she would try many times, Jessica could never fully remember the details of her first day with David after she watched him die.

Her first memory was being in the cabin's bed, somehow washed, wearing her own fresh-smelling nightshirt. A cool washcloth was draped across her forehead, and occasionally she felt David take it away and bring it back, damper and cooler than before. The blood smell was gone from her, but she could still smell it on him.

"You have a fever," she heard David say, and it reminded her of being a little girl in her bedroom, when she would stay home from school with the television playing *Partridge Family* reruns, and her mother would make her sit up to chew bittersweet, orange-flavored children's aspirin. And she'd dab cool water across her forehead, just like David was doing now.

She slept a lot. That much she knew. She awakened when she heard a noise—the clatter of some pot from the kitchenette, the running water from the bathroom, the cabin door opening or closing—and she would open her eyes and stare up at the wooden planks across the ceiling.

Once, she smelled food and it nearly made her vomit.

"Are you hungry?" she heard David's voice ask, floating somewhere above her. She shook her head without opening her eyes.

It seemed to her that she must have been lying there for many days, an eternity, though the daylight was always there. At some point, David leaned across the bed to close the heavy curtains across the picture window, making the room darker, and she remembered being glad.

And she was glad to smell his scent, his perspiration, the freshness of his shampoo, even the chemical pine scent from some disinfectant that had cleaved itself to him. She knew those smells. The blood smell, that was the one she hadn't known. That was the smell that pitched her into semiconsciousness, the one her mind retreated from, lulling her to a calmer place.

At last, David sat at the edge of the bed and kneaded her shoulder until she opened her eyes. He was wearing a UM T-shirt and cutoff shorts. He smelled like smoke. She could remember being confused about why he smelled like smoke. Much later, he would explain that he had burned the blanket and bedsheet because of all of the blood, and he'd paid Mantooth extra to replace them. She never knew what explanation he'd given him.

David was smiling at her. She was convinced by now that his image was part of some cruel, elaborate dream, so she did not smile back. Or, had the blood and moaning all been part of an equally elaborate nightmare? She didn't know which.

"Almost time to go, Jess. The boat will be here soon. We'll go pick up Kira, okay? Won't you be glad to see Kira?"

Kira. Oh, yes. Thinking of Kira, Jessica felt her mind emerging from its protective clouds. Kira was at her mother's. The weekend was over. It was time to go back home.

Jessica reached over to David and lifted his T-shirt so she could see his stomach. She saw a crooked path of hairlessness under the cluster of wiry hairs growing around his navel, nothing more. Nothing. She blinked, waiting to feel something. Whatever it was didn't come.

"You didn't have to do it that way," she said. David leaned closer. He hadn't heard her. She struggled to raise her voice slightly. "I wish you hadn't done it this way, David."

David gazed at her and nodded solemnly. "Okay," he said, "I'm sorry." He kissed her open palm. "I'm really sorry."

"You said there's more."

"Yes," he said. "Later. We don't have time now. Wait until we get back to Ochopee. I'll talk to you in the car."

David tried to stand up straight, but she held tight to his hand, pulling him back down toward her. Her words came without thought. "You have to say thank you to God, David. You told me we'd both see a miracle, and we did. You can't see a miracle without saying thank you. That's all He asks. That's all."

David stared at her tenderly and touched her cheek with his index finger. She saw a struggle in his face, words wanting to come, but he didn't speak at all. Then, he gently pulled his fingers from her grasp and stood up, walking away.

▪ 30

"Daddy! Mommy!" Kira cried, flinging the front door open to run out to the van as they drove into Bea's driveway. Jessica's heart surged to see her daughter dressed up in new matching purple shorts and a tanktop, her hair parted into two puffballs secured with purple barrettes.

Bea followed closely behind Kira, laughing. Bea was always overjoyed to see Jessica come home from vacation in one piece. And Alex would be next, Jessica knew. Her BMW was parked beneath the shade of the front yard ficus tree. Jessica was so glad to see them all, and yet it was a strain to pull the latch to try to open her door.

"Just stay in the car," David said, patting her knee, before opening his own door and climbing out. He called to Kira. "Come here, Duchess. What did Grandma do to your hair?"

Kira giggled as David lifted her into the air, hoisted her over his shoulders, and began to spin her around. Her laughs sounded nearly hysterical—half joy, half fright.

"David, you're going to drop that child," Bea muttered, walking past him to lean into Jessica's window. "Get your lazy behind out of this car. Dinner's waiting. How was the swamp?"

Before Jessica could open her mouth to answer, David walked behind Bea and knelt down, easing Kira to the ground. "The swamp was great, but poor Jess came down with something. She's not feeling well."

"Mommy's sick?" Kira asked.

"Just a little cold or something."

Bea reached over to touch Jessica's forehead. The gesture was so familiar, so warm, that Jessica longed to tell David she wanted to stay at her mother's house tonight. Just for one night, that was all.

"You've got a temperature. Snake didn't bite you, did it?" Bea asked. "You look worn out, Jessica. I don't know about this camping out in the swamplands. That's for white folks."

Weakly, Jessica shook her head and smiled. "No snakebite," she said, "but worn out, yes. Definitely."

Alex appeared next in her window, wearing a smart mauve dress from church. "Hey, girl. What's wrong?"

Jessica wanted to shrink from their stares. What would they see in her face? So much had happened. So much had changed. How could people go through changes and not show it on their faces? How could soldiers leave battlefields and simply go home to their families, after all they had seen?

"I'm just tired," Jessica said.

"Go get your bag, Kira," David said, playfully swatting her backside. "We need to get Mommy home to bed."

"Lord, well at least let me fix you some plates. Don't you leave me with all this food. Come help me, David," Bea said.

Alex stayed by the van window, smelling of Giorgio, the scent she saved for Sundays. She looked worried, gazing into Jessica's eyes. Jessica glanced away from her sister.

"Everything okay?" Alex asked.

"I don't think I'm cut out for camping," Jessica said.

"That bad, huh?"

Jessica nodded. When would her brain wake up?

"Well, I'm just glad you two are back. I couldn't believe it when Mom told me you were off to some island somewhere without a telephone. I just think of those slasher movies. I don't think I could go for that."

Jessica couldn't think of a response.

"You sure you're okay? Everything okay with David?"

"Why would you ask that?" Jessica asked, looking at her.

"Just asking, that's all. He seems like he's in a big hurry to go home. And he's smiling too much. He only smiles when something's wrong."

"There's nothing wrong," Jessica said, wondering how convincing she sounded to someone as insightful as Alex. She realized what a profound burden David's secret would be. She kept very few secrets from Bea, and none from her sister. Theirs was not a family of secrets. She'd even mentioned the incident with Mahmoud to Alex, and David's explanation. Now, there would be a barrier between them.

"Call me later if you feel like it. I met somebody last night. No big deal yet, but he's an immigration lawyer. . . . Well, I'll tell you later," Alex said, smiling.

Ordinarily, a love interest would have been big news to Jessica. Now, she had to force herself to feign a reaction. Nothing in her life, she began to realize, would ever be able to affect her the way it had before. Everything would seem trite and inconsequential compared to the past twenty-four hours.

During the drive home, Jessica tried hard to listen to Kira's excited chatter about how she'd spent her weekend. How the little boy next door was a meanie, how he'd broken the toy she got in her McDonald's Happy Meal. How Grandma watched The Lion King on video with her for the hundredth time. David filled up Jessica's silences, telling Kira about the woods and the cabin and the airboat.

Jessica's thoughts could not drift far away from the extraordinary story David had told her during the ninety-minute drive from Ochopee to her mother's house. He'd begun after taking a deep breath, and his tale had been barely punctuated by any pauses as he spoke, his eyes hidden behind his sunglasses as he stared straight ahead at the road.

My name is DAH-weet. I was born in what is now called Ethiopia nearly five hundred years ago. I am an immortal. There are fifty-eight others like me. Our blood lives forever, and our bodies heal. We do not age. We were not born this way, and our condition is not genetic. We underwent a Ritual.

We do not have extraordinary strength, and it is not our purpose to harm others. We are merely a race of scholars. Most of us choose not to mingle among mortals, but some of us do. We love, and we have families. I have had wives and children before you. I have either outlived them or been forced to abandon them.

We have a Covenant that forbids us to reveal our truth. For what I am telling you, I expect someday to be punished. I take that risk because I love you. I have been told that it is time for me to leave you, and I cannot. I hope we can all leave together.

David had also said much more frightening things while she sat and listened to his words. He told her that Mahmoud had been sent to spy on their family, that he had been watching them, probably for many months. He might even have wiretaps or monitors in the house, David said, so they could not speak any further of this unless they were somewhere private, like the cave.

Mahmoud may suspect what I have told you, so you must be very, very careful, Jessica. Our Covenant dictates that no one can know. You are a reporter, and therefore he would consider you highly dangerous to the safety of our entire Brotherhood. I am afraid he might try to hurt you. That is why we must go very soon. And we must watch Kira at all times. Our lives will be different now, but until we go we must behave as though nothing has changed.

Jessica had asked questions: Where would they go? Could they ever come back? What was the Ritual they underwent?

David said he was no longer sure about going to France, and he suggested Senegal, saying he considered the nation and its people among the most beautiful in Africa. There, Kira could refine her French and learn Wolof at the same time.

About the Ritual, he said nothing. But she sensed, in a way she had learned from living with him for so many years, that he had purposely chosen to keep silent on that point. So far, her questions far outnumbered David's answers.

What was in their blood? If he had not been born immortal, did that mean that anyone could become immortal?

Thinking of this as she rode with Kira and David in the van, Jessica felt her pulse quicken. She tried to let the thought go. She knew she would need time to absorb everything, so she couldn't dwell too much on any one aspect. She couldn't allow herself to think too much at all, or her fear would drown her. She wondered how she hadn't lost her mind already.

"Are we almost home, Mommy?" Kira's question drew Jessica out of her thoughts, but she felt dazed.

Where were they? David had just coasted off of the I–95 expressway ramp to Biscayne Boulevard, so they were ten minutes from home. Jessica was comforted to see all the signs of stable life she'd known—the Shell gas station, the convenience store, the empty glass office buildings glaring in the Sunday twilight. She was mesmerized by the normalcy passing her window.

"We're just about there, Duchess," David answered for her.

Jessica was anxious to return home, to crawl into bed, but she wondered if it might overwhelm her to suddenly compare who she was now to the person she had been only two days before, living in the same house. Would the idea of wiretaps in the bedroom make it impossible for her to sleep, to hold her husband?

And who was her husband, really? Who was he?

As usual, their secluded neighborhood calmed the fever in Jessica's mind. The shaded roadway was a sedative. She saw the DeNights' ten-year-old grandson riding his bicycle, and she could hear the jangling music of a nearby ice-cream truck. Her life might spin out of control soon, but for today, at least, she was returning to the sanctuary of what she had known before.

"Yayy! Look, Mommy. He's back!"

Jessica followed Kira's pointing finger as the van pulled into their driveway, and she smiled gratefully.

Teacake was posted on the front porch, his elegant tail curled around his front paws, waiting for them to come home.

▪ 31

After the night Raymond Jacobs never came home from Burger King, mornings were the worst time in the Jacobs house. In the mornings, Jessica woke up and heard muffled sobs through her mother's door. Bea seemed too tired to be sad as the day wore on, after she picked up Jessica from their neighbor's house and asked her how school went (although her eyes strayed somewhere else when Jessica tried to tell her, and for a long time Jessica knew her mother wasn't really listening). Bea cooked dinner, the family thought private thoughts in front of the television set, and then everyone went to bed, usually without tears.

Tears came in the mornings.

One morning, fifteen days after her father died, Jessica went into hysterics. The funeral was over. The hams and macaroni casseroles and sweet-potato pies people had brought to the house were mostly gone. The flowers had wilted. His death was an old thing, not a new thing. But, for some reason, Jessica woke up from a dream about riding on her father's bouncing knee, and a certain part of her didn't remember he was dead. She didn't remember as she looked at her Raggedy Ann and Andy clock and saw that it was only a little after six. She didn't remember as she slipped into her powder-blue house shoes and padded out of her room.

But when she passed the living room window on her way to the kitchen, where she planned to fix herself a bowl of Captain Crunch, she noticed a white car in their driveway. Whose car was that?

The memory, worse than any nightmare, stunned her: It was the car their neighbor, Mrs. Houston, was lending to them. The blue station wagon was gone now. The station wagon got wrecked when Daddy was killed in the accident.

Jessica cried so hard, her mother let her stay home from school that day.

Years later, the morning syndrome was repeating itself with Jessica. One morning, she woke up and saw David's bath towel tossed across the bedspread near her feet. She called out, "David, come hang up this wet towel before you get the room all musty!" She felt annoyed, just like she would have before. That was all.

For five whole minutes, sometimes staring straight at his face, she wouldn't think about it. Then, her stomach would plunge as she relived her bloody night with him. And she would gaze into his eyes and realize that those eyes were five hundred years old, that they belonged to a man she barely knew, and her heart would drop. Her husband, the father of her child, was a man she barely knew.

The first few nights, which Jessica hardly remembered, she couldn't bear to share a bed with him. She sat on the sofa downstairs, pretending to watch TV with Teacake on her lap, and she stayed wide awake each night. At bedtime, David stood on the stairs and tried to call her to him, but she only shook her head. Even talking to him was a struggle now, and she stopped trying once Kira was asleep. He knew to leave her alone.

So Jessica held herself, shivering sporadically in the warm room that was hers and yet no longer hers. She felt a deadness, a paralysis; a strange dream had enveloped her, leaving her frozen in this fog that used to be her life. Her mind was offering rational answers, trying to free her. Had it all been an illusion? Had David's horrible wound been less serious than it looked? Was David trying to trick her? But why?

Jessica couldn't even bring herself to pray about it, not at first, because her prayers seemed like empty rituals. David flew in the face of everything she'd known or believed.

The only real answer, the consistent answer, was that David was who he said he was, and she had seen what she had seen. He had died and come back. He would never die, ever.

Once she decided to try to accept this, Jessica felt the paralysis fading. She could even lie with David at night; she just couldn't touch him. Not yet. Even though she could feel how much he wanted her to in his cautious silence across the expanse of their bed.

"See here? This is me," David said after he took the damp towel away, slipping an old photograph into her hand. (He must have been relieved to hear her bitch at him, she realized; irritation was better than silence.) He raised his finger to his lips, a reminder that she couldn't respond out loud because of a spy. Real conversation had to wait.

The browning old photograph was ragged on the edges, but the image was almost startlingly clear: six black musicians in tuxedos, posing with their instruments at The Jazz Brigade's Summer Stomp, 1926. David's hair was cut shorter than he wore it now, slicked down, but she recognized him standing in the center of the photo with his clarinet, posing beside a man who wasn't dressed like the others, maybe a bystander or a fan. This was really David. In a photograph that was seventy years old. The thought was a kick in her stomach, and she cradled herself in the bed.

David looked alarmed. "What's wrong?"

She shook her head. "Nothing," she said.

Jessica had tried, in the past week, not to be shocked by David's mementos, or at least not to show it. She wanted to encourage his reminiscences because she knew she needed to hear them. This was a journey, David had said; and she was taking it with him whether she liked it or not. She tried to enjoy the moments they stole away to the cave after Kira was in bed, when he would sit beside her and begin to talk. If she felt overwhelmed, Jessica distanced herself by pretending she was listening to a history lesson. She'd spent enough years as a reporter encouraging sources to pour out their sorrows that she had become good at pulling back when she needed to. It was a survival tactic.

So, she didn't lose her head when David showed her a wrinkled program from the Kärntnerthor Theater in Vienna with a date reading 1824.

"Mahmoud and I got tickets by chance, through the man whose sons we tutored, a music patron," David told her in the hush of the cave, brushing his finger across the yellowed paper. "I wasn't happy with our seats, but it was a marvelous concert.

Startling. And he was there himself, as you know. You've heard how he had to face the audience to see our applause. Absolutely true. He was deaf by then. He died a couple of years later."

"Who?" Jessica asked, embarrassed by her ignorance.

David grinned. "Beethoven. This was the debut of his Ninth."

Jessica would experience many of these moments of unreality. Another night, David showed her a faded, handwritten document inscribed with a date from the 1840s for a slave named Seth, who was the property of a Lowell Mason in Louisiana. Rust-colored fold marks crisscrossed the paper. Though the words were hard to make out, Jessica recognized David's handwriting. "This was my pass," he explained. "I wrote myself a pass when I ran away. The ink faded here at the top because it got wet."

"Did you get away?" she asked. The whole while, Jessica's brain was telling her it was all right, she was merely asking a historical question. It wasn't like her husband, the man sitting here, had actually ever been a slave more than a hundred years ago.

"No. They caught me. And the woman who came with me."

"What happened?" Jessica asked.

David sighed, sifting the short hair on Jessica's forehead through his fingertips. "Well," he began, swallowing, "we were unarmed, but we fought them. And she died."

The sorrow in David's voice was tangible. Jessica could feel it moving through him, throughout the cave, and it shattered her mental defenses. This was David talking. Not only had he had other wives before her, he had *loved* other women who lived before her great-grandparents were born. And this long-dead slave woman still lived with him, in his thoughts. His past was as real as the blood she would find if she scratched the surface of his skin. It wasn't history. It was present still.

"What was the woman's name?" she whispered.

"Her name . . ." David started to speak, but his lips clamped shut and he drew a deep, difficult breath. He shook his head and squeezed Jessica's hand, silent.

His grief, at that moment, made her swell toward him. "And you've never told anybody any of this, David?"

"It isn't permitted. You're the first," he breathed.

"I don't know how you could live so many years and not tell anyone. I don't know how you could do that."

"I don't know either," he said.

"Thank you for choosing me. For trusting me."

David moved as if to kiss her, but stopped himself. "Her name was Adele," he said instead. He told Jessica about how the five men caught them when they stopped to take a drink at a river. And how they violated and lynched her while David watched. Afterward, for long minutes of silence, Jessica tried to think of words that wouldn't sound small and meaningless. She couldn't. She was horrified for him, and for her own faceless ancestors.

"For vengeance, I fought in the war, and I slaughtered men. Many men, Jessica. I died many times over," David said in a hollow voice Jessica had never heard. "I call that time the Century of Blood. I lost my soul."

"You can't lose your soul, baby."

"When you have seen enough. And done enough. Oh, yes."

She stroked the side of his neck with her index finger. How would she ever have managed all the hate David had felt, and must be feeling still? Thinking of all the men he said he'd killed, she wondered if maybe David had really lost his soul, after all. She would have too. Jessica had read The Autobiography of Frederick Douglass, and she remembered how wretched he'd felt as a child, even though he'd never known anything but slavery. She'd thought it must have been worse for people like her own ancestor from Ghana, whom Bea had told her about, who was kidnapped and brought to the United States as an adult, as a man with his own life, in the 1840s.

"What year did you come here, David?" she asked.

"Eighteen forty-four."

Jessica's heart spun as she began to realize the weight of David's words. "My great-, great-, great- . . . oh, I forget how many greats back it is—but my ancestor was brought here around that time, even though it was illegal. From Ghana. Isn't that amazing? Think of it. You might have known him. But he was a slave in Georgia. I guess you never met."

"No, most likely we didn't," David said. "But I do know him, Jessica. I know his heart. As much as I know my own."

"How could you stay here after all you'd been through?" Jessica asked. "Couldn't you get the money to go back to Ethiopia, to the others? At least you lived to see the end of slavery, and you had somewhere else to go, a home."

"No, it wasn't money. I could always find work as a tradesman, a skilled laborer, a technician. I was very advanced, understand, and wisdom has always been a precious commodity. Life was backward here. I planned to go home right after the war, and I did visit briefly in the 1890s. Ethiopia was being encroached upon by the

Italians, and I went to fight, to fend them off. But I returned here."

"Why?"

He sighed. "How can I explain? The other Africans here shared my wounds. Does that make sense to you? Just as I could never illustrate to any mortal all I have seen and felt in my lifetime, I could never expect my Life brothers in Lalibela to understand all I have seen and felt here."

David sighed again, a ragged sound, and she realized he was going to cry soon. He went on: "I was enslaved only a brief time. Yet, that short time, in its cruelty, stands out in my memory. I have never suffered more greatly than I did watching the senseless way Adele died, like a hunted boar. When my first wife died long ago, in Ethiopia, I thought I knew grief. But until you have witnessed the death of a loved one to another man's violence, you know nothing of grief. And when you do, it lives with you and changes everything you thought you were. When I was a boy, I watched my father lose his life, and I became a warrior in my heart. And when Adele was killed? I still don't know what that made of me. I am afraid to know."

Jessica blinked, rapt.

David took a long, labored breath. "Adele was the only glimpse of beauty in the midst of so much ugliness. Men who emptied their lusts inside of her still called her less than human. These same men sold their own children, and hers, as chattel. She told me these things at night, when we talked, as you and I are talking now. One by one, infants were wrested from her arms. And so, as much as Adele yearned to love a child, we did not dare create one because it would not be ours.

"I remember these events as well as I do eating breakfast this morning. It was a very short time ago. Yet, I have lived to see it buried. And Adele, and all of us, treated as though our pain was imaginary. It was not imaginary. It is with me every day."

Even in the darkness, Jessica could see David's frame shaking violently as he spoke. Suddenly, he sobbed and collapsed against her. For the next hour, he wept in her arms.

Maybe it was only a temporary phase, maybe it would pass, but at the times Jessica wasn't utterly swallowed by her fears of the future, she found herself in awe of David. It was like the awe she'd felt early in their courtship, when his intellect became more plain each day. Her new awe was even more keen.

One night, he brought the old Jazz Brigade photograph to the cave and told her how he started the group with a couple of buddies who used to have jam sessions in his living room. He pointed each man out to her, telling her their names, laughing about things they said and did.

"What was your name then?" she asked.

"Still Seth. Seth Tillis. They called me Spider."

He had this whole wonderful life as a musician, and a wife and children, and then the people from Ethiopia he called Searchers came. Just like that, he had to go. That was exactly what was happening now, he told her.

After hearing the story, Jessica began to unbutton her blouse. Then, she hooked her fingers to the fly of his jeans, resting the heel of her palm against the lump there.

"In the cave?" David asked, surprised.

She only smiled.

Standing over the bathroom sink later to shake dried leaves from her hair, Jessica wondered if this new ardor was a form of hysteria. Her eyes found the mirror; there, in her own troubled face, were the doubts. Was she clinging to David's physical body because that was all she could possess of him, since she believed she was about to lose him? He was becoming a mirage to her, and she was a mirage herself. A stranger in her own body.

One of two things would happen now: He would leave and they might never see him again, or they could run away with him. Either scenario was unthinkable.

But even if they all went to Africa for a year or two, then what? Wouldn't his friend Mahmoud find them again? At some point, wouldn't anyone be able to notice that David wasn't aging? Even Kira would be old enough to ask questions soon.

On these nights, with hard questions gnawing at her peace of mind, Jessica climbed into bed beside her husband and curled around him so tightly that she imagined she could squeeze beneath his flesh like a second covering. Touching him this way, his name and history didn't matter, because she knew him; the familiarity made her doubts vanish. They dissolved inside each other's body heat as though they wore their souls on their skin.

Now, she decided, it was time to learn the core of it all, the one truth he'd left unspoken.

"Tell me about the ritual that made you this way," she whispered to him.

Dawit shook his head firmly, covering her mouth with his palm. Then he sat up, gestured, and they slipped down the stairs and through the kitchen into the yard, following the path to the cave. Teacake followed them. He always settled between Jessica's crossed legs when they sat on the blanket they'd brought inside the cave.

"We call it the Life ritual. Khaldun is the blood's source. It's a passing of the blood."

"Did it hurt?" Jessica asked.

"Cramps and such, for a time. He baked a poisonous bud into loaves of bread and separated us into small groups, then he instructed us to eat. Its effects were swift. We couldn't breathe. We gasped and fainted. Then, as we died, Khaldun performed the Ritual on us, one by one. He recited an incantation and gave us drops of his blood."

"How did you feel when you woke up?"

"I don't remember. We were all in a state of disbelief, I think. I had a headache. I remember being thirsty."

"When you ate the poisoned bread . . . were you afraid?"

"Very," David said. "I've never been more afraid since."

"Then why did you do it?"

At this, David smiled. He reached over to try to pet Teacake, but the cat's head snapped to hiss at him. Why was he so touchy lately? Teacake seemed afraid of David now, as if he knew something had changed. David withdrew his hand.

"Why? A very good question. I've asked myself that many times, believe me. Many times. I just wanted to know . . ."

"Know what?" she asked, fascinated.

"I wanted to know everything," he said.

Jessica could understand that. She felt the same way, just as she wanted to know everything about David now. There wasn't enough time in a week or a month or a lifetime for all the questions she wanted to ask him.

"So, is Khaldun the only one who can do the ritual?"

At this, very suddenly, David met Jessica's eyes. She saw an ardent hopefulness in his face that scared her. "No, Jess," David said gently, his eyes holding her. "I can pass the blood too."

All of her other questions slipped out of Jessica's head. A dreamlike sensation tugged at her, making her lose her mooring in the moment. Her mind was shutting down. All she felt was fatigue, like she could sleep for a week. She knew this feeling; it came when a part of her began to give in to her doubts, reminding her that she no longer had even the simplest understanding of life anymore, that nothing was what it should be.

And that maybe her best times, her happiest days, were already behind her.

"Let's go to sleep, David," she said in a toneless voice.

That night, they slept in the same bed, but their bodies were far apart.

■ 32

Dawit had never particularly cared for Jessica's cat. Teacake shed everywhere, he was more temperamental and aloof than Princess had been, and he was too undisciplined with his claws. Once, after Teacake swatted at Kira and drew blood on her tiny wrist when she was two, Dawit raged and threatened to take the animal to the pound. It sparked one of his worst arguments with Jessica, one he sulked about for days.

But that history was instantly irrelevant the moment Dawit saw Teacake sitting on the porch. Waiting. Alive.

He could catalogue all of the happiest moments in his life—the promise of his marriage to Rana, his unblemished nights with Adele, his studies in Lalibela, the music in Chicago, the birth of Kira, the unequaled relief of his disclosure to Jessica—and the sight of Teacake alive ranked high among them. Dawit had been so preoccupied with nursing Jessica from the trauma of the weekend at the cabin that he'd forgotten to dread the return to the cat he thought he'd killed.

So, he was stunned on two levels to see Teacake. He'd forgotten Teacake was supposed to be dead. And, remembering that, he was amazed to find he was not.

Teacake pranced on the dining room table, mussing Dawit's newspaper in a bid for attention, but Dawit did not rebuke him. He nuzzled the soft fur at Teacake's throat, where he could feel the rough rumbling of the cat's purr. Teacake had shied away from Dawit for a while, apparently skittish from the memory of the injection, but he'd responded well to Dawit's kindness in the past two weeks. In the end, no matter what, pets always forgive.

"Do-It-Yourself Realty," a woman's voice chirped from the speaker on the telephone beside Dawit's elbow, full of that too-pleasant American artifice. For the past two minutes, the line he'd dialed had been ringing unanswered.

That morning, Jessica agreed Dawit could list the house for sale, just to see how it would fare in the marketplace. He bought the materials to post a FOR SALE BY OWNER sign in the front yard as soon as he dropped Kira off at school, and this company's advertisement in the paper claimed it would send someone to photograph the house the same day. By the time Jessica came home from work, it would be done. They would be that much closer.

All he needed was time enough to sell the house. He could not go back to his colony for ancient bars of gold or rare paintings, so he could ill afford to walk away from something so valuable at the time they needed money most. If Mahmoud challenged him, Dawit thought, he would explain he was selling the house because Jessica had always wanted a larger one, and she could use the money to move wherever she pleased. You know women cannot conduct business, Mahmoud, he would say. Let me at least give her this.

Surely Mahmoud would grant him the courtesy of a second visit before attempting to carry out his threats against Jessica or Kira. Would Khaldun even give his permission for such a severe tactic? Dawit doubted it; his teacher seemed to value mortal life. He remembered a remark Khaldun had made once, when Dawit returned from the battlefield against the Italians: *What do you gain from it, Dawit? Must a scythe prove itself sharper than a blade of grass? Let grass grow as it will.*

While the Do-It-Yourself clerk described the company's terms and prices on the telephone, Dawit stroked Teacake and kissed his cool nose, hardly listening. Occasionally, he couldn't suppress a small, anxious laugh. Teacake represented a possibility of lasting happiness Dawit had never allowed himself to fathom. Teacake's small beating heart was a promise, a new covenant. *Love that which is constant, like yourself.* Weren't those his teacher's own words? And here was Dawit's solution, unfolding with such simplicity that his mind could barely comprehend it.

Dawit would have the opportunity to watch Kira grow up, even after the Ritual. Berhanu, who had been twelve and his youngest Life brother when he underwent the Ritual, had confounded Khaldun because he was the only one among them who aged. Berhanu grew visibly taller and more masculine with each passing year, until he reached manhood. Then, as with all of them, his aging process stopped. So it would be with lovely Kira, he was certain.

In coming centuries, he and Jessica could have dozens of children together—and, once immortal, might Jessica pass the Living Blood to their offspring, as Khaldun believed? What a blessing if that could be so! Their future children would be immortal without the price of the Ritual; lasting life without the pain of death.

And they would be the first children of the Living Blood.

Dawit tried to banish his disobedient thoughts, but they were too seductive each moment of the day, especially when Teacake was within his sight. Dawit would never again have to wish for death to end his isolation, or envy mortals for the irreversible fact of their mortality. Could this really be?

"So, how's two?" the Do-It-Yourself woman asked.

"Uhm . . . two? For . . . ?"

"We can send the photographer at two."

"Perfect," Dawit said.

"That's a great area. You won't need it, but good luck selling your house."

Dawit smiled. "Thank you. I have a feeling my luck has permanently changed for the better."

Jessica came home at eight, an hour later than she'd told them to expect her, but Dawit was not surprised at her tardiness. On the telephone, he'd detected that her voice was distracted, the way it became when she was away from their home, immersed in that world outside. He did not want to lose her to that world. She insisted upon going to work, even now, and each day Dawit wondered if she might return with uncertainty or loathing in her eyes instead of gladness.

"I'm sorry, baby," she said breathlessly, wrapping her arms around Dawit's neck to kiss him. He savored her cleaving and her scent, closing his eyes. "Drug dealers. The usual."

Kira, though she'd been asking about dinner since the moment Dawit picked her up from school, had insisted on putting off eating until Jessica was home. After finishing a sheet of simple addition problems she'd been assigned as homework, Kira, while waiting, had promptly fallen asleep watching cartoons on a cable channel.

"Mommy's here, sweetheart," Jessica said, prodding her awake. Kira made a face, blinking at her.

Dawit had fixed curried chicken and Ethiopian *enjara* to eat it with (Jessica had complained *enjara* tasted sour to her in the beginning, not like any bread she'd known, but she'd adapted well). The food was barely warm by now. They ate together as Duke Ellington's "Solitude," one of Dawit's favorite pieces, played from the living room stereo. Teacake was curled in Dawit's lap, and Dawit did not move to stir him. Jessica did not remark on the FOR SALE sign posted at the end of the driveway. Instead, she focused on Kira. "Honey, after dinner I want you to bring your homework downstairs so Mommy can check it."

Kira shook her head, looking irritable. Her moods were the most sour when she first woke up. "Daddy already checked it."

Jessica chewed faster, appearing nervous. "That's okay. Bring it down for Mommy to look at too. 'Kay?"

Sulkily, Kira glanced up at Dawit, so he winked at her. Kira slipped a thin strip of a green pepper into her mouth, sucking it like spaghetti. "Okay," she said after a moment. Then she smiled and twisted in her seat to face Dawit. "Daddy, listen: *Nous prenons dîner à huit heures.*"

Dawit smiled and clapped, delighted. "We eat dinner at eight o'clock," she said, and with such a beautiful accent! "That was lovely, darling," he said, "but one correction: LE *dîner, oui?*"

"*Le dîner,*" Kira said, smiling back.

He asked her, in French, if she liked her dinner. Yes, Kira replied, she liked it because she was hungry. "*J'ai faim.*"

"Kira . . . want to tell me how school went today?" Jessica asked.

Kira didn't answer, playing with her chicken with her fingers. Dawit was surprised. It was as though Kira hadn't heard her mother.

"Kira, Mommy asked you a question," Dawit said.

Kira sighed, rolling her eyes. "*Je suis fatiguée, Daddy.*"

Dawit glanced at Jessica and saw that her face was drawn with anger. Kira knew her mother did not speak French, so she was purposely trying to annoy her. What was worse, it was as though she instinctively knew how to play on Jessica's most basic insecurities. As with past offspring, Dawit was surprised at how naturally intuitive children are, for better or worse.

"You speak English to me," Jessica said.

Kira didn't answer, her eyes on her plate, puffing her cheeks out so that she reminded Dawit of Dizzy Gillespie. This time, when Dawit looked at Jessica's face, her bottom lip was trembling.

"Kira Wolde," she began, "you better answer me, or I'm going to get one of my belts and whip your little behind. Do you hear me? Do you want a whipping?"

Jessica's hushed voice hung over the table. Neither of them ever spanked Kira, so the threat startled Dawit and made tears appear in Kira's eyes. Kira crossed her arms, her lips pursed.

"David, you better say something to your daughter," Jessica said icily.

"Babe, I think she's just—"

"And stop always making excuses for her!" Jessica shouted,

glaring at him. The anger in her eyes was the potent brand that accompanied ultimatums. He fell silent. Jessica pushed her plate away and leaped up from the table, near tears herself. "I don't need this. I must be crazy to put up with this shit."

As Jessica climbed up the stairs, Kira began to sob.

"Kira . . ." Dawit began, leaning toward her. "Were you acting that way because you were disappointed Mommy was late?"

Still sobbing, Kira nodded.

"Well, you shouldn't do that. It isn't nice to try to hurt people's feelings on purpose. A little later, you need to tell Mommy you're sorry. Don't be a baby. You're almost six."

He wished he could explain to Kira that Jessica's emotions were likely to be very volatile because the face of her entire world was changing. Kira's time for illumination would come soon, but not yet. Not quite yet.

Jessica had her good days and her bad days—and this was a bad day, Dawit decided. She'd been so much stronger, so much more accepting, than he'd imagined she would be, but she was still a mortal being forced to bring changes into her life. Mortals and non-mortals shared a dislike for change. He could not rush her. The balance was very precarious now. The slightest upset might push her away, and then it would all be lost.

After dinner, Dawit left Kira in her room coloring at her desk and found Jessica curled on top of the bedspread, talking softly on the telephone. The TV was playing a 1970s sitcom about a bigoted white-haired man he remembered vaguely. Dawit had his own affinity for romantic movie classics, a weakness Jessica teased him about, but at least he had an excuse; as he told her, until he'd returned with his phony documents to amuse himself at Harvard fifteen years before, he had never *seen* a motion picture. Some of them, especially the older ones, were charming and full of innocence.

" . . . Love you. 'Bye," Jessica said, hanging up, and Dawit recognized the voice she used with her mother. They spoke once a day, usually at this time. Dawit had not known parents in so long that he observed with amazement how strong Jessica's family ties were. Christina, too, had constantly been in her parents' bosom. He imagined she must have gone back to them, with Rufus and Rosalie, after he left them alone.

Jessica sighed, blinking. She was staring hard at the television screen, but Dawit was certain she was not paying attention to the program. Since she didn't speak right away, he busied himself changing into his bedclothes.

Jessica would have reason enough to grieve for her family, Dawit thought sadly. Once the Searchers realized that Jessica knew about the Living Blood, Bea and Alexis would be in danger if Jessica returned to Miami. Jessica was not likely to see much of her mother and sister for many years. And she would surely live to see them both die, as she would every other mortal on the planet.

But Dawit knew he could not explain any of this now. The process of disclosure with Jessica was not yet complete.

Dawit felt liberated by the small secrets he had divulged so far, but bigger ones still weighed against his conscience. He could not tell Jessica how Khaldun claimed that he had come into possession of the Living Blood, not now nor ever. Even if Khaldun's claim was unfounded, a true woman of faith like Jessica would never consent to receive blood that might have been stolen from Christ.

And, grievably, there was much more he could not tell. The worst secrets remained unuttered. The worst must never be uttered, and so he would never be free of them.

If only he had tried to think of more clever solutions than killing those mortals. Yes, killing was always the easiest method to quell questions or dissent, but he had come to dismiss mortal lives too easily. He had told himself he'd acted to fulfill the Covenant, and yet now he had willfully broken his word to Khaldun by revealing himself to Jessica. What purpose, then, had the deaths served? Death had been a favor to dear Rosalie—he must believe that—but he had killed the others in hypocrisy. Or, as Mahmoud said, in sport? Killing had been Dawit's first lesson in life as a child wrested from his father, after all. Killing, too, was as constant as he.

But it would cease. It must. The killing must end.

And even Teacake's secret could not yet be told. Dawit could not mention Teacake's condition because he knew she would be horrified by the violence of the Ritual inflicted on her precious cat. For now, that must wait.

Besides, he knew Jessica was not yet ready to face the question of whether to accept the Life gift. Her abrupt silence in the cave after he revealed that he could perform the Ritual told him that. He should have held his tongue! Once they vanished to safety in Senegal, he would begin to convince her. How could she refuse to spend eternity as a family? And what mother could forfeit the opportunity to protect her own child from death?

He must open her mind a little at a time. But first, their reacquaintance would continue. Tonight, perhaps he would tell her about his childhood so long ago, a time he'd nearly forgotten because he thought of it so little. He would tell her about his father, who died so bravely in battle. And his mother, whose lips curled at the edges like Jessica's. The image of his mother's full lips was all that was left of her in his memory. What had her face looked like?

"I shouldn't have acted like that at the table. I guess I freak out when I can't understand what you two are saying," Jessica mumbled after a long silence.

"It wasn't just you. Kira was being a brat, Jess. Want to go for a walk after she falls asleep?"

Jessica gazed at him thoughtfully. He recognized that look; she was examining him, struggling to understand. To accept.

"You're good with her," she said.

Dawit cocked his head dismissively. "You are too."

"No," she said, her voice unsteady. "It's not the same. I mean, I know she loves me too. But I remember how I felt about my father. To her, you're . . ."

"I'm one of the parents she loves," Dawit said. "That's all."

Jessica smiled, sitting up in the bed with her legs curled beneath her, a pose that made her appear very young. Her movements were stilted, as though she were dazed. In that instant, Dawit felt profoundly sorry for her. She looked weary of mind and spirit, the way she looked much more often since the cabin. He had stripped something from her, perhaps her sense of balance. He was asking too much, too fast.

At what point, he wondered, does the bent twig snap?

"Want to go to sleep?" he asked gently.

"No," she said, lifting her shoulders and straightening her back as she gathered her breath. "Let me make up with Kira, then we'll put her to bed and go take a walk. I want to hear your bedtime stories. I want to hear all of your stories."

Then, silently, Jessica mouthed his name: Dawit.

That night, as they walked in darkness, Dawit told his wife about the light across the African skies.

▪ 33

Kira had never been afraid of the man in the cave.

She was still wearing diapers the first time she saw him, when Daddy brought her to the cave to get away from the sun. She could barely see him then, just his shadow against the wall like a jellyfish, but she laughed. "Grannaw," she said, pointing, because she wasn't old enough to say "Grandpa" yet.

The bigger she got, the better she could see him. He looked like a real person now, with dark skin and a white moustache and a black baseball cap. He was always eating a Whopper. She was starting to think, even though she'd never tried it, that if she ever wanted to just sit on his lap or reach to touch him, she could. He was just that close.

It was magic, maybe.

Kira knew their house was in a magic place because she could hear the voices all around. Sometimes, when her window was open at night, she woke up because she heard fighting. Other times, it was laughing. On some nights, all the voices came to visit and the treetops sounded like the school playground through her window.

It didn't surprise Kira that Mommy and Daddy never heard the voices except for Night Song, who liked to play tricks with her whistles. Or that they never saw Grandpa even when they were all in the cave and she could see him perfectly clear, not just his jellyfish shadow, but the overalls and shoes he was wearing too.

There were a lot of things grownups couldn't see and hear.

Kira liked visiting Grandpa. She tried to visit at least once every day, after Daddy picked her up from school and she finished her coloring homework and went outside to play before dinner. Daddy thought she was playing with Imani, the dolly Peter bought for her—her especially favorite doll—but she wasn't. She was in the cave, talking to Grandpa.

She felt smart when she was with him. He could use any kind of words, big or small, or any language at all, and she always understood what he was saying. Sometimes they didn't have to open their mouths, not even a little, and they could talk with their heads.

> How's my little Pumpkin today?
> Tell me a story, Grandpa.

Before, Daddy was the best storyteller Kira knew, and Mommy was second-best. But Grandpa was the best of all, the bestest in the world. When he told stories, he could change his voice to sound like a woman, a lion, a sorcerer. He could make his eyes glow in the scary parts, and his laugh made her dance in the funny parts. When he talked, they weren't always in the cave anymore. She felt like she was in a tall tower, like Rapunzel, or flying on Aladdin's magic carpet.

"I'll tell you a story, all right," Grandpa said, moving his lips this time. "Did I ever tell you the one about Lin?"

Kira hugged Imani close to her so her dolly could listen too. She shook her head. "Who's Lin?"

"Why, Lin was a little boy who lived all the way across the ocean in China. He was a lot like you, Pumpkin. He was smart and handsome, the happiest little boy in the village. He lived with his Mommy and Daddy in a house at the edge of a forest. There were wet rice paddies all around, so the forest was the only place he could play. One day, Lin was walking in the forest looking for sweet berries to eat when he happened upon a fearsome red dragon."

Grandpa made his eyes turn bright red, and Kira laughed even though she hugged Imani tighter because it scared her.

"Well, Lin had heard enough about dragons to know that they can blow fire out of their noses, and they don't like little boys, so he was frightened and ran away. He didn't play in the forest for a long time. But one day, weeks later, he fell asleep beneath a sapling. When he woke up, he felt something warm and wet against the side of his face. He opened his eyes, and there was the dragon staring him right in the eye."

Kira gasped.

Grandpa held up his finger. "But then, Kira, a very strange thing happened. Lin realized the dragon hadn't hurt him and his eyes looked friendly, so he reached out and touched the dragon's long, scaly snout. It felt soft. The dragon smiled. From that moment on, Lin and the dragon were very best friends."

"Did he bring him over to his house?"

"The dragon was too big to go into Lin's house. You would need a palace for a dragon that big, and these were poor folk. But the two of them played in the forest, and the dragon was so big that Lin could climb on his back and sit between his wings."

"Like Princess!" Princess had been just like a horsey. Kira didn't want to think about Princess too much, or she'd cry.

"Yes. Exactly like Princess," Grandpa said, smiling a wide smile at her, just like Ms. Raymond did when she answered a question right. "And one day, Kira, while Lin was sitting on the dragon's back, the dragon spread out his massive wings and flew straight into the sky. Lin had never seen such an incredible place. The dragon and Lin lived there forever."

"But what about his Mommy and Daddy?"

Grandpa sighed. He bit into his hamburger. Kira wondered if he'd forgotten the rest of his story, but soon he went on: "The thing is, Kira, Lin's Mommy and Daddy were wizards. And wizards have wonderful magic powers, but they can't live in the sky. That's the price they pay for their magic."

Kira wasn't sure she liked this story anymore. She wanted to hear a fun story. "Wasn't he sad without his Mommy and Daddy?"

"Sad? Well, he was at first. Of course you are. It's scary to live in a new place. But let me tell you something: Lin had his very best friend in the world with him, the dragon. And he met people he didn't even know about: his parents' parents, and their parents, and all of the parents to the end of time. And they wrapped so much love around him, he couldn't help laughing all the time. He'd never been so happy."

"And . . . he didn't miss his Mommy and Daddy at all?"

"Oh, yes. He did, Kira. But whenever he thought about them, Lin just climbed on the dragon's back and they flew down to earth so he could see what they were doing. They were always busy—there's a lot of work for wizards—but they were just fine. And Lin's parents couldn't see him, but they always knew he was there. So they would smile. And then Lin would go back beyond the clouds, and he lived happily ever after."

Kira clapped her hands. That turned out to be a good story, after all! Grandpa would never tell her a bad story. Except once he made her cry because he said something mean about Daddy, but he promised her he would never say anything mean again.

> I know you love your daddy, Kira. I'm not saying he's bad. But can't good people sometimes do bad things? Maybe they don't mean to, but they can do bad things even to people they love.
> Daddy won't do anything bad!
> Shhhhh. I'm sorry, Pumpkin. We won't talk about your daddy.

"Are there any other Lin stories?" Kira asked.

"Oh, there are plenty of Lin stories. Lin gets into mischief every now and then. But I won't have time to tell you today. Your daddy is about to come call you. He sees it's getting dark."

"Are we really leaving, Grandpa? Like you said?"

"Yes, very soon. You'll know when it's time," Grandpa said. "It will be in a rush. Even little Imani will stay home. You won't have time to bring her. But Teacake is going to come."

"What about you, Grandpa?"

"Oh, I'll be here," Grandpa said. "I can't go. Not me. But you'll see me again just a few days later. You sure will. You won't be away long at all."

Kira heard Daddy calling her from the front porch. Just like

Grandpa said, Daddy was saying it was too dark outside. Grandpa was never wrong. Not even once.

Kira didn't tell Daddy and Mommy about Grandpa anymore. That one time she said something about him, they acted like she'd said some bad words. Like she was in trouble. You couldn't talk about some things with grownups.

"Before you go, Kira, tell me . . ." Grandpa said, leaning over to look at her face. He was smiling. "If you saw a red dragon, would you climb on its back? Would you fly into the clouds?"

"Is it a nice dragon, like Lin's?"

"Perfectly nice."

Kira grinned and nodded yes.

▪ 34

Lately, Jessica noticed in church, her mother was wearing pastel colors that beamed across her dark skin. Peach. Rose. Lemon yellow. For years after her father died, even for routine Sunday services, Bea only wore black in church. Then, she slowly progressed to other sober shades like rust or forest green.

Now, for some reason, a rebirth.

Jessica wondered if Bea's bright new look had anything to do with Randall Gaines, the retired optometrist who sang the male lead in the choir and always managed to glance at Bea during his slightly off-key solos. After church, they stood in the parking lot in the hot sun talking for twenty minutes at a time as the crowd melted around them and worshipers waved goodbye before running to the air-conditioned sanctuary of their cars.

Today, standing beside her mother with a polite smile as she listened to them one-up each other in conversation, Jessica was surprised to learn they'd been having regular meetings at Bea's house to discuss the Founder's Day program. They were also both on the community health committee. How cozy, Jessica thought.

Mr. Gaines was tall, like her father had been, with thinning salt-and-pepper hair and a West Indian accent. When he spoke to Bea, Jessica happened to notice, he sometimes lighted his hand across her shoulder before self-consciously slipping it away.

"See you Monday night, Bea," he said at last, nodding.

"Uh-huh . . ." Jessica muttered as they walked to Bea's car.

"Not a word out of you," Bea said.

"I approve," Jessica said, smiling.

"Oh, just hush." Jessica saw, right before her mother ducked into the car after opening her door, that she was smiling too.

This was another sign, Jessica decided. Everything was unfolding as it should. She could leave her mother now because Bea wouldn't need to rely on her company so much. In all of these years, her mother had never paid attention to any man, despite urgings from her daughters. Now, out of nowhere, here was this Randall Gaines coming to her house. Although it was none of her business, Jessica wondered if her mother was enjoying a sex life. Bea was only in her sixties, after all, and Jessica planned on enjoying sex with David until she was ready for the grave.

The thought stole the smile from her face: David would still be a young man then. Would he take an old woman, even a woman only Bea's age, in his arms? Jessica studied her mother objectively, noting that she was still honestly pretty. The skin on her face didn't sag, except slightly at the jowls. She had a few laugh lines, but no real wrinkles. The Benton women had always been blessed with uncanny youthfulness as they aged. Could David, or Dawit, or whatever she was supposed to call him now, love her when she grew into her mother's face?

If only she could keep her own face, always. Always.

Jessica caught herself, disgusted. Lord, what was going through her mind? *Surely every man is vanity*, she thought, remembering the words from the Book of Psalms. She was willing to sacrifice her salvation for a young, pretty face?

At her house, Bea turned on the CD boom box Jessica had bought her for Christmas two years before, playing her old-time gospel songs. Bea always complained that the heavy sound of the new drummer and bass player at church was more like a rock concert than a worship service. She preferred the tried songs, by Mahalia Jackson and The Staple Sisters and Alex Bradford. Jessica understood her point. The old songs were saturated with sorrow and joy like no others. Even a simple organ flourish or a soloist's earnest voice could bring unexpected tears to her eyes, like now. Out of Bea's eyesight, Jessica flicked a tear away with her fingertip.

Lord Jesus, am I doing the right thing?

Bea hummed the tune to "My God Is Real" along with Mahalia, taking a seat across from Jessica on her plastic-covered living room sofa. The plastic hissed beneath her weight. "What's going on in that busy head of yours?" Bea asked.

Jessica half smiled. "A lot more than usual."

Bea nodded, reflective. "Must be this Africa business. You and David have decided to go, then?"

Jessica's eyes, involuntarily, dropped from her mother's. So, Bea had heard about Africa. Up until now, Jessica had only mentioned France as a possibility. But she'd told Alex how David's editor knew a man in Senegal who had promised to let them stay in his house for at least six months. It was all working out, just like a master plan. Alex must have told Bea. Jessica could trust her sister with most secrets, but apparently not all of them.

"Well, you know what?" Bea went on cheerfully. "I'm not going to say a word about it. I wouldn't run off to Africa in your place, with a good job and Kira so young, but we've always been different people, you and I. And that's fine. God didn't make carbon copies. What's good for me isn't necessarily the right thing for you, and vice versa."

Jessica looked at her, stunned at her levelheadedness. "That's it?" she asked.

Bea pursed her lips, thoughtful. "Just remember I won't be here forever, and I don't want my grandchild to forget me. I don't fly, and I'm not going all the way across the world on any boat."

"We won't be gone long, Mom," Jessica said, but as she heard her own words she realized they might be lies. She didn't know how long they would be gone. More than at any other point in her life, she didn't know the first thing about what was to come.

"You just be careful with David," Bea said suddenly, intruding into her thoughts.

Jessica's heart honestly jumped. "Be careful?"

"You need to watch out in a new place, with laws that won't protect you. If things go wrong with you and David, you need to bring Kira right back here as fast as you can. David could take her away from you."

The warning made Jessica more uneasy than she'd felt all morning. She leaned back in the parlor chair, listening to Mahalia's assurance that, yes, God is real. And God would understand she was trying to do the right thing, keeping her family together. And God would protect them. Wouldn't He?

"Don't worry about us," Jessica said. "We're soul mates, Mom. I've never been more sure."

Bea nodded, but she didn't look satisfied. Jessica's seven years of marriage hadn't done much to ease Bea's doubts about David's history, or his vague explanations of how he was so self-sufficient and established at such a young age. Now, of course, Jessica could see how flimsily constructed all of David's lies were. An orphan. A trust account. Bea had always seen through him, even when love made insight impossible for Jessica. Thinking back, Jessica was alarmed at how she'd accepted his word at every turn. And here she was, doing it all over again.

"You don't trust him, do you?" Jessica asked.

Bea shrugged. "I want to. And I have to admit, he's done better by you than I ever thought he would. So there's no reason to doubt his intentions, really. There's something about him, though, honey. I respect that he's your husband, but I always had the feeling you should be careful."

"Why?"

Bea paused, then sighed and shook her head. "Too many unanswered questions. Who knows?" she said sadly. "Maybe I'm just jealous he's taking you away. Guess I always knew he would."

Hurriedly, Jessica looked toward the window, hoping to hide the tears about to make themselves known. Her mother, too, was silent, except for occasional humming. "Shoot, let me go heat up the food . . ." Bea said, standing.

There was plenty of food, since Bea had been expecting Alex to come today too. At Jessica's request, though, her sister made other plans. She would deal with Alex later, but she'd wanted this time alone with her mother. Proper goodbyes were best done in private. And she was looking for something from Bea, too. Direction, maybe. She felt as though she were perched on a white-water raft, bouncing against boulders with no idea if a calm pool or a crashing waterfall lay in her path.

The worst part of all, she'd decided, was not being able to tell the full truth about anything. She was growing apart from Bea and Alex in ways they would never know. How could David have kept his secrets for so many hundreds of years? Jessica had known only a short time, and she wanted to share it so badly that she ached.

"Mom, you remember how you went to visit Uncle Joe up in New York? And how the traffic made you miss your plane, the one that crashed?" Jessica asked, sampling from her plate of stewed turkey wings, collard greens, and rice and gravy.

"You think I could forget that?"

Jessica smiled. "That was a miracle. We always said it was, but I know it was now. I know miracles are real."

"Shoot, we raised you to believe that."

"I know, but it's one thing to hear it and another thing to see it. Right? I mean, before that airplane thing, I know you had doubts. Didn't you?"

Bea gazed at her across the table, one eyebrow raised. She

looked concerned. "Jessica . . . I hear you were in Bible class before you dropped by this morning. I thought you didn't have time for that. Why are you getting all this religion all of a sudden?"

"What do you mean?"

"What's going on with you?"

Jessica bit her lip, feeling a surge of joy as she remembered David's touch after he awakened from the dead. The image no longer filled her with fear. Like Christ, he had risen. She'd seen a resurrection. Maybe David was like a prophet, a sign of the messiah's return. His knowledge and incredible history had to be part of a plan. God hadn't seen fit to make it all clear to her yet, but she knew He would. She only had to stop questioning and *believe*.

"Nothing's going on. I'm just happy. I'm happy to have Jesus, that's all. And happy to have David."

"David's not taking you to one of those Jim Jones cults, is he?" Bea asked skeptically.

"Mom, quit teasing me," Jessica said. "I remember what you were like those first two weeks after that plane crashed. Playing gospel all the time, listening to all of the televangelists, reading us Bible verses at night. Don't even try to deny it. So I'm allowed to get a little too."

"Well," Bea said, biting her corn muffin, "I guess it's all right as long as you don't get any ideas about joining the choir. You know you can't sing, and they have enough trouble as it is."

"That must include Randall Gaines too."

"That's right, bless him. Love is blind, but I'm not deaf."

Together, clutching each other's hands, they laughed.

Sitting with her mother, listening to gospel and then James Brown, then Tina Turner—music David never played—Jessica forgot about the uncertainties outside. She'd thought this would be difficult, saying goodbye, but she and her mother drank sweet iced tea and laughed into the afternoon like old college roommates.

Neither of them had laughed that way in a long time.

▪ 35

As soon as he heard the mailbox clank outside his Biscayne Boulevard studio apartment at midday, Mahmoud left his bowl of lentil soup and opened the door to check for letters. The single piece of mail for him, addressed to Occupant, was a postcard advertising a tire company.

Mahmoud cursed. Did Americans ever receive real correspondence, or was the entire mail system the domain of advertisements? Not that these illiterates would know what to do with a pen if they ventured to take one in their pudgy hands.

He returned to his table to eat his soup, which, along with the flat loaf of Cuban bread he'd bought at a nearby bakery that morning, would serve as his day's only meal. This way, both his mind and body were lean. He would feast when his job was finished.

He must learn patience, he told himself. Not even three weeks had passed since he mailed the letter to Khaldun. It had barely had time to arrive, much less for Khaldun's response to return. The express letter's passage would have been delayed because Lalibela's only airstrip was closed during the rainy season, so it would be delivered by automobile. This one time, he wished their colony was equipped with telephones. If he'd remained in the House of Mystics long enough to learn telepathy, Mahmoud thought, Khaldun could have known his message instantly. But, then again, surely even Khaldun could not hear thoughts across so many thousands of miles.

Mahmoud's eyes wandered to the three black-and-white video monitors lined up on his furnished room's faded pinewood bureau. Alongside the bank of television screens, large reels spun on an audiotape monitoring the telephone wiretap.

" . . . Two bedrooms," he heard Dawit's voice say. Dawit's image was visible on the middle screen as he talked on the telephone while he sat at his computer. Mahmoud's pin-sized video camera, hidden within a groove on Dawit's VCR, broadcast an exceptional view of the house's living room and dining room table. A second camera, substituting for a nail in a wooden picture frame upstairs, showed a view of their cat sleeping in the middle of Dawit's bed.

Miami was flush with spy shops of every variety, which Mahmoud browsed for entertainment, but he'd brought his devices with him from Lalibela. Mortal wits could not match those in the House of Science. Mahmoud's simple wireless cameras and microphones were nearly invisible, broadcasting flawless images and sounds.

"And bathrooms?" a woman's voice asked on the tape.

"Only one, unfortunately. But the plumbing is new."

At last, there was movement in the third video screen, which had remained unchanged since early that morning. Mahmoud saw Dawit's wife take a seat in front of the camera, so close he could only make out her waist and chest. Her blurred, monstrous fingers came toward the camera, holding her key chain.

Where was she going?

Lighting a cigarette, Mahmoud lowered the volume of the telephone conversation and turned up the sound from the wife's monitor. She had someone with her, apparently. Mahmoud heard a man's voice briefly, though he was out of the camera's frame.

"You're shooting from the van?" she asked her guest.

"Hell, yeah. A photog had his equipment stolen at Evergreen Courts last month, at an antidrug rally for the kids," the man said. "Can you believe that? The asshole broke into his trunk while he was out shooting."

"I thought you had insurance for stuff like that."

"Don't worry about the photos. I'll use my zoom. Just point the guys out to me."

Mahmoud couldn't make out their voices after that because of a sudden explosion of loud music. Dawit's wife must have turned on the radio, where the camera was hidden in the eye of one of the knobs. No matter; there was nothing terribly revealing there anyway. She was working, posing no immediate threat.

Mahmoud turned down the volume on the vehicle's monitor, then raised Dawit's so he could hear the remainder of his telephone call. The tapes would capture whatever Mahmoud missed, and he would replay all of the tapes while they slept, as usual.

"How about three?" Dawit's woman caller asked.

"That's not good, I'm afraid, unless you just want a look at the grounds. I pick up my daughter at three. But anytime after three-thirty is wonderful. You can have a full tour."

Despite the rage Mahmoud felt—and he tried to control his rage, since rage dulled intellect—he found himself marveling at Dawit's hubris. Hubris was the only word that suited Dawit's behavior. He must think himself a god, to behave so—to carry on the sale of his house as though he would be allowed to walk away despite Khaldun's desire for him to return to Lalibela.

But if only that were the extent of it!

The monitor in Dawit's vehicle had captured evidence that would result in Dawit's imprisonment for all of time. Not only had he broken the Covenant, but he had told his wife so much shocking detail, more than Mahmoud had imagined any Life brother would ever dare. Only Allah could divine what more Dawit had revealed when they stole away from the cameras at night. And she a reporter who conducted investigations!

Her spell on him was so powerful that, with his own eyes, Mahmoud had seen Dawit allow the woman to raise her voice at him in front of their child! How had he come to this?

Dawit must be insane to behave this way. For that, Mahmoud pitied his dear friend. Khaldun was sure to be angry, but perhaps he could implore their teacher to show mercy on Dawit. He clearly was not in control of his actions, as his violence and poor judgment proved. The danger Dawit had thrust upon them was unintentional. And it was not too late to repair the damage.

Exactly when, he didn't know.

Mahmoud did not dare act until he had the words from Khaldun himself. Since no one had ever broken the Covenant, Mahmoud did not trust his own solutions, though he knew Khaldun would echo them. He needed Khaldun's sanction, and then he would finish it.

The entire business was regrettable.

"Dawit, Dawit . . ." Mahmoud said aloud, watching Dawit's wife's hands on the steering wheel of the van. "What insanity is this you have brewed for us all, you pathetic fool?"

The tapes played on for the audience of one.

▪ 36

Jessica tapped on the door frame of her boss's office. "Sy? We got great photos. I think we saw a transaction."

"Uh oh. Next, it'll be sting operations," a deep voice came from her left, surprising her. She hadn't realized Sy was in a meeting. A dark-haired man with round-frame glasses sat in a chair in front of Sy's desk, legs crossed. Jessica knew his face.

"Oops, sorry to interrupt. This can wait."

"No, Jess, come on in," Sy said, standing, indicating an empty seat in the corner. "This is Lieutenant Fernando Reyes. Believe it or not, your name just came up."

"Si, claro," Jessica said, shaking the detective's outstretched palm. "I remember you from my days on the police beat. But you weren't a lieutenant then."

"And you weren't on the I-Team," Reyes said, smiling. His brown skin looked rich against a light-pink dress shirt. Jessica remembered how female reporters used to joke that Reyes looked like Andy Garcia. He really did, she noticed.

Jessica sat, slightly breathless. She'd been hot as hell idling under the sun for two hours. She needed a cool drink.

"My name came up? What's going on?"

"Jess, Reyes is leading Miami PD's investigation of Peter's death. He's tying up some loose ends, he said."

Jessica nodded, gazing at Reyes, but she involuntarily looked downward at the mention of Peter's name. She couldn't distance herself from his death, no matter how much time passed. "Well, you know I'd love to help," Jessica said softly.

Reyes whipped a notebook out of his breast pocket and absently flipped through the pages. "I'll update you. Basically, we've scrapped the random attack theory. We believe someone was waiting in the car and probably knew when to expect him. And the wound was very clean, ritualistic. That leaves trying to figure out who would have the best motive to kill Donovitch."

Sy exhaled ruefully. "There's probably a club. He was a good reporter. Good reporters make enemies."

Sy had a point. In about a week, when her story on the drug dealers ran, Jessica could count on a few high-ranking enemies herself, including the county's deputy housing chief. Leaving the country for a while wasn't such a bad idea, after all.

"I don't know anything beyond what I told the other detective a long time ago," Jessica said.

"I've seen your statement. This is about something else," he said, finally stopping at a page in his notebook, which he scanned quickly while he spoke to her. "In trying to get a handle on what Peter might have been working on, we pulled e-mail messages he sent and received for a couple of weeks prior to his death. We're getting down to the nit-picky stuff now, but you never know where you're going to get a break. I'm sure you know what I mean."

Jessica lowered her eyebrows, confused. "E-mail? You mean you read Peter's messages? Aren't those private?"

"Jess . . ." Sy said in a calming tone. "The circumstances are extreme. E-mail is the newspaper's property. We read it if we have to."

"As I'm sure you know," Reyes went on, "the last message he sent was to you. 'Mr. Perfect is a trip.' That sounded like a code name for something, and we wondered what it could mean."

Jessica looked back at her editor, and was amazed to find him watching her with a sober expression, waiting for her response. Was she the only one outraged that Peter's privacy was being violated? Not to mention hers? These cops were desperate, playing spy games to feel useful, exercising pointless authority.

She hoped Sy hadn't seen the messages too. Lord, she and Peter had exchanged more than a couple of unflattering messages about Sy, meant as jokes. With Peter dead, the barbs would sound blunt and cruel. It wasn't right to unearth them.

But, Jessica decided, maybe she was overreacting. If she were in Reyes's place, wouldn't she have checked Peter's e-mail too? Her judgment was clouded by their friendship, that was all. Sy had asked her a couple of times if she wanted to help cover Peter's murder investigation for the paper, and she'd always said no. Now, she understood why she couldn't.

"Do you remember that message?" Reyes asked.

Jessica blinked. "I remember it. I saw it a few weeks later, when I came back from taking some time off."

"You did mention something about getting a silly message from Peter. I remember now," Sy said.

"We're curious," Reyes went on. "Donovitch sent it late at night, probably right before he walked out of the building."

Jessica half smiled. "Well, I hate to blow any theories, but there's nothing glamorous about the message. Mr. Perfect was our nickname for my husband, David."

Sy nodded, illumination washing over his face. He chuckled to himself. "Mr. Perfect . . ." he repeated, amused. "Good one."

Reyes's expression didn't change as he gazed into Jessica's eyes. "I see. Well, that makes sense now. So, do you happen to know if your husband might have run into Donovitch?"

"Run into him when?" Jessica asked.

"That night," Reyes answered, glancing back down at his notes. "The guard says . . . He came up at about nine-fifteen with a plate of food for you. Something like that. Left about an hour later. Does that sound familiar?"

"I wasn't here," Jessica said, the first words to emerge from her jarred mind. "I don't know."

"Well, your husband was here. Nine-fifteen, the guard says. So, I guess you were out on a story or something?"

Jessica's lips parted, then she closed them. She glanced back at Sy, whose hands were folded in front of his jaw, hiding his mouth. What the hell was happening here? This was an interrogation, not a conversation. Never mind this business about David being here, which she didn't know about. She didn't like the questions. She shouldn't say anything else now. She shouldn't have said anything at all.

"I don't think I can help you," she said.

Reyes smiled, his face still friendly. He extended a blue-embossed business card, which she took. "I understand. You weren't here. Could you do me a favor, though, and ask Mr. Perfect to give me a call? Just loose ends."

"I'll mention it," she said.

Reyes flipped his notebook closed. "So . . . I understand you and your family are moving to Africa soon. You must be excited."

"Yes," Jessica told Reyes coolly. "We're very excited."

Once again, Jessica shot a glance at Sy, whose face looked stony. Sy shrugged, his eyes apologetic. Later, he would tell Jessica he hadn't liked Reyes's tone either. He'd thought he only wanted her for casual chitchat. Even though Sy told her to forget it, Jessica thought he must have something ugly on his mind.

She didn't forget it.

She spent a half-hour on the telephone bitching to David about the cop's smug demeanor, how the interception of Peter's e-mail made her feel violated, how the cop treated her like she was a conspirator in something.

Be very careful what you say to him, David, she warned. The paper's surveillance tape was lousy, but some people were insisting they could tell it was a black man climbing into Peter's Mustang. ("That's why we can't see him," she overheard one guard say, and another piped up, "Too bad he didn't smile.") The more time passed, the more likely they would start grabbing at any wild theories they could.

She felt protective of David. Lately, she'd begun to view him as a sort of visitor to their modern world. It was as though Reyes was trying to lay a trap for him, and all because he wanted to bring her a plate of food. It was ridiculous.

David tried to calm her down, telling her it was no big deal. He asked for the cop's number, saying he'd be glad to call him and tell him everything he knew, which wasn't much.

"Well, okay," Jessica said, a little less agitated. "Anyway, Peter was in the library. I'm sure you didn't even see him."

"No, I did see him for a moment," David said. "Jess, listen, the lady just arrived to look at the house. We'll talk about this when you get home, all right, sweetheart?"

It wasn't until three hours later, driving home, that Jessica's irritation with Reyes dissipated enough for her to examine something else—even bigger—twisting the pit of her stomach: David had been at the paper the night Peter was killed, and he'd never mentioned it to her. Not once.

He'd had a conversation with their friend in his last hour of life, and he'd never thought to bring it up even as an anecdote.

Now, she understood

MR. PERFECT IS A TRIP.

Peter saw David bringing her food, got a laugh out of it, and shared a joke with her, expecting her to sign on and see his message later that night. Hadn't she mentioned to David at least once how much that message confused her? She must have. How could he not say anything?

Jessica was on the verge of whipping herself into full anxiety, nearly bearing down on the Lexus ahead of her on Biscayne, until she remembered that David had no idea who Mr. Perfect was. She'd never shared the nickname with him because he might think it was sarcastic. Of course David wasn't purposely trying to keep anything from her. She shouldn't let that cop's attitude taint hers.

Hell, hadn't David for weeks been telling her volatile secrets that most people would never trust anyone enough to disclose? He had trusted her not to freak out and bolt. He had trusted her not to betray him and sell his story to The National Enquirer. How could her own trust in David be so fragile? Especially when she and her daughter were about to start an entirely new life with him?

"It was thoughtless not to say anything," David said in bed that night, wrapped around her from behind. When he spoke, she felt the warm air from his lips between her shoulder blades. "But you were so distraught. It never crossed my mind to mention it before we heard the news, of course. It was such a routine meeting. And after . . . I suppose I thought it would upset you needlessly. I wish I'd seen something, like I told that Reyes gentleman, but I just didn't. So why bring it up?"

Jessica's eyes grew teary as she imagined Peter in his cartoon-inspired tie, laughing and smiling with David. What would have happened if David had waited just a few more minutes and the two had walked out together? Would David have been attacked too? Or would Peter's assailant have been scared off?

It was so random. It scared her that it was all so senseless. And it hurt. Her anger with David hurt. And her anger with Reyes. And especially her anger with the faceless killer. The anger had nowhere to go. "You should have told me," Jessica said, sobbing.

David's grip tightened around her middle, and he rested his forehead against the nape of her neck. "I'm sorry, Jessica. I didn't mean to hurt you or cause you discomfort. I wish I could go back and change it. I'd change all of it. Honey, I wish I could make it so it never happened."

I'm sorry, he kept saying. I'm sorry.

▪ 37

Jessica's dream was peaceful.

She was standing at the foot of the knoll, staring up at the cave, which was casting a splendid, tranquil white light. She saw the tall silhouette of her father centered in the cave's mouth. And Peter beside him? They waved, and she felt washed in joy. *I won't be going there,* she called to them. They nodded. They understood. *Hold tight to Kira for me,* her father's voice said, and the dream was over.

It was when Jessica woke up that her nightmare began.

She flung the bedsheets away from her skin. It was so god-awful hot. She touched her cheeks, her abdomen, and realized she was damp with perspiration. David shifted beside her, rolling away, but he was still snoring lightly. Glancing at his curled form, Jessica's heart plummeted to her stomach. She felt like she would vomit.

Four o'clock in the morning, the oak grandfather clock said in the moonlight. If David hadn't silenced its mechanism, the clock would be tolling right now.

Jessica couldn't sleep. Unconscious thoughts, free to roam while her defenses were weak, were surfacing in her anxious brain.

You know, like a flooring knife. For linoleum.

Again, Jessica felt a constricting in her throat that warned her she might be physically sick. Her heartbeat was in a fury. Weakly, she climbed out of bed and searched for her shoes beneath the frame. Once her sneakers were on, she walked quietly into the bathroom, closed the door, and flicked on the light above the sink.

She did not recogize the wild, red eyes she saw in the mirror. These were a stranger's eyes. The eyes of a woman wondering, for the first time, if her husband was a murderer.

David had never really liked Peter.

David had probably been the last person to see Peter alive.

David had a linoleum knife.

"Oh, my sweet Jesus . . ." Jessica whispered. She doused her face with a cool stream of water from the faucet. *This must be what fainting feels like,* she thought, *or diving from an airplane. You're falling, and where will you land?*

Okay, she thought, steadying herself by curling her fingers over the rim of the sink, *let's be logical here. There's no evidence, just a bunch of crazy notions. So what if the guards thought it was a dark-skinned man on the tape? She'd seen the tape herself, and all she could make out on the grainy image was a faint gleaming on the chrome when the killer opened Peter's door.*

And why would David do something so vicious? Just to prevent them from writing their book? No way. He would need more motive than that. David had been coming around on the book anyway.

The new voice from the recesses of her psyche shot her down. You think he came around on the book, the voice said. You don't know that man. That man mutilated his own insides with a hunting knife. That man was born in an era your history classes never even taught you about. He told you himself he slaughtered men in the Civil War. The whole time you've known him, you haven't even been calling him by his given name, which you can barely pronounce. You don't know the first thing about that man.

That man, the voice kept saying.

But what about David? Who was he? Was he real at all?

"Oh, my Lord . . . sweet Jesus . . ." Jessica whispered. What had she been thinking to stay with him? To agree to go away with him, and to drag Kira along? She must be certifiably insane.

Then, just when she needed to most, Jessica remembered her Scriptures, the words of Jesus in the Book of Mark. *Why are ye so fearful? How is it that ye have no faith?*

The work of God had unfolded in Jessica's own hands, which had been soaked in David's blood from the wound healed by a miracle. She alone had witnessed this, and there was no disputing what she had seen. She'd been chosen to see. And David had been chosen to show her. So, despite the slander of others, and her own weakness of mind, she must not let go of her faith. It was all she had.

Besides, there was a simple way to make her doubts vanish. She could find David's toolbox and hold the linoleum knife for herself. A killer would have disposed of his weapon.

Then, she could go back to sleep.

Downstairs, the darkened living room was crammed with packing boxes, and Jessica carefully felt her way around the stacks on the floor. Some boxes would be shipped to Africa, and others would go to charities. David packed each day while she was at work, despite her protests that she wanted to help. He'd packed his books and most of his music first. The shelves on the wall where he'd kept his CDs were bare, and already the house looked like it belonged to someone else.

In the kitchen, moving cautiously, Jessica turned on the dim light above the stove and opened the drawer where they kept the Durabeam flashlight. When she lifted the flashlight, an old ice pick clattered to the floor, making her jump. Kneeling, she glanced up, tense, to see if David would come.

She heard a sound on wooden stairs. She waited, still kneeling. Then Teacake, his plumelike tail standing straight up, came running into the kitchen. He mewed.

"Please hush," Jessica whispered, relieved, her heart flying.

With Teacake leaping ahead, Jessica unlatched the door leading to the screened-in back porch and tipped outside into the humid night air. The moon was nearly full, making the river flicker in white. She almost didn't need a flashlight on a night like this. When she navigated through the foliage to the shed, her cat didn't follow. He sat in the grass and watched her slip inside from a distance.

The first thing Jessica noticed was the scattered dried lizard skeletons on the concrete floor, at least a half-dozen. The reptiles' eye sockets were empty, eaten away by ants. Had David put some poison down? Good thing she didn't believe in omens, Jessica thought, or the wispy lizard bones would have spooked her right back into the house.

"Okay," she said aloud, to reassure herself with her own voice, "Where's that toolbox . . . ?"

The large toolbox was bright red and would be hard to miss, but she didn't see it on the worktable beneath David's carpenter's apron. She didn't see it on the plastic patio table or the folding chair in the middle of the floor. Now what? Was it in the car?

Then, she spotted it. The toolbox was near the stepladder in a far corner of the shed, beneath a paper bag folded down at the top. The bag was heavy to lift, but she moved it aside and carried the toolbox to the table to examine it.

Jessica didn't recognize half of the tangle of tools she found. Wrenches big and small, duct tape, screwdrivers. She took them out one by one and laid them aside, burrowing her way down. A knife! But it wasn't the right one; it was smaller, without the hooked tip. Damn. Where was the linoleum knife?

It wasn't in the toolbox. Jessica wiped perspiration from her forehead. More hurriedly, growing nervous, she searched the worktable, pulling out the plywood drawers and digging through them. Plenty of nails and small gadgets, but no linoleum knife. She scanned the various tools—his saws and shears—that hung from hooks on the wall. Damnit. Everything but the knife.

By now, Jessica was more frustrated than frightened. Her eyes and body were craving sleep, and she began to think of how ridiculous it was to rummage through her husband's things at four in the morning. She'd make up a reason to ask about it later.

"Would that make you happy, Columbo?" she asked herself aloud. She shouldn't have let Reyes get to her. Since she was fully awake now, her fears in the bathroom seemed alarmist. Ridiculous. It was only her mind still freaking out about David's immortality, she decided. The spells were less frequent now, but they still came.

As she replaced the toolbox, Jessica glanced once again at the folded paper bag. She hadn't checked inside, and the knife had probably been there the whole time. She lifted the bag, bringing it out to the stream of light from the overhead bulb.

The bag was filled with bottles. No wonder she couldn't find the ammonia last week. And here was the bleach. She lifted the bottles out of the bag one by one. Rat poison? Maybe he'd used that on the lizards. She also found a tin can of paint thinner and a half-empty bottle of rubbing alcohol. What in the world . . . ?

At the bag's bottom were three plastic syringes. Two were empty, but one was quarter-filled with a dark-red liquid. She lifted the third syringe and examined it in the light; the liquid inside, which was the consistency of a watery syrup, swept around the syringe's barrel as she turned it over in her hand.

The liquid was warm.

Suddenly, she knew. David's blood.

Jessica's mouth fell open. She gazed at the blood with awe. Why had David drawn this blood?

No, she had not found what she'd come looking for. But she'd found something else, something even more valuable. Her hand, grasping the syringe, began to tremble.

"Who are you, David? What are you?" she whispered.

Finally, she resolved, she would know.

"Excuse me? We must have a bad connection," Alex said.

"Quit playing. I'm serious," Jessica said, gazing around the newsroom to see if anyone could hear her. It was lunchtime, and no one was within earshot of her desk. She repeated herself, speaking slowly. "I'm going to bring you a blood sample so you can run some tests on it. But this has to be absolutely secret. You can't tell anyone you have it. No one can see you with it. And you can't show anyone the test results."

"This is a major research facility, not the free clinic. And what's with all this James Bond foolishness?"

"Alex," Jessica said, her voice dipping low, "Just this one time, I need a favor. This is off the record. I can't go to anyone but you. It's for a story. It's very, very important. I can't tell you anything else. It's very big."

Alex sighed, silent.

"Please?" Jessica whimpered.

"Girl, what have you gotten yourself into?"

"I can't tell you. I just need some tests run."

"What kind of tests?"

"I don't know. Screen it for diseases. I need to know if there's anything strange about it. And I bet you there is."

"Where'd you get this blood from?" Alex asked.

"I can't say."

"Well, whose is it?"

Jessica sighed. "Look. I can't say. Can you do this?"

This time, the silence was long. When Alex spoke again, there was no joking in her voice. "This doesn't sound ethical. And depending on how old the sample is, it may or may not even be much good. You know that, right?"

"It's a fresh sample," Jessica lied.

"What about anticoagulants?"

"Huh?" Jessica said. "Alex, I don't know. Look, I've put the syringe in an envelope, and I'm going to come by and slip it into your purse. I'll stay for lunch, but we won't discuss it there. You can only begin testing when the lab is absolutely empty. If you feel like you have to call me at home, just say you want to talk about the book I lent you. And I'll go to a pay phone. From now on, we call it the book."

"You know what?" Alex said after a moment. "You sound like you have lost your natural mind."

"Alex, will you do this?"

"All right," Alex said reluctantly. "Bring me the damn book."

David met Jessica at the door, grinning. "She made an offer."

At first, Jessica didn't know who "she" was, or what the offer was for. Then she remembered that their house was for sale, and how busy David had been showing it to prospective buyers.

"How much?" she asked.

"One hundred fifty."

"For this?" Jessica hadn't thought they'd clear more than ninety thousand.

"She wants to shut out any other buyers. The woman is a historian. She's very fond of the neighborhood, and she likes the river, the Indian lore, the burial ground, all of it."

As he hugged her and she thought about what this meant, Jessica whooped with joy. David had paid cash for the house, so everything they made from the sale was profit. They would have more than enough money to begin their new life, first in Senegal, and then wherever else they chose to go. Jessica was transported, at that moment, far from where her mind had been in the morning's early hours, when she was turning the shed upside down searching for a knife David may have tossed out a year ago, when the floors were done. There was simply no *reason* to suspect him.

Suddenly, she felt guilty. David trusted her, but she hadn't trusted him. And now she had stolen his blood.

David hadn't been to the shed yet, she guessed from his preoccupation with discussing details about the sale. As soon as she got a chance, she would grab that paper bag and throw it away. If David asked questions, she'd tell him she'd been cleaning and thrown out a bag full of chemicals.

After dinner, David was in such a playful mood that he started chasing Kira around the house, his head covered under a box with holes cut out for his eyes. They must have been playing the game earlier; David had painted the box with bold strokes of black and red paint, creating a horrible face. He was making convincing slobbering noises inside his mask.

"Daddy's the Box Monster!" Kira shrieked, ducking from him.

Jessica watched them, smiling, from the table. She expected to have to clean up a scrape or a bump any moment, as they came precariously close to knocking over the packed boxes. But she felt a familiar twinge of envy. They were having fun together.

Jessica picked up an empty box on the kitchen counter. "Where's the paint? I want to play," she said, pretending to pout.

"Up in Kira's room," David said, sounding muffled.

"Mommy's going to be a monster too!" Kira cried, excited.

As Jessica reached the top landing, the phone rang. Alex. She ran into her bedroom to pick up the phone. "Hello?"

"It's me, Sis," Alex said. She sounded weary. "Look, I haven't had a chance to start reading that book yet."

"Hello?" David's voice interrupted from the downstairs line.

"I've got it," Jessica said quickly, and she waited until she heard the click as David hung up the phone. There was a new squeal from Kira downstairs.

"There are too many people hanging around for me to do much reading, if you catch my drift. I have to crash."

"Okay. Just let me know," Jessica said, her words clipped. Alex sounded like she thought this was some kind of game. For all Jessica knew, their phone line could be bugged. In fact, David had told her it probably was, since Mahmoud had known about their plans to leave. Of course, explaining the bugged phone to Alex would mean explaining many other things she could not.

She should tell Alex to forget it, to throw the blood away. Why was she so curious about what was in that syringe? Was she genuinely interested because David was her husband, or simply because, as a reporter, she felt a deep need to know?

It was probably a little of both.

"We'll talk tomorrow. Go on home and rest," Jessica said.

"'Night, Double-O Seven."

Jessica cringed and sighed, hanging up. As usual, Alex wasn't being serious. Well, she thought, her sister would probably realize very soon that there was nothing at all to joke about.

PART FOUR

The Living Blood

If I let my best companion
drive me right into the canyon
'Taint Nobody's Biz-ness If I Do.

—WORDS AND MUSIC BY PORTER GRAINGER AND
EVERETT ROBBINS
(1922)

▪ 38

Mahmoud drew his curtains, blotting out the infernal midday sun. Then, before taking Khaldun's letter in his hands, he burned sage and lit the candle on his table. The movements of his fingers were deft and gentle on the envelope. His teacher's correspondences were rare, to be treasured.

The response was one line, written in Khaldun's script in ancient Ge'ez: *Redress Dawit's grievous error, but be humane. Return with Dawit soon.*

Mahmoud read the words several times over. He had expected this, but the impact of the statement was powerful. Khaldun did not intend to send additional Searchers. Khaldun expected him to contend with his friend alone. As it should be.

After this, his long friendship with Dawit would be no more.

In the candlelight, Mahmoud waited for sadness to come. It did not. He tried to revisit his earlier rage at his friend's transgression. That, too, would not come.

Mahmoud felt nothing. He was ready.

He blew the candle out.

▪ 39

The white glow from the television set bounced off the towers of boxes in the living room. "Was that cannon fire? Or was it my heart pounding?" Jessica heard Ingrid Bergman's voice say.

For the thousandth time, David was watching *Casablanca.* His face was full of such captivation that he could have been lost inside of unearthed home movies full of ghosts. His expression was the same when he watched *It's a Wonderful Life* or *The Philadelphia Story* or any of those old flicks that bored her, frankly, because they were full of nothing but white faces. David never got sick of them. His eyes searched the glimmering screen, unblinking, half mournful, half hopeful.

David was squeezed between boxes on the sofa, his elbow propped up on one to support his head, and Kira was asleep, curled up with her head resting on his thigh. What a sight they were, Jessica thought as she stood in the entryway with a bowl of frozen yogurt. Their silent sweetness made her wish for David's camera.

"Want to carry her up?" David asked quietly, peering back at Jessica. Her presence had broken his spell.

"I'll let you do that later," she said, smiling. "There's no school tomorrow. Let her cuddle."

"You're going to bed already?"

"Nope. I need to write some notes to my friends I've been putting off. You know—we're moving, more details to come. Just so they'll know we didn't vanish."

On the television, violins swirled a romantic fury as Humphrey Bogart and Ingrid Bergman shared a fervid gaze. "I'll turn it off if you want," David said.

"No," Jessica said. She leaned over David to kiss his forehead. "Watch the ending. Maybe she'll stay with him this time instead of catching the first plane out of Dodge."

"I'll be up soon," David promised, his eyes on the movie.

It was all happening so fast.

Signs of change were everywhere Jessica looked. That morning, David had repainted the bathroom, and the smell of the paint still pervaded the house. They'd taken down the picture frames and packed them away. The bookshelves in the bedroom, like the ones downstairs, were bare. Their house was in transition, and Jessica hated transitions. She wanted to be settled either here or in Senegal, but not caught somewhere in between.

What would it be like, she wondered, to live with constancy, the way David struggled so hard to live? And to live that way literally forever? Was it bliss or boredom? The three of them could freeze, like the features on David's face or the reels of *Casablanca*, and time would ramble on around them, meaningless.

It was a staggering, frightening idea. But it was a reality for David. And it could be a reality for her. Jessica was sitting benumbed by the thought, occasionally scribbling a line to her college roommate in Rochester, when the phone rang. "Hello?"

"Jessica," Alex's voice said, tight and unfamiliar. "I have to talk to you about this blood. I really do."

"Hello?" David's voice broke in from downstairs.

Jessica's heart thudded. "Honey, I'm on," she said to David, amazed she could think of coherent words. "You can hang up."

For long seconds, Jessica knew she hadn't heard a click. He must still be hanging on. He had heard. He knew. He would come flying upstairs any minute to demand to know why she'd given his blood to her sister.

"Who's this? Alexis?" David asked at last.

"Hey, David."

"Honey, I have it," Jessica repeated, and this time she heard a loud distortion and then a click as David rested the handset on its cradle. She waited, holding her breath. He was gone.

"Jessica?" Alex said. "I have to talk to you. I mean it."

"Okay. Just slow down. Are you at home?"

"I'm still at the lab. Should I come over—"

"No, not here," Jessica said. She'd better hope the line wasn't bugged after all, because they'd dropped any pretense of speaking in a code. Not that the code had been all that brilliant to begin with, she realized. Jessica's palm, wrapped around the receiver, felt clammy. What had her sister found?

"I'll be right there," Jessica said.

"You're coming now?"

"Give me twenty minutes." She couldn't contain her curiosity. "So, is it an interesting book?"

Alex didn't answer the question. She sighed. "Girl, I'm so tired. Just please bring your behind over here—*now*."

David had been surprised Jessica wanted to run out of the house so late—"It's almost eleven," he pointed out, looking at his watch— but she hadn't seen any suspicion in his face. Thank goodness. Maybe he hadn't heard exactly what Alex said, after all. She couldn't even remember what crazy story she'd concocted for him, something about girl talk. She hoped that David's trust would make her lame story sound as convincing as his early stories had to her. She promised to come back soon.

Alex met her in the near-empty parking lot beyond the side entrance to the university's hematology lab. Jessica parked the minivan next to her sister's Beamer, which was shining under the streetlamp. The lab was two blocks away from Jackson Hospital, where Jessica could just make out the red neon sign for the emergency room. It made her think of Uncle Billy.

Alex was wearing her white coat and thin plastic gloves. She looked exhausted, her eyelids open in slits and her face oily. "Long night, huh?" Jessica asked her as they walked through the dimly lighted hall.

At first, Alex didn't answer. "You don't know how long," she said finally. "Last night, too."

"So what did—"

"Let's wait until we get to my desk. We'll have privacy there," Alex said in a low tone. "There are a couple of folks still chilling here tonight. Now you've got me paranoid."

The plate on the laboratory door was engraved RESEARCH/HEMATOLOGY. The lab, inside, was bright from fluorescent lighting. As always, Jessica wondered how in the world someone who had grown up in the same house with her could make any sense of the forbidding-looking equipment, with the various test tubes and meters and computer displays. Alex had a small desk in a midsized office behind the lab. There were three other desks in the room; Alex's was closest to the window, which overlooked the parking lot.

The desk and rolling green chair looked old to Jessica, like furniture from the 1950s. Her sister's desk was beneath a mound of textbooks and paperwork, but there were small touches of sentimentality: In a corner, she kept a picture of Jessica's family taken when Kira was three. Alex also had a black-and-white photograph of their mother, from when Bea was Jessica's age or younger. In it, longhaired Bea was a different person.

Alex swallowed the last of a Diet Coke and threw the can into her trash bin with a spinning clank. She pulled off her gloves, throwing them away also, then rubbed her eyes hard with her palms. "Lord have mercy . . . I am so beat," she said.

Jessica sat across from her sister, stiff with curiosity. At first, Alex wouldn't meet her eyes. When she did, her bleary gaze was heavy with unspoken questions.

David's secrets, Jessica decided, must be in his blood.

"It's miracle blood," Jessica explained softly, unprompted.

Alex nodded so slightly that her head barely moved. "Yes," she said in a voice equally soft. "That's exactly what it is."

Jessica clasped her fingers together. "You've never seen anything like it."

"No," Alex said. "And that doesn't surprise you, I see."

"I suspected. I didn't know," she said. "What's in it?"

Alex sighed, pulling open a folder on her desk. She gazed at her notes a moment, then shook her head, overwhelmed. "If you were another hematologist, I could sit here and talk to you about it all night long. There's just so much. I don't even know. . . . Well, I'll start at the beginning and try to make it simple. We have a machine called a Coulter counter, which basically takes a blood sample and counts the red and white cells. The red-cell count was normal, about five million. Nothing strange there. Then I saw the white-cell count."

"White cells fight disease," Jessica said, feeling her body awakening with both dread and exhilaration.

"Right," Alex said, briefly meeting her gaze again. "I'm talking about *crazy*. The counter threw some figure at me that almost made me fall off the stool. An impossible number. Normally, you see fewer than ten thousand white cells—this number was in the millions, Jessica.

"I thought, well, this has to be off. Usually, when you see an elevated count—not *that* elevated, mind you—it's because the body is fighting off an infection. So I started to wonder what in Heaven's name this person could have. I did a blood smear to look at the sample under a microscope for myself. Of course, what I found didn't look like any damn blood cells I've ever seen before. Normal white cells are very flat, discs almost. These looked healthy, but they're much smaller and attached in threes. Like a Mickey Mouse head, if you can picture that. So I'm pulling out my books, checking out this shape, and I still can't find them. There's no record of them. Then, I noticed something else . . ."

"What?" Jessica asked, her mouth as parched as straw.

"These smears I took, these samples, don't clot. The blood is always fluid. I pulled the tube out of the refrigerator, where I was storing it, and the damn thing was . . ."

"It was warm," Jessica said. "The tube was cold at the top, but the blood was still warm."

Alex gave Jessica the another hard gaze. "Be up front with me. Where'd you get this blood? What is it?"

Jessica shook her head. "Don't ask me that, Alex. I can't tell you."

"Maybe you don't understand what we have in our hands," Alex said sternly, leaning closer to her.

Jessica remembered David in the bathtub, thrashing in the blood. And his vanishing wound. "Oh, I think I do," she said.

"No, I think you don't. But I'm going to tell you. The big problem with sickle-cell patients is their inability to fight off infection. We have a test called a serum opsonin, which helps us measure the blood's ability to fight off bacteria. You take a patient's serum and incubate it with bacteria. It's sort of a coat to make the bacteria a magnet for white blood cells. Then you add *healthy* white cells from someone else. The point is to see if the healthy cells can fight the patient's bacteria. That's what I decided to do with this blood you gave me."

"You mean you mixed it up with somebody else's blood?"

"That's exactly what I mean."

Jessica nervously played with her fingers, twining them. By now, she could feel nervous perspiration beading in the space between her breasts. David had said something about a Ritual to pass the blood, hadn't he? He never said anything about what would happen if his blood happened to touch another person's.

Suddenly, Alex stood up. "Come out to the lab. I want to show you this part."

There were specimens lined up across a counter in a far corner, near an aluminum double sink, each marked with numbers. The specimens reached from one end of the counter to the other, a dozen in all. Alex walked with Jessica to the far left end, where a slide-sized smear of blood was marked "1/8."

"What I did," Alex said, "was to dilute my patient's blood. That's a normal part of the test. I started at about an eighth of the blood's strength. And I added the blood you gave me at full strength. I call your blood the Supercells.

"The bacteria was gone before I could even slide it under the microscope to take a look. I thought I'd made a mistake, so I did it again. Same thing. Not a trace of the bacteria in the patient's sample. Just Supercells. So I decided to start improvising; I diluted the Supercells to one-eighth of their strength too. Then one-sixteenth. Pow. Same thing. Bacteria's gone."

Jessica surveyed the line of blood samples, her heart thudding as she followed the sequence of numbers: 1/32, 1/64, 1/128, 1/256, 1/512. The numbers grew higher, scrawled in red pencil.

"You understand what I'm getting at?" Alex asked her.

"I think so . . ."

"No matter how minuscule the dilution, the Supercells are having a picnic on the bacteria. Just eating it. They're somehow invigorating the patient's serum, and I mean on instant contact. I spent two nights monitoring these samples, testing and retesting. At really small dilutions, it takes much longer to have an effect. Eventually, there's none at all."

"When does it stop working?" Jessica asked, inching down the counter to try to see to the end. Then, she did: 1/4096. So diluted there was hardly any of David's blood at all.

"And this is the effect on someone else's blood? Not just by itself?" she asked, bewildered.

"Jessica, that's what I'm trying to tell you. I mean, I can't even think about what kinds of effects those undiluted Supercells would have when circulating inside a patient. Not a trace of harmful bacteria in the body, that's for sure. No viruses. The immune system would be beyond imagination. And this—the way this blood affects an outside sample—I can't even express the full meaning of this. The Supercells take over. They heal. They take what's weak and make it strong. It's just what you said. Miracle blood. That's exactly what it is."

At the end, her voice was shaking. Alex was speaking in a hush, like an awestruck child. Silently, she waved Jessica back into the tiny adjoining office and closed the door behind them. For a long time, the sisters didn't speak. The fluorescent bulbs buzzed above them, the only sound in the room.

David's blood could heal by itself? Did that mean if Alex gave a sickle-cell patient a transfusion of David's blood, it would wipe out the malady entirely? Would the same be true for other blood disease, like leukemia? My Lord. Or AIDS, even?

Alex, she guessed, was having the same thoughts. Alex was slumped low in her chair, as though all her strength was gone, staring at Jessica. Waiting.

"It's artificial, isn't it?" Alex asked finally. "I've read about work with artificial blood. What is it, some kind of DNA manipulation? Cloning cells?"

Quickly, Jessica shook her head. She stared at the floor.

Alex sighed. "I'm sure you know that if you weren't my sister," she said, "I would have been on the phone by now to every researcher I could think of to find out what this is. I would be flying in a team to prepare a study that would set hematology on its tail, from the *AMA Journal* to the *New England Journal of Medicine*. I would be on CNN and the *Today* show. Make no mistake. You understand where I'm going?"

"Alex . . ."

"I'm not talking about fame, if that's what you think. And this has nothing to do with journalistic ethics or whatever you were talking about when you gave me this sample. We're way beyond that. I'm a researcher. It's my life.

"And do you know what hurts me? There are a lot of folks out there who think researchers have discovered all of the cures for these diseases we have, from AIDS to sickle-cell to you-name-it, but we're just sitting on top of it because it isn't politically expedient or financially viable enough, or bullshit like that. I hear that all the time. Especially from us, because of that Tuskegee experiment with syphilis—a bunch of white doctors letting the brothers suffer on even though they had a cure. Let them die, one by one, just to see how syphilis fucks up a human being.

"I've worked with patients who would not have died if a treatment using these Supercells had been available. And the minute you put this sample in my hand, you gave me knowledge that could help save lives in ways I haven't even thought of. This is what I'm talking about. And if I have that knowledge and don't act on it, then guess what? What all the folks have been saying is true. Except, this time, they're talking about me."

A tear ran down Alex's face, which otherwise was rigid as stone.

Her chest tight, Jessica clutched her own cheeks with her fingers. Now she knew what people meant when they said their breath was stolen away. The implications of her sister's words were making her world spin again. Jessica wiped away her own tears.

Her voice was faint. "Alex, I know where the blood came from, and it doesn't matter. Even if I told you, it wouldn't change anything. It won't help anybody."

"Of course it would. Our team could meet with them to learn the process to create these Supercells and multiply them. Or we could help them broaden their research, open it up to testing on human patients. Anything would help, Jessica. If you let me know who's directing their research, I wouldn't even tell them where I got the name—"

"Oh, Lord Jesus . . ." Jessica said, wringing her hands between her knees as she stared at the floor. She was shaking her head.

"Take your time."

"Alex, it's David's blood."

Alex's face didn't change, as though she hadn't heard. She stared at Jessica, not blinking.

"It's David's blood. It's from his veins. Remember when I told you how his scars heal up? He told me why. He has unusual blood. I found a sample he'd drawn, and . . . I just wanted to know what was so unusual about it, I guess."

Without speaking, Alex turned in her chair to stare out the window, where their cars were parked side by side as a uniformed security guard strolled past. Slowly, Alex curled her hand into a fist that was so tight it looked painful.

"I broke my word to my husband by showing you this blood," Jessica said, "and that's on my conscience. It always will be, no matter what. But what you're talking about—the studies and the cameras and the research—he's been running from that his whole life. That's why he never told anyone, not even me. If it were me, Alex, I'd do it. I'd give up my freedom and my life and do whatever it took for doctors to poke holes in me and help people. But that's not our choice to make for him. He's made it. He wants to live his life."

"But . . . how is his blood—"

"All he knows is that he never gets sick." The half-truths were the best she could do, and Jessica knew she had said too much already. Too, too much. Jesus help her.

Alex folded her hands on top of her desk and rested her cheek there, as though her bones had collapsed. Her red, weary eyes faced Jessica. There was nothing in those eyes. "Okay," Alex said tonelessly.

"Okay what?"

"Take the blood back. Get rid of it. Take it away."

It took Jessica a few seconds to absorb what Alex had said. She meant to sweep it away, pretend it never happened.

"You can live with knowing about it, Alex? And that's all?"

"I don't know," Alex said in the same dead voice. "Guess I'll find out, won't I?"

Jessica watched Alex pour what blood remained in David's test tube down the sink, and she washed it away with a powerful stream of water. She gathered her slides together and dropped them into a McDonald's bag someone had left from lunch. She gave the bag to Jessica, who tossed it into a looming, empty garbage bin in the parking lot as they walked outside.

Jessica saw her sister gazing back at the bin, shoving her hands into the pockets of her lab coat. She wondered if Alex was just in shock, the way Jessica had felt when David told her the truth. Or, maybe she was thinking about all of her empty hours of research ahead, when she would always know she'd had the answer right in her hands. Now, Alex would be a hypocrite. Jessica realized she was going to cause her sister pain that she would never fully understand.

The security guard was reading a paperback in the light of his own car parked at the curb, and Jessica was glad he was nearby. Alex waved at him, and the guard waved back.

"I guess this is why you all are leaving," Alex said in the van's window after Jessica closed her door.

"Mostly. Yes," Jessica said. "He doesn't feel safe here anymore. The tree episode was a close call for him. If he ever went to a hospital . . ."

"Last I checked, there were hospitals in Senegal too." Alex's eyes glimmered.

"I know. He just needs to live somewhere we aren't known."

"I'm not going to lose you, am I? You better not go off without a trace or anything. Please don't do that."

Jessica squeezed her sister's hand. "Oh, no, Alex. Never. You'll hear from me. You always will."

Alex smiled at her in the darkness. "I feel like a fool tonight," she said.

"Why?"

"Because these past two days, staring at those slides, I was here thinking this was something to do with man. All those years of medical school, all that studying, I looked under that microscope tonight and thought I was witnessing the work of man. I should have recognized God's work right away."

Jessica nodded. God's work. That was it exactly.

"Keep God close to him," Alex said. "One day, when David is ready, he'll do the work he was born to do. You're right. It's not up to me or you to tell him when. But when that time comes, I'll be ready too."

Jessica felt wholly relieved at her sister's levelheadedness. Alex was really something else. Maybe it was right that she'd brought David's blood to her; now, she wasn't isolated. She needed her sister's friendship.

"It's not an accident I married him, is it?"

"No. Nothing is an accident, little sister," Alex said. "Not a thing in this world."

She leaned over into the window, and the sisters hugged for a long time.

▪ 40

Alexis Jacobs felt at peace. Lord knew she deserved it.

The lunacy of the past two days, from her racing heart to her adrenaline rushes, had served their purpose. She didn't have to spend any more hours mulling, wondering, obsessing. Now, she realized, she could rest her muddled mind for a while. Just relax.

Amazing as it was, she'd somehow put David's blood out of her mind—at least from a clinical standpoint. She'd have plenty of time to pore over the notes she'd made to reinforce what she'd known all along, that there *was* hope; there *were* answers.

Tonight, waiting for the elevator's slow climb up to her apartment, Alex was thinking about her sister. What was she in for now? She'd been moved to see the glow in Jessica's face, the way she was embracing a real-life miracle, ready to march with it. If only it weren't about David, yet again. Miracle blood. David could have two heads and be a charter member of the Ku Klux Klan, and it wouldn't matter to Jessica. Alex didn't know why, but Jessica had always been determined to hold on to him no matter what. And Alex had always tried to do her sisterly duty, questioning her at every turn: Didn't you jump in bed with him too fast? (Hell, seemingly overnight, Jessica had gone from gushing about her first date with him to gushing about how great he was in the sack.) What do you *mean* he won't get an AIDS test? (Alex had never forgiven David for that; though now, of course, she could see why he'd refused.) Isn't twenty-one a little young to be getting married? Hadn't you planned to wait longer to start having children? Jessica, don't you think you've let yourself get too wrapped up in what *he* wants?

Jessica had always had an answer, an explanation, an excuse.

It was like Jessica didn't feel whole without that man. Sometimes, from the way she interrogated Alex about her love life, Alex got the feeling her sister thought being single was some kind of curse. She never seemed to believe her when she said she was just fine, that she *liked* living alone. How else, except through being alone for a while, could you ever discover who you really are?

But Jessica didn't get it. And now what? Was David finally going to overshadow her entire life, taking her on some quest to protect his bizarre physiological secrets?

Alex was worried about her sister. But she wouldn't think about it anymore, not tonight. Tonight, she just wanted to sleep.

Alex expected her two cats, Sula and Zoe, to trip her at the door because she was so late and hadn't fed them since morning. But when she let herself into her apartment, the cats weren't in sight. She dropped her briefcase on the black-and-white checkerboard floor and locked her deadbolt.

Her apartment, in an eight-story Art Deco building on South Miami Beach, was furnished entirely in black and white, from the black leather couches to her zebra-pattern beanbag chair. Even Sula's coloring was black and white, and Zoe was pure black. When Alex's attorney friend, Kendrick, visited her, he tried to tell her she was psychotic for decorating her apartment to match her cats.

"Sula? Zoe? Mommy's home, guys," Alex called, shaking their box of cat food in the kitchen. Still not so much as a hello.

It was nearly one A.M. Maybe they'd reported her to the ASPCA and moved to a new home, she mused. Fine with her. She could save some money on kitty litter and cat food.

The light was blinking on the white answering machine on her kitchen counter. She pushed the button to rewind the tape and let it play while she poured food into her cats' empty dishes.

One message from her mother, of course. Next, Kendrick confirming their plans to see the Alvin Ailey dance company on Sunday. (Was he going to turn into something, with his fine self? Jessica, for one, would be relieved.) The last message, from only fifteen minutes before, was from David Wolde himself. Alex's heart jumped with renewed fascination; this man's blood, someday, might lend insights that could change world medicine. Her baby sister's husband.

"Listen, Alex, it's after twelve-thirty and I was wondering if it would be too unreasonable to expect my wife back here soon." He was pissed, not even pretending to be in a good mood. David pampered Jessica to death, but he never cozied up to anyone else. "Perhaps you can resolve whatever this is during the daylight hours?" the voice went on. "It's late, and this is very disconcerting. I'm debating whether to come search for her—"

Alex pressed the button to erase the messages. Jessica must have made up a hell of a story to get out of the house so late, and Alex knew she wouldn't help the situation by calling David if she didn't know the story herself. Jessica would be home soon enough, if she wasn't by now.

Where were those damn cats? They always hid when she brought strangers to the apartment, but any other time they were all over her as soon as she came home for another precious few minutes. Maybe they were asleep, which was exactly where she needed to be.

But first, she needed to chill out. If not, she'd spend another night staring at the ceiling.

Alex poured herself a glass of white wine from the half-full bottle Kendrick had brought, turned on her black torchère lamp to a dim setting, and put on her new Anita Baker CD. Then she opened the glass sliding door leading to her balcony, which stretched from her living room to another glass door in the bedroom.

The breeze smelled thick and nearly sweet to her, like the ocean coated with sugar. She left the door open behind her and leaned across the iron railing to gaze three blocks east toward the black water. From seven stories up, she could see the fanning leaves of palm trees and the Spanish-style courtyard with a fountain that had seduced her into buying the one-bedroom condominium, even though she still thought it was overpriced. She could watch that gushing fountain, with its green-shaded lighting inside the pool of water, all night long.

No more thinking about David or his blood. Not tonight.

Alex closed her eyes, enjoying her favorite refrain of Anita's song. She sipped the wine and savored the fine, pure taste. She could smell the ocean, and feel a restless calm, all around.

Alex heard the sharp crack against the back of her head before she felt it, and when she did, the pain was sudden and blunt.

Then, it seemed to be gone. What she felt afterward wasn't nearly as startling. It was liberating.

She was flying.

She was

▪ 41

"You're crazy," Sy said, standing over Jessica's shoulder at her computer terminal.

"This has to get edited. Am I right? Then let's get it done," Jessica said, her eyes locked on the type on the screen. She spoke rapidly, without inflection. "Who was it you asked me to call? I'm not going to get anywhere with the housing people in Washington. The best they'll say is that they'll conduct an investigation of the trafficking charges. I'll add that here." She pointed between two paragraphs, her finger barely trembling.

Kira was sitting at the desk in front of Jessica's, flipping through the pages of a coloring book she'd brought. She whirled around in the too-big chair. "Mommy," she said in a whine thinly disguised as a whisper. "Do you have crayons in your desk?"

"No, sweetheart. Use the red pen Mommy gave you."

"I used red already. See?"

"I'll look in a minute, Kira. I'm working."

Sy leaned over Jessica, his hands on her shoulders. "Don't do this, kiddo."

"What do you mean, 'Don't do this'? I am doing this. We can finish this in two hours, Sy. It's running Wednesday."

"Now we're leaning toward Sunday. We have time. You have more urgent things to take care of right now. I don't even know what the hell you're doing here."

Irrationally, Jessica felt enraged. "What am I doing? I'm doing my job. That's what I'm goddamned doing," she hissed, blinking back unexpected tears. Floodgates. Just waiting.

Her hand fumbled on the keyboard, highlighting a large paragraph in bright green. She gasped. She couldn't think of what to do. What if she erased it accidentally? What then?

Sy reached over to push the CANCEL key. The green went away. The paragraph was fine, untouched. Everything was fine. Fine.

"Where's David, Jessica?" Sy asked her patiently.

"I don't know," she said. "I think he's at home."

David had mentioned an errand he needed to run home for, something to do with an inspector's appointment, and he'd left Jessica with her mother and Kira at the hospital. And Randall Gaines was there, too, talking to Bea in a corner. Jessica hadn't wanted to be there anymore, that was all. So she took Kira's hand and told Bea she'd be back, and somehow she ended up in the parking lot and spent ten minutes in the sun looking for the minivan until she remembered that it was gone because David had taken it. So, she pulled open the door of a cab and told Kira to get inside, and here she was. Here she was.

Sy spoke softly. "How's your sister?"

"Fine," Jessica said, feeling moisture trying to slip from her nose, so she wiped it with her knuckle. "She's fine. No change. You know. Nothing new."

"Aunt Alex is sleeping," Kira said, waving her pen instructively at Sy as she spoke. "She hasn't waked up yet."

Sy squeezed Jessica's shoulder hard before turning to walk away. "You need to go, Jessica. I don't want to see you here when I get back from my cigarette break. You'll do more harm than good right now."

A sob caught in Jessica's throat. That's what Peter would have said. Exactly what Peter would have said.

It was all wrong, all wrong, all wrong.

Peter was supposed to be here. And Alex was supposed to be at work at her lab, not taped up and plastered and strapped in a bed in an intensive care unit. She was supposed to be waiting at the other end of her telephone with a smart-ass crack, not breathing into tubes from a machine, in a three-day-old coma. Three eternities. And more likely ahead.

Alex wasn't supposed to jump from her balcony and try to kill herself. Jessica never would have believed it was a suicide attempt—Alex was so clearheaded, with a heart so full of faith—

but the police found a note that Alex had typed to her and Bea on the screen of the computer in her bedroom: *first I'm sorry*, and then a verse from Ecclesiastes: *And I gave my heart to know wisdom, and to know madness and folly: I perceived that this also is vexation of spirit. For in much wisdom is much grief: and he that increaseth knowledge increaseth sorrow.*

Jessica had memorized her sister's words, sobbed over them, prayed over them. Those words kept her awake at night. She had brought Alex knowledge and sorrow.

Everything, everything was wrong.

"Mommy, this phone isn't working," Kira complained.

"Hang up and dial nine first," Jessica said, not thinking clearly enough to wonder whom Kira could be trying to call.

A glimpse of beauty inside ugliness is what David had said about Adele; that was how Jessica felt, right now, about Kira. Jessica had dressed Kira meticulously that morning, parting her hair into two short, neat puffs, giving her a shirt with a frilly collar to wear beneath her pink denim overalls and lace-fringed socks to wear with her loafers. Since the news of Alex's fall, Jessica hadn't let her daughter out of her sight.

She had done this. She had made this happen. She had lied and stolen and broken a promise, and she made it happen. Alex had been going along just fine, loving her life, and then Jessica had to bring her something, a secret, that made her want to die too soon. And now nothing would ever be right again. Nothing.

You can live with knowing about it, Alex?

Step on a crack. Break your sister's back.

"Hi, Daddy," Kira giggled into the telephone handset. "Nope. Guess where. Wrong. One more guess. No," she said, and laughed. "I'm at Mommy's work. Coloring my book. Yes. Right next to me. But can I talk to you first? Pleeeeeez? Okay, Daddy. Wait."

Jessica sighed, pushing the buttons to clear her computer screen. Sy was right. Nothing would improve just because she was hiding away here. It was time to go back to the hospital.

"Mommy . . . Daddy wants to talk to you," Kira said.

The telephone cord was too short to reach Jessica, so she stood and sat at the edge of her coworker's desk to take it. As she did, she rested her hand on top of Kira's head as though to balance herself.

"Bea has been looking for you for an hour, calling here frantic. What happened, Jess?" David asked her.

"I just had to leave," Jessica said quietly.

"All right, darling. I know how hard this has been, but stay there and let me take you back to Jackson. There was some news a short while ago."

"News?" Jessica asked, nearly whimpering, expecting grief.

"Alex opened her eyes. She's done it twice."

Overwhelmed with joy, Jessica sobbed. She couldn't speak.

"I'm on my way to you. Wait downstairs with Kira, *mi vida*."

Jessica mumbled something and hung up. A few coworkers were gazing at her from across the room, feeling too awkward to approach her. She understood. Hardship had no friends. It was a solitary task.

Kira was rubbing Jessica's elbow, gazing up at her with wide brown eyes. "Mommy, don't be sad," she said. "You're always sad. Please don't be sad."

Jessica sobbed again, wrapping her arm around her daughter. Oh, this child. She'd been so blessed to have this child.

"I'm not sad, Kira," she said into her ear. "How could I have a little girl as precious as you and be sad? I'm crying because I'm happy. People cry when they're happy too."

At that, Kira smiled. She found a napkin on the desk and wiped it across the tears watering her mother's face.

While Randall Gaines took Kira to the gift shop to look at a big white teddy bear that had caught her eye, Dr. Ivan Guerra led the family to the hall just outside of the ICU waiting area. Jessica could hear the television set playing a rerun of *Roseanne* as the physician fixed a hopeful expression on his young, mocha-complexioned face. He was the same doctor who had tended Uncle Billy, and the sight of him made Jessica fearful of unthinkable news. He must think their family was horribly accident-prone.

"I'm concerned about overwhelming her," Dr. Guerra cautioned, "so I want to limit her visitors to two right now."

David rested one hand on Jessica's shoulder, one hand on Bea's. "You two go," he said. "I'll go catch up to Kira."

Jessica had visited her sister's bedside all weekend, but she was always stunned by the sight of her. She did not look like Alex at all. Jessica didn't know if it was from medication or injuries, but her body looked swollen the way Uncle Billy's had. Her face, especially, was like a stranger's, round and fat. The rest of her was dwarfed by the beeping machines and devices hooked into her flesh, her nose, her invaded bronchial passage.

Alex's nose and jaw had been broken in her fall. She'd broken many other bones, including parts of her back—but somehow, when Jessica gazed at Alex's face, it was her sister's broken nose and jaw that most pierced her heart. With her bandages and swelling, she looked as though she had been severely beaten. The awful sight made Jessica ask herself: Who did this to you?

But Alex had done it to herself. Seven stories down. Her fall had been broken by a tall coconut palm and the thick clump of gardenia bushes near the courtyard's fountain, where she landed. If she'd fallen closer to that fountain, the police told Bea, she'd be dead for sure. Solid concrete all around. Somebody's watching over this lady, he said.

Bea clasped Alex's hand first, leaning over her. "Pumpkin . . ." she said, nearly whispering, "I don't know why it is that everybody in the family has to fall out of a tree this year."

Alex's eyes fluttered open, nearly startling them. She gazed at them with her eyelids half shut. Jessica laughed, excited, clutching her mother's shoulders. Thank you, Jesus. Thank you. Thank you.

"Honey," Bea went on, "you're going to be just fine."

Alex didn't move, but a snake of tears crept down the side of her face. With the edge of Alex's pillowcase, Bea wiped Alex's face; miraculously, Bea herself was not crying. "I know. I know, Pumpkin. You're scared. Anybody would be. But Dr. Guerra just told us some very good things about you. So you just leave it all in God's hands, and don't you worry about a thing."

Alex's lips moved, as though she wanted to speak, but Jessica and Bea both hushed her.

"You just rest," Bea said.

"The doctor said not to talk, Alex."

Alex worked her dry lips around, giving Jessica a glimpse of the thin metal wires holding her jaw in place. Again, she felt a gripping surge of anger. Was it Alex she was so furious with? Or only herself?

"We know you love us, Pumpkin," Bea said, as though they were holding a conversation. "And we know you're sorry for causing us worry. Just put that out of your head. Don't even think like that. We just thank the Lord you're still here with us, and the rest of it doesn't even matter. Want to see Jessica now?"

After drying her own face, Jessica took her mother's place and clasped Alex's hand, careful not to disturb her IV tube. Alex squeezed her fingers with surprising strength, and Jessica smiled.

"It's okay, Alexis," she said. She wished she could speak to her privately, just for a moment.

Was she upset about anything in particular? the police asked when Alex was first brought in. Yes, Jessica had said, dazed. She'd just asked me to come to her office to talk to her. *Did you expect her to try something like this?* No, Jessica said, her face afire with guilt. Never. She didn't understand. Yes, Alex must have been disappointed about the real origin of the blood, feeling as though something that she'd worked so hard to find was wrested away.

But suicide? She thought she knew her better than that.

Jessica leaned over the bed, estimating where Alex's ear would be behind the thick bandage wrapped around her skull. "We'll make it okay," she whispered. "There's a better way than what you did. We'll find a way, Alex. Both of us. Together."

Confusing sounds issued from Alex's mouth: a whisper, a grunt. "Sun . . . won . . . put . . . me . . ." The words sounded nonsensical.

"You can tell me later, okay? I can't understand," Jessica told her tenderly, stroking her fingers. "Don't talk now."

"Putch . . . me . . ." Alex's breathing was labored.

"What's she saying?" Bea asked.

"I don't know," Jessica told her mother, frustrated. Alex sounded like she was delirious, or maybe Jessica couldn't understand her sister's words because of the wires and tubes.

"Does she want to write it down?"

Jessica glanced back at Alex's face. Her sister's eyes were closed, though her breathing hadn't changed. She must be so weak. "You okay, honey?" Jessica asked her.

Alex squeezed her fingers in response, more feebly this time, her eyes still closed.

"We better leave her alone," Bea said. "We're not going far, Alexis. All right? We'll let you rest, but we'll be right here."

Very faintly, Alex smiled. No one but kin would have seen it.

There was no talking Bea into leaving the hospital, even though they'd tried ever since Alex was admitted in the predawn hours on Saturday. One of Alex's friends, a sister who was a resident at Jackson, had found a reclining chair and moved it into Alex's room while Dr. Guerra turned a blind eye, so Bea even had a decent place to sleep.

"You all go. Just go," Bea instructed Jessica, David, and Randall Gaines in the waiting room. She didn't look like a woman whose daughter was critically injured, barely out of a coma after a suicide attempt. Her hair was combed, her lipstick fresh. She was in control. Jessica couldn't remember much control at all in the awful days after her father had died. But, then again, maybe that was where Bea had learned it. Sorrows lining her pockets.

"Get some sleep, Mom," Jessica said, hugging her.

"You too, baby. You look like someone punched you under your eyes. David isn't beating on you, is he?"

"Oh, stop," Jessica said, laughing despite herself.

No, David wasn't beating her. Far from it. He was saving her. If Kira was the beauty in her life, David was the anchor.

She felt so much guilt. For stealing the blood. For showing it to Alex. And now, she felt guilty for the fight she started with David just before the telephone rang at two A.M.—the call she'd always known would come, somehow—when Bea was screaming that Alex had fallen from her balcony.

The night had been cursed. When Jessica came home after her meeting with Alex, she met David standing on the front porch with the car keys in his hand.

"Where are you going?" she'd snapped, defensive, trying to ward off his questions.

She was much later than she'd expected, since she'd stopped at an all-night gas station and mini-mart on Biscayne Boulevard to browse the well-lighted aisles and collect her thoughts. She read half of an article in *Essence* on black men who won't date sisters. She finally bought the magazine and a bag of potato chips, telling herself she couldn't avoid facing David forever. And having to lie to him, the hardest part of all.

"Jesus Christ, Jess, it's almost one-thirty in the morning. Where the hell have you been? I got a switchboard recording when I tried to call the laboratory. When I tried Alex, I got another recording. At your office, a recording. I was about to wonder if I should go look for you. I've been worried senseless."

"What about Kira?" Jessica asked. "Were you planning to leave a five-year-old kid sleeping in an empty house? David, that's so irresponsible!"

David looked hurt rather than angry. "You know I wouldn't have left her alone. What's wrong with you? Can't you see why I would be worried? You hurry out of here in the middle of the night, then you disappear and don't tell me—"

"You don't have to run after me like I'm some child!" She unlocked the door to go into the living room, where *Casablanca* was still playing. He must have started the tape again.

David followed her. "Jessica," he said, speaking slowly, as though she couldn't understand English, "it's one-thirty. What have I been telling you? Don't you realize how dangerous things can be for you? Haven't you grasped the implications of everything?" He silenced himself, obviously measuring what he would say aloud. His eyes said the rest.

"Is this what it's going to be like in Africa? I'm relying on you to make intelligent decisions and you're going to freak out over bullshit?"

Their fight ended when the telephone rang.

Until tonight, Jessica had forgotten about the argument with David—though, for those brief moments, she'd begun to ask herself if she could really go through with taking Kira to Africa with him, after all. And to wonder what the alternative was. Living without him? That was no alternative.

And now? Alex would need months of recuperation, and Jessica couldn't leave with her sister in the hospital. But if they didn't leave, what then? Would the others like David come after him?

Jessica felt smothered by the complications assaulting her. What next? Lord, why was she being tested so severely, without reprieve? Jessica's prayers had turned into pleadings for God to make His purposes clear.

"If you don't, Lord," Jessica said after brushing her teeth, staring at her worn face in the mirror, "Alex may make it through, but I don't know if I will. I'm telling you right now."

David gave her a thorough backrub, helping to deaden her worries and coax sleep to her muscles. His slightly calloused hands moved across her shoulders and her rib cage, his fingers tickled her spine. She was able to close her eyes, for a time, and forget. His freshly showered skin always smelled sweet, like a child's, even without cologne. She leaned against the smell, her arms wrapped tight around his waist, and kissed his bare chest. Holding him was the only thing that felt right.

"David . . . I'm sorry I went off on you on the porch the other night. You didn't deserve that. I was wrong to run out."

She felt his chest rise and fall. His breathing sounded loose, relieved. "You frightened me," David said. "I thought you had changed your mind. It would all be for nothing if I couldn't be with you and Kira. All of it." Suddenly, his voice was a whisper licking her earlobe. "Jess. I want to tell you more about the Life gift. About the Ritual. What I can do."

Jessica's heartbeat quickened. She was frightened at herself, at what she'd felt when she first stared at Alex's broken body in the hospital bed. That was how Uncle Billy had looked. It was how her mother might look someday soon. And so would she, and Kira, too. Broken by mishap or age or disease. She knew death was a celebration, but that wasn't the part God let you see. She didn't believe in pink-skinned cherubs playing lutes on beds of clouds. That was an artist's imagination, it wasn't real. She knew Heaven must be more wonderful than any living artist's painting could ever capture; but she couldn't visualize it as a real place when she closed her eyes. How could she? All that was real to her now, terribly real, was the ugliness of the rocky, inevitable passage. And if her sister had blood like David's, Jessica found herself thinking, she would have healed by now.

But they could not talk here, and Jessica was too exhausted to think about tramping outside to the cave. The mystery of David's ritual would have to wait. But not very long. Not long at all.

"Tomorrow," Jessica said. "I want to hear."

As she slept, one of Jessica's prayers was answered for her, only not in any way she had imagined. The answer came in the form of knowledge as ugly as death itself. It lighted with a stunning clearness that made her eyes fly open in the deep night.

At last, she knew what Alex had said in the hospital room.

Someone pushed me.

▪ 42

"Well, I'll tell you one thing. I don't care what the police say, I'm not leaving this bedside," Bea said, glassy-eyed, after the boyish-faced Miami Beach police officer left Alex's room. Alex hadn't been able to do much to answer his patient questions except turn her chin up for yes and to shake her head gently for no. No, Alex had nodded, she didn't know why anyone would want to kill her.

Bea and Jessica had demanded Alex be placed under twenty-four-hour police guard, but so far it hadn't happened. Well, god-damnit, Bea said, she would guard her child herself.

"If it was just some burglar, why would he leave that note? It makes my skin crawl to think of it. Hell, no burglar off the street knows his Scripture like that," Bea went on. "Somebody went after this child. That's what they had the intent to do when they went into her apartment. Only the devil himself knows why."

Alex, tired, had closed her eyes again and drifted to sleep. Jessica hated to see Alex sleep. Sleep looked like a coma. And a coma looked like death. It was all a precursor to death, wasn't it, in the end? If Alex did get better, it would only be for a time. Then, someday, she'd be right back here.

Bea walked to the table near Alex's head to arrange the cards from well-wishers. The playful greetings pictured balloons, Far Side hospital cartoons, and cats of every variety. Either her friends refused to acknowledge how serious Alex's condition was or they figured they could heal her with smiles. Maybe they could.

"You don't know what kind of loonies we've got running around this town. Somebody could sneak in here in the middle of the night and smother her with a pillow," Bea muttered.

"It's true. That really happens," Jessica told her mother, before her thoughts had a chance to catch up to her. "There was a woman in a nursing home in Chicago . . ."

Suddenly, Jessica's limbs seemed to draw up against her, flinching as though a blast of cold air held the hospital room frozen.

"David, where are you going?"

"Jesus Christ, Jess, it's almost one-thirty in the morning."

In her mind, Jessica was back on the porch with David, arriving home after Alex had told her about the blood, where she saw him there in the lamplight with his car keys gleaming in his hands. She'd naturally assumed he was on his way out somewhere.

But what if David had overheard her conversation with Alex and figured out she'd given Alex the blood sample? What if he noticed she'd moved the bag from where he kept it? (And why did he have the blood there, anyway? For her?) What if he'd waited for Alex in her apartment to make sure she wouldn't tell what she knew? What if—just suppose—when Jessica saw David on the porch, he was really on his way back in?

Would he have had time to drive across the causeway to Miami Beach, let himself into Alex's apartment somehow, and then drive back home to beat her home?

Maybe. Oh, God. Yes.

. . . he that increaseth knowledge increaseth sorrow

The unexpected thoughts were making Jessica feel breathless. She stared at Alex's troubled, sleeping face, helpless against a downy white pillow. A pillow. She thought about her mother's words, the words that had triggered her floodgate of living-color memories.

A pillow. Smothered with a pillow.

That's exactly what had happened to the Chicago woman Peter had told her about. Rosalie Tillis Banks. Death and a broken nose, all in the same quiet night.

Why think of that now?

They called me Spider. Spider Tillis.

Rosalie Tillis Banks's father was a jazz musician who had disappeared, Peter kept telling her. Vanished. David had been a jazz musician in Chicago in the 1920s. His name was Seth Tillis. He disappeared.

And David had been lecturing near Chicago when the old woman died, hadn't he? At Northwestern University's School of Music. She remembered how he called so often complaining about the cold, saying he missed her, saying he would give up lecturing after that.

Coincidence followed David. Alex had said there was no such thing as accidents.

But why? Why kill his own daughter? And could he really have tried to kill Alex? Jessica wondered if her grief was tearing a trail of outlandish imagination or equally outlandish truth. She must know.

Then, as Bea complained on about useless police, Jessica remembered how she could know, once and for all.

Sy stopped Jessica in the hallway before she could reach her desk. "The lawyers have a couple of concerns about the housing piece," he told her. "I know this is rough, but we're staring right at deadline. It would be a big help if we could get one more person on the record."

Jessica stared at him with more venom than she'd intended, but she couldn't help it. She couldn't believe Sy was holding her up to talk about something so mundane as a newspaper story when her life was falling on top of her, crushing her.

Sy saw something in her eyes and took a step back. "Well . . . when you get a minute, take a look. Make a couple of calls. How's Alexis?"

"Great," Jessica lied, just to be through with him.

From nowhere, a headache landed against Jessica's temples and rang beneath her skull. She knew it was here. That Chicago police report had been lost, but it found its way to her hands and she hadn't even opened the envelope. It wasn't until Jessica reached her desk and gazed at her bottom desk drawer that she realized she was only afraid. All along, she'd thought she was this great crusader for truth; but, in reality, she'd been doing nothing but running from it. Ignoring it. Well, no more. Not after today.

The manila envelope she found in her drawer was still smudged, as it had been the day the mail clerk first brought it to her desk. Cook County Police. The homicide report on Rosalie Tillis Banks.

The first time she'd seen this report, Jessica remembered, it was only a fax. All she'd seen was a composite sketch of a featureless black man, shrouded by a muddy reproduction. But this was no fax. If the composite sketch was in here—and she prayed that it was—she would see the murderer's face. It might all finally be settled.

GOOD LUCK WITH YOUR BOOK, the sister in media relations had written on a gummed yellow note on the first page. She'd drawn a smiley face.

It was all so long ago.

Jessica flipped through the pages, one after the other, not daring to skip to the back. The life and death of Rosalie Tillis Banks, who was referred to as V for Victim, fluttered between Jessica's fingers. S was Suspect. S, it said on page five, had asked for V's room number at approximately four P.M. But he had not asked to see her.

One page to go. Jessica could feel her heart's drumming resound to the joints in her toes. She turned to the last page, the composite.

"Hey, stranger," came a woman's voice beside her.

With a gasp, Jessica looked up. It was Em, whose hair was cut shorter than Jessica remembered and whose signs of pregnancy were beginning to show in her slightly puffy cheeks. Jessica mumbled something to her coworker, her mind dead.

Em glanced over Jessica's shoulder to see what she held so tightly in her hands. "What happened? Bad news?"

Jessica could not make a sound.

▪ 43

"Hi. You have reached Fernando Reyes with the Miami Police Department homicide division. I'm not at my desk right now—"

Her frame shaking uncontrollably, Jessica slammed the handset back down at the graffiti-marked pay phone. She'd already hyperventilated once, breathing for a full two minutes into a small paper bag she'd found in the van while she was still parked at the newspaper, and she felt the tightness in her lungs returning. Gulping at the air, not breathing. She'd forgotten something so simple as that.

Her van was parked haphazardly across three spaces behind AAA Liquors on Biscayne Boulevard, not even five minutes from her house. It was after four o'clock, so David had picked Kira up from school by now. When she'd left him that morning, she told David she would go to the hospital after work to visit Alex. She might be late, she said. *No problem*, David assured her, grinning. *Kira and I will go ahead and eat early then.*

The memory of David's grin, now, made Jessica shudder. Her fingers shook as she went through her large woven purse searching for the business card she'd taken from the Miami Beach cop that morning. And where was Reyes? She had to call someone.

You see, she would say, my husband is immortal. He also kills people, by the way. He killed his eighty-year-old daughter in Chicago, and when he figured out that my reporter friend and I might discover his crime, he killed the reporter too. You remember Peter Donovitch—the bloody windshield on CNN. Yes, that reporter. And when my husband found out that I gave a sample of his immortal blood to my sister, he tried to kill her. You could say he's on a roll. It's all perfectly clear, don't you think?

With a sob, Jessica gave up her search for the card and closed her purse. She could not say those things. She could not prove those things. And even if the police cordoned off the neighborhood and swooped into the house from SWAT helicopters, would that be something she'd want Kira to witness? Her father in handcuffs?

Jessica had changed her mind a dozen times in less than half an hour. First, she wanted to call the police. Then, she didn't. Then, she decided the only way to be safe was to call the police. And then she thought she mustn't.

What the hell should she do?

There was only one thing to do. It was the last thing Jessica had decided, the thought that made her race outside to her van in the moments before she discovered she'd forgotten how to breathe.

She had to have Kira with her. She had to take Kira away from David, far away. And then she could call the police, the National Guard, the Marines, whomever. Kira came first.

Oh, how her lungs hurt. What did a heart attack feel like? Weakly, Jessica climbed back into the van's driver's seat and fitted the drugstore's small paper bag over her nose and mouth. Immediately, the bag puffed with air, then she sucked the carbon dioxide back into her system. Puffed out, then back in. Out, in.

Slowly, the breathing came easier. It was time to go home.

▪ 44

Something was troubling the woman. Something new, beyond the hospitalization of her sister. She had been crying, breathing into a paper bag, at times wailing Dawit's name as she drove. Mahmoud regretted that he had not made an effort to replace the camera Dawit had packed away when he removed the picture frames from his upstairs bedroom. Since then, Mahmoud's surveillance had been limited to Dawit's living room, the van, and the telephone wiretap. This was revealing, but perhaps not enough so. Something was happening before him, and yet he could not see it.

Mahmoud had spent a brief thirty years in the House of Mystics, struggling to learn to channel his own psychic energies. He was a failure as a clairvoyant, he decided. He had learned to see his brothers' auras and read meaning into the subtle color changes that he witnessed as he sat across from them with his palms resting across his kneecaps. But he could not capture others' thoughts as Khaldun could—or even one so dim-witted as Jima, who lacked the capacity to learn more than six languages, yet who had challenged Mahmoud once because he'd known, at that instant, that Mahmoud was thinking what a tiresome fool he was. Mahmoud did not share this gift. He could not predict when the rains would end, or how many sheep would die, or when a Searcher would return with a Life brother from abroad.

But perhaps Mahmoud had learned a little something in that time, after all. If he had listened to his psychic senses, he would have remained at the Miami Beach apartment building to determine whether or not the mortal woman's sister had indeed died in her fall. Seven flights down! How could she have survived?

But she had.

And his senses were thrilling now, so much so that the hairs on his arm were erect. He might be treading failure. And this task, the one Khaldun had entrusted to him, was no ordinary challenge. The future of all his Life brothers might be in his hands.

He should have known this! Khaldun had hinted as much when he called Mahmoud to his chamber to describe the mission.

The time has come to bring Dawit back. The time has passed.

Finally! Mahmoud had been eager. He had no way of knowing, then, how lost Dawit had become among the mortals. He had expected his friend to welcome him, to travel with him. He had laughed with joy when Khaldun gave him his instructions.

But Khaldun's face had remained grim. His colorless irises held Mahmoud's eyes as he shook his bearded head back and forth.

You will find no reason to celebrate. After this, you and Dawit will be friends no more. He will not heed gentle measures.

Mahmoud had not believed this. How could he? Dawit treated Khaldun like the father he had lost to war as a child. Dawit's taste for mortals was disagreeable, but harmless. Dawit had chosen to separate himself many times before, and yet remained true to his brothers. He had left his fame and his family in Chicago the very night the Searchers found him. Surely disobedience was foreign to Dawit!

Khaldun, deftly, read Mahmoud's thoughts.

Your brother has a true heart, Mahmoud. But he has suffered much, and his soul is stricken. Fate uses the very strong and the very weak as its agents for change. Even we are not immune to change. Nor to fate.

His message had been very clear, but Mahmoud had failed to interpret it then; Khaldun had been trying to tell him that Dawit might bring destruction to their centuries of peace. Now, Mahmoud was watching the prophecy unfold. He had watched Dawit break the Covenant and reveal himself to his wife, a journalist; and Mahmoud had discovered that she shared the knowledge with her sister, a physician.

What more did he need to see?

Mahmoud stared at the monitors in front of him. Dawit and the child were in the kitchen, making dinner. They were out of his camera's scope, but he could hear the girl's laughter. He had seen Dawit's wife in the van, but now the van was empty.

Tonight, he decided. He must abandon his plan to visit the hospital in the surgeon's scrub suit he had found at a medical supply store, coupled with the false identification he had easily printed and laminated himself. The wife's sister and mother would enjoy one last night of life.

But not so for Dawit's wife and child. Mahmoud had considered many methods, but in his haste he had succumbed to crudeness. He would let himself into Dawit's house with the universal key that had worked without trouble at the Miami Beach apartment. He would visit Dawit's daughter's room first; a simple gunshot to the head while she slept. A silent gun was quickest.

He would visit Dawit's room next and shoot the sleeping parents. He would leave the bodies of the woman and child behind. He would carry Dawit with him; when Dawit awoke, he would sedate him long enough to finish the business of the two women at an appropriate time.

Four would be too much killing for one night, since he must act with caution. Two, then. In two nights, at last, he could begin his journey back to his brothers with Dawit and resume his normal life.

And, after this, he would tell Khaldun that he had lost his

appetite for the ranks of the Searchers. This was not what he had intended. Khaldun's warning was wholly true; there was no satisfaction in this for him.

Khaldun was right in what Mahmoud had heard him say many times: It was pure cowardice, nothing more, for an immortal to kill mortals unnecessarily. What nobility was there in stealing from those already impoverished? Mahmoud had never been a coward.

The monitors gleamed against Mahmoud's weapon as he loaded the cartridge with the heel of his hand.

▪ 45

He was standing behind the screen in the open doorway when she drove up, wrapped in shadows from the tree branches knotted overhead, as though he'd been waiting for her. He was now as much a fixture at this house as the plants around it and the uneven path leading to the door. Jessica didn't allow herself to sit in the driveway and think about what she was going to say or do. That was when she couldn't breathe. She climbed out of the van and trudged past the cave toward David, her legs reluctant to move.

"You're so early. What a great surprise," he said.

She felt naked standing in front of him. Helplessly exposed. Her awful knowledge was big inside her, glowing from her.

Absurdly, David was in an unusually good mood. He was wearing tattered denim cutoffs and a faded Charlie "Bird" Parker T-shirt she'd bought him for a birthday some years back, clothes that were as painfully familiar as his face. At this moment, he looked so much like a reflection of her that his simple presence felt staggering, nearly making her lose her balance.

She had braced herself to face a maniac. But he wasn't one. He was only David, even now. He was smiling, squeezing her forearm to gently lead her inside, closing the door after her. She noticed the sound of the deadbolt clicking into place, and she felt her muscles lock.

Suddenly, she was exhausted inside and out, maybe because of the thrashing in her chest from her overexcited heart. It would be easy to stretch out on the sofa and let him rub her feet.

"Mom-meeee!" Kira cried happily, her voice wavering as she bumped down the stairs.

"Hey, sweetness. Come here," Jessica whispered, meeting Kira at the bottom of the stairs, kneeling to hug her at eye level. She rocked with her, hanging on. "I missed you today."

In an instant, Jessica heard a click and saw a flash of light against the wall. Again, her muscles turned rigid. Her head whipped around.

David stood across the room with his Canon camera, smiling. He advanced the film manually with quick flicks of his thumb. "Perfect. That was a priceless shot. Stay just like that."

"Daddy's been taking pictures all day," Kira complained into Jessica's ear as the camera clicked again. Jessica felt lost in the temporary white blindness.

"You didn't smile, Jess."

"Sorry," she said, and the word sounded comical. What was she apologizing for? How in the world could he expect her to smile? "I think I'm just hungry."

"Ah. Then you're ready for our special treat for tonight."

"Pizza!" Kira announced.

"Kira and I made gluttons of ourselves on my homemade pepperoni specialty. I just need to grate some more mozzarella, and I'll make you one all to yourself."

"Great," Jessica said in the loudest voice she could manage.

Driving home, she'd imagined all sorts of scenarios where she would run upstairs and throw some clothes into a duffel bag, at least enough for her and Kira to stay somewhere overnight. But now that she was inside and saw how small the house was, she knew that was out of the question. Her purse was still on her arm, and that was all she could take. That and her daughter.

She had to do it now. If not, she might not do it at all.

She stood tall, clasping Kira's hand. "While you're doing that, I'm going to run with Kira over to that doll store down the street. It's only five minutes away."

Kira looked up at her, her face full of puzzled surprise. The doll store, which sold antique dolls as well as porcelain dolls crafted by Nadine, the proprietor, was a rare treat. That was where Peter found the beautiful black doll he'd bought for Kira at Christmas; thinking of Peter made Jessica's throat swell nearly shut.

David was frozen, confused. "Well . . . If you want to postpone eating, I'll go with you."

One of Jessica's purse straps nearly slipped from her shoulder, but she quickly yanked it back into place. "No. Please? I just want to be with her a little while."

David leveled a questioning gaze at her. She hoped the excuse would work; she'd maintained plenty of times that she needed to spend time alone with Kira—a source of contention, since he always wanted to be included too—but never so abruptly. He was going to argue. Then it would be lost, because Jessica could barely control a startling new quiver at her bottom lip, and she was sure Kira must be able to feel the unsteadiness in her fingers. She was afraid he would use his reliable old tactic, *Kira, don't you want Daddy to go too?*

Instead, David raised his camera once more and snapped a picture. For a moment, he was hidden behind the bright flash. "Will you be long?" he asked.

"I just want to show her a new doll I saw in the window today. It looks just like her." She had no idea where she was pulling the lies from, but she was thankful they were coming.

Kira was gazing at David, waiting. Jessica now saw that it wasn't enough that Mommy wanted to take her somewhere; Kira had to be certain it was okay with Daddy too. Seeing this, and realizing for the first time how much she had allowed David to win control of their daughter, Jessica felt a wave of near nausea.

"Have fun, Duchess," David told Kira, winking.

Kira grinned, squeezing Jessica's hand. "Let's go, Mommy."

"Love you, baby," David said, walking over to kiss Jessica's lips lightly. Jessica's stomach rattled. He kissed Kira's cheek. "You two hurry back."

As Jessica pulled Kira by the hand up the driveway, she had to use all her self-control to keep from sprinting, or running like someone crazed. She couldn't. David was probably at the door, still watching them go, probably an impulse away from begging to come too.

Teacake had already sprawled across the warm hood of the parked van, and he meowed as they approached. Kira reached up to try to pet him, but Jessica anxiously pulled her to the passenger's door. Fumbling for her keys, Jessica glanced back over her shoulder at the house. The door was closed. David wasn't in sight. Out of habit, she glanced up at Kira's open bedroom window. She didn't see him there, either.

"Will you buy the doll for me?" Kira asked.

"I don't know," Jessica said, biting her lip hard to keep from sobbing. She couldn't cry now, not until they were gone. Safely gone. Then she could do anything she wanted and explain everything to Kira any way she chose. "Get in, honey," Jessica said after she'd opened the door.

"Make Teacake get down," Kira said, worried, trying to climb up to her seat. The cat was gazing at Jessica benignly from his resting state, with no intention of moving.

"I will, honey."

After closing the door behind Kira, Jessica lifted her cat, feeling the hairy tufts of his underbelly, and brushed her nose across his fur. Another so-familiar scent, a comforting smell that reminded her of her bedroom, safe sleep. Teacake mewed, purring. She was about to cry again. Fuck it.

"Teacake's coming?" Kira cried, delighted, as Jessica tossed the cat into the backseat and slammed the door shut behind her before the cat could scramble back out. Unlike Princess, Teacake loathed automobiles. They reminded him of visits to the vet.

"Yep. We're all going."

Somehow, she managed to find the ignition with her trembling hand. She thought of the horror movies where the poor heroine can never get the car to start, but the van started immediately with a roar. Kira's door wasn't closed tightly enough, the dashboard display warned with a red light and a soft, whining alarm. She should have closed it harder. Jessica cursed, shaking her head. She wouldn't worry about that now. Put the van in reverse, she told herself. Go. Not too fast. Check your mirror; be sure not to back over anyone. Make sure no one is coming. You can't have an accident. Just *go*.

They were moving. The thought filled Jessica with a hysterical disbelief. They were driving. The oak tree posting their street number was trailing behind her in the rearview mirror, and they'd reached the intersection that would take them straight to Biscayne. They would vanish into the busy highway's rush-hour traffic. Next, the Interstate. After that, the Turnpike.

She'd done it. Sweet Jesus. She'd really done it.

"Mommy, my door isn't right," Kira pointed out, fussing with her seat belt. "Won't I fall out?"

"I'll fix it at a light, honey," Jessica whispered, blinking hard. Stay away, tears. They hadn't traveled far enough yet. Traffic had boxed them in. No one was moving. Brake lights everywhere. Teacake's clipped, frightened mews from the back pierced Jessica's brain, making her neck stiff. Like a baby's cry.

Jessica had hoped to barrel through the stoplight alongside AAA Liquors, but the light turned red too soon and she braked abruptly. Damnit.

"Fix my door now," Kira said. "Please?"

Jessica's mind was so dazed that she didn't even realize until she'd jumped out of the van to run around to Kira's side that she could have simply reached across her daughter to close the door. Once outside, she immediately felt vulnerable, naked. She'd left the sanctuary of the van in the middle of the road, with everyone noticing her. What if David had followed? Her fingers slipped when she tried to grab Kira's metal latch, so she had to wipe her hands on her slacks. "Careful, sweetheart," she said once the door was open, then she closed it with all her weight.

Somewhere, a car honked. She looked at the light, frantic. Still red. What asshole was out there honking?

Then, Jessica gasped. A red Ford Tempo was only three cars behind her in the left lane, and she nearly fell to her knees when she saw it. David's car! He'd been behind them the whole time.

For an eternity, Jessica stood frozen in the sun. It barely mattered, after the first few seconds, that she finally realized the Tempo's driver was a stocky Hispanic teenager, not David, after all. And he was honking at the car next to him, gesturing that he wanted to merge into another lane.

By the time Jessica climbed back into the van, only seconds before the light finally turned green, there was nothing she could do about the tears. She was sobbing. For those few seconds, standing in the middle of Biscayne Boulevard, she'd nearly collapsed because she thought she had seen David. Jessica was paralyzed with the realization that the life she had known was over. Simply over. Her rationalizations, her acceptance of David's history just to keep the peace, could not change that.

Kira looked at her with worried tears in her own eyes, but she didn't say anything. Jessica almost never cried in front of Kira, because she remembered how terrified it always made her feel when she saw her own mother cry. If Mommy couldn't make it better, then no one could. To a child, it meant chaos. And lately, all she'd been doing was crying.

"I'm sorry, Kira," she apologized through her sobs.

Through the window, Kira watched as they drove past the doll store's friendly yellow sign. She turned her head and craned her neck to watch it disappear behind them, then her eyes were back on Jessica, hopeful, as though she thought Jessica had made a mistake. Teacake's cries, which were close to Jessica's ears because he had curled up in a corner directly behind her, sounded frantic.

"Are we going away now?" Kira asked.

Still sobbing, Jessica nodded. She'd stopped in a turning lane, waiting for a break in the traffic so she could follow the signs pointing toward I–95. Almost there.

"What about Daddy?" A whine crept into Kira's voice.

"Daddy's meeting us. We're going to Disney World."

What a pathetic attempt. Even a five-year-old would have to be brain-dead to buy a story like that. But the assurance seemed to relax Kira, and she leaned back thoughtfully in her plush seat.

All of a sudden, she looked so remarkably small sitting there.

"Is the monster coming, Mommy?" Kira asked after a silence.

Jessica stared at her daughter. She tried to say "No, honey," and explain they were just taking a surprise vacation. But she couldn't answer or speak at all, not even to tell a happy lie.

▪ 46

Dawit believed he would go mad in the silence.

There was the large silence of the house, which he had so foolishly stripped of the music he'd always insulated it with to disguise the hours of emptiness. As he stood gazing through the window at the still yard, the gentle stirrings of insects echoed his loneliness, magnifying the absence of all other sounds.

In one terrible instant, he knew the silence was something more than what it seemed. He knew before Jessica's mother called from the hospital wondering why she had not heard from Jessica, saying there was news about Alex's upcoming surgery. He knew before he found the telephone number for Gallery of Dolls on Biscayne Boulevard, and the good-natured Bahamian woman who ran the shop said she had not seen Jessica. She was about to close up early because she had not had a customer since two, she said.

"Summertime," the woman complained. "Everything dies here in summer."

Then, Sy called shortly after five, asking Dawit to have Jessica call him immediately about some legal matter pertaining to an important story of hers that the newspaper would not be able to print without her input. She ran out without saying a word to anyone, Sy told Dawit. Was everything all right?

In the House of Mystics, which Dawit had never visited except to attend their ceremonies to predict the world's annual events, the conjurers would call it premonition. Dawit had felt it most strongly that day with Adele, when they stopped by the tree at the river. And now, again. He felt so severe a cramp deep in his belly that the pain alone brought tears to his eyes.

He sat on the windowsill hoping that the van would drive up and shatter his fears. Yet, the longer he sat and waited, the more certain he became. She could have driven to the doll shop and back twice, even three times, by now. For some reason he could not fathom, Jessica had taken Kira and was gone.

At first, he was stricken with worry. Dawit was reasonably certain Mahmoud was the one responsible for Alex's attack, though the failed attempt was so uncharacteristically sloppy. Dawit could not think of what reason Mahmoud might have for striking, except as a warning. He could just as easily harm Jessica and Kira too. Perhaps he'd threatened Jessica, and that was why she'd fled.

Or, perhaps Mahmoud had chosen a different route.

Mahmoud might have reached Jessica and told her stories of Dawit's history: his amusement with decapitation as a warrior, or of his unbridled sexual tastes in the brothels. Those things would shock her. Or, more likely, Mahmoud could have revealed to Jessica Dawit's most recent transgressions—his killing her friend and the old man, Uncle Billy. That certainly would have made her flee! Why had he never considered Mahmoud would do such a thing?

Now, Dawit remembered the odd slant of Jessica's eyes when she had walked into the house. He was certain he would see it in her face again once he developed the photographs he had taken of her; consternation, eyes vacant. He'd believed she was still distraught over Alex, and he'd intended to take her in his arms that night and lull her to sleep with gentle kisses to ease that expression away.

But what if, this time, her eyes were so empty because of him?

It could not be. And yet, yes, it was. It was.

Worry gave way to a new, foreign feeling: sweeping rage. He had been betrayed, first by Mahmoud, and now by Jessica. After all he had told Jessica, risking the wrath of his entire brotherhood, she would leave without giving him an opportunity to defend himself, to reassure her? And take his daughter besides?

Kira was gone. She had been in this house, this very room, not even an hour before. Now, she had been stolen from him.

Dawit found himself trembling from anger, sorrow, fear. All three emotions swamped his reason in waves as he sat helpless in the window. This pain, so thoroughly well known to his weary psyche, would not do. He would not resign himself to live in suffering. Not again. Never again.

"On my father's soul," he said, and he heard in his vow the voice of the warrior he had been so very long ago, "my wife and my child will be with me. I swear it."

He uttered the final words in a rasp he himself could barely hear, even in the silence. "Forever," he said. "Forever."

▪ 47

Jessica didn't allow herself to stop—except to pay a toll and ask the attendant for the quickest route out of the state—until they were in

Palm Beach County, more than an hour's drive away. She would have happily plowed on even then, but Kira's complaints about needing to pee had been constant. And although Teacake had finally quieted in the last few minutes, curled near Kira's dangling feet, the cat was panting and obviously needed water. Not to mention food. Hell, she herself hadn't eaten anything except a muffin at the hospital that morning. No wonder she felt so dizzy and sick to her stomach. It was nearly six.

"Where are we?" Kira asked drowsily, peering to try to see over the dashboard as Jessica coasted off the Turnpike.

"West Palm Beach. Remember where we stopped on the way to Disney World? All the drivers in the big trucks were here? And there are . . . bathrooms!" She tried to sound excited, to make it more a game than a nightmare.

Kira, scowling, didn't look entertained. "I'm thirsty."

"I'll get you a juice, then, okay?"

She didn't need gas, thank goodness. The van still had half a tank. This would be a quick stop. The full-service complex was like new, painted pink and aqua like the Art Deco buildings in Miami. The smells from the competing fast-food chains inside made Jessica's mouth melt with saliva. She was starving.

It wasn't until Jessica finished chaperoning Kira in the bathroom and stood in front of the juice machine searching for a dollar bill that she realized she only had two dollars and change left in her wallet. Her heart thudded. Feeling the familiar panic, she glanced wild-eyed throughout the lobby.

There was an ATM on the wall, next to an arrangement of touristy brochures of Florida attractions. "Thank you, Jesus," she whispered. She had plenty of credit cards with her, but stocking up on cash was the only way to be safe. She might as well take out the limit, however many hundreds the machine would allow.

"Mommy, Teacake is hot in the car," Kira said as Jessica slipped her Barnett Bank card into the machine.

"I know, baby. It's not good to leave him out there. We'll be back in two minutes, I promise."

The message on the ATM's screen startled her: INVALID CARD, it read with a beep. The saliva gathered, this time, in Jessica's throat. The machine advertised the Honor network's deep-blue logo, and Barnett was an Honor card. What the hell was wrong?

CONTACT FINANCIAL INSTITUTION FOR ASSISTANCE, the machine said, beeping again. Jessica held out her trembling hand, waiting for the card to be spat back out at her, but no card came. The next message that flashed across the screen in green was WELCOME, asking the next customer to please insert a card.

"What—" Jessica tapped on the screen with the heel of her hand. "What in the world . . . ?"

"Ate your card," came a drawling man's voice behind her, startling her. A bearded white man in a Grateful Dead T-shirt, which was stretched nearly threadbare across his big belly, stood in line, arms crossed. "Happened to me once when I forgot to make a deposit and I was bouncing checks up and down the seacoast. Just took the damn card. They can fix it at the bank."

"The bank's closed," Jessica said feebly, as though the stranger could offer some solution, some comfort.

The man shrugged, not saying anything else. Did he think she was asking him for money? And wasn't she?

"Mommy . . ." Kira prodded, yanking on Jessica's pant leg.

It came to her then. David must have done something to make the machine take her card. Maybe he had cleared out the account, closed it. Maybe the bank had some way of tracking her down, and she'd just revealed her location.

Jessica grabbed Kira's hand, pulling her without looking back at the man with the beard. She felt her knees shaking. They had to go. They weren't safe yet.

Jessica stopped frozen at the northward exit's automatic doors. She'd forgotten about the cat. He needed water. But she couldn't take care of it now. Running, pulling Kira with her, they escaped through the doors.

They should not have stopped. Jessica couldn't worry about eating now, or when they would have to stop for gas, or how nervous she would be in a short while, when the sun would be all but gone and she'd have to face the road at night.

"Mommy, why are we running?" Kira asked.

"We're in a hurry, that's all," Jessica said.

"Is Daddy coming?"

Lord God, I hope not, she thought. "Not yet, Kira," she said.

Jessica found the ramp to the Turnpike with a squeal of the van's tires. Teacake's awful cries started again.

What else was David capable of, besides making sure she would be broke? She didn't know. But Jessica felt very strongly, and with a deep sense of dread, that she was about to find out.

She'd decided on Georgia. She would take the Turnpike up to where it merged with I–75 north of Orlando, as the toll attendant had told her, and that would lead straight into Macon. Bea had a half-brother there Jessica knew only as Uncle Bigger—last name Gillis, or Giles, she couldn't remember which—someone she was sure David didn't know about. They could stop there, with family, and she'd decide what to do. She would have time to think safely.

Already, with a plan, she felt better.

She wished she'd been able to warn her mother somehow, but she was sure Bea was protected in the hospital with Alex. David wouldn't dare try to hurt them there; Jackson, the emergency room hub for the county, was never deserted at night like the nursing home in Chicago must have been. Once Bea realized that Jessica and Kira were gone, she would probably assume she'd had a fight with David. She would worry for a while, but not for long. Jessica decided she would try to reach her the next day, from Macon.

And the police. She'd have to do that too. The composite sketch she'd tucked back into the drawer in her desk would be proof enough for Reyes. She'd leave a message for him the next time she stopped, so at least he would be notified by morning.

David would be a fool to chase her now. Was she secretly hoping he would simply give up and go away without police involvement? Even now, after everything he'd done? That seemed to be the only fitting outcome: David had to go back to his home. Whatever he was, wherever he belonged, he was a freak in their world.

Damn. She'd told herself that she wasn't allowed to think about David, because the road was slick with drizzle and it was nearly impossible for her to see through tears. Her head would have to go somewhere else for now. She would concentrate on details.

It was nine o'clock, and she'd been on the road for nearly four hours. Orlando, the green road signs announced, was sixty miles away; already, each billboard for a gas station or tourist stop advertised tickets for Disney World. Every few miles, Jessica saw a new set of Mouse ears. Jessica was thankful Kira had curled up in her seat to sleep after tiring of the Alphabet game. She'd been stuck on Q when she finally dozed off. She would be disappointed that they weren't going to Disney World after all, though she probably already suspected that.

Jessica turned the radio on softly, finding a static-filled R&B station to make up for the loss of Kira's chatter. The closer they got to the city, the stronger the Orlando station's signal.

Because of the cat, she hadn't been able to save gas by driving with the air conditioner off and the windows open, not as hot as it was; Peter had once told her how, when he was in college, his cat died while he was driving on the interstate in a car without AC. So the luminescent gas gauge was past Empty, and she would have to stop for gas soon or be stalled. There was no choice. And Jessica needed to eat; the growling in her stomach was fierce, and she had a headache even a three-course meal and plenty of aspirin wouldn't help by now.

Cash wasn't an option. Since both her Visa and Discover cards were maxed out, she'd have to pull off at the next exit and find a gas station that took American Express. And she'd have to hope David hadn't thought of that too.

Most of Florida's large stations had mini-marts, luckily, so she could find some hot food, some Pop-Tarts and fruit for Kira to eat for breakfast, cat food, maybe even cat litter. Teacake had been quiet for two hours straight, but now he was scurrying close to her feet, worrying her near the brakes. Jessica loved Teacake, but she was sorry she'd brought him. That had been dumb. Another thing to worry about.

Damnit. They really needed to stop.

Alongside the Turnpike, gas stations and fast-food franchises advertised with lighted signs perched on mammoth poles above the slash pine treetops. She saw another cluster of lights rising a half-mile north of her, from three gas stations and a Comfort Inn.

A motel. Did she dare stop, to rest? No. As ludicrous as it seemed, she'd never sleep a wink, worried that David could find them simply by spotting their van in the parking lot. She wanted to get as far away from him as possible.

Gas and food only. Then, back to the road.

"I want to talk to Daddy," Kira said, barely awake after Jessica roused her, sounding closer to tears than she had all day.

"Shhhhh," Jessica said, kissing her forehead, which was striped in red from the neon of the gas station's window display. "You will. I'll try to call him, okay? But we might not be able to talk to him right now."

"Where is he?" Kira whimpered.

"He's going to meet us tomorrow, honey."

Jessica said all of this, somehow, despite the stone-sized lump in her throat. She planned to make a call, all right, but it wasn't going to be to Daddy. Her fortress of lies would crumble soon. Wouldn't it be best to try to slowly tell Kira the truth, that they had left Daddy behind? She couldn't do it. Not yet. When she did that, she would have to admit it to herself.

Kira cheered up a little inside the mini-mart, after Jessica told her she could pick any candy bar and plastic toy filled with bubble gum she wanted. Meanwhile, Jessica shopped the cramped aisles for necessities: a comb, travel toothbrushes, cat food, a cat dish, bottled water, crackers to snack on. There was cat litter, but no litter box. Forget it. Teacake would just have to shit in the van.

The greasy, shriveled hot dogs rolling on the pins of the roaster looked two days old, but the sight of meat made Jessica's stomach tumble eagerly. She fixed herself two, and had already eaten half of one by the time she made it to the counter with her armload of booty. Kira carried the Meow Mix.

The man behind the glass was middle-aged, a brother with glasses whose hairline formed a perfect, shining U. There was a paperback folded near his hands on the counter, a well-worn copy of Terry McMillan's *Waiting to Exhale*. Seeing the book made Jessica smile, at ease. It was good to see a brother reading a book by a sister.

"Durn. Looks like somebody forgot to pack," he said. "Who's this pretty little lady down here? What's your name, Sleepyhead?"

Kira didn't speak or smile, so Jessica answered for her. "Sorry she's grumpy. It's been a long drive," she said.

"This'll be all for you?" the man asked her.

"I'm going to fill up my van at pump one," Jessica said, handing him her American Express card with a silent prayer.

"All right. Lemme run it through, and when you come back in I'll give you the total."

Jessica watched, not blinking, as he zipped the card through a computer scanner. After a pause, the machine made a high blipping sound and Jessica exhaled, relieved. It had worked.

But the man made a face and zipped the card through again. "Error that time. Scanner could be acting up. If it don't go through this time, I'll punch in the number myself."

The same sound. Watching, Jessica's face was taut with anger, nervousness. She knew, as the man manually entered the card number on his machine, that it would not go through.

He looked up at Jessica, gazing above the rim of his glasses. "Says I've got to call. You had a problem with this card, miss?"

"I don't think so," Jessica said, a whisper.

The man regarded her a few seconds longer, his expression hard to read, then reached for his phone. "Sorry about this," he said.

Waiting, as he dialed and spoke to someone in numeric codes, Jessica finished eating her first hot dog. She had to struggle to swallow. What could she do without money? Had David trapped them here? If so, she would have to do better than leave a message for Reyes—she'd have to call 911. Right now.

The attendant was saying "Uh-huh" and "Is that so?" still looking at Jessica. Finally, he sighed, hung up, and spoke directly into her anxious eyes. "Well, miss, they're saying that card was reported stolen today."

Jessica closed her eyes, her chest sinking. "Damnit . . ."

"I won't confiscate the card if you can show me a picture I.D., but I think this is something you need to settle with those folks there."

Her hands unsteady, Jessica searched her wallet for her driver's license. "I don't believe this," she said. "This is my fucking hu—. . . My . . ." My fucking husband. She stopped herself, remembering Kira, and her eyes filled with tears of frustration. "This is a mistake. Here it is. My hair was longer then."

Very carefully, he examined the license, then Jessica's face. Finally, he smiled and handed both cards back to her. "It's prettier the way you have it now, I think. You favor that singer Toni Braxton. Girl sings her behind off," he said.

Jessica was flipping through her wallet to find an obscure card David might not know about. Damn him. She would just call the fucking police, then. He couldn't take her down like this. If he thought she was playing, he was wrong.

"Uhm . . . Maybe there's something else in here . . ."

The man pointed. "How about that Mobil card?"

"You take that?" Jessica asked him, stunned and grateful. She'd applied for it when she was a college freshman, and she hadn't even looked at the card in nearly a year.

"We better. We're a Mobil."

Jessica was so relieved, she nearly laughed. The Mobil card would go through, she was sure of it. If a glass partition hadn't separated them, she felt she would have hugged this man. He wasn't saying anything outright, and he wouldn't ask her any questions, but Jessica knew that he knew something was very wrong. And he wanted to help a sister out.

"I want to call Daddy," Kira said, reaching up to slap her Milky Way on the counter.

"I know you do. We'll call right after this nice man rings everything up. I'm going to get a key so you can use the bathroom in the back, and I'll call Daddy on the phone. See the phone right here? I promise I'll call and see if he's home."

Jessica glanced with sorrowful eyes at the man, shaking her

head. Silently, he nodded. When he finished, the total on the register came to only five dollars. Jessica knew the real cost must be three times that much, even more. Her mouth fell open.

"We're having a sale tonight," he said. "I'll add another ten for the gas, and you can sign the receipt now. Then fill her up."

"Thank you," Jessica said, too moved, embarrassed, and newly grief-stricken to even meet his eyes. The gas would surely cost more than that too. Suddenly, she'd become a charity case.

"Good luck with your phone call," the man said. Then he added, after a meaningful pause: "Hope it works out all right."

Jessica nodded, struck silent, blinking away her tears.

▪ 48

An unremarkable white Ford sedan pulled into the lot of the Yee-haw Junction Mobil station off Exit 193 on the Florida Turnpike, sidling to a darkened corner near two covered Dumpsters. The headlights switched off first, then the engine. For a few seconds, the driver sat in the car.

The driver was the sort of man few people notice. No facial hair, skin brownish, ambiguously dark. He wore jeans and an aqua-blue Florida Marlins windbreaker despite a temperature of seventy-eight degrees, and he walked across the oil-spattered concrete toward the gas station's mini-mart. He did not go in. Instead, he stood just beyond the window and peeked around to glance inside.

At first, he saw no one except a bespectacled black man reading a book at the cash register. Then, carefully scouting the brightly lighted aisles, he saw the woman in the rear, standing at a pay telephone with an armload of bags. He could not see the girl, but she must be there. As he'd paced himself a kilometer behind the van, Mahmoud, from his handheld video monitor, had seen Dawit's wife awaken the girl and take her inside.

The fates were working in his favor, Mahmoud decided. He had no tracking device planted in the van, so while his video monitor allowed him to see Dawit's wife and hear her every word, he could have easily lost her when she surprised him by fleeing with the girl. His chase began too late. In fact, he'd guessed incorrectly that she would be driving on I-95 until he heard her talk to a toll taker at a tollbooth west of him on the Florida Turnpike. That gave him not only her location, but her destination. But, in fact, once he found the Turnpike, he had somehow driven past her and was two minutes north of the West Palm Beach truck stop when he heard her tell her daughter they were stopping there.

Now, Mahmoud knew he would not have much time. He could not do his work here at the gas station because the attendant's partition was bulletproof, no doubt—Americans, unluckily for him, were always at war with one another—and the attendant was likely to shoot back. That would be catastrophic.

Instead, Mahmoud walked purposefully toward the van, where both front windows were partially open. Seeing Mahmoud and recognizing his scent, the cat stood at the window on his hind legs and cried out. Mahmoud tried the driver's door. Locked.

Mahmoud heard clicks throughout the vehicle as he slipped his thin universal key into the lock, and he opened the door with ease. When the cat tried to jump past him, Mahmoud struck out, making the animal fly against the passenger's door. Teacake hissed at him, scrambling upright, then vanished somewhere in the rear.

The rear. Should he simply stow away and surprise them?

No. With all of the bags of purchases the woman needed to pack in the van, she might find him too soon, before they were on the expanse of the dark, open road.

Mahmoud found a knob beneath the steering wheel and pulled it, making the hood click open with a hollow sound. He glanced once more toward the mini-mart's window and saw no change. A few seconds more and he would be done.

The bright floodlight above him enabled him to see the vehicle's fuse mechanism. His fingers darted across the tiny fuses, then he jiggled them with the precision of a surgeon. Not too hard. Not enough so that the van would not start. But enough, he hoped, that once she started the vehicle, the bumps on the road would jar a fuse out of place and cut off the vehicle's power supply.

He did not have the time to be as meticulous as he would have liked, so as Mahmoud closed the van's hood he knew there remained many unknown variables. Would it stall too soon? Not at all? He would have to tail her and see.

If this plan failed, he would shoot out her tires at a later point, when there was little traffic, and complete his task that way. He shook his head, mortified at the idea; a shoot-out on the roadway, like a crass American movie. Dawit would have laughed with him about such a plan, had it not been his own wife and child.

"Car trouble?" a man in shorts asked as he walked past, with an accent betraying his home as slightly north of Leeds, England.

Mahmoud smiled amiably. "All fixed now," he said.

▪ 49

Miami International Airport, a city in itself, was alive tonight. There were families everywhere Dawit looked: fathers leading daughters by the hand, mothers scolding sons, college-age couples shuffling together with backpacks and weary faces. They were all colors, all nationalities, with myriad purposes. These beings were so furious and passionate in the way they lived out their short years; that was why Dawit believed he was drawn to them. The confused din of languages in this place reminded Dawit of *Casablanca*, like North Africa during the war. A place to be penned in by other people, and yet suffer the keenness of being alone. It made him long to board one of these airplanes, almost regardless of where it would deposit him, and escape the sorrow of his last stay among the mortals.

Dawit's ears picked up fragments of countless mingled conversations. A German couple arguing over where to spend the night. Teenage girls from Brazil worrying because they didn't know where their parents had wandered. An old Argentine man complaining to his adult son that he was too old to walk so far.

But at the heart of all the words was love. Companionship. Life had cast these individuals together, and they were bound to one another. If someone got lost, a loved one would search until he was were found. They would fight and argue and complain, yet always remain tied to someone. It was human nature, mortal or otherwise.

So few people were alone here. Only he.

At instants as he gazed at the crowd of people, Dawit was certain he saw Mahmoud appear in front of him, approaching him. Let it be, Dawit thought. If Mahmoud came, he would simply go. He would not argue. He should have gone from the first.

Dawit collapsed against one of the pay telephones at a circular telephone bank, drained of the will even to stand straight. If only he could melt into the earth and vanish, smothered in darkness, his thoughts silenced.

How much did he really love Jessica? Even Kira? Was it that he'd loved the novelty of enjoying a family at last? Perhaps it could have been any woman, any child. If that were true, he could find satisfaction anywhere else, with time. He could start again.

Dawit swallowed a sob, imagining Kira's face. And remembering Jessica's intimate touch, her laugh. The utter completeness he'd felt the few times the three of them were truly alone. He'd never been able to convince Jessica that those moments were the only ones worth hoarding. Of what lasting value was her job? Why couldn't they have schooled Kira at home? How ironic it was that mortals, who had the least time of all, were willing to waste so much of it away from people they loved.

Their time had been too short. No, mortals were not interchangeable. He must have them back. No matter how improbable his blind efforts, or how long the search, he would find his wife and daughter.

Sighing, Dawit picked up the telephone handset and dialed the number he had memorized by now. He had been calling every half-hour even before he decided to leave the house. Once at the airport, he had never wandered far from the telephone. Far-fetched though it was, it was the only hope Dawit had.

"Cardmember services," a man's voice answered.

Dawit repeated his name and account number in a monotone voice. He'd spoken to a woman named Valerie twice before, but this was someone new. He told his story again. Any word?

"Hold, please," the man said, and Dawit could hear the keystrokes on his computer. Dawit closed his eyes. This was his sixth call. He was growing more and more certain that his plan was useless, after all. His uplifting moments of inspiration would be stripped from him, leaving only despair.

"Mr. Wolde, there has been activity. It was at a service station upstate from you, not even ten minutes ago."

Dawit had so longed to hear these words, that he was at first confused: Was the man's voice real or only his imagination? He stood straight up, holding the phone with both hands, but he couldn't open his mouth to speak.

The man laughed. "Want to hear something funny? It's a Mobil station in a town called Yeehaw Junction. God, that sounds like the name of one of those bad comedies from the seventies."

"Where is that?" Dawit breathed, finding his voice.

"I'm not sure exactly. If you want, I can give you the number. At least you can find out what the thief looks like."

When Dawit called the gas station, he did not identify himself. He asked for directions, discovering that the station was near a Turnpike exit. South of Orlando. Yes, the man from the gas station told him, there was an airport nearby if he wanted to fly— a small one forty minutes east in Vero Beach. "We sure ain't got one here," he said.

"Was there . . ." Dawit swallowed hard. " . . . Was there a woman there? And a little girl?"

"Who's asking?" the man said.

"Her husband," Dawit said, his heartbeat resounding through his frame. "Sir, I need to find her right away. We've had a terrible misunderstanding."

There was a pause. "Okay, well, she may still be at the pump. You that girl's daddy? I heard them say they was going to call you. Hang on."

Surely this must be a dream after all, Dawit thought. He felt no sensation in his fingertips in the long seconds of silence while he waited to hear his wife's voice on the telephone. Was it over at last?

"Hey, man, sorry about that," the attendant said, returning. "They must've pulled out. I didn't hear where they're going. But that little girl would'a been real happy to hear your voice."

Dawit hung up, unable to utter a polite goodbye or thank you. No man deserved such a cruel prank of the fates! Had he called five minutes sooner, he might have spoken to Jessica and convinced her to go to the airport to wait for him. Could it be true that Jessica had tried to call him? To say what? To explain why she'd left?

When Dawit checked the messages on his home answering machine with the remote code, the only messages he heard—and there were five—were from Bea, and one from Sy. By now, Dawit's face was streaked with tears. How could he have allowed himself to hope?

He would not swallow this defeat. Whether she considered him an enemy or a friend, he would find her. He would have to take a plane; if he couldn't find a flight leaving immediately, he would charter one. But to Vero Beach? He visualized Florida's geography, calculating Jessica's speed at sixty-five-plus miles per hour. No, he should fly north to Orlando instead, which might even out their pace. He might have a prayer of catching her.

"Wait for me, Jessica," he whispered, running toward the ticket counter for Florida Air. "If you have a heart, and your God has any mercy, let me come to you."

▪ 50

Just as Jessica was beginning to wonder if there was any civilization at all along the quiet Turnpike stretch through Osceola County, and then past the Disney World signs in Orange County, the radio abruptly shut off. A too-loud commercial for a car dealership had been playing, and Jessica was about to reach over to adjust the volume when, as if reading her mind, the radio clipped the booming announcer's voice in midsentence. Silence.

For the longest time, she really thought it was only the radio. She fiddled with the knob, clicking it on and off, but it didn't make a sound. The radio's panel was no longer lighted, either. Weird. They'd never had a problem with the radio before.

Returning her eyes to the road, the next thing Jessica noticed was that the roadway was pitch-black except for the cones of light from a station wagon passing her in the fast lane. She sat up straight, straining to peer through the windshield past the dots of water from the last brief rain shower. Well, shit. How were people supposed to see the damn roads out here without streetlamps? Had it always been this dark?

Jessica lifted her foot from the accelerator slightly, slowing down, and she glanced at the speedometer. Too dark to read, like the rest of the instrument board. What the hell . . . ?

Her hands suddenly tightened on the steering wheel as she felt a surge of cold fear through her limbs. She couldn't see anything, she realized, because all of the vehicle's lights were off, including the headlights. Making a small, panicked sound, she tried to flick the headlights on and off. Nothing. Just like the radio. And the AC, she realized, was gone. Had the battery died? How could that be, when the car was still running? This couldn't be happening. It couldn't.

"Oh, my God . . ." she said, so loudly that Kira stirred. She pushed the button to unlock the doors, and heard them click. Okay, there must be some kind of glitch in the electrical system. No big deal. The car was running. The locks were okay. The only thing was, she didn't have a fucking radio or fucking headlights so she could see where the fuck she was going in the middle of fucking nowhere.

Jessica bit her lip hard, struggling not to cry. There was only so much crying she could do in a day, and she was way past her limit. Her eyes hurt. Her back hurt from sitting rigid behind the steering wheel for five hours. Kira was probably going to wake up soon and start fussing again about wanting to see David.

Jessica told herself, just trying the words on for size, that they would have to stop. That was it. She couldn't endanger Kira by driving out here without lights. The eighteen-wheelers had been barreling down the road around her like demons, making the van shake as they sped past, and she couldn't take a risk that one of them wouldn't see them plodding along until it was too late. MOTHER, DAUGHTER KILLED IN FIERY TURNPIKE COLLISION, the headline would say. She'd written plenty of those stories herself.

Jessica put on her blinker, moving to change lanes so she could get closer to the shoulder on the driver's side. A thundering honk made her swerve back to her lane and brake hard. Lord have mercy, one of those monster trucks had been speeding right alongside her. The van shuddered as the truck passed, and she heard road residue spray against her windshield.

Kira, startled, cried out, "Mommy?" Then she sat up and started crying, an emotional collapse. She'd had all the scares and confusion she could take.

"It's okay, honey," Jessica said from habit, making a second attempt to move toward the shoulder despite her frenzied heart. Her hands would have been shaking if they weren't wrapped around the steering wheel. She felt herself shaking inside, to her bones.

One of the battery connections must be loose, that was all. She could fix that. If not, she'd turn on the hazard lights and they'd just sit. It was about 10:15, not late enough for the real crazies to start swarming, and despite her paranoia it was unlikely that David was right behind them. A Florida state trooper would see them, give them a jump-start, and they'd go.

"It's dark," Kira sobbed as they came to a stop in a small clearing where the road met a hidden woodland.

"Honey, I know, but there's nothing to be afraid of. We're just giving the van a little rest, okay? Go back to sleep."

Another sob, a heartbreaking sound in the darkness. Jessica leaned over to kiss Kira's forehead, which felt hot and damp to her lips, as though Kira had a budding high temperature. "Kira, Mommy needs you to be a big girl now. Please. I promise, everything is fine. I'm getting out to look under the hood. I won't go far."

She felt under her seat for the extra flashlight that was always rolling around when she didn't need one. She finally remembered to check the glove compartment, and there it was, buried beneath the van's registration papers. She turned it on, and the light was faint. But at least it was light.

Jessica saw Kira's blinking, reddened eyes. Kira's sobbing had stopped as soon as the light came on. Children were so afraid of the dark. Maybe the flashlight reassured Kira, but the weak beam only heightened Jessica's sense of isolation.

"Stay in the van with Teacake. I'll be back in one minute."

Kira grabbed Jessica's wrist before she could move. "Mommy, do you promise nothing bad'll happen?" The sound of her tiny voice, a fragile whisper, filled the van.

Jessica shined the light toward her own face, forcing herself to smile for her daughter. "Would this face tell a lie? Huh?"

Kira shook her head, sniffing. "No."

"Well, then. Nothing bad will happen. I promise. I just need to see why the lights on the car don't work."

"Daddy can fix it."

"Well, Daddy's not here. So Mommy's going to fix it."

Jessica thought about cutting off the engine, but decided against it because she'd learned never to shut off a car that was threatening to stall. Keep the engine going. If it stopped, it might not start again without a jump. Already, the engine was making a strange choking sound that warned her it might not be running much longer anyway.

The overgrown grass nearly reached Jessica's knees, tickling the tops of her feet in the flats she'd worn to work. She felt prickly briars clinging to her cotton slacks as she walked around to the hood. The flashlight tucked under her chin, she maneuvered her fingers beneath the grease-caked underside to spring the hood open and prop it up.

Belts were turning and the engine hummed, parts of it shivering occasionally with the worrisome sputters she'd heard. She felt a glow of heat from all of the working parts, and she reminded herself she'd need to be careful about touching anything. She found the battery and concentrated the light on it; the connections looked secure, even as she nudged them with the flashlight. She felt the uncomfortable realization that the battery was not the problem. It was barely six months old and still looked new. It must be something else.

While Jessica inventoried the rest of the parts to try to guess what was wrong, the engine abruptly gave up. Now, the silence was as vast as the night.

Kira, she thought.

Kira could be bratty when she was restless. Kira was old enough to know better than to open her car door while a vehicle was moving, but she had a fascination with the keys. She'd probably reached over and turned them, click, and now they would be stuck.

But Jessica didn't have much time to think about this. Without the reassuring sound of the car engine, Jessica became aware that she was a black woman alone on a deserted Southern roadway; all of her mother's stories about the civil rights movement and the headlights that had followed her late at night flooded her at once.

Jessica had grown up hearing about beatings and shootings, and the deaths of Mickey Schwerner, Andrew Goodman, and James Chaney in Mississippi. Even thirty years later, Bea didn't like to drive alone on roads anywhere in the South. And forget racists. Wasn't Florida the home of Ted Bundy and the Gainesville murders?

Jessica was thinking about all of these things when she first noticed the car. It was parked maybe thirty yards behind the van on the same side of the road, barely visible in the dark except when other cars passed and washed it in a brief, revealing light.

A light-colored car. No siren on top, so it wasn't a police cruiser. It wasn't the highway patrol. It was just a car sitting in the darkness with no lights inside or outside. As though it had been abandoned. Or it was waiting.

Jessica slammed the hood closed, her heart pummeling her breastbone with the terror she'd been living with all night. She didn't remember passing another parked car when she pulled over. She was sure she would have noticed something like that. So had it pulled over behind her, following her? Instinct made Jessica turn her flashlight off, so her movements wouldn't be visible.

"Did you fix it?" Kira asked when Jessica climbed back inside and closed her door. Thank goodness the locks didn't need power to operate, but she wanted to make sure the sliding side door was latched tight. She climbed to the backseat to check it. Locked. Teacake, who'd been hiding since they left the gas station, meowed from behind her and made her jump.

Jessica was breathing fast, reminding her of the way she'd hyperventilated earlier that day. She returned to the driver's seat, took a deep breath, and touched the ignition's keys. Sure enough, Kira had messed with them and shut off the car.

"Mommy, are you mad at me?" Kira asked, knowing Jessica knew.

Still breathing hard, Jessica shook her head. She closed her eyes, tightening her unsteady fingers around the keys. Jesus, she prayed, if I have ever done right by you and your Word, please let this car start up this one time. I won't ask it again, Lord.

Jessica turned the keys. There was a click, and a distant rattle somewhere beneath the hood, but that was all. The next time she tried the key, pumping her foot hard on the gas pedal, there was no sound at all.

Jessica exhaled, whimpering. She tried again and again, but the van's engine was dead. Nothing, nothing, nothing.

Well, she knew she couldn't run. Now she had to figure out what or whom she thought she was running from. Jessica crawled into the seat farthest to the back, pushing aside a bag of groceries, and peered out of the rear window at the car.

Still hadn't moved, still dark. She couldn't tell whether or not anyone was inside. If it was someone who wanted to help, why would they park so far behind them? Why turn off the lights? It seemed to Jessica that it had been a long time since any other cars had driven past. They were alone, really alone. Jessica had never felt more helpless.

"Kira," she said unsteadily, patting the first seat's back, "come back here, honey. I want you to lie down on the backseat and go to sleep. We're going to take a nap now."

"Did you fix the car?"

"Not yet."

"We're staying all night long?"

"Maybe so. Come on, now. Hurry up and do what Mommy says."

"But I'm scared."

"I know, baby," Jessica said, grabbing Kira's arm to help her make her way from the front seat without stumbling. "I know."

It was drizzling again. Jessica's senses were so awake, she could hear every drop that spattered the top of the car, an ominous drumming above her. And Jessica heard another sound too. She heard the *whomp* and the lingering echo of a car door slamming shut. She whirled back around to peer through the rear window.

Someone was coming, walking toward them with a slow stride. It wasn't even so much that she could *see* him, because she couldn't. She knew that he'd turned off his lights because he hadn't wanted her to see him. But she knew he was there. She knew she would see him soon, when he was closer.

Kira was curled up on her seat. "Mommy, I only got up to Q in the Alphabet game," she said, "and now there's no other cars."

"Mommy needs you to hush and be very quiet now, Kira," Jessica said, unable to hide the shaking in her voice.

"Or else, the boogeyman will hear?" Kira asked. "Does the boogeyman live in the woods?"

"Shhhhhhhhh."

There. Jessica could see him now. He was the boogeyman, all right. Jessica would have been relieved to see David at this point, would have kissed his feet, but this wasn't a black man. He had lighter skin, very short hair. He was wearing a sports jacket, either for the Florida Marlins or the Miami Dolphins. He was still twenty yards away, walking toward them.

Panicked, Jessica scrambled from the back of the van, past Kira, to climb back into the driver's seat. She pumped out her heartbeat on the accelerator, turning the key, praying something would catch, some miracle would start the van. Utter silence.

"Mommy," Kira whispered, "I think somebody's out there."

Whoever it was couldn't be up to any good, so Jessica didn't want to wait around to ask him for a proper introduction. They could run on foot. That was the only thing left. They could run into the rain, right into the road if they had to. There were head-lights coming now, way in the distance, and they could take their chances that somebody Christian-minded would stop for a woman and a young girl waving in the road.

"Mrs. Wolde," a man's voice called from somewhere behind the van, startling Jessica so much that she yanked the keys out of the ignition and clutched them in her fist.

"My name is Officer Rhodes, with the Orange County Police. Your van's license tag was reported to us by police in Miami. They've been looking for you. Your husband is in custody for a murder. Can you please come out of the van?"

Jessica's mouth fell open as her brain swam in mingled shock, relief, dread. He was with the police, after all! Fernando Reyes must have gotten her message instantly when she called from the gas station. David was already in custody? She gazed anxiously out the rear window at the man, who stood ten yards behind her. Why was he still so far back?

And why was he holding a glistening metal gun, both hands cradling it beneath his beltline? Though his voice was professional and soothing, the man's stance looked confrontational. "I'm sure you're understandably nervous. No one is implicating you in the murder. We just want to make sure you and your daughter can return safely to Miami. I understand your sister is very sick, and your mother has been looking for you."

Jessica sobbed. It really was over. Lord Jesus help her, it was over. David was really in jail. This awful escape, this awful heartache, was over.

"Mommy, who is that?" Kira whispered, sitting up.

"It's the police, baby. They're here to help us," Jessica said, burying Kira's head against her chest.

Jessica was reaching for the lock on the sliding door when she saw, as a passing car bathed the officer in light, that he was making a movement she'd seen countless times in movies: He was cocking the weapon he held, as though readying to fire. She also saw his face, which was both familiar and unfamiliar. She couldn't help thinking that she'd seen him once before, with a beard.

Jessica pushed open one of the side windows, allowing a breath of damp air into the van. "Who are you?" she screamed out. "Why do you have a gun?"

"Mrs. Wolde," the man said patiently, taking a step toward the van, "there's no reason to be upset. The gun is merely a precaution. I know you're in a very excited state."

"Stay back!" Jessica screamed at him. To her dismay, the man ignored her, taking two more steps toward the van. He held the gun in one hand, at chest level, taking aim. *"Who are you?!"*

"Mrs. Wolde," the man said, this time with a very different voice, a lower-pitched voice with an accent she did not recognize, "don't force me to be discourteous. This will be easier for all concerned if you bring the girl out of the van. Do as I say and I'll spare her. You have no alternative."

Jessica's mind went white, stripped of rational thought. All she had left was instinct; she dove to Kira's seat and huddled over her, sitting on the floor of the van. Both of them sobbed.

There was an explosion, or at least it sounded like one. A gunshot shattered the van's rear window and exited through the windshield, spraying glass on all sides of them. Jessica screamed, hugging Kira so tightly against her that she thought she would break. There were glass shards on the seat cover, in her hair. What nightmare was this? What hell was this?

"My patience is gone," the awful voice said. "Come out now, or you'll both be found dead where you are."

"O-kay-kay . . ." Jessica stuttered, barely able to speak beyond the trembling of her jaw. She tried to raise her voice so the man could hear her strangled words. "Please . . . don't . . . hurt us."

"Open the door. Bring the girl too. I'll not repeat myself," the man said.

To Jessica, a woman who believed in miracles, it wasn't so extremely remarkable that, at that moment, a bright light seemed to fill up the van just when she was praying most earnestly. It was many seconds after she heard the roar of an engine and tires screeching across the asphalt and gravel that she first realized another car had come from somewhere.

She heard a sound—an impact, like a heavy sack filled with cracking wood—and then nothing except Kira's breathless sobs. An eternity passed, and then she heard someone's footsteps trampling through the grass. She wanted to move, but couldn't.

She expected a gunshot next, but it didn't come.

Instead, a face peered down at her in the window. She wasn't the least bit surprised to see that it was David's.

▪ 51

Dawit drove thirty miles before he turned on his blinker to signal that Jessica should follow him off of the road (not that she had much choice, since the front bumper of the car she drove was secured to his car's back bumper with a chain and padlock he'd found in Mahmoud's trunk). It was midnight. They would be meeting I-75 soon, toward Gainesville. He'd wanted to stop before then.

Kira sat in the seat beside Dawit, her thumb planted in her mouth, leaning against the door with her eyes fully alert. Dawit had not seen her suck her thumb in at least two years.

"You okay, Duchess?" he asked, touching her hair.

Kira nodded. She stroked the cat, who was at last quiet in her lap. After the initial moment when she saw him, when she ran out of the van to leap into his arms with hysterical-sounding laughter and tears despite Jessica's warning to keep away, Kira had not said a word.

Jessica climbed out of her car. "Why are we stopping here?" she asked, standing at Dawit's window.

Though Dawit tried, once again, he could not make eye contact with his wife. The beauty of her face stung him deeply, and the pain surged in him as anger. He looked past her at the thicket beyond the roadway, trying to determine whether or not the tree cover would suffice. It would.

Not looking at Jessica's face, Dawit held out his palm. "Give me your car keys," he said.

For a moment, she didn't respond at all. Then he heard a far-off jingling and realized she must have thrown the keys some-where. So this was her silent retort. The sting came again.

Foolish woman. Did she think he was going to leave her alone and give her an opportunity to ferret out the keys in his absence? And how did she propose to drive the car, chained as it was?

Dawit opened his car door, pocketing his own keys. Where had he found the self-control to refrain from striking her? As a boy, he'd once seen a villager set his dogs on his wife because she uttered an unkind word to him at the marketplace. He remembered the sight of her bloody carcass even now. With Jessica, there was no end to her offenses against him. Running away, endangering his daughter, forcing him to practically hold her at gunpoint with Mahmoud's weapon to convince her to go with him.

"We'll drive this car, then," Dawit said evenly. "But I liked Mahmoud's. At least his air conditioner produced something besides warm, stale air."

Dawit still felt weak when he imagined what he had seen. He was speeding north and chanced upon the van stalled on the road. If he had not seen them and swerved back around on the median at the moment he did, Mahmoud would have shot Jessica and Kira. Dawit had not even seen Mahmoud the first time he passed, driving at ninety miles per hour. He had not seen him until he came back, when Mahmoud was in the direct path of his headlights.

"Where are you going?" Kira whimpered.

"Your mommy and I have to take care of something. We have to use the bathroom."

"I have to go too."

"We're going in the woods. You just stay here. We'll stop at a real bathroom for you very soon. I want you to lie down and close your eyes. Keep them closed. Do what Daddy says, Kira."

He leaned over and repeated the words in urgent French, staring into her wondering, frightened brown eyes, just as he had less than an hour ago, when she was in the van and Jessica was clinging to her, half hysterical.

"*Come to Daddy, Kira. It's safe to come to me.*"

"*No! Kira, stay here. Don't go near him.*"

"*Kira . . . avec moi. Maintenant, mon bébé. Avec moi.*"

And so Kira had come, wriggling from her mother's arms to leap into his through the rear hatch door he'd opened by reaching through the shattered glass. Now, as she had then, Kira obeyed when he spoke their private language, the language of entreaties. She slumped down in her seat until she was curled in a ball beside the cat, and he tugged her hair before getting out of the car.

The tree cover was too thick to drive the car into the brush, as Dawit had originally hoped to do, so he would have to empty Mahmoud's trunk. Because Jessica had thrown the keys away, Dawit had to pry open the trunk with a tire jack. This took ten minutes of too-precious time, more to blame on Jessica. She stood behind him, watching, waiting. When the trunk popped open, Dawit was assailed by the scent of blood from the fractured corpse.

"Lord Jesus," Jessica said, taking a step back. "I can't do this. I can't."

"If you were trustworthy, I would leave you in the car with Kira. Since you're not, you'll accompany me. I won't make you help carry him. I wouldn't want you dirtying your hands."

Dawit hoped Kira was sleeping by now so she would be spared this sight. Dawit had wrapped Mahmoud's body in one of Princess's old blankets, which he'd found on the floor of the cargo bin in the minivan. A few bloodstains had seeped through in a macabre pattern, but not many. Aside from the damage to Mahmoud's crushed face, most of his injuries were internal. Dawit grunted, heaving the two-hundred-pound load across his shoulder firefighter-style.

Jessica gasped, stepping away from him. "David, don't make me go. Please. Why didn't we just leave him back—"

"Someone would have found his body where it was."

"So what?"

"The coroner would have had a mild shock in the morning when his corpse woke up in a bad mood, don't you think? Come. Let's be quick so Kira won't worry. Turn on the flashlight."

Dawit staggered down the embankment, squeezing between the straight trunks of thin pine trees, following the weak beam of light that Jessica directed in his path as insects flurried around them. Dry twigs snapped beneath their feet, and Jessica made a frightened sound. Just a bit farther, he assured her, slipping into ingrained habits of tenderness. They needed to go far enough to keep Mahmoud out of sight from the road. When they finished, he would have to haul Mahmoud's car another few miles north and then leave it on the shoulder. Even if someone found the abandoned car with its mutilated trunk, it was unlikely they would discover the corpse before dawn, when it would be a corpse no more.

"I'm trying to protect Kira from all this, David, but I'm not going to allow you to kidnap us. You hear me? You can't use her to control me. I'll tell her the truth if I have to."

Dawit's ears burned as he tossed his burden against the trunk of a peeling paper tree. Ignoring Jessica, he propped Mahmoud into a sitting position, the bloody head dangling forward beneath the blanket. It was more kindness than Mahmoud deserved.

"I know you killed Peter," Jessica said, her voice a venom. "And I know you tried to kill Alex. I left a message for a policeman in Miami. They're looking for you right now."

Dawit spun around to peer into the flashlight beam glowing

from where his wife stood behind him. His mind could not swallow her words. How could a woman who'd been so understanding through so much, his own wife, have become so heartless as to turn him in! Would this horrid night never end in its cruel surprises?

"You shouldn't have done that. You're wrong about Alex."

"I don't believe you!" Jessica shouted. "You know you pushed her because of what she found out, how your blood heals."

Dawit staggered, this time from disbelief. Betrayed, yet again! "You . . ."—he could barely form the words—"You told your sister about me? How did you get my blood?"

"From the shed. In a syringe."

Dawit raised his fingers to his temples, as though to steady himself from fainting. Had he been careless enough to leave his blood in the shed when he finished the Ritual with the cat? He should be smitten down for his own stupidity, if that were true. And it was, apparently.

Dawit laughed in surrender, hanging his head.

Jessica looked at him as though he were a specter. "What are you?" she hissed.

"What am I? I'll tell you what I am," he said, stepping toward her. "I'm your salvation, Jessica. Your sister will die soon, and perhaps your mother too. Don't you see what you've done, you fool? Mahmoud is our least concern. I thought he'd chased you as a tactic to prompt me to go. But it's worse than I feared. He must know what I've told you. Mahmoud wants you dead because Khaldun wants you dead. Every day you live, you endanger us all. And you have told your sister too? Who else?"

"No one," Jessica whispered, apparently frightened by his words. Dawit imagined he could feel her trembling, and he longed to hold her despite his rage and sorrow. He was now orphaned in every sense, for the second time; he must be anathema to Khaldun and his brothers. He could no longer claim his home in Miami, nor his true home in Lalibela.

"Mahmoud attacked your sister to protect the Covenant, just as he has attacked you and Kira tonight," he said, weary to his soul.

"But what about Peter? And Rosalie Tillis Banks—"

"Rosalie is none of your business," Dawit said, his body rigid. At the sound of Rosalie's name, carelessly tossed at him, his heart had dropped. "My daughter is none of your business. You didn't see what had become of her. Until you have been in my place, and seen your own child as she looked, you have no right to ask me about her."

"Tell me why you killed Peter," Jessica said. "Just tell me why. Was it because of Rosalie? He never made the connection, David. Neither of us had. I don't understand why."

Dawit took a deep breath, gazing up at the thick darkness above them. Black-gray nimbostratus clouds hung against the skies. "Killing Peter," he said slowly, "was a mistake."

His confession bound them in silence. Then, he heard her sob. She'd known, he realized, but she had not believed. Not until now.

"I would live my entire lifetime from the beginning and suffer everything twofold," Dawit said softly, "to regain that one night, Jessica. To correct that one night. That night, I laid a path to this one, so full of rage and distrust. You have harmed me now in more ways than you will ever know, but I forgive you everything because my forgiveness is unconditional. And you, my love, have forgiven me everything but this."

"I won't go with you," Jessica sobbed.

"That's your choice. I won't hold this gun to you. But Kira is going with me. I suggest you get as far away from Mahmoud as possible by morning. And I can guarantee you that your sister is not safe where she rests. Your police officer friend's energy would be better spent with her."

Jessica's sob turned into a wail, half vengeful, half frightened. It reminded him of a wail from another horrible night in the wilderness, when she'd watched helplessly while his body met death. If Dawit had not thought she would strike him, he would have surely hugged her now. Instead, he turned and began to walk back toward the car, where Kira was waiting.

"What can we do?" Jessica called after him.

He paused, but did not turn to face her. "Very little. But there is one way, at least, they cannot harm you or Kira."

"What is it?" Jessica whispered.

Walking on, Dawit didn't answer because it was unnecessary. She knew. The words need not be spoken. The answer was coursing, silent and hot, through his very veins.

▪ 52

Teacake was dying. It was the last absurdity.

As the shabby rental car rolled beneath the summer sun, David and Kira were in the front seat, and Jessica sat with the cat in the back. Teacake had hurt himself somehow. She'd noticed a small trickle of blood in one of his ears, so maybe he'd been injured from flying glass. Or hit his head somehow. She didn't know. He was lying flat and quiet on the seat beside her. So quiet. His eyes were open, but looked glazed. And he wouldn't drink the water from the eyedropper David had bought at the Walgreen's west of Pensacola, right before they crossed the Alabama state line. Jessica told him to buy it, along with whatever other things he wanted to pick up, because Teacake looked dehydrated. But he wouldn't drink. The drops of water were rolling back out of his mouth, dribbling on the stubbly hairs on his chin.

It figured. Like Job, she'd lost everything else she cared about, so why not the cat she'd raised since he was a fur ball of a kitten? Don't even get started, she thought. She couldn't dwell there, or she'd start screaming and David might turn around and have to knock her in the head with the gun he was carrying in his jeans. That would be a sight for Kira.

See, Kira, you think Daddy's this nice guy because he saved us from that other maniac, but did you know he's a maniac himself? Did you know that?

Every few minutes, Jessica caught David gazing at her in his rearview mirror. For a strange half-second, their eyes would meet where their minds couldn't. Then she would look toward her window and stare out at the long, unfamiliar miles.

She could run. At Walgreen's—the only time David had left her alone, except in the filthy bathroom of the burger place at the last truck stop—Jessica sat in the car and realized she was free to go. David had Kira. He always took her with him wherever he went, his unknowing hostage, his peace of mind. But that was okay. If she jumped out of the car to run to the pay phone just across the street, he wouldn't have gotten far with Kira yet. The police would find them.

But what if they didn't?

In the end, Jessica was relieved when David and Kira walked back outside through the store's glass doors. Her chance was gone. No more decisions to make. All she had to do was ride in the backseat and wonder if David would ever actually shoot her, wonder what it would be like to live for five hundred years, wonder if Alex was all right, wonder what Peter had felt when his throat was slashed. And stroke her cat's tummy while he died.

"I saw an M!" Kira cried to David, pointing somewhere out of the windshield. "There."

"You're telling tales, Kira. That's not nice," David said.

"It is too there."

"Then where's the M in Dairy Queen, young lady?"

"In the middle," Kira said, and she was beset by giggling.

"Spell it."

"D-A-I-R- . . . Kira began, and laughed again, " . . . M-Y . . ."

Unexpectedly, Jessica chuckled once, deep from her chest. She didn't even know she'd been listening, but a part of her mind had decided to laugh. David glanced at her in the mirror, surprised. Too bad for him if he expected to see her smiling. Jessica couldn't remember the last time she'd smiled in days. She couldn't even remember where smiles came from.

"Just for that, you lose a point," David said to Kira, his eyes still on Jessica in the mirror. "You have to find L all over again too. I'm still ahead of you."

Jessica's eyes locked with his, just that fast, and her stomach and chest and every loose part inside her seemed to gather, and she realized what she'd been thinking all this time she'd been staring outside: I'm still in love with him.

"Mommy, what's wrong with Teacake?" Kira was staring at the cat's wide-open eyes. Until she spoke, Jessica hadn't noticed that Kira had clicked free of her seat belt and was leaning over the seat to gaze back at them.

"He's very tired," Jessica answered hoarsely. Her voice was gone now too. Soon, she feared, everything would be gone. "I think he needs to rest."

"He's not the only one," David said. "Look out for a motel so we can pull over before the sun gets unbearable. More than it is already, I mean. Okay, Jess?"

Jessica looked. His eyes were there again.

Dawit was beginning to realize how selfish he'd been. He'd thought so much of his own losses that he hadn't considered Jessica's. He had never seen her look so wretched.

In fact, he had brought her nothing but wretchedness. Her life would have been better without him. He'd known this in the beginning.

Stay away from that woman, he'd told himself the first day he noticed her. You will make her life a misery, as yours always has been. You will bring her the same pain you brought Christina and Rufus and Rosalie.

"David, why did you fall in love with me?" Jessica had asked so often, especially when they were first married. To him, the reasons were obvious, but they were impossible to explain. How could he tell her that when he saw himself reflected through her eyes, he could forget what he was? He'd wanted her in his bed because of her face, her youthful shapeliness, the challenge in her defiant eyes. But he'd lost his heart to her because she was everything he was not. And for everything he'd known he would teach her, he had hoped she could teach him too.

What did she see now? Would she ever again touch him, or always tremble away?

He wanted her still. Despite all the turmoil of the past twenty-four hours and the worse suffering that he knew remained, all he could think as he stared in the mirror at her face was that he wanted so badly to make love to her and hear her whimper her pleasures in his ear.

He wanted to hear her say that she loved him, even if it was a lie, or to at least assure him that she'd loved him once. He, who had taken love so much for granted. Christina's love had been of no real value to him. And Adele's love only showed its true power when she was no longer with him.

Could he even name the others? Rana, of course. His first.

But what of the women in Cairo, the chieftain's daughter in Ife, the naive bargirl in Paris (Monique? Charmaine?), the noblewoman he'd toyed with in Gonder before losing his hand to her husband's sword? They had all loved him. So was this what they had felt when he was gone, this horrible longing to step backward in time?

Oh, to take it all back. To take everything back!

Couldn't Jessica see that this was why he could not leave her and Kira? He could never leave anyone again. And if he must spend eternity longing to see the love missing from Jessica's angry eyes, then the punishment suited him. At least he would always, always have Kira. He must never give Kira reason to hate him as Jessica did.

Dawit clutched his daughter's hand. It was sticky from the Coke she'd spilled from the burger place when she tried to push her straw through the plastic top. "My legs hurt, Daddy."

"They've probably fallen asleep because you can't move around enough. We'll stop soon, Duchess. Then you can stretch."

First, to find lodgings, for rest and an escape from this horrible sun. Next, the Ritual. He had all he needed in the bag he'd brought from Walgreen's. Dawit's heart leaped from both joy and fear. He would do it sometime before morning. He could not dwell on it long, or he would lose his nerve.

And tomorrow? More driving. He hoped he would be able to

locate his contact in New Orleans, the man who could manufacture passports and birth certificates for Jessica and Kira. Fifteen years had passed since he'd seen the red-haired man—he'd never known his name—and he had no phone, but Dawit knew how to find his secluded bayou home. It was unlikely he would have moved, even after all this time. He'd told Dawit, in his butchered English and with an ironic twinkle in his eye, how his family had owned the overgrown parcel of land since the days of slavery.

This would be Dawit's last return to the region stamped with his suffering. They would be away from here at last, beginning fresh. And living, at last, a life without unhappy endings.

▪ 53

From somewhere, there was light.

Mahmoud's eyes flew open and he blinked hard, his senses momentarily stunned. His head was covered, he realized. He smelled blood directly beneath his nose. Beyond, he smelled pine trees all around him, and a fainter scent of exhaust fumes. When Mahmoud tried to move, his body grew so rigid that he had to clench his teeth in pain.

Suddenly, the rough fabric covering his face was whipped away and Mahmoud was greeted by the fresh, dew-drenched scent of morning.

"Come now," a familiar voice said. "This is a very strange resting place, brother." Could it be his imagination? He was seeing his Life brother Kelile, the jokester, grinning widely beneath his wiry moustache. He had no skullcap, but he was dressed traditionally in a white tunic and white linen slacks. His clothes seemed to glow against his dark skin.

Kelile, with a grunt, reached beneath Mahmoud's armpits to pull him until he was sitting up straight. Someone behind Mahmoud began to yank the blood-spotted tarp from his shoulders to free him. Startled, Mahmoud turned to see who it was. Teka, the technological master from the House of Science! He, too, wore a white tunic and pants. How could his brothers be here? Was he dreaming?

Mahmoud's thoughts were interrupted by pain. He cried out, feeling as though his limbs were being torn apart as they tried to bring him to his feet.

"The devil has shit on you," Kelile laughed in Amharic, touching Mahmoud's soiled Western clothing. "What is this shambles?"

"Are you an illusion?" Mahmoud asked.

"No, my brother," Kelile said, squeezing his shoulders hard. "No illusion. Flesh."

Despite his confusion and pain-wracked body, Mahmoud grinned. No joy could compare to the unexpected appearance of two Life brothers, and such well-respected Searchers. No other Searchers could boast the swiftness of Kelile and Teka, especially guided by Teka's devices. What a happy reunion! Khaldun always said Searchers should not think of themselves as individuals: They were a smaller family created to preserve the peace of the larger family. Mahmoud held Kelile and Teka in a long, hearty embrace.

As he leaned against them, he was barely able to stand. What had happened to him? The van with Dawit's wife and daughter had stopped along the roadside. He'd fired his gun at them. What next? Instantly, Mahmoud remembered the oncoming headlights, the grill of an automobile upon him. And its deadly impact, mercifully swift.

"Dawit must not have changed much," Kelile said. "By your appearance, I see he still has the heart and strength of ten men."

"Not so. Do not be fooled. He is resourceful, but he is not the Dawit you remember," Mahmoud said sadly. "It is not so much Dawit's victory you witness here, but only my own failure. That is why Khaldun has sent you, I'm sure. But so quickly?"

"Sit, Mahmoud," Teka said, indicating a patch of grass covered with pine needles. "You are in a very poor state."

"Yes," Mahmoud said, avoiding their eyes as he sank to the ground. "I am full of shame to be found this way."

Kelile laughed. "Such dramatization! Stop wringing your hands, Mahmoud. You should rejoice. It is to your honor that Khaldun has sent us—not because he feared you would fail, but the opposite. Be glad you have not succeeded!"

"Explain," Mahmoud said, confused by their smiles.

"Dawit's wife and child live still?" Teka asked anxiously.

Mahmoud's heart sank. "Yes. At the instant I—"

"Don't explain," Teka interrupted. "Be grateful. We must tell you something, and then you will understand. Khaldun asked us to fly here, to come quickly. After he mailed your instructions, he had a dream that so excited him it flung him from his bed."

"Not a dream," Kelile corrected him. "Remember? He said he was awake when he saw these things. A vision."

"A message came to him," Teka continued earnestly. "He was greatly changed by it, and frantic that you be stopped. He dispatched us the very same day. The message was this: Dawit's wife and child must live. They are no threat to us."

"Nonsense!" Mahmoud responded.

Kelile shrugged. "Yes, I know. I thought perhaps he'd had too much wine. I, too, have had many strange visions after—"

Teka shot Kelile a grave look. "Khaldun would not enjoy your ridicule."

For a moment, Mahmoud was too awed to speak. This could not be so! Khaldun was not one to change his mind, nor one to heed dreams or visions. Khaldun, who never spoke of God, was professing a divine vision? And was so transformed by the experience that he would then send other Searchers to prevent him from finishing his work?

"My brothers, hear me," Mahmoud said. "Dawit has broken our Covenant. I believe he is once again with his wife, and he has told her more than any mortal should know. I have heard with my own ears how he described the Ritual to her, all of our most sacred history! And I believe Dawit somehow means to give her the Living Blood. I am sure of it."

Looking solemn, Teka and Kelile nodded. "All of these shocking things you say were also in Khaldun's dream. We are much aggrieved," Teka said. "We know Dawit's intentions. But Khaldun was emphatic: Dawit's wife must live, and the infant as well. Your work here is done. No blood will be shed. You will return with us. Not in shame, Mahmoud, but with satisfaction."

"But . . . Dawit—"

"Dawit will come of his own will," Teka said. "This is what Khaldun has told us."

Mahmoud felt as though his breath had been stolen from him. Then the mortal woman's mother and sister would live, and she and her child would live, and Dawit would go unpunished? Khaldun, who had taught the Life brothers to cherish the Covenant above all else, would have them sit idly by while Dawit tried to pass his Living Blood to a mortal? What purpose did the Searchers serve, then, if Life brothers were free to behave like gods?

Mahmoud pulled on Teka to stand, forgetting his pain. "I will not believe this of Khaldun. Forgive me, but he cannot know what he does."

"Mahmoud," Teka sighed, "we've all struggled to understand. It is not in keeping with our beliefs, so we must trust in Khaldun. Perhaps this knowledge is for him alone. Dawit's wife and infant must live. Her infant is chosen, he said."

"And he said it more than once. He repeated it many times."

"But you see? Khaldun is mistaken. There is no infant!" Mahmoud said. "Dawit has a daughter of five years. This is the infant? Why should Khaldun be concerned with her? She is chosen for what?"

"This," Teka said, "you must ask Khaldun."

Kelile grasped Mahmoud's chin with his fingers, shaking his face playfully. "Be cheerful, Mahmoud. At least now you can make peace with Dawit."

Peace! How could that be so? Could he still love a brother who had betrayed them—even if it was Dawit? What if Dawit returned to Lalibela, not alone, but with a newly immortal wife and girl-child? And how many others might follow?

How could Khaldun fail to fathom the dangerous implications of welcoming outsiders to their fellowship? Once exposed, their race of immortals could not long live in peace. They had all witnessed mortals' treachery to their own kind: How could Khaldun entrust the fate of the brotherhood to them?

"Think of the consequences," Mahmoud said quietly, his voice calmed by the heaviness in his heart. "With his blood, Dawit is bringing fire to humankind. Their greedy race, when it has fire, burns everything to cinders. All of us will be in that fire's path."

For a moment, neither Kelile nor Teka spoke. They knew it was true.

"We've been instructed not to interfere with Dawit or his mortals," Kelile said gravely. "What is left for us, then, Mahmoud? Disobedience?"

His question might not be rhetorical, Mahmoud realized. The Searchers existed only to protect the seclusion of their brotherhood, a task they had done well for hundreds of years. Khaldun himself had given them their mission, just as he had given them the Life gift. Without Khaldun, they would have been nothing but mortals themselves; left, by now, in the memories of no one. If Khaldun said they must not act, they must not. The decision was not theirs.

"No, brothers, I will heed Khaldun," Mahmoud said. "But remember I have said this, because from this time on, all is changed: We will long regret this day. My soul tells me so."

Teka and Kelile did not answer. The three men stood in silence. Beyond the tree line, Mahmoud heard the sounds of early-morning traffic speeding past them on the Turnpike, the mortal drivers oblivious to the extraordinary strangers hidden from their sight.

But oblivious, Mahmoud wondered, for how long?

▪ 54

ALABAMA. MISSISSIPPI. Now, a new sign said LOUISIANA. Jessica was in a new state every time she opened her eyes.

She hadn't realized she'd been sleeping until the car jolted to a stop in the parking lot of a strip-style, one-story motel called the I-Ten Inn. WELC ME TO LOUIS ANA, the red letters on the marquee read. The row of look-alike doors and windows stretched in front of her, and there were few other cars in sight. David must have picked the most out-of-the-way motel he could find.

David dangled a motel key in front of her, cutting off the car's engine. When had he gotten out to register? She must have slept through that too. And she was still so sleepy that everything played in front of her like a dream.

Kira, ecstatic to be out of the car, was racing back and forth across the walkway, half skipping, half running. She's going to fall and break her neck, Jessica thought, but she didn't have the strength to lean over to call to her through the open window.

The heat. Jessica couldn't move. She was so hot, her clothes clung to her skin. She knew Teacake was lying on the seat beside her, and she couldn't stand to look at him. She didn't want to deal with one more bad thing, today or ever.

"Where are we going?" she asked David in a cracked whisper.

"Nowhere right now. We're stopping to rest."

"I have to call my mother," she said in the same frail voice.

"I already took care of that. I called security at Jackson and threatened to come back and finish the job I started when I pushed Alex off her balcony. And I said I'd get the old lady too. I'm sure I sounded convincing, since you've already made me a fugitive. They'll have plenty of protection."

Jessica stared at him, confused, blinking. "You pushed Alex?"

David sighed. "No," he said patiently, as though he were speaking to Kira, keeping his voice low, "I said that so they would pay attention, Jess. You know what really happened to Alex."

Jessica no longer knew what to believe of David. He could be claiming he'd called her mother just to placate her. All the world was a lie. Even God, apparently. Her so-called God had abandoned her. She felt tricked. After David's recovery at the cabin, she'd believed he was touched by holiness, and nothing could be further from the truth. So much for faith. Why had God led her to David at all in the beginning, and now led him back to her?

"I still have to call her, David. I know she's worried . . ."

"Later. Not now," David said. He got out of the car and opened her door for her. Always the gentleman. "Come on out."

No. She couldn't go that way. If she did, she'd have to climb past Teacake on the seat. "The cat . . ." she began.

David was silent, apparently examining Teacake. He sighed, and she could only imagine what he must be seeing. "The cat's fine," he said inexplicably.

The cat was fine? Her heart leaping, Jessica ventured a glance. Teacake's blank eyes met hers. Jesus help. Teacake didn't even look like a real animal anymore, he looked like something somebody had stuffed. His mouth was horrid, frozen slightly open. She turned away, nauseated. "He's dead, David."

"Shhhhhh. Don't say that. Kira will hear. I'll take care of Teacake. Come on out. I can't leave you in the car."

It all felt so painfully familiar, just as when Jessica had walked into her house for what she'd known would be the last time. Inside the cramped motel room, as Jessica dropped her purse on top of the plain bureau, she thought of their countless family vacations that had begun this way. The room was bare and smelled clean in the way motels could, a smell that was foreign and new and full of promise.

Her eyes shot toward the nightstand between the double beds right away, looking for the telephone. Nothing there except a brass banker-style lamp. Not even a Bible.

"No phone. Sorry, this isn't exactly the Fontainebleau. We get what we pay for," David said evenly, following her gaze. He clapped his hands together once, turning toward Kira. "But there's a TV. Let's see if we can find any afternoon cartoons."

"It's time for Muppet Babies, Daddy. The clock says two!"

"They might have different cartoons in Louisiana, Duchess."

"Lew-see-ANNA . . ." Kira repeated, bouncing on one of the beds.

While David fumbled with the television knobs to try to clear up the reception, Kira scooted off of the bed and began to creep toward the closet. "No, Kira," Jessica said, speaking for the first time since they'd walked into the room.

Kira looked back at her, sticking out her lip. "I want to play with Teacake."

"Teacake's still sleeping," David said, walking over to lift Kira up and carry her back to the bed. "You stay put. You can play with him in a few hours. Maybe when it gets dark."

Jessica glared at David, feeling a fluttering across the back of her neck. He was insane. If she'd ever doubted it, she knew it now. Why the hell had he carried a dead cat into the room and hidden him behind the mirrored closet doors? He should have left Teacake in the car, then gotten rid of him and told Kira he ran away. Anything would be better than such a gruesome lie. Teacake must have been dead for at least two hours. What if the carcass started to smell? And what if Kira snuck into the closet? The poor child would be hysterical.

And that would make two of them, because Jessica was about to be hysterical herself. She couldn't hold it in much longer.

Jessica realized she could barely keep her balance. She shuffled to the bed where Kira sat and collapsed beside her, swaddling her like they were two fetuses in a womb. Could she protect her daughter now? And would someone protect her?

My God, my God, she thought, remembering the Book of Psalms from Sunday school, why hast thou forsaken me?

There is one way, at least, they cannot harm you or Kira.

Why art thou so far from helping me?

Tell me about the Ritual, David.

O my God, I cry in the daytime, but thou hearest not.

It's miracle blood.

Jessica couldn't move. Her thoughts were running wild, zipping circles in her head. And she was so, so sleepy. She wanted to touch Kira's face, but her limbs felt like they were a dozen times their normal weight. Jessica gazed across the room, and she found David staring at her. Behind him, she could see her own reflection, and Kira's, in the bureau mirror.

"You put something in my drink," she said, knowing for the first time as she said it, "the one from the burger place."

"It was just a Sprite, Jess." His lies never ended.

"Why do you want me to sleep?"

David didn't answer. He was leaning against the bureau, his arms folded in front of him. He was still beautiful, and his beauty made him more terrible to her. Jessica's eyelids fought until they closed, but she forced them open again. "Not Kira, David. Don't give her anything. Promise me," she said.

"Don't give me what?" Kira broke in, pulling her attention away from the crashes and frenzied classical music playing on the cartoon. It sounded like Bugs Bunny. Kira nudged against Jessica. "Don't give me what, Mommy?"

"Promise me, David."

"Will you stay with me?" David asked Jessica. A soft plea.

Tears came to Jessica's eyes. She hoped Kira wouldn't look at her face and see the tears, since Kira's happy oblivion was the only joy Jessica had. What was David asking of her? And what was she agreeing to by not running from him?

"Nothing's going to happen to you," David said slowly. "And nothing is going to happen to Kira. Trust in that."

"What's going to happen, Daddy?" Kira asked, bouncing impatiently. She hated it when they talked around her.

"Nothing, Duchess," David said.

Jessica's eyelids won. Again, she slept.

She didn't know how much time had passed. The TV was still on when her mind woke up, but it was playing a news program. Something about a deadly flood in India. Armageddon knocking, her mother always said. She didn't open her eyes at first, but she stirred because she smelled pizza in the room and heard paper bags crinkling as Kira and David unpacked food he must have had delivered. She was hungry, too, but she was more sleepy than hungry. She wouldn't get up yet. Just a little more rest.

Something heavy landed with a thump on Jessica's chest, and her startled eyes flew open.

There, in her face, were Teacake's green eyes. He meowed.

Jessica screamed. And then she screamed again, watching her dead cat scamper across the floor in a blur of bushy orange fur. Once her mouth was open, her screams couldn't stop.

"Baby? Honey? Listen to me. Please be calm and listen. I gave Teacake some of my blood. Do you understand? I never told you, but he's undergone the Ritual. That's why he woke up after he died. The same thing happened with me, remember? It takes a few hours. Just like at the cabin. Okay, Jessica? Tranquilo, sweetheart. Please?"

In an instant, the muddy cloudiness gave way to clarity.

David had been repeating the same words again and again, breathing fast. They were scuffing the motel's cheap plastic bathtub, where Jessica had tried to hide herself behind the smudged curtain. David was wrapped around her, nearly on top of her, smoothing her hair back with his palm. The top of her forehead, by now, felt raw and irritated from his touch. She shook her head away from him, resting her cheek against the plastic shower wall.

"When did you do that?" she said, barely loud enough to hear.

"Just before we went to the Everglades. That same morning, in the shed. I wanted to be certain I could do it."

"You just . . . gave him your blood?"

"That's why you found the syringe. I injected it."

"And that's all? That's all you did?"

When David didn't answer, Jessica could hear the muffled sound of Kira's sobs in the next room. She must be standing in front of the closed bathroom door, reeling in terrified confusion. She'd just seen her mother acting like a nut, flinging the lamp to the floor, hiding in the bathroom. Lord have mercy.

"Kira . . ." Jessica whimpered.

"I know. I'll go to her in a minute." He squeezed her shoulder tight, pulling her toward him, not letting go. "I want to make sure you're all right. I never intended any of this to happen this way, Jessica. I planned to tell you. I wasn't thinking when I opened the closet to let him out. Kira heard him crying . . ."

Jessica blinked, swallowing. She would never forget the sight of Teacake's eyes so close to her face. Remembering, her body trembled. She swallowed back a new sob.

"And it worked just like that? Just by injecting the blood?"

David sighed. He stroked her forehead again, and she couldn't move to escape his touch. "Basically."

"But you said something before about . . . how you had to eat poisoned bread. You told me that."

"Yes."

"You did something to Teacake? Something to poison him?"

"That's not the important thing. You saw the result."

"But you . . ."—she could barely speak, so she struggled to swallow again—". . . you want to do that to me? And Kira?"

"I want you and Kira to be safe, Jess. Always."

"You want to kill us?" Jessica whispered.

"No," David said. He looked so big this way, staring down at her like some demigod out of Greek mythology, his voice reverberating against the stall. "I want to give you life."

When they opened the bathroom door, Kira wrapped her arms around Jessica's legs, still crying, like she wanted to touch her and prove she was real, still Mommy. The sound of her child's cries tore holes inside Jessica. It reminded her of the strangled cries the night of Kira's worst asthma attack, when she couldn't breathe. And the morning Princess died. Jessica, dazed and nearly losing her balance, clutched the top of Kira's head with her hand and struggled to think of how to make the crying stop.

"Don't worry, Duchess. You poor creature. Mommy is fine," David was saying, reaching into the Walgreen's bag he'd left beside the sink. "It's all better now. Mommy had a bad dream."

Yes, Jessica thought, and this is it. It hasn't ended.

David opened his palm to her. He held four red-and-yellow capsules. "To help you relax. You've been so excitable," he explained.

"What . . . ?"

"Sleeping pills." He poured tap water into the motel's plastic cup. The sink's faucet was a trickle. "Go on."

Jessica would never recall a conscious decision to take the capsules in her hand and toss them into her mouth, where they felt thick against her dry tongue. Her thoughts were disjointed, hazy. She remembered wondering why he was giving her four instead of one or two. Still, she took them. And, as she drank the water, she felt them glide down her throat, one after the other.

She was trusting him. For the second time in her life, she felt truly wed to David Wolde. The Bride of Frankenstein.

Teacake, her precious little monstrosity, was nowhere in sight. Probably hiding under the bed. Jessica couldn't blame him. That's exactly what she wanted to do.

Kira cried on. Jessica crouched to the floor so she could hug her and see her teary, contorted face. Her hair hadn't been combed in nearly two days, and looked it. Comforting Kira gave her a reason not to cry herself. Jessica even managed a smile, somehow. "Kira, Mommy's okay. Sorry I scared you."

"Here. These will calm Kira," David said.

Jessica looked up and saw that he had three more capsules in his hand. For some reason, she couldn't believe her eyes. Seeing the pills made her swell with rage, and she panicked as she remembered she had just swallowed four of them herself.

"You're not giving her any goddamn pills!" she shouted, wondering herself where the loudness had come from.

David shrank away from her, surprised. "They're just . . ."

"You don't give a five-year-old girl sleeping pills, David! What are you trying to do, kill her?"

As soon as she said it, realizing what David was doing, she felt the second wave of terror and hysteria. She had to hug Kira close to keep her screams at bay. They had to get away from him. The sense of urgency felt more keen now than it had when she'd gone home and whisked Kira into the van, when escape seemed so easy. He was going to kill them.

Jessica took Kira's hand and clung to the edge of the sink to try to stand. She imagined that she was tearing across the room, dragging Kira behind her, running and screaming to the front office to tell the people who ran this place that her husband was crazy.

But she still stood in the bathroom nook with Kira and David. She felt so dizzy, she could barely stand. She was holding Kira's hand. She took one step with her, and then another, trying to pull her. She sobbed, realizing how weak her efforts were.

"What did you give me?" she cried. "What's in that bag?"

"My love, the pills will help you sleep. That's all." He tried to put his hand on her shoulder.

"Don't touch me."

"Jess . . . you're going to frighten Kira."

"Run, Kira. He's going to hurt you!"

"Jesus Christ, Jessica," David said, angry, grabbing her and practically lifting her from her feet as he dragged her toward the bed. "Stop it. Lie down and be quiet. You're delirious."

Jessica could feel Kira trailing behind them, tugging on Jessica's shirttail. She could hear her baby crying. She wanted to hold her baby. "Kira, he's going to hurt you—"

David had pushed her to the bed, pinning her shoulders down to keep her from moving. His weight was intractable. He was staring hard into her eyes. She did not know him. Even during moments of this drive to Louisiana, seeing those eyes, she thought she did. No matter what else he might have done, Jessisca's one certainty—despite the hidden gun in his waistband she could feel against her hipbone—was that David would never do anything to hurt her, and especially Kira. Now that certainty was shattered. She did not know her husband at all.

"Not her," she was saying, little more than a mumble. Soon, very soon, his face, this room, would be gone. "David, not her. Don't do it to her. You hear me? Please. Not Kira. What if it doesn't work? What if . . ."

"Just rest. In the morning, everything will be fine." His voice was so calm it was frightening.

In her mind, Jessica saw a horrific image of David's blood-drenched corpse springing to a wild-eyed sitting position in the bathtub on the island.

She whimpered, her chest heaving. Then, as her eyelids flickered, she imagined something else, so vivid it looked real.

Skeletons of dead lizards scattered all over the floor.

▪ 55

Lou Reed's hearing wasn't the greatest, but his olfactory senses were sharp as hell. He could smell a Smiley's pizza from yards away and peg the kind of topping with an accuracy that shocked even him. The one coming now was a plain pepperoni. How could anyone order pepperoni pizza when the fliers in the motel rooms, plain as day, said Smiley's specialties were barbecued shrimp or crawfish pizza? No imagination, he thought, flipping stations on his thirteen-inch color TV to find a show that might make him laugh for a change.

The kid ducked inside the motel office, waving, a pizza box in his hand. Yep. Pepperoni, all right. Shame.

The kid had probably stopped in to fish for a brew, since Lou kept his minifridge under the counter well-stocked during baseball season. As long as Lou had the Braves and his Amstel Light, he didn't care if there weren't any guests all night long.

Which was probably a good thing, he figured ruefully, since business was shot to hell since the Motel 6 opened down the way. Goddamn chains had money to advertise, and people liked a name they recognized. It was an indisputable fact of American consumerism.

"Second time here tonight," he remarked to the kid, studying his pimply face and wondering why he didn't use any cream for it. Wasn't he past the age when he should be thinking about girls?

"Told you it was a good idea to put fliers in the rooms," the kid said. "Between you and the Motel 6, we're over here five, six times a night."

"Tell that cheapskate Smiley to give you a raise then."

"Yeah, right. Hey, Lou Reed, what happened in Two?"

Lou Reed. The kid always called him by both of his names because he thought it was funny he had the same name as that singer who did "Walk on the Wild Side." Most times, he came in here singing it and was about to drive him crazy.

"Nothing going on with Two I know about. Black guy checked in with his kid this afternoon. Then they came by an hour ago when he used the pay phone to get a pizza."

The kid's eyes bugged. Really, Lou thought, if he got rid of those glasses and found some acne cream, he'd look all right. "You kidding me? Didn't you hear all that screaming?"

Lou flipped to another channel. He hated that loud *Roseanne*. "What do you mean, screaming? Maybe he was yelling at the kid."

"Naw, Lou Reed, it was a woman screaming. I give him his food, he pays me, he gives me a dollar tip, and I'm walking to my car when I hear this woman screaming her head off. And I hear this crash, like something breaking."

Now, the kid had Lou's attention. Some drunken shithead had broken a window just last week throwing a bottle of whiskey at his wife, and Lou was still trying to pay for that. Lou didn't even remember seeing a woman when the black guy and his kid checked in, unless she was out in the car. What the hell was wrong with these men beating up on their wives? If he ever tried to lay a hand on Glo, she'd kill him. He almost chuckled at the very idea.

But this wasn't funny. A guy beating his wife wasn't right, especially in front of a kid. Maybe he was beating that cute little pigtailed kid too. The guy in Two didn't look the type: clean-cut, well spoken. But the whole world was going to hell in a handbasket nowadays. Nothing but psychos.

Of course, Lou reminded himself, this pizza kid once told him he watched *Natural Born Killers* at least once a week, and the goddamn video was two years old. He probably wasn't the most reliable source, considering he must have a sick imagination.

"I'd check out Two, if I were you," the kid said, turning on his heel. "Hey, that—"

"Yeah, yeah . . . that rhymes," Lou said, waving him off.

"No beer tonight?"

"Later. Not while you're driving."

"Damn, Lou Reed, you sound like my stepdad. Walk on the wild side," the kid said, and vanished with his pizza.

Lou didn't waste any time. The invoice from A-Anytime Window & Glass was sitting on the desk right in front of his face, and he wasn't going to put up with any more crap from the guests. He grabbed his master key and made his way around the counter to walk outside into the humid night. Room Two.

Eight o'clock and only five guests in thirty units. Not that early summer was ever a busy time for him, but things were looking dire. Might be time to sell soon, if anyone who'd been offering a couple of years back would still be interested.

The black guy's car was a gray Plymouth, probably a rental. Nothing special about it. Florida plate, from Orange County. Lou took note of the tag number, KAT 161. Easy enough to remember.

He listened in front of the freshly painted door for a half-minute. He heard music from the TV's built-in radio, but that was it. Should he barge in on these folks over some kid's wild imagination or just go on about his business?

Thinking about his broken picture window and the price tag to fix it, Lou knocked.

After a few seconds and some shuffling, the door cracked open.

Black guy stood there, a slice of pizza in his hand. Plain cheese, congealing. Must be way cold by now.

Right away, Lou glanced over his shoulder to peek inside. He saw the little girl sitting on the edge of the bed, stroking a woman's hair like she would a doll's. The woman was black too, with short hair. Sleeping, or seemed like it. The kid had the sniffles and didn't look very happy, that was for sure. And the lamp on the nightstand was crooked, knocked out of whack. Maybe something really had happened in here.

"Can I help you?" the black guy asked, not annoyed, but over-polite with a voice that really meant "Get lost."

"Just checking to make sure everything's all right," Lou said.

"Fine. Thanks," the man said. He smiled as an afterthought. "Good night."

It wasn't anything Lou could put his finger on. The black guy hadn't been very sociable, even when he came down to use the phone, but then again, some people were friendlier than others. There was just something about the little girl's face, her mussed hair, the way she was stroking the woman like that. Didn't look right. He wasn't even sure why. He'd have felt loads better if it had been the woman who answered the door.

And the black guy was something else again. There was something in his eyes.

Now that damn pizza kid had Lou's imagination going too.

KAT 161.

Well, just for the hell of it, he could call Glo's brother at the state patrol and see if the license tag meant anything special. Craig loved shit like that. Nothing better to do, sitting behind a desk with a broken ankle. And still blaming Lou for it. Hell, it wasn't his fault the fat SOB couldn't dodge a tackle.

Lou walked back to his office toward the phone, singing, "*Doop de-doop, doop, doop-de-doop doop, de-doop, doop . . .*"

Damn that pizza kid, anyway. Never should have told him my goddamn name, Lou Reed thought. Now he'd be hearing that song in his head for the rest of the night.

▪ 56

All difficulty is relative, Dawit realized. His labors as a slave, his breathless combat with other men, his terrible disembowelment at his own hands, the suddenness of his life's sorrows: All of these things had been difficult. These trials were the timber of his being, whatever he was.

Why, then, had nothing seemed so difficult as this?

Kira was sitting on the bathroom sink's countertop, her legs swinging back and forth, the tip of her neon-orange sneakers occasionally brushing against his thighs. Her eyes were moony, and she gazed up at him, hardly blinking.

"I don't want any pills, Daddy," Kira said.

He had not been prepared for an argument. Nor for the doubts, even distrust, plainly written on his child's young face. He felt, suddenly, like a masked Nigerian *Egungun*, the face of death.

"They'll make you sleepy, that's all, Kira."

"I don't want to go to sleep. I want to watch the Disney Channel. When are we going to the Magic Kingdom? Mommy said."

"Tomorrow, we're going to see a man in New Orleans," Dawit said. "He's going to give us papers to go on an airplane to Africa. Just like we planned."

Kira stared up at him, then glanced toward Jessica's unmoving form on the bed. She made no move to take the pills.

"Is Mommy sick?"

"No, Duchess. She's only resting."

"How come . . . when I shake her, she won't wake up?"

"Because she's very tired."

"Did the pills make her tired?" Kira's wide eyes were questioning. She blinked, waiting for his answer.

"Yes, I think they did."

"Daddy . . ."—Kira reduced her voice to a whisper—"Mommy didn't want me to take them."

Dawit felt his extended palm trembling. This was nothing short of torture. How could he proceed? "Kira . . . it would make Daddy very happy if you would take the pills. *S'il te plaît?* Do it for me."

Once again, Kira's eyes ventured toward Jessica, who had been motionless for the past half-hour. He'd brought the bottle of thirty-milligram capsules of Dalmane from their medicine cabinet because he knew the drug acted quickly; Alex had given Jessica a prescription after Peter died, to help her sleep, but she'd only taken one dose. They were too strong, she complained.

He'd emptied two capsules into Jessica's soda earlier that day, twice the recommended dosage. And the four additional capsules Dawit had given Jessica, while very strong, would not be lethal, he believed. Nor would Kira's. Sleeping pills were too uncertain a means of death. He did not have the time, nor the equipment, to take the risks he had taken with Teacake, waiting for their bodies' metabolic reactions to a poisonous compound. For true precision, with both Jessica and Kira, death must be at his own hands.

He only needed them to sleep. He would not be capable of harming his child unless she were thoroughly unconscious.

Kira gazed at the capsules. Tears brimmed in her eyes.

"Oh, Duchess . . ." Dawit said, sucking in his breath. With his free hand, he touched her smooth, warm face. "Why do you cry?"

"Daddy, did you hurt Mommy?" she choked.

Now, Dawit's own tears came. He leaned over to speak directly into Kira's face. "Of course I didn't hurt Mommy. I would never do that. Never. I gave her the pills so she would sleep, and so she is. You see? I only want you to sleep too. What makes you think I did something to hurt her?"

Blinking rapidly, Kira didn't answer. She was crestfallen.

You truly are a monster, Dawit thought. Any other man would abandon this plan. Instead, you lie to your own young daughter.

"Kira . . . Do you trust me?"

Biting her lip, Kira nodded. He heard a sob in her throat.

"Then take the pills, Duchess. Please." He held one to her mouth, not quite touching her soft lips. "All right?"

Bit by bit, Kira opened her mouth. Dawit deposited the first capsule on her waiting tongue and gave her the cup filled with tap water. "Don't chew. It's not like baby aspirin. Swallow it down whole, like your food. That's very good. Let's try another."

He heard another half sob as Kira tried to swallow, but she gamely took all three. Then, she leaned over to wrap her arms around his neck, and he could feel her tiny heart racing against his chest. She was terrified, he realized; and yet, because she was a child, loving him was all she knew.

Dawit's own throat felt swollen as he lifted her, feeling her weight against him as he stood. This betrayal will remedy itself in the end, he thought. He could save her forever only through temporary suffering. He walked toward the bed where Jessica lay.

"There's no Disney Channel on this TV, Kira. Do you want Daddy to tell you a story?"

When Kira didn't answer or stir, Dawit was at first alarmed. Had he miscalculated her dosage? Could the drug have acted so quickly? He'd counted on having time to finish the Ritual on Jessica first, before her breathing became too impaired from the high dose of the sleeping pills. "Kira?"

"Lin," she said softly.

"What, Duchess?"

"Tell me the story about Lin and the dragon."

Despite himself, Dawit smiled. "I don't know that one. You must have heard that one at school. But I can tell you a story about a beautiful princess named Kira who lived forever and ever."

When Dawit reposed Kira on the bed alongside her mother, her eyes were already closed. He watched Kira's steady breathing, then laid two fingers across the carotid artery of her throat, where he could feel her pulse, which still raced. Gazing at her, his entire face was damp, smarting from tears.

"Forever?" Kira whispered softly, drowsy.

"And ever," Dawit said, and leaned over to kiss her forehead.

Dawit knew he did not have much time for thinking, but for one moment, after he had attached the very basic pulse monitor he'd found at the drugstore to Jessica's arm and readied the syringe filled with his just-drawn blood, he realized that he could choose another, much simpler, path.

He could leave them here in peaceful sleep and go his own way, allowing them to live the rest of their mortal lives without him.

If not for Mahmoud and the Searchers, he realized, he could have considered this option. In fact, he would have: Because, for all of his selfish impulses and deep love for them, he knew there would not be bliss in either route. His relationship with Jessica was fundamentally changed. By now, the only solutions were bad ones.

"The blood . . . is the vessel for Life . . ." he began in Hebrew, jogging his brain so he would not do the unthinkable and forget the incantation. Only a handful of words. He could not fail.

Teacake sat on the opposite bed, grooming himself with one dainty paw raised. Yes, Dawit reminded himself as he glanced at the cat, he had done this before. He could do it again.

Jessica's pulse was low, only sixty, the monitor said.

" . . . The blood flows without end . . ."

He did not have time for hesitation. Already, the proprietor had investigated the room once, probably because of Jessica's screams. He must finish this and check out at the first morning light, when Jessica and Kira would be forever awake.

His hand still unsteady, Dawit grasped the readied syringe. He raised his other palm to Jessica's cheek and touched it. Already, her skin felt clammy. He rubbed his hand across her face, her jaw, her chin, until it rested on her throat, which he touched with loving gentleness.

"A short sleep, my love. My life," he said, and leaned over to kiss her lips.

Then, as if electrocuted, he seized the appropriate spots on Jessica's throat and squeezed with all his might.

His own heartbeat was a roar in his ears. He stared hard at the pulse monitor, waiting for the number to begin to drop.

Even an unconscious body fought, he learned to his horror. Jessica's entire frame tensed, and her mouth dropped open to gasp for air. He expected to see her eyes open next; if that happened, he would be forced to let her go. Mercifully, her eyes remained closed and she slept still. Her body itself, deprived of oxygen, was acting upon instinct.

And her heart was quickening, not slowing.

Dawit felt a cramp in his hand, but he pressed on, making certain no air could pass through her throat. Perspiration dripped into his eyes, momentarily blinding him. One minute passed. More.

At long last, Dawit saw between blinks, the monitor indicated that her heartbeat was slowing. He lowered the hypodermic to Jessica's exposed forearm, ready to plunge.

Forty beats per minute, the monitor said. Thirty-five.

She was dying. She was truly dying. Jessica's face was changing colors, literally beginning to glow a purple shade. Beneath her brown skin, her face was bright red.

Thirty beats. Twenty-six.

Dawit gasped, longing to release her. How much time had passed? Why was death so slow? How had he subjected himself to this utterly inhuman torture?

Twenty beats. Eighteen.

"You are fighting, Jessica . . . For God's sake, don't . . ."

It was an eternity before the monitor dropped to twelve beats per minute. Then, ten. Then, at last, five.

Dawit could not wait for the monitor to show a zero. Her heart would stop a few seconds before the crude device could record it. Still holding her throat in his death grip, Dawit jabbed the needle into his wife's arm and pushed the plunger, exactly as he'd done with Teacake. His voice shook.

"The blood is the vessel for Life. The blood flows without end, as a river through the Valley of Death."

When Dawit released Jessica, the monitor at last read zero.

He stared at it, forgetting to breathe.

Zero.

"What have I done?" he wondered aloud, collapsing against the bed as his legs folded beneath him. He could not bear to look at her face. He had killed her. And now, he must wait. How long?

Two hours? Three? Even more? From person to person, it varied. He could not attempt the Ritual on Kira until he knew Jessica's own passage was safe.

Dawit sobbed. He stared at his own hands as if they were covered in blood. "What have I done?" he asked again, and there was no answer except the squeal of a saxophone from the radio.

Teacake jumped from the bed. He rubbed against Dawit, purring. Dawit clung to the cat and stroked his fur, holding the animal as if for dear life.

▪ 57

There were a host of reasons Alexis Jacobs was dying in Miami as a team of surgeons barked orders over her and injected her with life-saving drugs she would have been intimately familiar with if she'd been conscious to see the procedure.

She was hemorrhaging badly. That was the first thing. Her heart was distressed. Her body, still traumatized from the fall, was too weak to withstand the shock of surgery.

But the deeper reasons had nothing to do with physiology.

Alexis knew that Bea had been keeping things from her, but it was only a few hours before surgery, when she was semiconscious and most people assumed she couldn't understand what was going on around her, that she lost her will to live.

Bea's friend Randall Gaines, talking to a nurse, had finally explained why Jessica had not come to visit in at least two days. Jessica was missing.

But it was worse than that, even. As it turned out, the police thought David was the one who had pushed Alex off her balcony. They thought David had killed Jessica's friend Peter. And David was missing, too, presumably chasing Jessica.

The most unbelievable news had been uttered in a low tone: Jessica's empty van had been found, the windows shot out. Her baby sister and little niece might be dead.

She would have shaken off the tidings as fantasies conjured up in her semiconsciousness except for the simple fact of her mother's absence. Bea, who had been at her side for days, had been gone for several hours. Even when Alex's eyes were closed and she couldn't see, she knew it. Her mother wasn't there. And only a firestorm of tragedy could be keeping her away.

Alexis had told herself she would try to hang on for her mother, because God only knew what she must be going through.

But when a body is ready to die, it's hard to will it not to. It takes a kind of energy some people don't possess, and even people who can muster it have to focus, sometimes for hours on end. For two hours, Alexis had been focused.

But now, her focus and her energy were slipping fast.

Because, the truth was, the world that was waiting for her after all her fighting wasn't a world she wanted any more to do with. It was a world without her sister and Kira. It was a world filled with uncertainty at best, and heartbreak at most. So, even thinking of poor Bea, escape was a welcome blessing.

"We're losing her," Alexis heard a voice say. She knew the voice. Victor Dunn. Victor Dunn, who barely passed anatomy, the one everyone had nicknamed The Resident from Hell, was on the surgical team operating on her? Lord help her now.

"Adrenaline," another voice, an unfamiliar voice, said.

Adrenaline. They must be desperate. This was really going to be it, this time. There would be no going back. And if Jessica and Kira were gone, she'd see them on the other side.

That was when something happened that Alexis would forever describe as a vision. Not a dream. It was a place she visited, something she witnessed for herself from a shelter in her psyche. She was standing beside Jessica, but they weren't dead. They were in bright sunlight. There was a little girl with Jessica. She was sure of it. And Bea, standing behind them. Alexis and Jessica were wearing white. And they were standing before a throng of people, the most black people Alexis had ever seen gathered in one place. And the people were smiling. It was a sea of smiles against dark, beautiful skin.

And she could hear music, the most lyrical harmony of human voices she had ever heard, a praise sung in a lovely language that wasn't English. Zulu, she knew somehow. A sound full of hope. And Alexis was *healing* people. She didn't know how she knew. She just did.

What she didn't know was that, hundreds of miles away in a motel room outside New Orleans, her sister was having the exact same vision and gathering the same resolve to live, but under very different circumstances. The sisters' souls touched.

A great peace settled over Alexis, because she'd seen herself somewhere she'd always wanted to be, doing something she'd always wanted to do, and she realized it was all within her grasp. All she had to do was fight. Just a while longer. Life was something worth having, after all.

"Sinus rhythm. We got her back," Alex heard a voice say.

But Alex didn't need to hear that to know her heart was beating fine.

▪ 58

"Here's an obscure one that goes way back for you real aficionados," the announcer on the radio said. "The Jazz Brigade, a group out of Chicago, with a song recorded in nineteen twenty-six that George Gershwin credited as the most influential of its day: 'Forever Man.'"

Then, Dawit heard the sound of his own aged clarinet. Lester's piano. Al's banjo. Cleve's trumpet. A seventy-year-old memory, music played by an ensemble of dead musicians, and he was hearing it here, of all places. And now, of all times.

Dawit looked at the clock glowing lime green from the television set. It was midnight. Though it was relatively early, Dawit interpreted the song as a sign that he could peek over the edge of the bed at Jessica's pulse monitor. Before he had a chance to read the tiny digital display, his heart melted inside him.

Jessica's chest was gently rising and falling as she slept.

Rising to his knees, he clasped her hand and kissed it. Then, her neck. Then, both of her covered breasts, burying his face in the fledgling warmth of her bosom. He had done it. She was still his. He had preserved the first half of his family.

Sixty-five beats per minute, her pulse monitor said.

Dawit stood, stretching his legs, and leaned over the bed to examine the second monitor he had attached to Kira. His daughter's pulse was slower, only fifty beats per minute, and felt weak to his touch. Her breathing sounded harsh, and her poor chest was fluttering. The medicine might be complicating her asthma. He must work on her now, or she would die from the Dalmane alone.

Now, the most difficult part of his task.

The telephone in the motel office was ringing. Lou Reed was still there, packing up his magazines and paperwork to go home to his wife in the two-bedroom house they'd built only a few yards behind the motel. His hours were noon to midnight, and he didn't like to work a moment before or past.

Lou picked up his telephone, hoping it wasn't some Johnny-come-lately calling for directions. He wanted to hit the sack.

"I-Ten Inn," he answered.

Lou barely recognized his brother-in-law's voice. When he'd talked to Craig at least three hours ago, he'd sounded half asleep. Now, he sounded like someone had set him on fire.

"Holy Jesus, Lou, you and Glo be careful," Craig wheezed.

Must be news about the license tag on the Plymouth. Lou's skin pricked. "What's going on? We onto something?"

"Hell, yeah. He's wanted for murder, and they say the woman and kid have been kidnapped. He's armed, Lou. Don't go near that room again. You're lucky he didn't shoot you in the ass."

"Well . . ." For a second, Lou was speechless. This was like something out of *America's Most Wanted.* "Is anybody coming?"

"Only the fucking cavalry," Craig said. "Five minutes. You get home to Glo. I just called over there. Make sure she's okay."

"I'll be damned," Lou said, still stunned. He remembered the black guy's eyes, the way he'd smiled as cordial as could be. "You just never know about people, do you?"

"Cut the philosophizing, man, and get home to my sister."

Kira's throat was so delicate, strangling her with his oversized adult's hand felt like a crime against all nature. Dawit had steeled himself, remembering his ordeal with Jessica, but this was something else again. When Kira's body stiffened beneath his grip, Dawit's layers of self-preservation peeled away and he felt himself shaking all over. The syringe in his hand trembled so violently that he could barely clasp it between his fingers. A droplet of blood spilled from the raised needle, too soon, and rolled a path of crimson across his daughter's forearm.

This was too, too familiar. Like Rosalie.

Goodbye, Daddy.

Kira's pulse monitor, unlike Jessica's, plunged steadily. It didn't linger as her heart fought for life. Her child's heart lacked either the strength or the will to resist him.

Sixteen beats, the monitor read. Twelve beats.

"I love you, Duchess . . ." Dawit whispered through tears.

He waited for his daughter to die.

▪ 59

Jessica's new life began unexpectedly, and very badly.

She awoke with a paralyzing headache, one that hurt her crown and temples so much that she almost made a sound. Her mouth was dry. And her arms and legs were tingling beneath her skin, as if she could feel the delicate streams of her own blood tickling through her veins. She was fully aware of the texture of every article of clothing she wore, from her soft cotton blouse to the clinging nylon of her knee-highs wrapped around her toes. Her back was sore against the mattress from lying still too long.

When she opened her eyes, she saw a dizzying reflection in the mirror from the light on the nightstand. Then, the room around the light crept into focus.

There, in the mirror, she saw a frozen image from a bad dream. David was leaning over Kira, strangling her with one hand, his arm locked rigidly above her. She closed her eyes, believing she must be hallucinating. But then she looked again, and the awful visage was still there. And, strangest of all, she saw her own aghast face beside them.

It wasn't until Jessica felt a movement and heard David's grunt that she realized he and Kira were on the bed next to her. It took all her strength to turn her head to watch her husband murdering her child.

No moment in her life had foreshadowed what she felt as she watched. Horror was too small a word. Rage was only the beginning. And she was far beyond helplessness.

The parts of Jessica's mind that weren't stunned made frantic plans. Grab the gun from David's pants and shoot him. Knock him over. Push him away. Close your eyes and scream to the Heavens until someone comes to rescue Kira. Someone help Kira.

Her weakened body would not obey; parts of her were literally still dead, only numb flesh. All she could do was watch, blinking with disbelief.

Kira, she thought. My baby.

And then, right on time, there were three solid knocks on the door. Jessica heard a man calling David's name. And then hers. The loud knocks came again.

David looked up at the door, startled. His eyes, for the briefest moment, met Jessica's. His face flooded with guilt, remorse. But his straining hand never once left Kira's throat.

Jessica tried to open her mouth to beg him, and could not.

The door, on its own, flew open with a slam so loud that the sound rattled in Jessica's aching skull. From nowhere, white men in dark uniforms flooded into the room. One, with a beard, had a gun pointed the way she'd seen Mahmoud pointing his the night the van stalled. Were these the Searchers, come to kill them at last?

She was so amazed at the sight of the armed men that she hardly realized David was screaming at them. His voice sounded half human. "Leave me!" David was shouting. "You don't know what you're doing! You'll kill her!"

"Get away from the little girl. Now," the bearded man with the gun said, looking as frightened and enraged as Jessica felt.

David looked away from the men, his head bowed over Kira's chest. He still choked her with one hand, but was doing something to Kira's arm with the other, movements Jessica couldn't see.

But she heard. David was whispering. Jessica could just make out his voice, uttering words in a language she didn't know. And yet she did. "The blood is the vessel for Life . . ."

With his free hand, he fumbled for his waistband.

Instantly, Jessica saw something red explode against the wall behind David, like a splatter of color in a kaleidoscope. Then she remembered hearing gunshots. And she saw David's mouth contort without making any sound as he stumbled backward from the mattress. He was wearing a white shirt; three dark-red stains, like large ink spots, made a perfect triangle across his chest.

David fell against the wall, gasping. His pupils had rolled upward, and all Jessica could see was whiteness where his eyes should be. " . . . The blood . . . flows . . . without end . . ."

Jessica saw something on the bed beside her, something she knew had flown from David's hand. A syringe of blood.

Only then did she really know, and she nearly swooned where she lay. David had killed Kira so he could save her. And his Ritual had been interrupted. With that realization, to Jessica, nothing else existed in the room except Kira and the syringe.

Suddenly, Jessica screamed. She summoned even her still-sleeping parts. She found the syringe with her fingers and held it. David, very probably, had not had time to inject Kira. She must do it herself. And when she did, Kira would not die now, or ever.

She would never die.

But Jessica did not move, and this time it had nothing to do with her sluggish muscles. The clarity of this moment, this one moment, made her feel wide awake for the first time in days. She understood, her mind strangely naked of barriers. Hold tight to Kira for me.

She could not give Kira this blood. The blood was a temporary respite with an everlasting curse: exile from wherever all children's souls go. Hold tight to Kira for me. Could God be so cruel? Holding on to Kira only meant letting go.

Jessica heard wounded sobs, and of course they were her own.

David's voice was faint as he lay crumpled against the wall, seeing nothing, breathing the last breath of a corpse. " . . . The blood flows . . . without end . . . as a river . . . through the Valley . . ."

Of Death, Jessica thought, half insane, already mourning. When she tried to speak, this time her mouth refused.

Of Death.

The men—police officers, Jessica realized now, sitting up in the bed with a blanket wrapped around her because she was shaking uncontrollably and one of the officers had decided she must be cold—fussed and worked over Kira on the dingy carpeting for what seemed like hours. They were afraid to try to put her in the waiting ambulance until her heart started beating again. And for some reason, it would not.

While Jessica waited, the things she noticed puzzled her.

For instance, she'd see glimpses of how Kira's hair was standing on end, and she wished it was neater so they could see what a beautiful child she was. And she noticed how Teacake, every few minutes, stuck his head out from beneath the bed to see what the commotion was about, then darted back into hiding. And how, even though David hadn't moved in the longest time, his mouth was open slightly, trying to finish his sentence even now.

Her mind would not let go of the details. Maybe it was so that while she watched everything around her, she wouldn't really see it for what it was. This was her family.

These strangers were trying to comfort her, and yet they didn't know Kira had thought they were going to Disney World on this trip, and that she had asthma, and that she had asked Jessica once if there was such a thing as a good monster; or that David, for all the terrible truths she'd told the police, was the most loving and perfect husband and father anyone could imagine. Wasn't that strange? They just didn't know.

The first gurney was for David. She watched two ambulance technicians, dressed in white, lift her husband's limp body, making his wrists swing back and forth. One of the men pushed David's eyes closed first, then they covered him with a sheet. Like he was gone for good. Why had they done that?

Oh, yes, Jessica remembered. They didn't know.

"He's not dead," Jessica called out to them as they rolled the gurney past her. One of the officers, a sister, squeezed Jessica's shoulder beneath the blanket and gave her a pitying look. Her haircut reminded Jessica of Alex.

"He's not dead," Jessica said again, looking at her earnestly.

Funny. Jessica didn't think the police were supposed to get emotionally involved, and yet this sister had tears in her eyes. The officer took Jessica's hand and rubbed it.

"Mrs. Wolde? I want you to try to walk outside with me," she said softly, as though they were the only people in the room.

Jessica didn't stand. Instead, she looked at the doorway and saw a second gurney waiting. Kira's. She looked again at the floor, where three paramedics were huddled over her daughter, pushing on her chest, doing something to her throat, nearly blocking her from Jessica's view. All she could see was Kira's tiny orange sneakers on her feet, twitching occasionally when the men jolted her body.

One of Kira's laces was untied. Someone had to tie Kira's shoe, Jessica thought, or else she might trip.

Then, as if it had been waiting, grief washed over Jessica; a waterfall, unrelenting. The officer was trying to help her stand, but now Jessica was on her knees. She was making a sound from her chest she herself didn't recognize.

"It's all right, Mrs. Wolde," the officer was telling her, trying to lift her and lead her to the open doorway. Jessica lurched again, and a man grabbed Jessica with his sturdy arm. "She'll be all right, Mrs. Wolde. We need you to wait outside."

Yes, Kira would be all right.

Maybe David had finished the Ritual before he died.

Maybe she could have her back.

"She's dead now, but you check on her," Jessica was saying as the police led her into the darkness, where a small crowd of more strangers parted to clear her a path. She saw the men in white close the doors to the first ambulance, locking David inside.

"In the morning, you check on her. See if she's healed. Don't forget to check on my baby. You hear what I'm saying? The blood heals," Jessica told the sister, clinging to her sleeve.

No one was saying a word. Jessica had never heard such a silence. All she heard was the sound of her own heartbeat, thumping stronger in her ears, and she drew in a breath as if she'd never before tasted the night.

▪ 60

Kira didn't know how she'd gotten there, but she realized suddenly that she was back at home. She was in the cave. And it was still night, so dark she could barely see.

But she wasn't alone. It was too dark to make out Grandpa's face, but she could see his outline from his glow, like moonlight. She laughed, calling his name. For the first time since she'd seen Mommy crying when they were driving in the van and Daddy wasn't there, she wasn't the least bit scared. When Mommy and Daddy had been fighting over the pills, she'd been the most scared of all, maybe the most scared ever. Now, she felt like laughing.

Hey, Pumpkin. Didn't I say you'd be back soon? He was talking to her without moving his mouth.

"Grandpa, guess what happened! A man came—"

"Oh, I know all about that," Grandpa said, breathing out a sigh as though the man with the gun and the shot and the fighting was all nothing. "That stuff ain't important. Is it?"

Kira, smiling, shook her head.

Now, she could see him. It was like the sun came out, shining only on Grandpa, and she could see him better than she ever had. She could see light glowing on every hair on his moustache, every line on his dark, dark face. She'd never seen anything so wonderful. So magical.

"Kira, do you remember the story of Lin?"

"And the red dragon. And they were best friends. And they flew into the sky."

"That's right," Grandpa said, smiling. "Well . . . Grandpa told a little fib. That isn't really a story about a boy named Lin all the way in China. I made that up. It's a story about you."

"Me?" Kira asked, delighted. She felt Grandpa's light glowing on her face too. The cave was warm the way her covers felt when she curled underneath them if her window was open on a cold night. "But you said Lin's parents were wizards."

"Right again, you smart girl. Lin's parents are wizards. And your parents are wizards too. What did I tell you about wizards?"

Kira remembered every word. It was her favorite story. "Wizards have a lot of work to do. And they have powers. And they can't live in the sky."

Grandpa was proud of her. She could see it in his face. He looked happy and sad all at once, and he wanted to hug her.

"Turn around, Kira," Grandpa said. "Look outside."

When Kira turned around, she saw something amazing. It was a long red snout, scaly all over, sniffing at the mouth of the cave. Bright red, like a lobster Daddy cooked in the big pot. Even more red than that. A black tongue longer than her arm darted out, nearly touching her.

A real dragon! Kira was scared. "Grandpa!" she cried, about to run to him.

"No, Kira," Grandpa said. "Look again."

Oh, Kira realized, she was just being silly. It wasn't a dragon at all. The animal's fur was really black, and she heard a loud, deep bark. It was only Princess. Where in the world had Princess been so long? Mommy and Daddy had been looking for her.

Princess lowered herself on her haunches, looking like she was smiling, her big pink tongue hanging from her mouth. She crawled into the cave, her big tail wagging back and forth. Princess looked real and not real, almost like a cartoon.

Kira had tears in her eyes, but it was from being happy. She leaped to Princess and hugged her big neck. Princess smelled the same, just like before.

"Are you happy to see Princess, Kira?"

"Yes!" Kira cried.

"Well, see if you can climb on her back. I think she wants to take you for a pony ride. Remember how she did that?"

The entire cave was glowing now. The sun must have come out for real. Kira could barely see Princess for all the light.

"Like the dragon?"

"Could be," Grandpa said.

Kira started to scoot one leg over Princess's back. Then she stopped and tried to see Grandpa again. "Grandpa . . ."

"Yes, Pumpkin?"

"Can I ever come back?"

His face was the light, Kira saw. That must be why everything was so warm and felt so good, because it was all from Grandpa. She couldn't see him anymore, but she could hear his voice around her.

"For visits? Of course you can. Anytime you want. Just like Lin. And you'll see, Mommy and Daddy will be just fine."

So, Kira clasped Princess's neck and wrapped her legs over her dog's back. Princess stood up, very gently, so she wouldn't knock Kira off. When Princess began to run, Kira felt a cool wind brushing her face. She felt a bump-bump, bump-bump as Princess's paws hit the ground with every leap. Princess was giving her the fastest pony ride of all!

Kira closed her eyes, smiling. Soon, there were no bumps at all, just the wind and the light, and Kira held on, held on, with all the strength she could find.

▪ 61

For a day and a half, the entire time Jessica Jacobs-Wolde had been admitted to Southeastern General Hospital in New Orleans, she had uttered only the same two words, and she said them with regularity when anyone on the hospital staff visited her.

No blood.

Today, she'd already said it six times. Finally, Bea had to protest, chiding the slim Creole woman who'd been encouraging her to do what the doctor wanted: "The child said she doesn't want any blood tests. Can you please just let her be?"

Reporters were also calling, some of whom she knew. Even Sy called once—it didn't surprise her that he got through to the room—but Bea answered the phone and told him, please, not to give them any more pain just now.

Jessica wished she could do her own talking. Her mother had been through so much already that she hated to be another burden. The problem was, she just couldn't think of any other words. Every time she tried, her mind wrapped itself up tight. The only thing she really knew was that she was alive because David must have given her his blood. And if the doctors did any tests on her, they would find the same thing Alex had found. And Jessica didn't want that to happen. Not now. Not yet.

Jessica had known instantly because of the way her body felt once the headache was gone: fresh, untried. But to be sure, she scratched her wrist until it bled the first night, and the injury was gone by the time she woke up six hours later. Only a slight tickle was left to mark the spot. So now, she was sure.

Bea had learned that Jessica was at a hospital in New Orleans as soon as Alex got out of surgery in Miami; Jessica didn't think her mother had slept at all in at least two days, and looked it. But Bea's behavior hadn't changed. She talked on, never letting go of Jessica's hand. She was telling her stories about so-and-so down her street, whomever the young assistant pastor was supposed to be sleeping with, something funny she'd heard on a television talk show at Jackson. And how Randall Gaines had stolen a kiss from her outside Alex's room, talking about getting married. "Man must be going stir-crazy," Bea said. He'd insisted on flying with her to Louisiana, then turned right back around to go to Miami so Alex wouldn't be alone.

Listening to Bea's voice, Jessica imagined her mother was smiling. But whenever she looked at her mother's face, she only saw hurting, the parts Bea couldn't bury. And when Bea came back from her long trips to the bathroom, her face looked swollen and her eyes were watery and red. But then she'd start her stories again.

"I think you're going home today, baby," Bea was saying. "Alex will be so glad to see you. She had some hairy moments, but she made it through surgery like a fighter. She'll have to go to rehab, and the doctors say she should be able to walk. It may not seem that way now, but this family is blessed. It really is. You just have to keep sight of that, Jessica."

Another doctor came into the room, the same one she'd seen in the beginning. He was very young—almost too young, Jessica thought—and red-haired. He had freckles up and down his arms. The doctor smiled briefly, but he didn't try to look happy for her, since he knew she had nothing to be happy about. He sat at the foot of her aluminum bed, pulling her chart from its slot.

"Mrs. Wolde, you sure we can't convince you to let us do blood work? You had dangerously high levels of a drug called flurazepam hydrochloride in your urine sample yesterday, and some other irregularities we'd like to study."

"No blood," Jessica said, for the seventh time.

"Jesus help, we've told you people—" Bea began.

The doctor half smiled, holding up his freckled hand to signal his surrender. "We're not trying to harass you, I promise. We only want her to leave us in the best condition possible. And there is one thing worth rejoicing about, Mrs. Wolde. Despite your ordeal, the baby seems fine."

Jessica was sure the doctor had just been speaking to her, but she couldn't seem to recall what he'd just said. Even Bea was silent this time, letting go of Jessica's hand slightly.

Had he really said something about her baby?

"Kira," Jessica said, half sitting, unexpectedly thinking of something to say. She'd wondered why it was taking so long for someone to tell her that Kira was all right. She'd only been afraid to ask, hiding from an answer she didn't want to know.

The doctor blushed bright red, seeing their faces. "No," he said. "You mean your daughter? I'm sorry. I really am. I'm sure someone must have told you what happened, Mrs. Wolde. Rescue was never able to revive her. Her windpipe was broken. The autopsy—"

"What baby is fine?" Bea asked in a tight, strained voice, cutting him off, not wanting to hear anything else about Kira.

"Mrs. Wolde, you're six weeks pregnant. Did you know that?"

Bea gasped. Her eyes, wide open, swept to Jessica's. Jessica was still confused about what the doctor was saying.

"We learned that from the urine tests. That's one of the reasons we wanted to examine you more thoroughly. A drug like that isn't healthy for a fetus."

At first, Jessica thought the sound was coming from her, but it wasn't. It was coming from her mother: a bruised and exhilarated sob. Bea leaned over to hug her. She was close to hysterics, and Jessica wondered how she'd kept it in so long.

As much as Jessica wanted to cry with Bea, she could not. She was beginning to understand things now. About Kira being gone. Gone. And about an unborn child she didn't know anything about, who must have been conceived . . . when? That night with David at the cabin. When she didn't have her pills.

A baby inside her. A baby being nourished with her new blood.

Jessica couldn't be happy. And she couldn't yet bear to be sad. She was a statue in her mother's arms.

"So, like I said, at least there's a little good news."

"A miracle," Bea was sobbing. "Jessica, do you hear? You're going to have a baby. Another baby. Oh, Lord Jesus, thank you. It's like the Bible says, 'you giveth and you taketh away.' It won't be Kira, Lord, but we know you had your reasons for taking her. We don't understand, but please help us. Help us. And thank you, Jesus, for this baby. Thank you."

In Jessica's overwhelmed mind, only one thought could fight its way to her lips: "David's gone. Where is he?"

She felt her mother turn rigid. The doctor shared an uncomfortable glance with Bea, clearing his throat before speaking. "Jessica, how did you hear about that . . . ?" Bea whispered.

"Vandalism," the doctor said. "Mrs. Wolde, I'm sorry. Sometimes when you get these sensational cases and people see things on the news, there are curiosity-seekers. Vandals. The last I heard, someone must have broken into the morgue. They . . ."

"They haven't found him yet, Jessica," Bea finished for him. "But they will. I know he was your husband, no matter what sickness in his mind made him do what he did. I know you want to bury him."

Jessica didn't know anything about vandals or curiosity. She just wondered when her husband had awakened, and where he'd gone. And if he'd left alone.

"Kira, too?" Jessica asked.

"Baby, those were sick people, disturbing all the bodies. They thought Kira was gone at first too. But someone had only moved her from where she was supposed to be. She's still there. Don't you worry. I saw her, the little precious heart. You can bury your child."

"Someone just wanted a look, I guess," the doctor said. "Like I said, it's because of all the news. I'm sorry you had to hear about this, Mrs. Wolde. I know it can't make this easier."

No, nothing could ever make this easier. Nothing could. She'd had a daughter named Kira, and now she didn't. She felt devoured by the immensity of it all; Bea was a widow, and any child with dead parents was an orphan. But there wasn't even a word for her. Nobody had thought to make one up. Some feelings couldn't even be put in a dictionary.

No wonder people say they wish they could die, she thought. No wonder.

Somehow, Jessica realized, when this doctor finally left her and her mother alone, she would have to find a way to do a lot of talking. She had a lot to explain. She would have to do it today, because she couldn't hold it all inside the way David had. She couldn't be all alone, knowing the things she did.

"Don't think about what you've lost, Jessica," Bea said, her sobs gone. "Think about that beautiful baby God has left you. That's your light, you hear? It's yours forever, Jessica. No one can take this child away."

Jessica stared at her mother, her eyes filled with rapture, and wondered how in the world she already knew.

■

PART FIVE

Wizards

And the angel said unto her,
"Fear not, Mary: for thou hast
found favor with God."

—LUKE 1:30

▪ 62

KwaZulu/Natal
South Africa

DECEMBER 31, 1999

The driver didn't need directions. As soon as Dawit showed him the magazine story he'd torn out, telling him he was looking for the children's clinic, the driver grinned with recognition and reached over to open the back door to his mud-caked Land Rover.

"You're from Soweto?" the driver asked, peeking at Dawit in the rearview mirror as the car rumbled across a dusty road hedged by tall stalks of green sugarcane. A sun-faded Nelson Mandela victory button swung from his mirror on a leather string.

"No. From Ethiopia," Dawit said after a pause. He could have chosen any nationality. He had as much right to North America as to Ethiopia, and belonged to Nigeria as well as Senegal and Egypt.

"You fooled me with your Zulu."

"I study languages," Dawit said tonelessly, forcing himself to look away from the smudged article he'd been carrying for days, the story about the children's clinic he'd torn out of The Atlantic. The story about the clinic was a sidebar to an update on the new South Africa: MIRACLE WORKERS, the headline read.

"I have five languages: Zulu, SiSwati, Xhosa, Afrikaans, and English," the driver said, veering so wildly that Dawit thought he was going to run over a boy pulling a wooden cart. Chickens flew out of his automobile's way in the road. "How many have you?"

Dawit smiled. "Those, and a few others," he said.

"What takes you to the clinic? You have a child in need of healing?"

Dawit blinked, his smile withering. He should have

expected the question. It was the first time in two years anyone had asked him if he had a child. No, he realized. He did not.

He raised his index finger to the bridge of his nose, silent, weathering the paralysis brought by mourning.

"I have other business there," he said at last. "What do you know about the clinic?"

The driver shrugged, turning on a cassette of American pop music, Michael Jackson or someone. Jessica had made Dawit listen to a few of Michael Jackson's songs many years ago, in that long-past life just finished, and the singer's childlike voice was difficult to forget.

"I'm a bachelor. No kids, so I just hear the stories," the driver said. "You should hear the way the old women talk. Crazy things. They say you can take your children there, no matter what is wrong, and they will heal them. How many times have I driven whole families to this place? And all of them wanting miracles. One child, they say, came back from the dead. A boy."

Dawit stiffened. "That can't be," he said.

"Hey, listen, I'm only telling you what I've heard. Don't think I believe this craziness. I just drive. Soon, the way everyone is talking, there will be a paved road to the door. And camps for all the people waiting to get inside. You'll see."

"I'm sure you're right," Dawit said uneasily, licking his lips. "Who runs this clinic? The government?"

The man laughed hard, slapping the steering wheel. He sounded like he would choke. "The government! Don't talk crazy. The government clinic is to the east. The only miracle at that clinic is when they have enough supplies. Of course, it's less crowded now because no one takes their children there. All the children go to the clinic run by the Americans."

Americans!

The article in the magazine had been vague, not even including a photograph or mentioning the names of the people who had organized the clinic; it only said a new clinic had appeared within the past year, that it had the Zulu excited, that it was a folk symbol of promise among South Africa's blacks.

"You're sure they're Americans?"

"Black Americans," the driver said. "That's what they say."

Dawit closed his eyes, only now daring to believe that his intuition had good impetus to lead him all the way from Nigeria, where he'd been living quietly in a Lagos flat since leaving the States. He'd wanted to be alone with his sadness, yet he was still drawn to cities, where he could walk streets anonymously and be swallowed by crowds. For these years, he'd sat in his room in darkness, occasionally allowing himself the comfort of five or six jazz cassettes he'd bought. At night, he drank so he could plunge into a sleep that was, he imagined, like a sort of death. Someone, presumably an American, had left the magazine open on a bar counter, and he'd seen it, blurry eyed, by chance.

The magazine had led him to her.

"Just over that way. There it is!" the driver said, pointing.

The squat white concrete building, obviously built recently in a rural section still being developed, looked like it was large enough for only three or four rooms. As the driver had said, there were a few families sitting outside in the shade of newly planted fiddle-leaf fig and African tulip trees. A woman in a colorful headdress sat on the stoop, nursing a baby while two near-naked children played beside her. Nearly two dozen people waited outside.

There was no sign identifying the building as a clinic. The only sign was printed in Zulu, hand-painted and posted to one of the trees: UNCULO UTHOKOZISA ABADABUKILEYO. "Singing makes all the sad people happy because it is the voice of happiness," it said.

In keeping with the sentiment, Dawit saw three adolescent girls leaning against the building, singing words in Zulu in a soft harmony that reminded Dawit of an American spiritual. Africans had taken their music with them to America, black Americans had ushered it back, and now there was no separating it, Dawit thought.

"You picked a good time. There aren't many here today."

Dawit's hand shook as he gave the driver a handful of crumpled rand without counting the amount, climbing from the car. "Thank you," he said. "Wait here. If I'm not back in a few minutes, you can go."

"With this, I can afford to wait all afternoon!" the driver called to Dawit as he walked up the path carved in the grass.

Dawit excused himself, passing the nursing woman, and went inside, where three large white ceiling fans swirled above his head. The floor was unvarnished, uncovered concrete, and the only real light was from the sun streaming through the large picture windows. Metal folding chairs lined the wall, all of them occupied by women and children talking, sleeping, or simply rocking in their seats, obviously ill. One young shirtless boy gazed up at Dawit with such hopefulness that it haunted him. He would see those eyes in his sleep, he imagined.

"*Yebo*," greeted a pretty Zulu woman, who sat behind a simple wooden desk at the rear of the room, beckoning him. "We're out of chairs. You should try to come early, before the crowds. We may not get to you just now. There are twelve in line before you. Fill out this paper and say what's wrong with your child. You came from one of the cities? Jo'burg?"

"Much farther," Dawit said. "I'm here to find a woman I knew in America. Jessica Wolde. Is she here?"

The woman shrugged. "Only Doctor Alex is here."

"Yes," Dawit said, his heart surging. "Alex is her sister."

"Doctor Alex's sister?" the woman asked, and a wondering expression passed across her face. "Yes, I know of the sister. She lives in the house just behind the clinic. But she doesn't take visitors. Only her relatives, and the children."

Dawit rested one palm on the desktop to steady himself, feeling his strength leaving him. She was here, after all!

"I am a relative," he said, finding it difficult to speak. "I am her husband."

The woman's eyebrows jumped with her obvious surprise. More than surprise. Dawit wondered, for a moment, if she had heard stories about him. He was certain he felt curious eyes on his back from onlookers in the chairs. A wiry boy who looked ten, dressed in a white dress shirt and navy shorts—a school uniform— peeked around the corner at him from one of the hidden rooms.

Dawit swallowed, uneasy beneath the woman's gaze. It was not quite fear he detected in her eyes; it was something else, more like wonder, reverence.

"May I see her?" Dawit asked when she didn't move.

"You, the husband, are the one the same as her?" the woman asked, sounding embarrassed, as though she should not ask.

"The same . . . ?"

Dawit made a slight turn, shifting his eyes to the onlookers behind him. An older woman with a smooth mocha face was gazing at him with tears ready to fall. Seeing that Dawit watched her, she smiled a toothless smile.

"Sipho," the receptionist said, startling Dawit as she called to the uniformed boy, "take the master to the house."

Instantly, the boy's hand was inside of Dawit's, squeezing. "Come with me, master," he said in English. "Come to the back."

Before the boy led Dawit to the courtyard outside the sliding glass door, Dawit heard the old woman say something to the child sitting beside her, a single word.

Magic, he heard her say.

In the large courtyard, chickens pecked at seed hidden in the overgrown grass, and six uniformed girls and boys shrieked and ran, trying to hit one another with a red ball. "Sipho! Sipho!" a slightly older boy called, poised to throw the ball to him.

Urgently, annoyed at the boy, Sipho shook his head. He looked up at Dawit with apologetic eyes. "They were sick, master," the boy told Dawit, as if in explanation. "Like me. Doctor Alex likes us to play here. She wants the sister to hear us laughing."

All of the windows and doors to the large two-story house twenty yards behind the clinic were open, and a child occasionally ran out with an orange or a can of soda. It was as though the house belonged to them, Dawit thought. Hearing the laughter, surrounded by the children's energy, Dawit blinked back tears.

Kira should be here, he thought.

Then Dawit saw someone he recognized, an older man squatting outside the door with a bucket, washing paintbrushes. At first, he could barely remember where he knew him from. But as the man stared at him, slowly rising to his feet, Dawit remembered him; he was Bea's gentleman companion named Gaines. Dawit detected the same expression—not anger, but mere wonder—on his face.

Sipho sensed a hesitation in Dawit's step, and tugged Dawit's hand with a laugh. "She is in here, master. The sister. Do not be afraid. Come inside."

Gaines stood in the doorway, a giant. He was an old man, but he looked conditioned and strong without his shirt, probably from labors. The sun had made his face look hard, and he did not smile. "That's far enough, Sipho," Gaines said in his West Indian English. He held Dawit's eyes, as a man. Then he cocked his head toward the house's cooler interior, extending one arm. "Let's go, David. This is the way. She's upstairs."

He was welcome in Jessica's home? Would Jessica welcome him as well? Dawit's mind swam with a sense of unreality. He had not expected to come this far, and now that he was here, what next?

Crying wildly, a toddler in an oversized T-shirt with short, curly hair ran into Dawit's path as soon as he walked inside. Dawit felt small fingers grasping his trousers. Gaines lifted the child into his arms, cooing. "What happened?" Gaines called to someone over his shoulder.

"She won't listen, and she grabbed the broken glass in the kitchen. Her finger is bleeding," a teenage girl said, running to

Gaines. They examined the child's hand, and Dawit saw a trickle of blood snaking around her tiny index finger. "You see how she's cut? There, there, little one. Let me wash it in the sink."

The toddler howled and squirmed as Gaines passed her to the girl, but Dawit forgot her as soon as he saw a shadow at the top of the stairway. He watched with anticipation, and then Jessica appeared. She seemed to glide rather than walk, her step was so graceful, and she wore a striking white head wrap and long white dress, probably provided by a local dressmaker. He had never seen her look this way. He was awed by her sudden sight.

"What in the world happened?" Jessica called down. She sounded newly awakened.

"She cut herself, madam. I'll wash her finger."

"Jessica," Gaines said, drawing Jessica's concerned gaze away from the child. "There's someone to see you."

For the first time, she saw him. He saw her clasp the railing with her long fingers, but she still looked regal, untroubled. No wonder they worship her, he thought. He, too, wanted to drop to his knees before her. He could not find words to greet her. Jessica bowed her head, as if struck, then turned and hurriedly walked back to the room she had come from without speaking. Hungrily, Dawit watched her every movement until she had vanished.

"Guess you better go on up after her, David," Gaines said.

Jessica's was the third upstairs room, at the end of the hall. It was furnished sparsely with a white wicker bookshelf, a desk pushed beneath the window, and a wicker armchair, where Jessica sat with her hands folded. A colorful mosaic of Zulu beads hung on the wall, but nothing else. Dawit heard a meow, and Teacake settled himself in Jessica's lap. A second pair of eyes stared at him.

Dawit did not move from the doorway, since he was not certain he should enter. It would be an invasion, he believed, just as his very presence felt like an invasion.

"I knew you'd come one day," Jessica said, speaking first. Her statement was a fact, stated with neither joy nor malice.

"You've never been more beautiful," Dawit said, the only words that seemed appropriate. Had he won even the slightest smile from her? He could not say from where he stood. "And this . . . what you do here . . . I am amazed."

This time, she did smile slightly. She seemed to relax, leaning back in the chair while she stroked the cat. Her smile, very soon, took a wistful turn. "Sipho probably brought you back here. We have to force him to go to school. He never wants to leave. When his mother brought him, his leukemia had progressed so far that everyone thought he was dead."

"My driver said something about bringing children back from the dead," Dawit said, and was immediately sorry. At that instant, he saw Kira's framed kindergarten photograph on Jessica's desk. He was transfixed by the suddenness of her smiling image. Since he'd been stripped of his possessions at the morgue and had no photographs of his own, this was the first time Dawit had seen his child since the night in the motel room, when her eyes had been filled with fearful tears. No, even worse. His last sight of her had been in cold death, when he found her naked, sallow corpse. The memory was an indictment. Dawit looked away from the photograph.

"What do you want, David?" Jessica asked, the civility leaving her voice. He knew the toughness there was a mask for sorrow.

David had to swallow twice, a struggle, before he could speak. "The things I want are impossible," he said. "So instead, I think I only wanted to see you. And to warn you, Jessica. What you do here is very dangerous. Already, everyone is talking. This clinic . . ."

"You said yourself it's amazing."

"Of course it is. I don't dispute it." He held up the magazine story. "But you see? Already, stories are appearing in print. You know investigators will come. You won't be permitted to operate without—"

"When that happens, we'll move," Jessica said calmly. "We've already scouted alternate sites."

Dawit's heart pounded. She was serious? "Jessica . . . You're going to bring yourself grief. The people already think you're magic. They know."

"We've never told them about the blood," Jessica said. "I can't help what they think."

"The blood wasn't intended to be used this way."

Now, for the first time, Dawit saw unbridled anger in his wife's eyes. He shrank from those eyes. "How can you stand there and tell me how this blood wasn't intended to be used? You?"

"Jessica . . ." Dawit said, near tears. "Don't punish yourself this way. I understand how it must feel, healing these children, protecting them from early death, but you know why you're doing it. And you can't bring her back."

This time, Jessica raised her finger, her eyes still afire. "Say that one more time, David, damn you. And this conversation will be over."

Dawit, defeated, felt his insides sinking. He wondered how he still had the strength to stand. He had hoped things would go better than this, though now he didn't understand how he could have imagined such a thing. He wished he were still hidden in Lagos, that he had never found her. How could he have chosen to relive this pain?

"You hate me," he said quietly.

"I did," she said, gazing at the air as if reading her own thoughts. "Maybe I still do. I don't want to. That hurts too much. I didn't ask you for this, what you've done to me, but now it's done. And good things are happening because of it. So maybe you've blessed me. And I can't hate you for that."

When Dawit didn't respond, Jessica went on in a detached voice, outside herself. "We learn more about the blood every day. Alex does her research at night, when she finishes with patients. Blood diseases are easiest: leukemia, sickle-cell. Most viruses. It takes a little longer, but HIV too. We're very excited about that. But we lost a girl with heart disease. We haven't figured that out. We can't give sight to the blind or anything. And some more progressive cancers. . . . The blood helps, but it's not enough. . . . But we'll find a way."

"You're going to save all the children in the world?" Dawit asked her gently, trying to point out the fallacy in her thinking.

Jessica nodded. "Yes. I hope so," she said.

Dawit sighed. "You know they'll die. You'll heal them of one thing, but something else will take them. That's why Alex will never find all the answers, Jessica. Without the Ritual, the blood alone cannot prevent death."

"But even so . . ." Jessica said in the same removed voice, stroking her cat. "We can give them a chance to live, at least. They deserve that."

And so, Dawit realized, this is how it would end. He could not remain here with Jessica, and she would not go with him. One day very soon, her work at this children's clinic would end with some heartbreak, or Jessica would be studied like a circus oddity in medical laboratories. And he had done this to her. He alone.

"I admire all you've built here," Dawit said. "The clinic. This house. And you are surrounded by people who love you. Those things are good. But if you learn nothing else from me, Jessica, learn this: Do not stake your attachments too deeply. In a very short amount of time—it will amaze you how quickly—one by one, they will all be gone. They are mortals, and you are no longer of them. And you and Teacake, alone, will remain."

For the first time, Dawit saw tears in her eyes. Had he at last gotten through to her?

"Is that your lesson?" she asked him. "I'm sorry to hear that, because you always said just the opposite. Love what you have while you have it, before it's gone. Isn't that what you were always trying to tell me?" Her damp eyes glimmered.

For the first time during his visit, Dawit again felt like a husband to his wife. Their thoughts were resting in a comfortable place, remembering.

"I did," Dawit said. He did not say the things that further anguished his mind: how inhumane it was that circumstances would ever see fit to bring people together to love for a short time and then force them to part; or, nearly as cruel, to bring love to people who, even while living, could never be together.

But he must hope for something, at least. In that, he might find purpose in the endless, waiting years.

"Lalibela is a city built of stone in Ethiopia, with underground churches adorned with paintings and magnificent religious relics that are centuries old. Many liken the city to Jerusalem. Coptic priests, the very devout, live there," Dawit said. "And so do we. There are fifty-nine of us, and we dwell in six houses of learning. Our teacher is a bearded man named Khaldun, whose name means 'Eternal.' There are many among us who believe he is the closest thing our Earth has to a God. He gave us this Living Blood we share. He is, in a sense, my father, Jessica. That makes him yours. And Lalibela is our home."

He blinked, beholding the sight of his wife in her magnificent dress of white, sitting in this room washed in sunlight. This was not Jessica as she had been. She had buried so much of herself; all he could see in her face was everything that was missing. He did not know her. The discomfort of trying to speak brought sharp tears to Dawit's eyes.

"One day—when all of this is gone, or perhaps before—when you have nowhere else, you should go there. And you will find me. For all of time, I will be waiting for you."

He did not remain to hear her answer, or to hear her utter the word goodbye. That said, Dawit turned and walked down the stairs, past Gaines's stare at the doorway, around the playing children and chickens in the courtyard, and through the clinic of miracles.

Outside, his driver was still waiting.

▪ 63

As soon as Jessica heard the irregular clump-clump on the stairs, she knew Alex was coming. The hurried sound pulled her back into herself somewhat. Even now, the sight of this whitewashed room felt distinctly false, as though it weren't real. This was not her life. This was not her. But, yes, it was. An African sun was shining through her window, brightening the colorful Zulu beads hanging on her wall. Those beads had been a gift from a grateful mother. A mother whose child had been spared by her blood.

Alex came limping into the room, sweat dripping down her face. She was wearing her lab coat—that, at least, was not so unfamiliar—and she probably still had patients on her exam tables. This was their clinic. Their new place.

Could David have really been here, in this room, only ten minutes before?

"Where's your cane?" Jessica asked, forcing herself not to think about David. Instead, she thought of Alex. It was ironic; for all the testing her sister had done with her blood, drawing new samples as she needed them, sometimes enough to make Jessica feel light-headed, Alex had never once injected herself to see if it might help her back mend properly or make her limp disappear. "It's not here for me," Alex always said.

"Girl, please, I left from down there so fast, I forgot all about it," Alex said breathlessly. "Sipho came running in with some foolishness about 'the sister's husband,' and then Daddy Gaines said David was here. Bea is downstairs saying she's faint. What happened?"

So, she would have to think about David, after all. Not David, she reminded herself when tears threatened, Dawit. That was who had been here. David, who was so much a part of her that she still couldn't bring herself to sleep on his side of the bed, had never existed. He'd been a fantasy conjured up for her by Dawit. A lie. She'd wanted the lie so much, she'd believed it. And knowing that David was a lie wasn't enough to keep her from missing him.

"He came," Jessica said.

Alex inhaled abruptly, sitting gently on the bed beside Jessica. She nudged Teacake out of her way, staring at Jessica with wide eyes. "All the way out here? How did he find you?"

"He read about the clinic in a magazine."

Alex's mouth dropped open. "Jessica . . ."

"Don't worry. We knew people would find out. Daddy's already bought the land in Botswana. All we have to do is move."

"That's not what I mean, Jessica. If David found you, what about those other—"

Jessica shook her head. "They would have come by now. I don't think they will. I just have a feeling."

"You and your feelings."

"The thing is," Jessica said, speaking words she still could barely bring herself to believe, "I'm one of them. Maybe they respect that." She heard her own words repeated back to her: One of them? What did that mean? She was one of what?

"Jessica, David is one of them, and you see how they messed up his life. But I guess we'll have to just pray on that and leave it alone. What did David want? What did he say?"

For all of time, I will be waiting for you.

Now, Jessica could not stop the tears she'd fought since David was here. She hid her eyes behind her arm, hoping to force the tears back to where they'd come from. Instead, a tiny sob escaped.

"Oh, Jessica . . . girl . . ." She felt Alex's arm slip around her, and her sister's head rested on her shoulder. "I know. You don't think I understand, but I've watched you, and I know. Let it go, Jessica. It isn't natural not to cry. Let it out."

Furiously, Jessica shook her head. At last, the wall was coming. The room had been trying to melt, trying to take her back to Miami, to her own house, to the family she'd once had, the little girl. Ki—. No. She would not think her name.

When Jessica chose, she could make that time seem like a century ago, and she could make the place it had held in her heart feel cold and barren; not fragile the way it had felt when she'd walked toward the stairs and seen David there. When she'd wanted to run downstairs into his arms and have him hug her and tell her it was all a dream. He was back now, he would have said, and it's over now, Jess. It's over. The way he'd comforted her in the cabin.

The feeling was gone, now. Jessica blinked, her mind remarkably clear. She heard the boys arguing outside, some childish dispute, Sipho's voice louder than anyone's. It helped. Sipho would not be alive today if not for her, if not for what had happened.

Jessica moved away from her sister's embrace, patting Alex's knee to tell her she was all right. "It just shocked me a little, seeing him."

Alex gazed at her with perceptive eyes. She knew there was more, that Jessica had pushed it away, but Jessica prayed she wouldn't try to draw it out. "Well, why did he just run in and out like that?" Alex asked at last. "He didn't even want to see Beatrice?"

Beatrice! Bee-Bee had cut herself, Jessica remembered. She'd seen the blood. And Katie was a great help around the house, but the teenager was no nurse. And she wasn't a mother. "Shoot, I have to go downstairs."

"Jessica," Alex said, dead serious, holding her sister's wrist. "You told David about his daughter, right?"

There was a commotion, more footsteps on the stairs. Bea appeared, holding her smiling namesake in her arms, and Daddy Gaines followed behind her, buttoning his shirt. Jessica's mother looked fifteen years younger since she'd started dyeing her hair black, wearing it in cornrow braids. Jessica saw a drop of blood on Bee-Bee's T-shirt, but her tears were forgotten. Bea, straining, lowered Bee-Bee to the floor, and she ran between Jessica's knees. "Par-ty, Mommy!" she cried.

"You come here," Jessica said, lifting her up to rest her plump little buttocks on her knee. She'd grown so much! Jessica was still amazed at how much Bee-Bee looked like neither her nor David, but like Jessica's father when he was a boy. That was the first thing Bea had said when her grandchild was born. "Did you cut yourself, Bee-Bee?"

"Look, Mommy." Grinning, Bee-Bee held up her hand for Jessica to look at it. Jessica checked each finger on that hand, then each on the other. There was no mark, and the blood was gone. But of course the mark would be gone.

"That was almost twenty minutes ago," Daddy Gaines said. "Cut's long healed by now."

"Jessica, you answer my question," Alex said. "Did you tell him?"

"What was David doing here?" Bea whispered. She, like Jessica, rarely spoke his name.

"Would you all please hush?" Jessica said, focused on watching her daughter play with her own fingers. No matter how often it happened, she couldn't get over how quickly Beatrice healed. The crazy girl sometimes hurt herself just to watch the marks go away, as if playing a game. That was probably what happened this time too. "He just came to see me, that's all."

"Why didn't you tell him about Bee-Bee?" Alex asked.

Because it would have hurt him more to leave us if he'd known, Jessica thought, understanding for the first time. And he had to leave. There might be a time when it would be different, but for right now, he had to leave.

"Daddy went away?" Beatrice asked, startling Jessica. Her smile had faded, her magical little fingers suspended in midair.

Jessica met her daughter's eyes beneath her beautiful crown of black curls. Again, she was startled at something that shouldn't startle her; she'd never said a word to Beatrice about her daddy, or shown her a picture of David, but Beatrice knew things. She always had. Jessica forgot she couldn't keep things from her.

"You'll see him someday, Bee-Bee. I promise." She hadn't planned to say that, and didn't know why she had, but the words filled her chest with comfort.

Beatrice scrunched up her face, concentrating. "La . . . li . . ."

"That's right. He's going to Lalibela. That's far away, in a country called Ethiopia."

The taller Bea had her hands on her hips. "I wish somebody would tell me what's going on. I don't like David Wolde showing his face here. When I saw him, I nearly—"

"Mom, please," Jessica said wearily, stroking Bee-Bee's hair. "He's gone now. I just think it means we'll have to leave here soon, that's all. The rest of them probably know we're here too. So we better get back to work."

"Well, you all can do what you want," Bea said, "I may go to Botswana, but I'm not going to any durn Ethiopia. You hear? I'm tired of all this moving."

"I said soon, Mom. Not now," Jessica said, smiling at her. What would she have done without this woman? And Alex, too. All of them had accepted so much, purely out of love. They didn't exactly sit around talking about Jessica's condition—What was the word in Spanish? Her inmortalidad—but they knew. Their knowing made it easier for Jessica, like she had some kind of disease they were supporting her through. Everything was changed, and nothing was changed.

For now, they were here.

Daddy Gaines finished fixing his shirt, tucking it into his pants. "I think Jessica needs to be alone," he said, always intuitive. "Alex, you have a clinic full of patients. And Bea, I wish you would help me get ready for the party. I can't blow up all those balloons."

"Par-ty!" Bee-Bee said, squirming out of Jessica's arms. She danced on the floor, bouncing on her fat, sturdy little brown legs.

"What party?" Jessica asked. She felt dazed, disconnected, again.

Alex leaned close to Jessica, whispering in her ear. "New Year's, remember? It'll be the year two thousand, girl."

Of course. That was why she'd thought David might come today. She'd been expecting him, for some reason, since Christmas. She was both dismayed and relieved that he had come. "Two thousand," Jessica repeated, imagining David's face from the picture he'd shown her with his jazz group, so long ago. "I can't believe I forgot that."

Would all of her photographs one day look that way too? Would that photograph of Kira on her desk one day be yellowed and frayed? Would it turn to dust before her eyes?

Kira. She'd actually thought her name. And she was still fine.

The comfort Jessica had felt earlier, talking to Bee-Bee, began to glow from her. She was all right. But she wouldn't be doing much partying tonight, Jessica thought. She would make an appearance because the children were always happy to see her—"the sister," they called her—but then she would leave them. Tonight, more than other nights, she would need to stay in her room. She would read some passages from her Bible. And she would pray. What was it that had kept her from praying for so long? Only anger?

If the answers weren't in the Scriptures, maybe she could find them in herself, in her heart. She was a part of something. Her new baby, this remarkable first child of the Living Blood, was a part of it too. She could feel the power between them, more than a parent-child bond. It excited her. But she would be lying if she tried to convince herself she wasn't more afraid than ever. She was.

Her life was bigger now.

But she was just about ready. That was the most amazing thing of all.

"Par-ty... P-A-R-T-Y..." she heard Bee-Bee saying as she made her way down the hallway with Daddy Gaines stooping low to hold her hand. Jessica watched her from the bedroom doorway, and Bee-Bee twisted her head back to stare straight into Jessica's eyes with a smile lighting up her round, coffee-brown face, as though she were sharing a secret.

Despite the hurts, which went to her soul, Jessica's spirits soared.